BLACK ICE

TOR BOOKS BY SUSAN KRINARD

Mist

Black Ice

BLACK ICE

SUSAN KRINARD

TOR®

A Tom Doherty Associates Book
New York

BLACK ICE

Copyright © 2014 by Susan Krinard

A Tor Book
Published by Tom Doherty Associates, LLC
175 Fifth Avenue
New York, NY 10010

www.tor-forge.com

Tor® is a registered trademark of Tom Doherty Associates, LLC.

Library of Congress Cataloging-in-Publication Data

Krinard, Susan.
    Black ice / Susan Krinard. — First Edition.
        p. cm.
    "A Tor Book."
    ISBN 978-0-7653-3209-7 (trade paperback)
    ISBN 978-1-4299-5595-9 (e-book)
    1. Valkyries (Norse mythology)—Fiction. 2. San Francisco (Calif.)—Fiction.
I. Title.
    PS3611.R5445B53 2014
    813'.6—dc23

                                                                    2014015444

Tor books may be purchased for educational, business, or promotional use. For information on bulk purchases, please contact Macmillan Corporate and Premium Sales Department at 1-800-221-7945, extension 5442, or write specialmarkets@macmillan.com.

First Edition: August 2014

Printed in the United States of America

0 9 8 7 6 5 4 3 2 1

BLACK ICE

1

Anna Stangeland woke abruptly, clutching the pendant so hard that the worn edges nearly cut into her fingers. The sheets were halfway off the bed as if she'd been thrashing, though she knew a person didn't move when she dreamed.

Orn hopped down from the headboard and settled on the bed, cocking his head so that one bright eye was fixed on hers. She shivered, expelled a shuddering breath, and released her hold on the flat piece of stone, letting it fall back to her chest.

"Another one," she whispered to Orn. "At least this time wasn't bad. But sometimes . . ."

Sometimes it didn't matter if it was bad or not. She still felt she was living someone else's life.

And she was.

She threw her legs over the side of the bed and peered at her alarm clock. Only four a.m. She felt as if she'd hardly slept, and all the dreams she'd had before seemed to march through her mind like an army of ghosts.

Leading that army was Mist Bjorgsen. The dreams about her had always been vague before she'd come here, filtered through the weave and weft of time and memory.

She didn't want to believe what she saw in those dream-memories.

Half-blind with lack of sleep, Anna stumbled to the kitchen for a cup of coffee. Orn rode on her shoulder until she sat at the small table, the mug cupped between her hands a spot of comforting warmth in the chilly apartment, and then hopped down to the table top.

"Yes," Anna said wearily. "You were there. You usually are, except—"

Except when Mist strode through her dreams.

Anna dropped her head into her hands. The dreams were becoming more and more nonsensical and bizarre, and here she was, unemployed and just moved into a very small and expensive sublet apartment in San Francisco. She still had no idea why she'd taken it into her head to leave New York, where she'd had a perfectly good job and a very decent life.

"Okay?" Orn croaked.

"Fine." She reached across the table to stroke his breast feathers. "I'm going to have to look for job leads today. No one'll be hiring during the holidays except the stores, and I have enough to tide us over until January. But at least I can check things out and see what might be available in the new year."

Orn bobbed his head as if in approval, and once more Anna wondered how much he really understood. He was smart. Very smart. But he was still a bird, even if he was the best friend she'd ever had.

With a sigh, she finished her coffee and braced herself to face the very thing that scared her the most. Orn in his usual place on her shoulder, she dragged herself to the small second room she'd set up as an office and opened the desk drawer.

The photograph was buried underneath a pile of unsorted papers, as if Anna could somehow forget it had ever existed. Until the end, Oldefar had never spoken of the young woman who stood beside him in the snow, both of them armed with Sten guns, determined and relentless. Geir had kept the photograph hidden until Anna's great-grandmother, Helga—once called Horja—had died in a boating accident.

Anna knew why he'd kept it to himself. Mist had been a remarkable woman. She was beautiful in a strong way, with her bold, high cheekbones, firm chin, and direct gray eyes. Very Norse, and very much a warrior.

Geir had loved her very much, Anna thought. He had hidden that love deep in his heart during all his faithful years with Helga, though Helga and Mist had also fought side by side and regarded each other as sisters. So Anna's dreams had told her.

Orn nibbled at her ear, his powerful beak as gentle as a mother's caress. She closed the drawer, fingering the pendant with its crude etching of a raven and the Runes inscribed above. The etchings were almost invisible now, rubbed away by the caressing fingers of those who had worn it.

But the stone still carried a heritage of unflinching courage and dedication to freedom and the good. Anna had tried to live up to that heritage, but she had never done anything heroic. A computer programmer generally didn't get many opportunities to perform acts of daring, gallantry, and valor.

Discouraged all over again, Anna returned to the small living room and turned on the TV, soothed by the drone of mindless infomercials as she dozed on the couch. It was still an hour before sunrise when she surrendered to hunger and made a breakfast of yogurt and toast, puttered around on the computer and prepared to wait until a reasonable hour to venture out—if there was such a thing as a reasonable hour in a city that still hadn't adapted to heavy snowfall and single-digit temperatures.

Another stupid reason for moving here, she thought, when New York was having something of a warm spell.

She was blearily examining her two business suits when Orn flew in to settle on the brass footboard of the bed and chirruped like an inquisitive cat.

"Find Mist," he said.

She swung around, doubting what she'd heard, certain that she'd misunderstood Orn's cartoonishly squeaky voice.

But she'd been with him too long. She hadn't imagined it. Orn simply stared at her, and for a moment she felt as if she were gazing into the eyes of a very intelligent and determined human being.

"Find Mist," he repeated.

Anna jumped back into bed, covered her head with the blankets, and pretended she'd never woken up at all.

Mist paced out the perimeter of the battered chain-link fence that surrounded the factory compound, considering where she ought to place the reinforcements. They wouldn't be literal in the physical sense; with luck, they'd be much stronger.

Since the sudden and unexpected arrival of Mist's sister Valkyrie, Bryn—along with Bryn's biker club, the Einherjar—Mist had been helping the newcomers set up camp in the abandoned factory and adjoining warehouse across the street from Mist's loft. It was up to Mist to make the place as secure as possible, especially since the Jotunar, Loki's frost giants, would be watching for any weak spots in Mist's defenses. And she still had to set up another barrier ward to prevent her neighbors from noticing how weird things were likely to get in the vicinity of her loft. As long as they *could* be hidden.

But after the energy she'd expended in fighting Loki Laufeyson— gods, was it only twenty-four hours ago?—and especially since she hadn't been consciously aware most of the time she'd been using it up, Mist wasn't sure she'd be able to handle even the most basic magic.

The prospect of failure scared her, but not nearly as much as the threat of Loki's ultimate victory. She put her doubts out of her mind and drew on the tools of her former trade as a swordsmith and knife maker, recalling how she'd used the same images to dispose of certain frost giants' bodies after the savage battle with Loki's Jotunn lieutenants in the gym. It took surprisingly little effort to create and fix the images of the weapons in her mind and inscribe their blades with the appropriate Runes, tracing the staves with imaginary fire.

Once each one was complete, she chanted a spell that pulled steel from the wires themselves, turning them molten and fusing the blades into the fence. Soon there was no indication that the Rune-blades had ever existed, but they were there, invisible and potent guards against intruders—at least, of the human variety. And, if she was lucky, the Jotunar as well.

If the Einherjar tracking her progress were impressed, they didn't speak a word as she traced a careful path around the fence to the section directly surrounding the factory. By then she was beginning to feel the strain of the prolonged use of her abilities. The price for this kind of magic was relatively minor: increasing exhaustion, exacerbated by her lack of sleep, and the feeling that she was running on fumes that were about to evaporate. She wasn't in any danger of entering the fugue state that had consumed her when she'd made use of the ancient magic—the elemental forces that she couldn't yet control—but she knew she couldn't keep it up much longer.

Still, she managed to finish just as her strength was beginning to give out. She completed the final Bind-Rune that would permit the single gate to open and sat on a broken piece of concrete. A red-headed biker called Vixen offered her a canteen full of lukewarm water, which Mist took gratefully. The others maintained a respectful distance.

Mist gulped the water down and returned the canteen with gruff thanks. She didn't feel ready to deal with the other Einherjar when she'd barely had time to absorb the monumental changes in her life—the changes that had engulfed her since the elf Dainn had appeared to warn her that everything she'd believed about her former life was wrong.

At the moment, all she wanted was hot coffee and a fire in her living room hearth. And the discussion with Bryn that couldn't be put off any longer

"I saw the world changing," Bryn said, taking another sip of cold coffee. "It wasn't just the weird weather. I could have put that down to global warming, but I knew that wasn't the problem."

"You always had a talent for sensing weather changes," Mist said, nursing her own coffee as she sat on the couch facing Bryn in the armchair.

"Hard to miss that these days," Bryn said, glancing at Rick Jensen, her devoted lieutenant. "But like I said, it was more than that. I'd already been hanging around biker clubs for years, joining one for a while and then dropping out to find another one, moving all the time. I didn't have the Cloak anymore, but I couldn't settle. Until about eight months ago, when I started looking for anyone else who seemed to sense the same changes I did."

"I guess you found them," Mist said wryly, listening to the roar of gunning engines across the street.

"Sorry about that. I'll have a word with them. Wouldn't want to upset the neighbors."

They'll have a lot more reason to be upset before this is over, Mist thought grimly. "So how did it happen?" she asked.

"Rick was first," Bryn said, setting her mug on the end table beside the chair. "We both happened to be in the same bar at the same time. The weird thing is, this strange old lady dressed like a rag doll was responsible for our meeting. She just sort of walked up to me, dragging Rick along with her, and said we had to meet."

"Weird old lady?" Mist repeated. "Who?"

"Never got her name. Guess I should have found out, huh?"

Mist clasped her hands together, uneasy down to her bones. Was it possible the "lady" had been Freya, pushing help in Mist's direction?

No, that didn't make sense. The goddess could have found all the Valkyrie herself if she could locate Bryn. And she couldn't take physical form, in any case.

"Rick and I hit it off right away," Bryn said, "and since neither one of us was hooked up with clubs, we decided to ride together."

"As friends," Rick pointed out hastily.

Bryn snorted in amusement. "After that, we kept picking up more men and women every couple of weeks. I only named us the Einherjar when I figured out why we were all coming together."

"A name of significance," Dainn said.

Mist started, amazed that she'd briefly forgotten the elf was there. But he'd been listening attentively all the while, standing with his back against the wall near the door. He'd cleaned himself up, and most of his minor wounds had pretty much vanished, but he was still far from his usual handsome self. She doubted *she* looked much better.

A nasty fight with a deadly enemy, involving all kinds of magic Mist was only beginning to understand, could do that to a Valkyrie. Or to an Alfr who'd been cruelly manhandled by the godling who'd betrayed him.

More than manhandled, Mist thought. Humiliated, abused, shamed. And Mist knew Dainn hadn't forgotten a moment of it.

But he'd hidden important things from her and behaved stupidly, putting everything they'd worked for at risk. It had been his own fault, hadn't it? Or was it really hers?

"Worry only about what you have the power to change." Dainn's words, and excellent advice. It was cursed hard not to worry when she felt she ought to have the power to change everything.

Kirby poked his head into the room, eyes wide.

"Here, kitty kitty," Bryn said softly, rubbing her fingers together. Kirby hissed, tail puffed nearly to the size of his body, and squirmed into the small space behind the sofa, where he remained safely ensconced.

Lee was watching it all from the top of the bookshelf at the back of the room, aloof and unafraid. Kirby, Mist thought, was the smart one.

"Don't take it personally," Mist said. "He's shy around strangers." She sighed and fought to keep her eyes open. "Go on, Bryn. Why *were* you all coming together?"

"Well, I finally figured out that every one of them had some kind of ancient Norse blood. My guess is that a few are even descended from the gods, or elves—"

"Alfar?" Dainn asked. "That would have been a rare occurrence."

"Maybe," Bryn said, flashing a frown in the elf's direction. "But everyone knows the gods didn't always keep it in their pants where mortals were concerned."

No kidding, Mist thought, her mind turning again to the battle with Loki, Freya arriving in all her glory to help her Valkyrie daughter defeat the Slanderer. But her victory had been brief. Mist had little memory of the fight, but Dainn had told her that Freya hadn't completely materialized in Midgard. Loki had sent the goddess away, leaving Mist with Odin's Spear, Gungnir, in her possession once more.

Freya should have been back in touch—of the mental kind— quickly enough, but Dainn had been unable to make contact with her, or even sense the Shadow-Realm of the gods in the great Void, Ginnungagap.

It might be only a temporary communication problem. If it wasn't . . .

Mist closed her eyes. She might have to be the leader of Midgard's resistance to Loki's scheme of conquest, but she was *not* the hero Dainn thought she—

"I figure all those Norse heroes and kings and such, the ones who had close dealings with the Aesir, they passed on some kind of understanding maybe ordinary folk didn't have," Bryn said, interrupting Mist's shamefully self-pitying train of thought. "My Einherjar were feeling whatever I sensed months ago. Not that they have magic like you or the elf, but I think they always knew that something big was coming."

Something like the very real possibility that Midgard was about to become a bloody battlefield.

"And how did you find *me*?" Mist asked.

"One was that weather business again," Bryn said, raising two fingers. "It was getting bad in a lot of places, but it had turned truly bizarre in San Francisco and the West Coast with all the snow. The only way it made sense to me was if the center of the change I felt was in this city." She shook her head. "Freya's daughter. I can still hardly believe it."

"Neither can I," Mist said.

"And what was the other thing?" Dainn asked.

"Well, that weird lady in rags said I had to find my family. Since I don't have any family except the Sisters I last saw over fifty years ago . . ." She looked at Mist. "I did a little research. Since you didn't bother to change your name, and it's not exactly a common one, I put those two facts together and brought the Einherjar to look for you."

Mist nodded, but she wasn't completely convinced. She couldn't be sure it wasn't her own inherited glamour that had brought her Sister to her—the glamour that could compel other people to fall under a spell of love and lust, or even summon them from far away.

"You okay?" Bryn asked, leaning forward. "Hel, after what you went through last night, maybe you need some rest."

"I can't afford to rest now," Mist said, glad she hadn't filled in all the details of the battle with Loki.

"If you do not," Dainn said, "your magic will suffer. And you must eat."

"You're not my mother," Mist snapped.

"I assure you that I do not aspire to that role," he said, with a trace of his familiar, acerbic humor. "I hope I would treat my offspring better than your own mother has you."

Better than ignoring one's offspring until the time came when one had no other choice but to acknowledge the theoretical "child" for reasons that had nothing to do with love.

As Freya had treated Mist.

"Please," Mist said with a rough laugh. "As if we needed more Dainns in the world."

"I quite agree," Dainn said softly.

Bryn looked back and forth between them with an expression that made Mist wish she and Dainn had a big chunk of the Great Void between them.

She wondered how Bryn would feel about Dainn when she learned who the elf really was. Dainn Faith-breaker, traitor to the Aesir.

But Mist wasn't about to mention that now. She caught her Sister's ear. "Listen. I want to make sure your people understand what they're riding into. We have to find the other Treasures, keep Loki from getting too far ahead of us, and be prepared to fend off attacks at any time—all while we try to reestablish our connection to Freya and Ginnungagap."

"That's a pretty tall order," Bryn said. "You *do* expect other mortals to help save their world?"

"I'm counting on it," Mist said.

"How do you plan to get them?"

"They'll be coming for the same reason you and the Einherjar did," she said, trying to convince herself that what she said was true. "I'm working on buying a few warehouses that can be set up as dormitories. Meantime, we need to put your people through their paces, find out what battle skills they have and what they need to be taught."

"One benefit of being descended from gods, elves, and heroes," Bryn said, "is that they all have excellent reflexes and natural fighting ability."

"With knives, maybe, and hand-to-hand," Mist said. "But I'm not talking about bar brawls or fistfights. Since we're still confined to ancient weapons—"

"—because firearms and bombs and such won't work for either side in this fight," Bryn said, confirming what Mist had told her earlier.

"Right. Your people will have to be good with swords, spears, and axes, and learn how to use them both to kill and disable. The most important thing is to get them up to speed quickly."

"I'll take care of that," Bryn said.

"You'll be covering a lot of ground alone." Mist rubbed her gritty eyes. "I won't soft-pedal this. It's going to be tough, and even though it was something of a draw the last time we fought, Loki still has the advantage. He just can't bring any more Jotunar over from Ginnungagap, at least not until—*if*—the bridges open for our allies in the Shadow-Realms."

"But you think Freya closed the bridges?"

"We're still not sure. One way or another, you're going to be facing all kinds of magic from Loki and the giants he already has. People are going to die."

"We know that," Rick said, running his hand over his perspiring pate. "We have from the start."

Mist nodded. "Okay, then. We'll need regular patrols to keep an eye on the Jotunar and whoever else Loki has crawling around the city stirring up trouble," she said, "and we'll need to keep on top of the local news, papers, and Internet for any strange goings-on. San Francisco is at the center of this, so at least we won't have to be scouring the whole world or even the entire country for signs of his influence. Loki's going to look for followers who are easily corrupted, who want money or power or both. If any of your people have dealt with street crime—"

"You think we'd naturally know people like that, huh?" Rick cut in. "Just because we ride bikes? Because maybe we're not pretty, like your boy here?"

"I'm sure that's not what she—" Bryn began.

Rick got to his feet. "Bryn says we're supposed to follow you without asking any questions. You want to test us. What if we want to test *you?*"

2

"Rick!" Bryn said, rising to face him.

But Dainn was already within reach of the biker, his expression far from friendly. Mist could hear his heart rate increase, see the twitch of his upper lip. His eyes were all pupil. His fists clenched, and she could feel the hair rising on the back of her neck.

She got up slowly. "Dainn," she said.

He didn't so much as glance at her. Rick's eyes narrowed in calculation, as if he had somehow identified the source of Dainn's unexpected behavior.

But neither he nor Bryn could possibly imagine what Dainn was capable of.

"Dainn," she repeated, slowly and distinctly. "Stand down."

"Rick, go round up the Einherjar," Bryn said in a voice that brooked no disagreement. "I want to talk to them as soon as possible."

With a grunt and a glare at Dainn, Rick obeyed, slipping past the elf without touching him. Dainn watched him leave, his muscles tensed as if he'd pursue and bring the biker down like a starving wolf hunting a stag in winter.

"Dainn," Mist said quietly.

He turned to stare at her, shivered violently, and shook his head. He was about to leave when Mist called him back. He leaned against the wall, shoulders hunched, head down.

"Oh-kay," Bryn said. "What was that all about?"

"You tell *me*," Mist said, standing between her Sister and the elf.

"Why the hostility from Rick, just because I asked a reasonable question? Why did he suddenly decide he had to test me?"

"I'll have a talk with him," Bryn muttered.

"I apologize," Dainn said, his voice hoarse and almost unrecognizable. "There will be no trouble on my part."

As if Dainn could make such a guarantee, Mist thought grimly. "We can't afford internal conflicts now," she said to Bryn. "You and I have a lot more to cover, but you'd better take care of your people. We can go over details later."

"I'll need to send some of them out for provisions, too," Bryn said, watching Dainn out of the corner of her eye. "They've pretty much eaten you out of house and home. And we'll need another refrigerator. Can't expect the Einherjar to go without beer."

Neither the human nor the divine ones, Mist thought. Though she'd be lucky if she ever saw Odin's eternal warriors again.

"I'll keep you posted," Bryn said. She hesitated, glancing at Dainn again. "Can I have a word with you, Mist? In private?"

"Stay here," Mist ordered Dainn. He remained where he was, staring at nothing. The women went into the kitchen.

"If it's about Rick and Dainn—" Mist began.

"It's about us, back during the war," Bryn said, her piquant face very grave. "You asked me before how I survived the Nazi attack in Norway, when you thought I was dead. I never got around to telling you, with all the other things. . . ." She sighed. "That rag lady who introduced me to Rick and told me to find my family? I saw her, or someone just like her, when I was lying in the snow. At least I *thought* I did. And then I woke up in a cabin, alone and healed of my injuries. There was a kind of . . . voice in my head that told me to go and keep on going without looking back."

"So this 'rag lady' has been following you around since the war?"

"It almost seems like it, doesn't it?" Bryn said. "But I didn't see her in all those years in between. I should have gone back to Norway, but I never did. I'm sorry I abandoned you, sorry I never tried to find you again."

"You were killed and came back to life," Mist said. "How could you return to the place where you died?"

"But I let you carry that guilt for decades. I want to apologize for that."

"I accept," Mist said. "At least we've found each other again, and we'll win our war this time."

"Thanks." Bryn smiled crookedly. "If that lady turns up again, I'll be sure to tell you right away. But I think I'd rather be dead than see her a third time."

"That's enough of that," Mist said. She took her Sister by the shoulders and kissed her cheeks. "If you think of any other details that might matter, let me know."

"I will." Bryn bobbed her head, birdlike, and strode out of the kitchen.

Mist returned to the living room, mulling over what her Sister had told her.

Who *was* that cursed rag lady?

Maybe they had another hidden ally. She could only hope.

"What's all this with Rick?" she asked Dainn as she walked through the door.

"I am sorry," Dainn said, his gaze locked on the carpet at his feet.

His humility and genuine regret flushed all the anger out of Mist's body. He'd been there for her, suffered for her, and still she never seemed to know what to say to him.

"Bryn doesn't know about you yet," she said, "and I want to keep it that way until I'm ready to explain."

Dainn looked up. "Would it be wise to tell her who I am?"

"Are you talking about your identity as a condemned traitor to the Aesir, or about the part of yourself you almost put on full display a few minutes ago?"

"Either, or both," he said. "Bryn, like Vidarr, might choose not to work with such a traitor. And she will rightfully fear what I can become."

"I told you I wanted to help you control it."

"Yes. But now you must rest."

She sighed at his stubborn persistence. "You're the one who looks like Lee dragged you out of the gutter," she said, heading for the kitchen again.

"I believe I have, on occasion, looked worse," he said.

Mist flashed back to the day she'd found him, sprawled in the mud and dressed in filthy, ill-fitting rags. She almost smiled.

"I'd say it's a draw," she said.

"Nevertheless, I must remind you—"

"I thought we agreed that you're not my mother," Mist said, falling into one of the kitchen chairs. Her head ached like Hel, and she wished she had the energy to go get the ibuprofen out of the bathroom cupboard. She made do with massaging her temples, digging her fingertips hard into the muscle.

Dainn sat at the opposite side of the table. "Mist."

She knew from the tone of his voice that she wasn't going to like what he was about to say. She dropped her hands and regretted it immediately. "Spit it out," she said.

"Are you certain you can trust these mortals?"

"You were just wondering if they'd trust *you*," she said as he leaned against the counter. "I knew Bryn for centuries before the Last Battle, and we fought side by side in the Second World War."

"Yes," he said. "But it is her followers I doubt."

"You convinced me to become the leader of our army, such as it is," she said, "and now you won't trust my judgment?"

His gaze slipped away from hers. "You are right, of course."

His sudden acquiescence didn't make her feel much better. She took a breath, eager to change the subject. "What about Freya?"

"Nothing has changed. I still cannot reach her."

"You can bet Loki will keep looking for potential bridges," Mist said. "All we can do is try to keep up." She glanced at the clock. "I can't believe the kids haven't come down yet."

"You *did* instruct them to stay upstairs," Dainn reminded her.

"I didn't think they'd be so obedient." She frowned, remembering all too well how slippery Gabi and Ryan could be, and how badly they wanted to stay in spite of all the danger. "Can you go check on them? They should know at least some of what's going on."

"Are you sure I can be trusted alone with them?"

"If you're talking about what happened in the gym—"

"I tried to kill Ryan."

"That's not going to happen again. Ryan still believes in you."

"Because he has a . . ." Dainn trailed off, his expression both grim and bewildered.

"A crush on you?"

"He is hardly more than a child, even in mortal years, and you and I both know that the dangerous consequences of his visions are likely to become worse the longer he remains here."

"That's why Tashiro and I are working on getting him and Gabi away as soon as possible. But I hope you'll be a little gentle with him until then."

"Would that not be even more cruel?" Dainn asked. "Gentleness, as you call it, will only encourage him to believe—"

"That there's some hope for him?" Mist said, feeling an unexpected tightness in her chest. "He's not an idiot. He already knows there isn't."

Dainn looked at her, his entire body as rigid as stone. She knew what was going through his mind now, even though he'd only let her see it on rare occasions. Just as she had done her best not to let him . . .

Pummeled by the sheer force of his stare, Mist found herself remembering the kiss, the one that had brought her back from the fugue state she'd experienced during much of the fight with Loki.

If things had been different . . . if there had been any way it could possibly have worked . . .

"I think I'd better eat something," she said, rising to look in one of the ransacked cupboards. She found a package of ramen noodles and a jar of peanuts.

"Protein," she said, setting the jar on the table. "This is going to have to do until—"

She never finished the sentence. There was a woman standing in the doorway. Dainn followed her gaze and nearly leaped out of his chair.

It was the first time Mist had "seen" her mother as a physical entity in Midgard, though the goddess had twice shared Mist's body to fight Loki. Yet Mist couldn't possibly doubt who stood before her.

Freya wore flowing robes that alternately revealed and concealed her lushly curved figure. Her golden hair hung in abundant waves around her shoulders, and the scent of primroses hung heavy in the air. Her beauty was startling, but her eyes were cold, turning her seemingly benevolent expression into a cruel parody of itself.

Dainn had said he couldn't reach her. Yet here she was, as if she'd taken strength from last night's fight and had finally completed her physical transformation.

Or it would have seemed that way if Mist hadn't been able to see right through her.

"Freya," Mist said, quickly overcoming her shock.

The goddess didn't even glance at her. She strode into the kitchen and faced Dainn as if she didn't know her daughter was there. Fury radiated from her body in almost tangible waves.

"Traitor!" she spat.

Dainn stared at her, his face blank with astonishment. "Lady?" he said.

"Freya!" Mist said, coming up behind her mother. The goddess ignored her.

"You know what you were to have done," Freya hissed at Dainn, "and already you have failed." She gripped Dainn's arm, and he collapsed to his knees with a groan of something between pain and ecstasy.

Without thinking, Mist grabbed Freya's shoulder. The goddess twitched slender fingers and sent Mist flying back to slam against the wall. Dainn began to rise, but Freya snatched a handful of his hair in her fist and forced him back down.

Mist scrambled to her feet and went after Freya again. "What are you doing?" she demanded. "How did you—"

"You know the penalty," Freya said to Dainn in her gentle, savage voice. "There is no hope for you now."

Dainn closed his eyes. "I know," he whispered.

"Dainn!" Mist said. "Get up!"

He, like the goddess, seemed not to hear her. But he began to change, and all at once she saw a shimmer around him, a brilliant light, as if his body were dissolving in the heat of a dying sun. It caught Freya in its radiance, and Mist was struck with a burning pain as if she, too, were catching fire.

Dainn slumped to the floor. Freya vanished. After some indeterminate length of time, Mist found herself lying on the floor as well, Gabi crouching beside her. Ryan was with Dainn, who was on his knees and breathing harshly.

"*Madre de Dios!*" Gabi exclaimed. "Are you okay?"

"We heard someone scream," Ryan said, his voice tight with anxiety as he peered into Dainn's face.

Mist touched her throat and realized she must have been the one screaming.

She *never* screamed.

"I'm okay," she said, getting to her feet. "Dainn?"

He looked up from the floor, his eyes bloodshot. "You saw her?" he asked.

"Did I *see* her?" Mist glanced from Gabi to Ryan and helped Dainn to his feet. "She was talking to you!"

"*Quién?*" Gabi asked. "Who was here?"

"I felt it," Ryan said, his voice dreamy. "It reached all the way upstairs."

"Is Ryan all right?" Mist asked Gabi. "No seizures?"

"No," Gabi said. But she looked scared, and that wasn't normal for the feisty teenager.

"What did you feel?" Mist asked Ryan.

Suddenly Ryan blinked, and the dreaminess was gone. "I don't know," he said, his expression collapsing into misery. "Light. A shape of someone. Something dangerous."

"We're not in any danger now," Mist said, "so I'm going to have to ask you and Gabi to go back upstairs. We'll talk about this later."

"Sure," Gabi said with a moue of disgust. She took Ryan's arm, and he didn't resist.

Once they were gone—presumably—Mist led Dainn to a chair and made him sit. His face was bathed in sweat, as if he'd felt that strange fire that had burned around him like an exploding star.

"Okay," she said, dragging another chair close to his, "what the Hel just happened?"

"Freya," he said slowly. "She was here. But she wasn't."

"Odin's balls, what does *that* mean?"

"Did she speak to you?"

"No," Mist said, wishing she could shake him. "What are you trying to say? That she wasn't real?"

"I don't know."

"You sure as Hel *acted* like she was. You felt her touch you?"

He rubbed his arm slowly. "Yes."

"But she ignored me completely. What in gentle Baldr's name did we just see and hear?"

He wiped the perspiration from his forehead with the back of his hand. "I have no explanation."

"She called you a traitor," Mist said. "She said that you'd failed in something you were supposed to do, and there was no hope for you."

"I don't remember."

"You betrayed the gods," she said, "but what did you fail to do?" His blank expression didn't change. "You have no idea what she—it—meant by all this?"

"No."

"*Fy faen,*" Mist swore. She had that all-too-familiar feeling that he was holding something back. "Did you feel anything else, any physical sensations while she was talking to you?" she asked, thinking of the light.

He flushed. Seeing him turn red was a somewhat novel experience. She had a feeling what had caused his embarrassment, and it wasn't any kind of illumination.

She let it pass. "Could Freya be projecting part of herself to Midgard again, like she did in Loki's apartment?"

"I am as interested in finding the source of this . . . manifestation as you are."

"Then you *do* think it was an illusion."

His shoulders slumped, and she knew she wasn't going to get anything more out of him now. "Maybe things will seem clearer once you've had some sleep," she said, scooting her chair back from the table. "I'm going up to talk to the kids. I don't want to push Ryan, but he did see *some*thing."

Dainn met her gaze, a hint of real panic in his eyes. It was gone an instant later.

"It would be best to keep him as quiet as possible," the elf said. "Let me think on this before you question him. I will look after the young mortals for now."

"If you're sure you're all right."

"Yes."

Mist rolled her aching neck in a slow circle. "Good. I need to take Bryn on a quick tour of the area. She and the Einherjar need to know what to watch out for. But keep your cell phone with you, just in case something like this happens again while I'm out."

He pulled the jar of peanuts toward him and opened the jar. "As you say."

"And I meant to tell you—I've left a message for Tashiro. He may be coming over sometime today. Keep it under control, okay?"

"Yes," Dainn said, clearly none too thrilled at the prospect of seeing the lawyer again. But as long as he didn't let his dislike of Koji Tashiro spill over into something more dangerous, she could relegate it to the list of secondary problems she just didn't have the time or energy to handle.

She started toward the hall, relieved that she wasn't going to have to deal with any more arguments. She didn't even make it to the door.

"Mist."

"Curse it, Dainn," she said, looking over her shoulder. "I have to—"

"If this were the time of the Roman Empire," Dainn said softly, "and you were the victorious general of a great military campaign, I would stand behind you on your chariot and proclaim, 'Remember that thou art mortal.' But since you are not mortal, I would remind you that you are not yet a god."

The Runes glittered in midair, ice rimmed with fire, dancing above Loki's open palms. Again the ice cracked, and the burst of heat singed Loki's hands. He swore and shook out his fingers, cursing with such force that a tumbler on his bar counter shattered, slivers and chunks of glass flying outward to strike the cabinets, ceiling, and wall.

With a grunt of annoyance, Loki lay on the couch with his feet up on the armrest and replayed the battle for the hundredth time. Ever since it had ended—more or less in a draw, after the usual taunts and threats from Freya—he'd possessed far from his usual capacity for magic.

Of course it hadn't started with the Lady. Mist had come to him alone, and in the beginning she had revealed extraordinary abilities that had seemed to be entirely her own. She had made use of the elements, of the moon and sun, of fire and water. In every way she had seemed astonishingly adept, wielding her magic as if she had absorbed not only her mother's skill, but something considerably more dangerous . . . and ancient.

But when Freya had appeared—and there had been no mistaking

her arrival, or her appropriation of Mist's body—Loki had believed that the Lady finally intended to take full possession of her daughter's flesh, mind, and soul.

He had assumed that when she had left with Dainn, believing she'd put Loki in his place, she had succeeded. But now Freya seemed to have vanished, along with all access to Ginnungagap.

The reason for the Lady's disappearance, and how Mist had escaped her, remained a mystery for the time being. But Loki very much doubted Freya's hint that she'd closed the bridges herself.

Playing with the stopwatch on his Rolex Cosmograph, Loki reminded himself that he had certainly drawn the correct conclusion. There must have been a "glitch" in the pathways between the Void and Midgard, a malfunction that Freya had chosen to claim as her own, deliberate work. And while he had been unable to gain any sense of Jotunheim's Shadow-Realm beyond the veil that separated it and the other realms from Earth, he wasn't prepared to believe that his allies were beyond his reach.

As long as the Lady stayed out of the picture, the penalties he had expected to pay for breaking the rules of their "game" for possession of Midgard could be ignored with impunity. In fact, as far as he was concerned, the game was over. He had his current crop of fifty or so Jotunar, and Mist's allies were badly outnumbered.

But Mist herself . . .

Loki stretched to work the dull aches out of his body. He had always assumed that Mist relied on her mother's proximity and aid to work magic of any real significance. Given what he'd seen her do during the battle, he had begun to doubt that assumption.

When next they met, with or without the Lady, he intended to test his new theory. Perhaps then he would learn how she'd escaped her mother's fatal embrace, if Dainn had played any part in that extrication . . . and if the elf finally confessed the full extent of his treachery to his new lady-love.

Curling his lip in disgust, Loki got up and went to the bar, clearing away broken glass with a spell that reduced the shards to harmless atoms. He glanced toward the panoramic window with its view of the busy street below, taking note of the weather. The snow had been heavy all night, gradually lessening as the morning advanced; weak sunlight struggled to part the sullen clouds without much success as the city's inhabitants battled their fellow Yuletide shoppers for the most coveted toys, objects of desire for both the adults and their mewling offspring.

Objects of desire.

Filling his glass with brandy, Loki called up a more pleasant image, remembering how weak and helpless Dainn had been after he'd revealed his "real" beast, the very physical monster he could barely control. If he'd hidden that particular aspect of his "problem" from Mist, he would have to work very hard to keep it a secret. And that would make him weaker still.

Loki laughed at his own conceit. Whatever he might wish to believe, he knew very well that Dainn was no lightweight. He was thoroughly, utterly dangerous.

But the elf was bound to his enemy as well. Closing his fist over his aching palm and the deep slash that had yet to heal, Loki smiled at another pleasant memory. His and Dainn's blood had intermingled, palm to palm and heart to heart.

In spite of the battle and bloodshed, in spite of Loki's treatment of the elf, in spite of the beast, something very powerful still bound them together.

Someone knocked on the door between the hall and Loki's living room, interrupting his revived satisfaction. Loki poured himself a fresh drink.

"Come," he said.

The Jotunn—Grer, one of his less intelligent minions, but sufficiently functional in his work—stepped into the room and bowed. Loki smiled sourly. Since his former chief, Hrimgrimir, and his two cronies had died at Dainn's hands, the others had been somewhat more respectful of their master. They knew they might not survive without his protection. And he wasn't about to let them forget it.

"What is it?" he asked.

"You requested regular reports, my lord," Grer said in an apologetic tone that did nothing to mitigate Loki's annoyance.

"Get on with it," he snapped.

"Nothing new since the other Valkyrie arrived at Mist's loft with her mortal followers."

Arrived, Loki thought, without the Treasure she was supposed to have guarded for the Aesir, Freya's Falcon Cloak.

"Nothing of this Ryan Starling whom Hrimgrimir thought so important?" he asked.

"He has not left the house since he and the girl were seen with Mist and Vali Odin's-son outside the loft."

Loki shrugged. Hrimgrimir had told him little about how he'd found the boy or why he considered the mortal of such value, but he couldn't be worth pursuing if he'd had so little impact on the game.

"Are you ready to send my little gift to Mist?" he asked Grer.

"Yes, my lord. He is ready."

Loki imagined the chaos said gift would cause. The spy might not harm Mist unduly, but she would be forced to waste whatever magical energy she had at her disposal just to defend herself. And to kill her assailant, of course. The irony of the situation greatly appealed to what others so dismissively referred to as Loki's sense of "mischief."

Such an inadequate, petty word.

"You will observe carefully," Loki said, "and report the results to me. In detail."

"Understood, my lord."

Loki dismissed Grer with a flick of his fingers, set down his glass, and strode to his private elevator. It glided past each of the lower six stories without stopping, coming to a gentle rest at the basement—one not even San Francisco's famed earthquakes could disturb.

The Jotunar posted outside the short corridor stepped aside, and Loki sketched a few Runes over the heavily warded and very thick steel door. It opened on silent hinges. He went on to the door at the end of the corridor and opened it using spells that, like encrypted passwords in a secret government facility, changed every time he visited.

The room behind it was nearly bare save for a small child's bed, a chest of drawers, a bed table, and a comfortably padded chair for the nurse. Various toys and equipment, including what the mortals called a "squeeze machine," were neatly stacked against the wall or piled in a large wooden box.

As usual, the boy sat cross-legged on the bedspread, rocking gently forward and back, forward and back, staring at the wall with no expression on his apparently ten-year-old face. His nurse rose from her chair as Loki entered, her gaze carefully averted.

"How is he?" Loki asked as he approached the bed.

"No change, Mr. Landvik," the woman said, her voice cracking with the nervousness she tried so hard to conceal.

"But you look worried, Miss Jones," Loki said, cocking his head. "Have you some problem to report?"

"No. No." She swallowed and looked up. "He is . . . quiet. Sometimes I can get him to play, but—"

"I request that you see to his basic needs and provide him with stimulation when he seems to require it. I do not expect you to perform miracles."

He didn't wait to see her face crumple with abject relief. He continued to the bed and sat in the chair beside it.

The boy gave no sign that he recognized Loki. He didn't even look at Loki's face. He simply rocked and rocked, sometimes making small, unintelligible sounds as if he saw or heard something or someone beyond the scope of Loki's senses. And yet Loki knew there was powerful magic locked inside the boy's soul, with limits he could only begin to guess at.

Power that had become almost completely inaccessible to him.

Aware that the boy might feel his frustration, Loki suppressed his emotions. There had been a time, in Ginnungagap, when Danny had been more responsive. He had always been reserved and quiet, strange and sometimes incomprehensible. But he had also helped locate the bridges that would have allowed Loki and his Jotunar to reach Midgard before any of the Aesir could manifest physical form and escape the Void.

Would have, Loki thought with a grimace. Freya had discovered the bridges before he could make his move, and so he'd had to agree to the game and the rules he and the Lady had set between them.

As far as he knew, she was ignorant of Danny's true abilities. She knew the boy existed; when she and Loki had met again in Ginnungagap, Danny had been with him. But her ignorance did Loki little good now that Danny would no longer speak to him in even the simplest words. Loki had not only failed to pierce the barrier between them, but had also driven the boy deeper into himself.

"Danny," he said softly. "Do you hear me?"

3

The boy didn't react. Loki sighed and tried again. "I need your assistance. There are people who would very much like to hurt both of us, and you can help me stop them."

Blank eyes flickered toward Loki and then focused inward with a finality Loki recognized all too well. He glanced over his shoulder at the wall, where Miss Jones had pinned up several of the boy's drawings on a blackboard.

Whatever his limitations in verbal communication, Danny could express himself very well with crayons. Scrawled on various pieces of drawing paper were the images of Loki and Miss Jones and even Danny . . . or the way he apparently saw himself, with lines radiating out from around the crude shape of a small boy, hands flung up as if to cast or repel magic.

That meant he was at least partially aware of his own nature, as well as the presence of the two people he saw every day. But the other pictures were more interesting: Jormungandr, Fenrir, and Hel—massive serpent, monster Wolf, and goddess of the dead, respectively—Danny's half-siblings, from whom Loki had kept Danny carefully separated while they inhabited the Void. Even Sleipnir, Odin's eight-legged steed and another of Loki's offspring, appeared in one of the drawings.

Danny had never seen any of them, and Loki assumed that somehow he had plucked those images out of his parent's mind. Such a capability surprised Loki not at all.

But there were also sketches of Freya and figures Loki thought might be elves. Had they, too, come out of Loki's mind? Did Danny recognize them as his parent's enemies?

Loki reached out to touch the soft wisps of reddish-blond hair that framed the boy's face. Not quite his mother's, but doubtless it would darken with time. Never as dark as his father's, of course.

The thought of revealing the child to his other parent was a pleasure Loki intended to savor as long as he could. It had to be delayed until just the right moment . . . the moment when the shock would give Loki a needful advantage.

Shaking his head, Loki cupped the child's soft cheek. "Centuries we were prisoners in Ginnungagap," he said, "and no more than ten years to you. But you were kept safe. And I promise you will continue to be so. My son."

He was utterly unprepared when Danny's eyes cleared and focused on his. The boy made a peculiar gesture with one hand.

"He wants his paper and crayons," Miss Jones said, her voice stronger and more assured than before.

"Then give them to him," Loki said. He studied Danny's face as Miss Jones provided the boy with a lap desk, a large sheet of white paper, and a small box of crayons. Without hesitation, Danny selected several crayons and laid them out on the paper. He began to draw, an outline in black, which he quickly filled with the same color.

There was no mistaking the image. The raven's beak was open, its wings spread as if it were about to launch itself heavenward. Danny chose a blue crayon and scribbled in the sky, filling it with swirls of darker blues and purples as in a van Gogh painting.

"Here," Danny said distinctly. And then, just as suddenly as he had come alive, Danny lost interest. He released the paper. It drifted gently to the floor, and Miss Jones picked it up.

Loki rose and snatched it from her hand.

"Here," Danny had said. A word meant to present a gift, or something else entirely?

After a final examination of Danny's expressionless face, Loki left the room, warded the doors with great care, and took the elevator to his office. Pushing all other thoughts aside, he picked up the phone.

His orders were simple and clear. It didn't matter if they made no sense to his Jotunar. He wouldn't make the kind of mistakes his enemies clearly expected of him.

If Danny had just given him a warning, he planned to be very well prepared.

The Jotunar were everywhere.

Mist sat on the back of Bryn's bike and jerked her head toward the deserted gourmet ice cream shop at the corner of Twentieth and Third. "See that guy in the khakis and light jacket?" she asked. "Frost giant. Only a Jotunn would be standing outside eating an ice cream cone in this kind of weather."

Her Sister chuckled, though there was little humor in the sound. "I guess they haven't got their disguises down just yet."

"They've certainly had time to work on it, though it takes some magical energy to maintain the more human form and not revert to their usual size." Her gaze swept the street. "There's always a sort of . . . smell about them, and sometimes an aura of cold that feels different from the surrounding air. Can you pick out the others?"

Bryn frowned in concentration. "That guy in the business suit who's let three streetcars go by without boarding any of them."

"Good catch," Mist said. "Sometimes they seem to forget we're watching *them*, too. Loki's arrogance seems to rub off on them."

"Wouldn't that be dangerous? I'm sure he's not a very forgiving boss if they screw up."

"He's not. But—"

"There!" Bryn said, pointing north. "Oh, shit." She snapped her hand back. "I think he made me."

A man in a construction worker's hard hat and jeans was striding away from them, head down against the wind. He didn't look back.

"It's okay," Mist said. "Loki's spies may make themselves scarce for a while, but they'll be back soon enough."

Bryn flexed her gloved hand. "What I wouldn't give for a good fight right now."

"I know," Mist said wearily. "But since we wouldn't be stupid enough to fight Loki and his frost giants where mortals can watch, neither will he. No one wants the authorities to get involved in a rash of swordfights, let alone magical contests."

"Too bad we can't just grab a couple of Jotunar and ask them what Loki's doing."

"Too risky," Mist said. She sighed and scooted off the bike. "Bryn, we have to talk about what happened with Rick and Dainn."

"Now?" Bryn asked, staring after the fleeing Jotunn.

"When we get back to the loft," Mist said. "There are a few more things I have to explain to you. You can—"

Her next words were lost in a gasp as a very large man crashed into her, bearing her to the ground. She pushed at him, struggling to escape the huge hands attempting to crush her trachea.

Bryn was on top of the Jotunn a moment later, but the giant fought like a rabid animal, slamming Mist's head against the asphalt and throwing Bryn from his back as if she were the little brown wren she so deceptively resembled.

Without thinking, Mist raised a ward around them, temporarily hiding her, the Jotunn, and Bryn from mortal sight. It was a mistake to waste her magical energy; she knew in less than ten seconds that she wasn't going to be able to rely on her physical battle skills to defeat the Jotunn. The tattoo around her wrist clamped down like a fiery manacle. The wolves and ravens, endlessly chasing each other over her skin, seemed to twist together into one writhing creature.

Something was wrong. Wrong that the frost giant had attacked her in the first place, wrong that he was openly trying to kill her where mortals could witness it. In a minute or two, he might even succeed.

Struggling to keep the Jotunn from choking the life out of her, Mist began to gather her magic.

Odin stared down at Dainn from his great throne, the two wolves Geri and Freki at his feet, his ravens Huginn and Muninn—Thought and Memory—perched on the back of the chair, ever watching. To either side, in a semicircle of smaller thrones, sat the twelve who had decided Dainn's fate: four of the Aesir and Vanir, four of the Alfar, and four of those Jotunar allied with the gods.

Dainn was alone. Only two of the Aesir revealed any regret or doubts about his sentence: Bragi, bard of the gods, and Freya, whose beautiful eyes were filled with sorrow. Not one of Dainn's people, judges or observers, had spoken for him.

"I have told you all I can," Dainn said.

Settling back, Odin gestured with his right hand. "Thor," he said.

His son, tall and broad-shouldered, his flame-colored beard framing his broad face like a copper gorget, strode forward from his place just behind Odin's throne. In his magic glove he clutched Mjollnir, the great Hammer. His Belt of Power, Megingjord made him appear larger and more imposing than he already was.

The room was silent as the Giant-slayer stopped before Dainn, his small eyes bright with contempt. With one swing of Mjollnir he could crush every bone in Dainn's body, and Dainn wondered if that was to be the manner of his death. It would be a relatively merciful one.

He glanced one last time at Eyfrith, High Lord of the Alfar. The elf's expression was remote, as if he stood in Alfheim among the tall trees and had nothing to do with the judgment at all. The other three elves gazed in any direction that did not encompass their former brother.

"You will take the traitor to Mount Ornoradet and destroy him there," Odin said, "and then return to the battle lines."

Return, Dainn thought, to a war the Aesir could not possibly win. The Last Battle, the end of all things until the rising of the new world, was about to begin.

Because Dainn had failed to stop it.

Thor grabbed Dainn's arm, nearly snapping bone. Dainn didn't react. He had been judged a traitor, but he would not give any of the gods and giants and elves in this hall the satisfaction of witnessing his pain.

"Stop."

Freya rose from her chair, flowing out of it like honey from a jar, all soft limbs and diaphanous robes. She turned to Odin, bowing her head.

"All-father," she said, "I ask mercy."

Peering down at her from his one good eye, Odin rested his elbow on his knee. "Mercy?" he asked. "What have *you* done, Lady?"

Her smile lit the hall more brightly than any thousand torches. "Not I," she said. "I ask mercy for this elf, who attempted to warn us of Loki's plot even when he knew it would mean his death."

"After he betrayed us," Thor snarled.

"Because he had hoped to prevent Ragnarok," she said.

They all fell silent again, thinking, Dainn knew, of the coming of Surtr and the Homeworlds engulfed in flame, as prophecy foretold.

"We have heard the evidence," Eyfrith said.

"Yes," Freya said. "But this elf came to us of his own accord, when he might have tried to escape."

"He would not have succeeded," Thor said, twisting Dainn's arm with such force that he could barely suppress a grunt of pain.

"But he can do no harm now." She looked at Dainn. "Will you fight and regain your honor?"

"Fight against Loki?" Thor said with a short laugh. "Even if the All-father would permit it, the traitor would be useless to us. Laufeyson has stolen his manhood, and his magic has deserted him. There is nothing left but a traitor's soul."

"Then let him fight himself," Freya said. She climbed to Odin's throne and whispered in his ear. The ravens flapped their wings, half rising from their perches. The wolves growled and bristled.

Odin was silent long after Freya had retreated to her chair and adjusted her gowns over her round thighs and naked breasts. Thor turned to face his father, a defiant thrust to his jaw, and nearly pulled Dainn's shoulder out of its socket.

"Father," he said. "You cannot allow—"

"Silence," Odin said. He looked slowly around the room, at the other Aesir and Vanir, the Alfar and the giants.

"There is one thing an elf fears more than death," The All-father said, his gaze resting on Eyfrith, "and that is to lose his reason."

"Reason?" Thor repeated in disbelief. "He has none left to take." He knocked Dainn over and pressed down on Dainn's back with his boot. "I can make a cripple of him before I—"

He broke off as Odin rose ponderously to his feet. "He shall live," the All-father said, "but not as an Alfr." He stared down at Dainn. "Of all the elves, you were the exemplar. You could never be shaken. Your mind was as lucid as the clearest pool, never sullied by any flaw but pride. And still you cling to what is left of it." He held out his arm, and Huginn flew to perch on his shoulder. "This is my judgment. I trust it will satisfy you, Lady."

Closing his eyes, Dainn lay very still. He didn't know what was to come, but it would be terrible. Terrible enough to make him long for death.

"I curse you." Odin's voice came from somewhere above him. "I curse you to become that which you and all Alfar most fear. And that you shall remain until the fire consumes us all."

With a hoarse cry, Huginn dived onto Dainn's back and stabbed the base of his neck with a beak like the blade of an ax. Agonizing pain engulfed Dainn's body, acid burning its way outward from the wound through the center of his chest, down to his fingertips and toes and up to the crown of his head. Something stirred in his soul, a darkness that had no bottom, no limit. And with it came rage. Blinding, mind-destroying rage.

Thor stepped back, his expression frozen in astonishment. Dainn scrambled to his feet. He was strong now—stronger than he had been moments before, stronger than any elf. He saw the horror on Eyfrith's face, on the faces of the other Alfar.

They saw what he could only feel.

With a snarl he wheeled and raced for the door. Golden mirrors hung in the outer hall, framed with horses and wolves and serpents entwined and racing endlessly around the glass.

The face reflected in the glass was almost his own. But such a wild and savage visage had never belonged to an Alfar.

Nothing like true thought passed through his mind then. He loped out of the hall like Managarmr chasing the moon and raced across the gardens and through the neat woodlands of Asgard, past the Einherjar guarding the borders of the Aesir's Homeworld and over the bridge to Jotunheim, seeking his betrayer.

He slipped easily past Loki's guards and found their commander lying on a couch heaped with furs, speaking with one of his Jotunn generals. The Slanderer sat up as he saw Dainn. A dozen conflicting expressions swept over his sly, handsome face, one after the other.

"Dainn!" he said. "What an unexpected pleasure."

The Jotunar guards advanced on Dainn, but Loki waved them away. The giants, bristling with armor crudely hammered out of vast plates of iron, lumbered out of the tent.

"Now," Loki said, watching Dainn warily. "You look quite out of sorts, my love. Was Odin less than appreciative of your message?"

Loki knew where he'd gone, of course. He would have expected Dainn to approach the Aesir once he'd learned how he had been deceived, how he had been used to advance Loki's cause.

But Loki would *not* have expected Dainn to return. Or to look and behave as he did now.

An animal. A savage. A killer.

"Have they sent you with a message?" Loki inquired, feigning indifference. "An offer of truce, perhaps? Surely not of surrender, as sensible as that would be."

"No message," Dainn said, struggling to keep his voice even. Composed. Normal. He started toward the couch. Loki stiffened, and Dainn could feel him gathering defensive magic, ready to strike out at a moment's notice.

"They rejected me," Dainn said. "Odin cursed me as a traitor. They would not heed my warning."

"A pity," Loki said. "But nothing has changed as far as I'm concerned. Don't think I hold you responsible for turning on me. I could have expected no less of my honorable elf."

"Honorable," Dainn croaked.

"Whatever you think I may have done, it is for the good of the Homeworlds," Loki said, throwing all his persuasive charm into the lie. "I will put an end to Ragnarok, just as you wished. There will be no more war when I have control." He held out his hand. "Join me, Dainn. Remain at my side. I will value you as they do not and never can. You will have a place of honor in the world I create."

As if he were still dazed by the Aesir's repudiation, Dainn crossed the remaining distance to the couch and stumbled against it. Loki laid his hand on Dainn's cheek.

"I am still what you loved," he said softly. "Only this body has changed." He rolled onto his back and pulled Dainn down with him. Dainn shuddered, still holding his rage in check. A moment longer. And another, as many as it took to feel Loki relax and sigh and tangle his fingers in Dainn's hair.

Faster than Thor's lightning, Dainn struck. His fingers closed around Loki's neck. Instantly Loki was fighting back, searing Dainn's hands with ice and then fire, blackening Dainn's flesh.

Dainn never lost his grip. He closed his eyes and found the creature inside him, unleashed the darkness, sent it hurtling into Loki's mind.

"*No!*" Loki's voice cried, soundless, into Dainn's own mind. "*You can't do this!*"

"*Can I not?*" Dainn asked, tightening his grip. The beast inside him reveled in Loki's terror, his pain, the way Laufeyson's will began to crumble, his soul to shatter. "*You stripped me of everything I had. I gave you what you wanted, and you rendered me harmless. I am helpless no longer.*"

Loki's mouth sagged open as the beast's attack began to have its effect, clawing through Loki's brain, shredding his thoughts. The black maw opened wide, like that of Fenrir about to swallow the All-father. Jaws closed, teeth pierced, and sentience pumped from the wounds like blood from an artery.

"*Dainn*," Loki's voice came again, weak, dying. "*If you kill me . . .*"

An image sprang into Dainn's mind, one the beast could not understand. But it made Dainn stop, loosening his hands, and Loki surged up beneath him, his breath sawing in his lungs as he tried a final, desperate counterattack.

It wasn't enough to stop the beast. But it forced Dainn to see beyond the red haze of the thing's Helish vision.

See what he could not bear to accept. And as Loki struck, gathering every thread of cold in the air to form a rope capable of strangling even the creature Dainn had become, the world exploded. Dainn was hurled to the floor by some force that seemed to come from inside and outside himself at the same time, a force that jolted the earth beneath him and wailed with a thousand despairing voices. It ripped Dainn in two, gutting him from heart to groin, and he screamed.

Bare footsteps raced toward him, and a thin hand touched Dainn's arm, searing down to the bone.

"Dainn!" it said. "Are you okay?"

Lunging up, Dainn struck at the blurred shape above him. The hand caught his wrist in a desperate attempt to stop his attack. Dainn knew he could have broken the hold and reduced the figure to shreds of flesh and muscle and bone, but he stopped. Breathed. Remembered.

"You're okay now," Ryan said, sitting on the edge of the bed. "It was just a nightmare."

"What did you see?" Dainn asked hoarsely.

"Nothing. I mean, no visions or anything. I just heard more yelling." He touched Dainn's sweat-soaked hair almost tenderly. "Is there something you want me to—"

"Did I hurt you again?"

Ryan flinched. "No. You were dreaming."

Dainn pushed Ryan's hand aside, swung his legs over the side of the bed and fought off a wave of dizziness.

"Where is Mist?" he asked.

"She went to show Bryn the Jotunar spies," Ryan said. "I couldn't slee—" Suddenly his gaze turned inward, and his face went white. "Mist . . . something's happening. She needs—"

Dainn was already moving. "Go upstairs and stay with Gabi," he said, heading for the hall.

"Dainn!" Ryan called after him.

Ignoring his state of near-undress, Dainn ran barefoot to the kitchen door.

4

The fire gathered in Mist's chest—fire, ice, stone, wind, all the elements that made up the ancient magic she had used so recently against Loki.

She drove it back and tried to concentrate on the Rune-magic she knew she had some hope of controlling. She slammed the Jotunn's snarling face with brands forged of Rune-steel, burning into his flesh. He hardly reacted, but she had the smallest chance to roll out from under him. She tried to get to her feet, fell to one knee, and heard Bryn shout a warning as the Jotunn attacked again, this time with a blast of bitter cold that Mist only evaded with a hastily conjured shield made of heavy billets. It held together just long enough to turn the blast aside.

Her forge-magic wasn't working.

Wielding the sword she'd "sung" to full size from the knife on her belt, Bryn hacked up at the Jotunn's chest. He slapped her away again. Mist desperately searched her mind for a different approach.

And she recalled the inconvenient fact she'd managed to shove aside whenever she was in danger of remembering.

She was half-giant herself. She could raise the cold and ice without relying on the ancient magic. She could accept what she was and call on her full Jotunn strength, as she had done so unwittingly in her first battle against Loki Laufeyson's minions.

Bryn fell back against her, her jaw bloodied and her nose apparently broken. "Any ideas?" she gasped.

"Yes," Mist said. "Stand out of the way."

Watching the Jotunn, Bryn moved aside while Mist closed her eyes and reached within.

It was difficult. It went against everything she believed in. But she let it flow into her, felt her unknown father's heritage swell her muscles and transform her heart into a piston. Her blood ran like an Arctic river through her veins. When the Jotunn came at her again, she drew on the frigid core of her body and built a hammer out of ice, its handle her arm and its head shaped around her hand.

As if he felt the change in her, the Jotunn faltered. She swung the hammer at his head. He staggered, losing his balance.

Mist had just begun to call up another Jotunn weapon when Dainn arrived at a run and charged Mist's adversary.

The Jotunn swung around, his fist connecting with Dainn's jaw. Dainn recovered instantly, tearing into the giant's flesh with fingers shaped into claws, drawing azure blood. The Jotunn answered in kind, striking Dainn in the chest with razor-sharp blades of ice. Very red blood stained Dainn's T-shirt, and he coughed sharply.

There was no question in Mist's mind what he would do. He'd go at the Jotunn until he'd killed the enemy or was too badly injured to fight.

Mist snatched at the cold around her as if it were a solid thing and drew it through skin and muscle, right down to the bone. Her very core turned to ice. She flung a blizzard of crystals toward the Jotunn, each one a tiny needle capable of piercing the skin and puncturing muscle. The white cloud swallowed him up, and he fell, his arms wheeling and thrashing as if he were trying to fend off a swarm of angry bees.

Then he crashed to the ground and lay still, his entire body sheathed in an inch-thick layer of frost. Dainn was on him an instant later, straddling him with the intent to kill in every line of his body.

Mist grabbed Dainn's shoulders and pulled him off. He met her gaze, jumped up, and circled her and the Jotunn like a jackal waiting for a lioness to abandon her slaughtered prey.

He was still very close to the edge. If she pushed him too hard . . .

"Why haven't you killed him?" he demanded, his voice as rough as sandpaper.

Letting go of the cold, Mist felt her body return to its normal state, her flesh warming, her skin flushing with honest red blood. The tattoo was once again no more than a lifeless marking on her wrist.

"I don't kill helpless enemies," she answered Dainn, "unless I have no other choice."

Dainn made a sound halfway between a growl and a laugh. "Helpless?"

"How did you know what was going on?"

"I—" Dainn broke off, and it seemed to Mist that some of the violent energy went out of his body.

"You were supposed to be asleep," she said. "Were you watching me?"

"I was . . . dreaming," he said, his face stricken with some ugly memory.

It must have been one Hel of a dream, Mist thought. "So you woke up and rushed out and immediately decided I needed help."

"I could see the Jotunn was—"

"You can't keep trying to protect me every time you think I'm in trouble. And if you'd been paying attention, you would have seen that I was winning."

"Hel, yes," Bryn said, coming up behind Mist. "I don't know what you did, but it was impressive." She eyed Dainn as she might a rabid mongrel. "I've never seen one of your kind fight the way you do."

Dainn stared back at her, his upper lip twitching.

"Save it," Mist said, nudging the Jotunn's body with the toe of her boot. "Right now we have to figure out what to do with this."

"And what *will* you do, if not kill him?" Dainn asked.

"Look," she said, "there has to be a good reason he just attacked us out in the open like this." She glanced around, abruptly aware that her ward was dissolving. She was amazed it had stayed up so well when she was fighting for her life. "We need to find out what that reason is. And that means we have to bind and confine him and leave him able to speak, so he can tell us why he did it."

"*If* he'll tell you," Bryn said, wiping a smear of blood from her nose.

"You leave that problem to us," Mist said. "I need you to take care of your injuries and make sure there's nothing else going on that we have to worry about."

To her profound relief, Bryn nodded and walked away . . . though not without a final, probing glance at Dainn.

"Where will you hold the Jotunn?" Dainn asked when Bryn was gone.

Mist rubbed clotted blood from her cheek with the sleeve of her shirt. "There's a large storage closet off the gym," she said. "Let's put him in there for now."

Together they lifted the giant and carried him into the narrow alley behind the loft and through the kitchen door. The storage closet was the size of a small room, cluttered with equipment Mist no longer used, stacks of worn towels and junk Mist had never found a permanent place for.

They laid the giant down on the concrete floor. Dainn stepped back. Mist bent over the Jotunn, looking for signs of consciousness.

Like a sudden eruption from a seemingly long-dead volcano, the Jotunn bolted up and locked his hands around Mist's arms. Her blood literally turned cold, and her skin crackled with a thin film of ice that almost immediately began to penetrate her flesh.

Acting purely on instinct, Mist blasted the Jotunn with Rune-staves pulsing black and red like coals in an old-fashioned forge. They struck the Jotunn full in the chest, and with no sound other than a grunt he fell back, clutching the blistering, smoking wound.

Dainn leaped toward him. Mist intercepted the elf and half threw him against the wall, setting one of the metal shelves to rattling. Her tattoo pinched her wrist.

"Curse it!" she swore. "I told you not to interfere!" She noticed the blood on his shirt and groaned silently. "Loki's piss, will you just keep quiet?"

He rose into a crouch. "Will you destroy him now?"

"No," she said. "And you're going to stay right there while I see how badly he's injured."

"He tried to kill you. Again."

"You don't say." She looked back at the Jotunn. He was quiet now, his eyes closed, breathing more or less normally. But the wound was serious. She couldn't think of anyone she could ask to deal with it.

And she had fallen back on a terrible kind of magic. Magic she feared might reveal the same darkness in herself that Dainn carried along with his beast.

He'd told her that there was no wickedness in her. She knew he was wrong.

"Now is the time to question him," Dainn said, "before he dies."

"Giants are as tough as Aesir when it comes to healing themselves," she said, more to convince herself than Dainn. She stood and searched the metal shelves for the stack of towels. "These are clean," she said. "I'll give him a field dressing, and we'll—"

"Did it occur to you that this attack may have been intended as some kind of distraction?"

"I don't think so. Someone would have alerted us by now if there'd been an attack on the loft or camp."

The Jotunn groaned and began to stir again. Mist bent over him. "Who are you?" she asked.

He stared her out of his ice-blue eyes. "Send the elf away," he said in a deep, rumbling voice.

"It would be better for you if you just cooperate," she said, cutting the towels into strips with her knife.

"The Lady Mist may have scruples," Dainn said, "but I do not."

"He almost killed you once already," Mist said to the Jotunn, playing along. "But I can protect you. Did Loki send you to attack us?"

The giant rolled his head to one side and closed his eyes. Mist's fingertips ached with cold as she began to bind the wound.

"Dainn," she said, "go outside and make sure everything's okay."

"I will not leave you alone with him."

"How many times do I have to tell you—" She drew a quick breath and pressed her fingers to his neck. "He's unconscious again. We'll have to tie him up and leave him for now."

Her hands beginning to shake with exhaustion, Mist concocted a binding spell, twining Rune-staves of steel into a fine rope to tie the Jotunn's hands and feet.

"Gleipnir it's not," she said, rocking back on her heels. "But he'd have to be in very good condition to break it." She could feel Dainn gathering another argument and raised her hand. "Trust me, okay?"

After a moment he nodded, and they walked back into the gym together. Dainn was very warm, perhaps in contrast to the chill that still hadn't left her bones. Strangely enough, his presence calmed her, quieted her horror at how badly she'd injured the Jotunn. She was aware of the danger lurking inside him, but the smell of him, the sound of his breathing, the—

She didn't get the chance to complete the thought. The ground beneath her knees heaved and shuddered, and she and Dainn instinctively reached for each other. The gym floor undulated like a gentle swell on the ocean, setting the sword rack to rattling and the walls to swaying. There was no nearby structure sturdy enough to shelter beneath.

Mist held her breath until the earth settled again and the waves receded. She released Dainn hastily and ran for the door facing the street. Dainn caught up and flung the door open just as she reached it.

Absurdly, the old tale flashed through her mind . . . how the Aesir had bound Loki under the serpent, condemning him to eternal torment as the snake's venom dripped into his face.

Loki's thrashing was said to have caused earthquakes. Like this one.

Once she and Dainn reached the street, they nearly collided with Rick and Bryn.

"Did you feel that?" Rick asked breathlessly.

Mist didn't bother to answer. She looked past Rick to Bryn.

"Is everything all right at the camp?" she asked.

"We were just on the way back to the factory when the quake hit," Bryn said. "Where's the Jotunn?"

"Confined. He won't—"

"Mist," Dainn said, drawing her attention. "The young mortals are alone."

"When's the last time you saw them?"

"When Ryan made me aware that something was wrong with you."

"Odin's balls." She turned back to Bryn. "Do whatever you have to, but be prepared for aftershocks." She spun and sprinted back to the loft, Dainn a step behind her.

The building seemed relatively untouched save for a mug lying in pieces on the kitchen floor and a bit of loose paint and plaster scattered across the carpet runner in the hall. There might be more damage they couldn't see, but Mist wouldn't have cared if all the paint had flaked off every wall in the place. Not as long as the kids were safe.

They found Ryan lying on the living-room couch, his arm over his eyes. He rolled onto his side as soon as they came in.

"Are you all right?" Mist asked, kneeling beside the couch.

Ryan's skin was flushed, and he wouldn't meet Dainn's eyes. "Gabi and me know what to do in an earthquake," he said.

"Where is she now?"

"She came down for a minute when the earthquake started, and went back upstairs when it was over." He sat up. "You're okay?"

"It's *you* we're worried about," Mist said, looking him over carefully. "There was that thing with Freya this morning, when you said you saw something dangerous. And Dainn said you told him I was in trouble. Did you know the earthquake was coming?"

"No." Ryan bit his lip. "I don't understand why I'm seeing things when they happen instead of in the future. It's all messed up."

"What happened when you told Dainn I needed help?"

Ryan ducked his head, as if he'd been accused of a heinous crime. "I only knew you were in some kind of danger."

"Well, it's been dealt with," Mist said, willing her heartbeat to slow. "But you *know* what could have happened once Dainn got involved."

"I knew he'd be okay."

"He didn't completely lose control, if that's what you mean," Mist said. "It might have turned out differently."

"No," Ryan said. He met Mist's gaze defiantly. "Will you believe me if I tell you what else I saw before the earthquake?"

"Unless it's something dangerous to us, it can wait. For now—"

"It was about *you*."

Something about the way he said the words convinced Mist that the coming revelation wasn't going to be pleasant. Dainn, his expression stuck in typical robot mode—a cursed sight safer than his other guise—retreated through the door to the hall. Obviously he shared her inexplicable sense of dread.

"Go on," she said to Ryan, masking her unease.

He glanced toward the door as if he wished he could call Dainn back. "What do you call those stars when they explode?" he asked. "Novas, right?"

A nova. Like the bright light she'd experience when "faux-Freya" had confronted Dainn in the kitchen.

"Ryan," she said, "when you came down to the kitchen this morning, did you—"

Male voices in the kitchen brought her to her feet. One of them belonged to Koji Tashiro. The other was Dainn's, and it didn't sound very friendly.

5

Mist strode into the kitchen. The two men stood about six feet apart. Dainn's expression was stony, Tashiro's wary and puzzled as it had been very early that morning when the Einherjar had arrived to interrupt his discussion with Mist. He still hadn't recognized Dainn as the savage fighter in the gym, where Mist and the elf had taken out a trio of Loki's Jotunar, but his brain was obviously working hard to resolve his faulty memory and overcome the blocks Mist had placed there.

"Ms. Bjorgsen," Tashiro said, his dark eyes meeting hers as she approached. "Are you all right?"

"Fine," she said, keeping an eye on Dainn. "No one's been hurt."

Tashiro glanced from Dainn's blood-stained T-shirt to Mist's scraped face and took her hand in a firm grip. "I'm glad to hear it."

"You happened to show up at an odd time," she said, pulling her hand from his.

"I was concerned about you and Ryan," he said. "It's pretty crazy out there."

"How bad is it?"

"I saw a few buildings with some structural damage, car accidents, that kind of thing, but it doesn't look as if too many people were badly hurt. The ambulances and emergency personnel are out in force." He noticed the broken mug on the linoleum. "I hope the earthquake hasn't done any significant damage to your property."

"None that I've found so far. I guess we were lucky." She hesitated.

"I'm sorry I had to ask you to leave earlier this morning. I just didn't expect my friend's arrival with a whole biker club, and that was about all I could handle at the moment."

"I understand completely," Tashiro said. He laid a fine leather briefcase on the table. "Under the circumstances, I think we can hold off discussing Ryan a little longer."

Mist glanced at Dainn, who was very quiet. And very watchful. Tashiro had threatened him during the battle of the gym, judging him to be psychotic or on drugs. And though Mist had told Dainn what she'd done to erase Tashiro's memory of the events, he was still on a hair trigger where the lawyer was concerned.

"I don't think we should wait," she said. "If you'll excuse us for a minute . . ."

She took Dainn's arm. It was all steel cables and clenched muscle, hot under her hand. She pulled him into the hall and stood between him and the kitchen door.

"Listen to me, Dainn," she said. "I don't have time for a pissing contest right now. We have a missing goddess, closed bridges, a Jotunn in the closet, ten Valkyrie to locate, no idea of when more allies will show up, and a very unpredictable beast to control. Of course, that's not counting trying to figure out what Loki's going to do next."

"The greatest danger sometimes hides itself in the least obvious forms."

"Then you aren't talking about yourself."

"My . . . other half is not known for its subtlety."

If he was cracking a joke, Mist thought, he was in better shape than she'd thought. "Look," she said, "Tashiro obviously doesn't remember—"

"You cannot expect him to remain ignorant if he continues to see you. Are you prepared to tell him the truth if he discovers your deception?"

"Considering the legal problems we're likely to face once this battle for Midgard really gets underway, he may come in handy for more than getting Ryan—and Gabi, I hope—to a safer place. I think he might be trusted with the truth."

"He has a personal interest in you," Dainn said, "caused by your—"

"I know," she snapped. "But even if his interest had nothing to do with the glamour, it wouldn't be any of your business." She glanced back at the kitchen door. "I'm giving you an order. Leave Tashiro alone. In fact, I think it would be a good idea if you stay away when he's here."

"It would be better if I stay away from everyone, would it not?"

"That's not a bad idea." She regretted the words as soon as she'd spoken them. "If you can just hang on until we can work on your problem—"

"And what of *your* abilities? You did well against the Jotunn, but you must strengthen your mastery of the Galdr, and without gaining considerably more control you cannot risk the ancient magic."

"I haven't forgotten. But you said yourself that we both have to be careful. Do you think you can you still teach me?"

He bowed his head. "I wish I could answer with certainty. You have exceeded every skill I possess save in the Alfar magic, and have learned more rapidly by intuition and instinct than any formal lessons can impart."

"Then I guess I have no choice but to stumble along as best I can."

She rubbed her wrist, which hadn't stopped aching since it had come to life during her altercation with the Jotunn.

Dainn looked pointedly at the tattoo. "It has burned you again," he said, statement rather than question. "Was it the fight with the Jotunn? This seems to occur most often when you face battle."

But that wasn't precisely true, Mist thought. Now that Dainn had forced her to think about it, she realized the same thing had happened when he had first touched her, when she'd learned that Loki was in Asgard, and when she'd joined her mind with Dainn's. The use of magic wasn't the only trigger, either.

"I don't know," she admitted. "It never did this before you and

Hrimgrimir arrived. Maybe it's when something big is going on, whether it's a battle, or magic, or . . . Hel, I don't have an answer."

"Under what circumstances did you acquire it?"

"Wolves and ravens," she said, tracing the interlocking figures. "I remember wanting to prove my loyalty to Odin."

"But you are not certain?"

"It's been a long time."

"But clearly it has some significance."

"Everything does these days," she muttered. "Have you made any more progress in figuring out what that Freya business in the kitchen was all about?"

He looked away quickly. "Not as yet," he said.

"Then I want you to do me a favor."

"Other than avoiding Tashiro's company?" he asked stiffly.

"Macy's," she said.

Dainn blinked. "The department store?"

"You never did strike me as a Patrick James kind of guy, elf or not. But you're still wearing Eric's clothes, and you need your own. I don't care if you come home with destroyed jeans and bright pink polo shirts, but I want to take everything out of Eric's closet and burn it as soon as possible."

"I understand the sentiment," Dainn said without so much as the trace of a smile. "But will the stores be open after the earthquake?"

"This is San Francisco. People here consider quakes a minor inconvenience unless they're a lot worse than this one was. Christmas isn't about to come to a crashing halt when it's just around the corner."

"Can you trust me with such a task now?"

"At the moment, you're less dangerous out there than you are here." She hesitated. "If you have any doubts . . ."

In spite of everything that had happened, the elf hadn't lost all his pride. Mist could feel his anger ebbing.

"I promise that I will not run mad in the streets," he said.

"Unless you bump into Loki, or his Jotunar," she said. "I'm giving you another order, Dainn: if you happen to meet any of them, you stay away."

Dainn shuddered, and Mist knew he was remembering yesterday's pain and humiliation all over again. "I will not engage them," he said, very quietly. "Do you wish me to acquire anything else?"

"No. Just take care of business as quickly as you can and come back home."

By then, Tashiro will be gone, she thought. *And I can start working on all the other problems.*

The only question was, which one she should tackle first?

When she focused again, Dainn had gone. She returned to the kitchen, where Tashiro was removing an accordion file from his briefcase. He looked up as she came in.

"Your cousin seemed a little upset," he said.

Hilarious, Mist thought. "He tripped over something during the quake," she said. "He'll live."

"I see." Tashiro fiddled with the file. "I thought maybe he'd taken a personal dislike to me. How close a relative is he?"

"Distant," Mist said, in a voice meant to discourage any further inquiry on the subject.

"Distant enough to be jealous about you?"

"Hardly. What would he have to be jealous of?"

If Tashiro felt the rebuke, he was careful not to show it. "How *is* Ryan?" he asked.

Since she couldn't tell him the full truth, she settled for part of it. "He'll be better off when he's settled in his own life," she said.

Tashiro nodded. "These are the papers pertaining to Mamie Starling's will and Ryan's inheritance," he said, pulling two folders from the file. "I did a background check on Ryan before I started looking for him, so I have a pretty good idea what he's been through." He grimaced. "His parents disowned him about a year ago, and since he's nearly eighteen they won't have any responsibility for him much longer. He certainly won't need their financial assistance."

"That's good. There's something else I want to talk to you about. There's a girl—"

She spent the next half-hour telling him about Gabi—whom he had met but didn't remember—and asking the lawyer if he could arrange for the girl and Ryan to stay together.

"I'll make inquiries," Tashiro said, tucking the files away. "Could be tricky since the girl is still a minor. It's certainly unorthodox, but I'll see what we can do." He smiled. "I have an in with a few judges here and there."

"Thanks," Mist said with genuine gratitude. "I'll need to give you a retainer. What do you—"

"No retainer," Tashiro said, raising his hand. "I do pro bono work pretty frequently. I'm not exactly living hand to mouth."

Because he was the scion of a very wealthy family. Mist knew that much about him, in addition to the fact that he could wield a mean katana.

"I'd rather give you something for your work," she said.

He gave a courtly little bow. "Your company is more than adequate compensation."

Mist kept a lid on her irritation. As Dainn had reminded her, Tashiro's interest was probably ninety-nine percent attributable to the glamour she'd used to tinker with his memory.

"Anything else?" she asked, quelling his hint with a hard glance.

He didn't seem to notice. "Can I speak to Ryan now?"

"He's been feeling a little under the weather, but I'll check."

When she went into the living room, she found Ryan curled up on the couch in an obvious state of distress.

"Are you all right?" she asked. "I know we didn't finish our conversation . . ."

He sat up, arms folded across his chest. "I'm fine," he said in a perfect tone of feigned indifference.

"If you feel up to it, Mr. Tashiro would like to speak to you."

"Now?"

"Now."

He hopped off the couch and almost ran to the door. Mist took a deep breath, and realized what had set him off.

Dainn had been in the room. Mist had the feeling that he'd had a serious and very personal conversation with Ryan while she'd been with Tashiro. And evidently not a cheerful one.

Choked with unexpected sadness, Mist returned to the kitchen. Tashiro was sitting alone at the table.

"Where's Ryan?" she asked.

"Apparently he wasn't quite ready to talk to me," Tashiro said.

"I'll speak to him," Mist said, wishing she could grab a beer. "I appreciate your help."

"It's my job. Is there anything more I can do for you?"

"Nothing, thanks. Take care with the driving."

Tashiro rose. "I'll be seeing you again very soon, then."

With a short nod, Mist escorted him to the front door. Just before he climbed into his car, she saw a faint shimmer around him, a blurring of his outline into something long and silvery. She blinked as the shape seemed to flow into the car, and a moment later Tashiro was behind the wheel and waving good-bye.

Rubbing at her eyes, Mist retreated into the house. She was tired, and hungry. If she was beginning to hallucinate, she'd have to do something about that.

With a sharp shake of her head and a quick laugh, she went to find a beer.

Orn perched on the hanging lamp close to the apartment door, watching for Anna's return.

He didn't like being separated from her now. Everything had been shaking and swaying just like his perch when she carried his cage from one place to another.

But now the shaking had stopped, and it wouldn't have been so bad if that was all he had to think about. But he and Anna had hardly been apart since Rebekka had died, and it was very important that they stay together.

Orn bobbed his head and rocked from foot to foot, confusing pictures racing round and round in his head. For a while, after Anna had taken him across the big water, he had been stupid . . . happy if he had his treat sticks and the comfort of Anna's shoulder.

But so much had changed. It was *here*. All here, the things he needed to find. Including himself.

He mantled his wings, stretched his neck, and felt his body begin to change, feathers turning black as soot, beak lengthening. He looked on the world through different eyes, but his thoughts were the same.

Find Mist.

He crouched, launched himself through the open cage door, and flew into the room where Anna shed her false feathers and soaked herself in a pool of water. He made a solid landing on the shiny, square stones in front of the frozen water thing—the *mirror*, he remembered—and studied himself intently.

"Pretty bird," he said. "Pretty bird."

But the sound came out as a croak, deep and mocking. He tilted his head right and left and circled slowly until he had seen all of himself.

He really was not as pretty as before. His eyes were small and dark, not big and bright yellow. His was missing his beautiful red tail. But his feathers were glossy, his vision keen, his talons sharp.

With another harsh croak, he flapped his new wings and let them carry him into the place where Anna got her food. There were parrot treats, if he wanted them. But he didn't. The thought of them made him feel the way he had when he'd been sick and Anna had forced him to go to the nasty, smelly place with all the other sick birds.

He knew there was something better here. After poking his beak into various corners and opening two containers of man-food, he decided to look into the cold box. He thought about what he wanted for a while, staring at its door.

He waited patiently, and at last there was a pop and a flash of light and the door swung open. Pleased with himself, Orn landed on one of the shelves and found the meat, all wrapped in something Orn knew was supposed to keep it nice for people. He didn't need it to be nice. He grabbed the package in his beak, flew back to the counter and began to tear at the stuff covering the meat, shredding it until it was scattered everywhere and the meat was laid bare.

It was not quite as good as he remembered. The meat was dry, there were strange flavors in it and not a trace of blood. He bolted it down anyway, and then, sluggish and drowsy, gathered up all the little bits of wrapping stuff and pushed it into a hole under the place where the water came out of the silver spout. It was very hard to fly back to his cage, and as soon as he settled on his perch he became a parrot again, tucked his head under his wing and forgot all about the black bird.

He had been sleeping for a long time when Anna came back. She stopped just inside the doorway to stare at Orn.

"I must have dreamed it," she muttered. "Are you okay?"

Orn bobbed his head, though he knew Anna didn't really believe he understood her. "Okay," he said. "Okay."

"Good." Anna threw down the pouch she always carried over her shoulder, shed her outer false feathers, and sat on her long, low perch, a short burst of air coming out of her soft mouth. "Can you believe it? Only two weeks in this city, and my first earthquake already." She looked around her nest. "Thank God this place is okay. It's a madhouse out there. We're lucky it mainly broke roads and buildings and not people."

Orn flew to the back of the soft perch—*couch*, he thought—and rubbed his beak against her head feathers. She reached behind her to stroke his breast.

"You must be hungry," she said. "Just give me a minute to—"

"Look," Orn said, wanting her to understand that they couldn't wait much longer. He let his feathers change, and then his shape, and very soon he was not a parrot anymore. He hopped down to stand beside her.

Anna went very still. She stared at him for a long time.

"I'm crazy," she whispered.

"Not crazy," Orn said.

Her body began to shake all over, just like the *earthquake.* "Where is Orn?"

"Here."

Her clawless top feet—hands—reached toward him and snapped back a heartbeat later. "Orn is a parrot," she said. "An African Grey parrot."

"I am Orn," he said.

Reaching inside her coverings, she pulled out the flat stone and held it up as if he had never seen it before. "The raven," she said. "The raven on the pendant."

Orn plucked at the false feathers over her perching legs. "Find Mist," he said.

"You're not real."

"Find Mist," he said, making his voice harsh and low.

"Mist is dead. She died many years ago."

"No," he said, rustling his feathers in annoyance.

"Are you . . . talking about her descendents? Even my great-grandfather . . ." She stopped and began to make the sounds humans made when they were happy, or sometimes upset. When she was finished, her mouth was very flat.

"What do you want?" she asked.

"Who I am," he said.

"Who you are? I don't understand."

"My name. My . . ." He couldn't find the word, though he knew exactly what he wanted to say. It had to do with the future and what he was supposed to do.

"And you think this Mist can tell you?" she asked, her soft face still strangely wrinkled.

He bobbed his head, glad that she finally understood.

Anna let the stone fall back on its thin, shiny rope. "We'll talk about it tomorrow, Orn."

"Now," he insisted.

"I need to lie down." Anna spread herself flat on the couch and covered her eyes. "Tomorrow."

Tomorrow wasn't *now*, Orn thought. Tomorrow would be too late.

6

Anna woke to the persistent sensation of a sharp object poking at her face. She opened her eyes to see Orn's bright yellow eye, upside down and inches from hers.

"Go," he said, very distinctly. "Go *now*."

She sat up, pushing Orn away. He fluttered to the arm of the couch and began to pace up and down its length, squawking and bobbing his head in agitation with every step.

Spearing her hand through her mussed hair, Anna glanced at the clock. She'd fallen asleep on the couch, and she wasn't sure she was even awake yet, considering that she kept seeing a black bird—a raven—superimposed over Orn's familiar gray and red form, and shouting in a strangely human voice.

She bolted up from the couch. Smoke was seeping through the narrow gap between the front door and the carpet, and Anna choked as she felt the air grow too heavy to breathe.

Instinct told her to run for the window, but if the fire was out in the hall, someone else could be in danger, as unaware of what was happening as she'd been a few moments ago.

Orn flew to her shoulder and gripped so hard that his claws bit through her blouse. He screamed incoherently as she ran for the front door. She grabbed the doorknob and yanked it open.

To nothing. No smoke, no sirens, no people shouting or running, nothing to indicate that there was a fire in the building. But there had to be; the choking stench and the smoke were too strong to explain any other way.

"Danger," Orn hissed in her ear.

Shaking with the rush of adrenaline, Anna stumbled back inside her apartment, closed the door, and leaned against it. This wasn't like the usual dreams about the war. But it couldn't be—

Smoke billowed out of the bedroom, shocking her into action. Her eyes stinging with tears, Anna got to the door just as the flames consumed her bed, leaping up to catch on the drapes. Orn snatched a beakful of her hair and virtually dragged her toward the window, tugging and tugging until she was standing right in front of it. She hardly felt the pain.

"Run!" he cried. "Run!"

Think, she told herself. Even if she'd only imagined the fire in the hall, her own apartment was burning. She had to call 911. She grabbed her cell phone from the kitchen counter, only to find that the phone had never recharged when she'd plugged it in. She snatched at the land line phone, the one she never used. All she heard was a busy signal.

Dazed with shock, she staggered into the hall again. Nothing had changed. She sucked in a breath of clean air and leaned against her door. It was searing hot.

Ms. Hudson stuck her head out the door of her apartment just down the hall. "Anna, is that you?" she asked, blinking her nearsighted eyes. "I thought I heard you yelling."

Anna stared at her. "Don't you smell it?" she shouted.

"Smell what?" Ms. Hudson said, wrinkling her small nose. "Is something leaking? This damned earthquake is going to cost me a fortune."

Anna raced toward Ms. Hudson, who began to retreat into her apartment with an expression of alarm. Grabbing her wrist, Anna dragged her to her own door.

"Don't you feel it?" she said, pressing Ms. Hudson's palm to her door. "My apartment is on fire!"

Staring into Anna's eyes with real fear, Ms. Hudson twisted her hand free and backed away. "You need help," she said. "I'll . . . I think I'll just call for . . . an ambulance. Yes. Stay calm, Anna. I promise—"

Anna dashed for the lobby door, Orn flying right behind her. Blinded by terror, she ran into the street, intent only on getting away and barely noticing the startled faces turning toward her. She could already hear the boots drumming on the pavement, the shriek of a whistle as the hunters tracked their prey.

There were places she could hide. Safe places where no one would look. She clung to the shadows, her heart slamming under her ribs, and ran until she found the alley she was looking for.

As long as they weren't using dogs, she was safe. She dove under the thick pile of rubbish and found the small, hidden doorway beneath. She could just crawl through it by falling to her stomach. Orn squeezed in behind her, and together they huddled in the dark behind the false wall of the building as the hunters rushed obliviously by.

Anna lost track of time. She had left her watch behind, but she knew several hours had passed since she'd escaped, and keeping on the move would be better than staying hidden indefinitely. She took a breath and stuck her head through the low doorway, surrounded by the stink of the rubbish. After a moment she crawled out, and Orn followed.

It was well past curfew, and Anna couldn't see anyone on the streets. The soldiers were gone. Shivering in the cold, she remained where she was, frozen by indecision.

"Anna."

She didn't recognize the voice, but she knew who it was. Orn settled on her shoulder, all glossy black feathers, arrow-shaped head, and pointed beak.

That was when she realized everything she'd experienced since she'd left the apartment had been a dream like all the others, a flashback to a past not her own.

Only one part *had* been real.

"Anna," Orn said. "Find Mist."

"Where?" she whispered.

He spread his wings and began to fly.

Dainn stood on the traffic island across the street from the office building, staring up at the sixth floor while determined shoppers—unfazed by the recent disturbance—flowed around him, jamming the sidewalks and dodging small pieces of glass and rubble. Police were directing stalled traffic, the din of horns overwhelmed tinny music from storefronts, and snow was softening the edges of every surface, broken or otherwise. The sun had set some time ago, swiftly vanishing behind the taller buildings as if it couldn't wait to abandon its fruitless attempts at bringing some measure of warmth to the world.

His fingers tightening around the flimsy handles of the shopping bag, Dainn dropped his gaze to the men standing on either side of the building's doorway. They looked quite ordinary, though one was smoking very close to the door in defiance of the citywide ban. They seemed not to notice Dainn at all.

But they saw him. They knew him. And after a few moments they went inside, the smoker tossing his still-glowing butt on the sidewalk to be trampled underfoot.

Dainn continued to wait. Loki didn't come out, and neither did the Jotunn guards. They had no reason to fear his presence. He had been drawn here almost against his will . . . and Mist's explicit instructions. Drawn by his need to understand Freya's "appearance" in the loft that morning.

He'd suggested at the time that the Lady wasn't quite real. Mist had theorized that the manifestation might have been Freya's projection of herself, but Dainn knew that such had not been the case.

He hadn't told Mist that it could have been an illusion created by one who, for all his cleverness, should not have been able to perform such a feat. Created to hurt Dainn, and not in the physical sense. If

Mist were to discover the meaning of the illusion's accusations before Dainn was ready to explain, she would lose her ever-fragile trust in him when she needed him the most.

And when will *you be ready?* he mocked himself. In spite of the silence from the Void, the odds were great that Freya would return and the bridges reopen. He had told Mist that Loki had managed to send Freya away after their battle because she was not yet fully "in" the world, but it had been Dainn's own act of desperation—a single kiss—that had jarred the Lady out of Mist's body. Or so it had seemed.

He still had no clear idea of how the break had been achieved. He couldn't grant himself the credit of having done it solely with his own magical skill, let alone sexual potency. But if at first he had deceived himself into believing that he might placate Freya and keep her away from Mist when the Lady *did* return, the incident in Mist's kitchen had reminded him that Freya would surely condemn him for the traitor he was.

A traitor to *her*, and to her foul plans for her daughter.

He stared at the reflections of passing pedestrians in the windows, blurs of color that ran together like the senseless images of a dream. Loki had *seen* Freya possess Mist's body, but he would have realized soon after the fight that the Lady had not returned to the loft in her daughter's shape.

Laufeyson would never believe that Dainn had truly harmed Freya, even if he accepted the possibility that Dainn had helped separate mother from daughter. But Loki could guess how Freya would respond when she met Dainn again. What words she would speak. How her fury would turn the scent of primroses to the stench of scorched earth.

And Loki knew how it would look to Mist, still ignorant of her mother's true intentions for her.

Dainn's breath of laughter condensed and was torn apart by the falling snow. Ironically enough, If Loki had hoped to open a new rift between Dainn and Mist, he hadn't succeeded. Any suspicions

Mist might have harbored had fallen prey to more immediate concerns. And still Dainn kept his silence, hoping that by discouraging Mist's use of the ancient magic he could prevent Freya from finding a way back into her daughter's soul.

You deceive yourself, he thought, blinded by the delicate ice crystals that caught on his eyelashes. If he could only eliminate the beast, he might be free to use the full extent of his magic to teach Mist in the way she must be taught in order to defend *herself.*

He might as well wish that the conflagration that had burst inside him when he had faced "Freya's" accusations had consumed him and allowed him to arise, perfected, from the ashes.

Dainn was about to turn back for the loft when a person emerged from the door. A very small person, no more than nine or ten years of age, who carefully closed the door behind him and stood just outside it, dark eyes seemingly blind to the holiday pandemonium around him.

He had taken no more than a single step onto the sidewalk before Dainn was sweeping him out of the path of oncoming pedestrian traffic. The boy clung to him with absolute trust, his small arms firm around Dainn's neck.

A shock passed through Dainn's body. He stepped back into the comparative shelter of the slightly recessed doorway and set the child on his feet without releasing his grip on the boy's thin shoulders.

The child had come out of Loki's new headquarters. He might have wandered into the building, separated from his parents, but Dainn could not imagine how such a thing could have occurred without the interference of the Jotunn guards. Who had mysteriously vanished.

Taking the boy's hand, Dainn guided him carefully along the periphery of the sidewalk, looking for a safer place to speak. It was the boy who stopped him, his unexpectedly strong fingers tugging on Dainn's with an insistence he couldn't ignore.

He pulled the child into another doorway and knelt to look into the boy's expressionless face.

"Papa," he said in an oddly flat voice.

"You're looking for your father?" Dainn asked.

"Papa," the boy repeated, his gaze fixed on a point above Dainn's shoulder.

"Where did you last see your papa?"

There was no answer. It was if the boy hadn't heard him. Nor did he respond to Dainn's other questions, no matter how simply they were phrased. Perhaps he had been so terrified of being separated from his father that he had withdrawn into himself, blocking all outside stimuli from his mind.

Dainn scanned the area. The wisest course of action would be to find a police officer, who could take charge of the boy and find his parent.

And yet . . .

"Thank God!"

Dainn turned at the sound of a woman's voice and met her dark, terrified gaze.

"I thought he was lost!" she said, brushing the snow from her black hair. "One moment he was with me, and then he just disappeared."

"He is unharmed," Dainn said.

"Thank you so much." The woman reached out to take the child's hand.

Dainn put his arm around the boy's shoulders to keep him close. "He said he was looking for his father," Dainn said. "Since he appeared to be lost, I was taking him to the police."

"The police?" The woman's eyes widened as she searched the crowd. "No. Oh, no. His father asked me to take Danny out while he was conducting business, but he . . ." She pressed her hands to her mouth. "Oh, God . . . he'll be furious."

The woman wasn't feigning her fear. Was her employer such a monster, or was she merely reacting as most mortals would to the near-loss of a child and the possibility of facing a kidnapper?

"I was merely concerned for the boy," Dainn said, seeking to ease her agitation. "I would never have done him harm."

"I'm sorry," the woman said, composing herself again. "Of course you wouldn't. I'm grateful. But Danny's autistic, you see, and I'm afraid all this will have been too much for him."

Dainn knew little of the disorder, but he was aware that it could afflict a mortal with difficulties in interpreting and interacting with the world and other people. It certainly explained the boy's detached behavior in the midst of so much commotion.

"I'll take him home now," the woman said. "Again, I'm very grateful, Mr.—"

"Alfgrim," he said.

"Thank you, Mr. Alfgrim." She reached for the boy's hand again. This time he took it, though he seemed to act less of his own volition than in response to some inaudible command.

With strange reluctance, Dainn let them go. But some inexplicable compulsion drew him after them, and he made careful use of his magic to create a small spell that altered the flow of air around him, wreathing him in snowflakes and hiding him from their sight.

When the woman reached the doorway to Loki's building, the Jotunar were there again. They held the door open for her, and she and the boy walked through. Danny turned at the last instant, and his eyes, focused and clear, found Dainn's through his camouflage.

Dainn stood watching long after the boy had gone inside. Clearly the child was in some way connected with Loki. His father was presumably within the building as well, perhaps in Loki's employ.

And yet the boy's penetration of Dainn's camouflage suggested that he was more than a mere mortal's child. What Jotunn would stand so high in Loki's esteem that his offspring would merit his own nurse and such intense concern?

None of the possibilities in Dainn's mind gave him any comfort. The feeling that something was wrong persisted. The beast inside him growled, disturbed by Dainn's unease.

Or perhaps by something else entirely. As he began to turn away, Dainn felt a tug on his senses somewhere above him, an unmistakably magical one that smelled neither of Loki nor Jotunn but something utterly different.

He looked skyward. Amid the white, rising between the upper stories of the buildings and bright decorations, flew a black bird. It appeared to be circling as if searching for something or someone, spiraling lower and then rising high again, ever moving east toward the bay.

Dainn had not been in San Francisco long, but he knew that ravens were no common residents of this city. And this was no ordinary raven.

He glanced at the Jotunar across the street. Only one stood guard now, and Dainn had no doubt that he was not alone in sensing the intrusion of alien magic into Loki's domain.

As Dainn was considering whether it would be best to wait or follow the raven, he heard the rumble of a motorcycle emerging from the alley next to the building. The Jotunn rider looked up as he pulled into the heavy traffic, searching the sky.

There was no question in Dainn's mind that the giant had been sent out to follow the bird. And once again Dainn faced a choice. He could pursue the Jotunn and thus the bird, or report to Mist.

The Jotunn was weaving recklessly among the stalled vehicles, moving out of sight, and Dainn knew he would make little headway by boarding any of the immobilized streetcars, buses, or taxis. Traveling on foot was the only option, and he was a very fast runner.

Shedding his camouflage, he raced along the street just parallel to the sidewalk, the shopping bag swinging at his side. Horns honked and faces turned to watch him pass, but he quickly left each group of observers behind. The bird, too, had vanished by the time he reached Third Street.

"Hey, Mist. You trying to freeze us to death?"

She turned from the open doorway, glancing back at Vali. Odin's big, bluff son was joking, of course; like her he was half Jotunn, and it would take a lot more than a mortal winter, no matter how un-natural, to make him feel even the slightest chill.

"I haven't seen *you* in a while," she said—genuinely grateful, in spite of her seemingly endless store of worries, that she hadn't had to contend with yet another player in this crazy battle circus. There were things to be said for the reclusive tendencies of a computer geek. Even a godly one.

"Yeah," he said, joining her as she closed the front door. "I know I've been pretty much holed up in the computer room since I got here. I guess a lot goes on outside my door I never seem to notice." He cleared his throat. "I heard about that Jotunn who attacked you. You need any help?"

"It's under control," Mist said, walking ahead of him into the hall. "Nothing to worry about."

"What're you going to do with him?"

"I don't know yet. We need to find out *why* he attacked us."

"Maybe I can talk to him. He may be an enemy, but I'm still half Jotunn."

"So am I. It doesn't seem to have helped." She looked back at Vali. There was real hurt in his eyes.

"Sorry," she said. "I'm not in a great mood right now."

"Understandable," he said, his expression clearing. "I mean, with the quake and all. But it wouldn't hurt to let me try, would it?"

"I'll think about it."

To her relief, he let the matter drop and stood aside to let her precede him into the kitchen. "I've got some stuff to show you, if you've got the time."

"Stuff?"

His ruddy face broke into a wide grin. "Come on. This shouldn't take too long." He clumped into the back hall and squeezed ahead of her through the door to the computer room, dropping into the chair in front of the largest monitor. The room was filled to the rafters with a half-dozen other servers and peripherals and equipment Mist didn't recognize. She could hardly believe it had once been "Eric's" office.

"You asked if I could combine magic with computer technology," Vali said, his thick fingers dancing with surprising agility across the keyboard. "I figured out something I think will be very useful."

Mist stood behind him, resting her hand on the back of the chair, as the display on the screen changed from one incomprehensible series of letters and numbers to another. The only thing she recognized was an occasional Rune scattered among the other symbols. Runes that didn't appear on any normal keyboard.

"You see?" he said, triumph in his deep voice. "Pretty good, huh?"

Feeling more than a little foolish, Mist leaned closer. "I'm sure it's great, Val, but I have no idea what you're showing me."

He blushed. "Oh. Sorry. The important thing you have to know is that I've written a few programs using Galdr that will make our search for your Sisters a lot easier. One of them"—he pointed at the screen—"runs all the database queries faster than the best mortal-made programs. This one"—he switched to another screen of gibberish—"breaks into systems the most skilled hackers have never been able to bust open. And this—" He rolled his chair to another, slightly smaller monitor and pressed a key. "This is my crowning achievement. It tells me whenever anyone else is accessing the same databases I am within a twenty-four-hour period." He rocked back in his chair and grinned up at Mist. "It's specifically set up to detect specific search parameters and patterns, and I've keyed the spell to detect Loki's influence. That means we'll get a warning if Loki is finding the same information we are."

"So we'll know if he locates one of my Sisters or the Treasures around the same time we do, or maybe even before."

"Or maybe even before, unless I've really messed up somewhere."

Mist slapped his shoulder. "Great work, Val. I knew you could do it."

The freckles splashed across Vali's cheeks and nose stood out like a galaxy of stars against a clear night sky. "Thanks, Mist," he said. "You made me believe I *could*." He grinned. "Haven't touched a drop since I set up here."

"That's because you know how much could depend on you and your skill."

"I'll need some relief eventually, if one of these Einherjar knows anything about computers."

"Or someone else might come along," Mist said. Hopefully without her "help."

He studied her with a frown that produced impressive chasms in his pale, broad forehead. "Speaking of relief," he said, "have you had any sleep at all since those bikers showed up?"

"I've already been scolded about that," Mist said wryly, remembering what Dainn had said of ancient Roman generals. "Good thing we aren't mortal, isn't it?"

"If we were," Vali said, "maybe we could go on pretending this isn't happening."

"Until it all came crashing down on our heads."

She turned to go. Vali nearly knocked her over in his haste to stop her.

"Shit," he said. "All this, and I forgot to tell you the most important thing. I think I've found one of the Valkyrie."

7

———

"Show me," Mist said, following him back to the large monitor. He sat again and opened a screen that seemed to be some kind of unfamiliar e-mail software. There was a single message in the inbox, its sender and subject line composed of random letters and numbers.

"Encrypted," he said. "Whoever sent this knew what she was doing." He clicked on the mouse, and suddenly the random letters and numbers resolved into real words.

The e-mail was from someone called "PapaBull" at a domain Mist had never seen or heard of. The text read:

"Message received."

Mist glanced at Vali. "What exactly does this have to do with my Sisters?" she asked.

"Papa Bull," Vali said. "That sounds like a male bovine with offspring, right?" he asked. "But it sounds a lot like something else, too." He looked into Mist's eyes. "Think. Does 'papa' mean more than just father?"

"Not unless it's a word in some language that means something else." She snapped her fingers. "The Latin word for 'pope.'"

"Exactly. So let's say the sender means pope, not father. What about 'bull'?"

"Bull," Mist mused aloud. "Papal bull. Isn't that some kind of charter?"

"From the pope, marked at the end with a lead seal called a 'bulla.'"

"So you think Papa Bull is Papal Bulla? What does that tell us?"

"There's a sign that makes up part of the pope's signature. Guess what it's called."

"Vali . . ."

"Rota."

Mist nearly fell out of her chair. Rota. As in the Valkyrie who had been assigned to guard and protect the Treasure Jarngreipr, the iron gauntlet that allowed Thor to handle and catch his hammer, Mjollnir.

"I put a lot of feelers out there," Vali said. "Careful ones, yeah, but the kind that someone who knew what to look for might pick up on."

"Could it be that easy?"

"*Something* has to be," Vali said. "Anyway, I'll work on it. No sign that Loki's caught on to this, but I'll have to keep it under wraps as much as possible."

Mist slapped his shoulder again. *Three out of twelve*, she thought. Only two Treasures, yes, but it was a start.

Except that Vali's much less pleasant brother, Vidarr, had demanded Gungnir—Odin's Spear, the Treasure the All-father had set Mist to guard—for his part in helping Mist find Loki when Dainn had gone to confront their enemy. And she still didn't know what he planned to do with it.

Either she could wait around for him to show up and demand the Spear, or she could go to Vid and make one more attempt to convince him that they had to work together. He hated Dainn, he hated Freya, and he hated *her*, but even Vidarr's formidable temper couldn't permanently erase his sense of self-preservation.

He had to realize he couldn't stand against Loki alone, especially if . . .

She sucked in her breath as the wolf-and-raven tattoo began to burn again.

"What's wrong?" Vali asked.

"Let me know if there are any new developments," she said, turning for the door. Her mouth filled with the taste of metal, and her skin seemed too small for her bones. It felt as if she were touching a live wire, conducting some violent energy that had nowhere to go.

Whatever she was sensing, she had a terrible feeling that it had to do with Loki. And Dainn still hadn't returned.

She walked out to the street and looked up at the sky, half-expecting a bridge to open up overhead and deposit an army of angry Jotunar right in her lap.

Get your ass back here, Dainn, or . . .

Or she might never be able to trust her own judgment again.

The drawbridge was only a mile and a half north of Dogpatch, and Loki knew he was inviting trouble.

Not that he feared the prospect of an imminent contest with Mist. After their recent duel, she probably wouldn't be expecting him to venture near the very border of her "territory." If his original theory concerning her role as a mere conduit for Freya's power held true, she would have no help from her mother now.

Even if his *new* theory was correct, she'd have enough on her plate dealing with the Jotunn she'd taken prisoner.

"Any luck, boss?" Hymir asked.

Loki's new chief of giants, appointed after Hrimgrimir's unfortunate demise at Dainn's hands, watched his master's face with an expression reminiscent of a fighting dog eager to launch itself at anything its owner might throw in its path. Loki's other escorts, Grer and Ide, kept a watchful eye on the surroundings, though at near-midnight China Basin was deserted. Choppy winds drove into Mission Creek from the bay, clear of snow but cold enough that even Loki could feel it.

He left Hymir's question unanswered and focused his inner senses. It was faint, so very faint, but he was certain there was the smallest crack in the invisible wall that had descended between Midgard and the realms of the Void, a crack suggesting that the lack of communication with the Shadow-Realms was not a matter of Ginnungagap's "disappearance" but of some obstruction. A crack he could widen and use to bring his allies into this world.

He rubbed his hands together, raising a spark in the moist air, and examined the framework that would anchor his spell. Lefty O'Doul Bridge was hardly a significant landmark in San Francisco. But every metaphysical bridge between Midgard and Ginnungagap's Shadow-Realms was somehow associated with a feature in the city's landscape that connected one place to another, and this unprepossessing structure was the one that had drawn him.

He opened his left hand, gathering the finest crystals of ice from the air and the earth surrounding the bridge. He closed his fist, and when he opened his fingers a tiny spider crouched on his palm, its faceted body reflecting the moonlight like a diamond.

Loki tossed it into the air, and it began to spin a webwork of ice strands as fine as sewing thread, firmly anchored them to the trusses and deck of the bridge. Loki kept the web stable as the spider did its work, spreading his hands wide and chanting the Runes: Kenaz, the Torch, for the energy of transmutation; Laguz, Water, to access and acquire that which is hidden; Uruz, the Ox, for the power of will. Each stave stretched until it, too, was no more than the width of a single hair. He tossed the attenuated staves toward the spider, who wove them into the filaments of ice, blocking the road and forming a structure that could have stopped an army of bulldozers in its tracks.

When it was finished, the spider crouched in the center of the web, waiting silently. Loki closed his eyes, drawing again on the air and earth. The already stunted grass in China Basin Park blackened and shriveled, and jagged cracks formed in the deck of the bridge, radiating outward from Loki's feet like the warped spokes of a giant wheel.

A flame leaped to life in Loki's hand, dancing joyously. It was not the magic of the mother whose name he bore. He hated its source, but it was far too useful to him to reject. Shaping the flame into a sphere, he flung it at the center of the web.

The spider exploded, sending shards of ice flying in every direction. The web caught fire, melting the ice outward from the tiny opening where the spider had lain. A hole was forming . . . an aperture that could be the beginning of—

"Boss!"

Hymir's voice shattered Loki's concentration. The flame went out, and the fragile strands of the web evaporated.

Loki swung around, grew to match the Jotunn's height and struck Hymir across the face. The giant fell back, eyes wide with shock. Loki was advancing on Hymir again when he became aware of the reason for the Jotunn's warning.

A motorcycle was approaching at breakneck speed, its rider bent low over the handlebars. The Jotunn skidded to a stop, turning the bike in a half circle, and leaped from the seat.

"My lord," Haurr said, dipping his head, "a raven has come."

The image of Danny's drawing sprang into Loki's mind. "Where?" he demanded.

"Heading this way," Haurr said. "I followed it from headquarters, but I didn't think I should get too near. There's a woman who seems to be with it."

"Who?"

"Mortal. I've never seen her before."

"Show me," Loki said.

Haurr and the other Jotunar ran for the nondescript but fast car Loki had procured for them while he mounted the bike. He watched the charcoal-colored sky as he rode, paralleling the car and finally allowing it to move ahead.

He saw the bird before Hymir signaled from the window of the automobile—a black bird, filmy moonlight limning its feathers with silver and catching the obsidian sphere of its eye. It made no sound, but Loki knew it instantly.

"*Odin*," he breathed, gunning the engine to keep pace. Not the god, of course. That was impossible. But even as the raven winged overhead, the All-father's magic painted the night sky like a jet's contrail.

If one of Odin's messengers was here in Midgard, it had either come through at the same time Loki had first opened the bridges to this world, or one of the supposedly "closed" bridges was functioning again.

Loki braked hard and brought the bike to a halt. He lifted his hands skyward, pulling ice out of the sky above him. His hands began to tremble as he drew it down, shaping a vast sphere with a binding of Merkstaves and flinging it after the bird as it streaked northward.

The spell missed its mark. The sphere dissolved before it could make contact, and the raven flew on as if it had never felt the slightest disturbance in the air behind it.

Perhaps it hadn't, Loki thought. Perhaps, intent on some other goal, it had entirely overlooked his presence.

And there was no sight of the mystery woman.

Loki waved at the car that had pulled up beside him. "Follow it," he said.

"Mist."

Dainn had come up so quietly on the sidewalk that she hadn't heard him at all. He was carrying a Macy's shopping bag, one straw handle half torn off, and looked very different from the last time she'd seen him.

His taste in mortal garments ran to rather un-elflike black and deep, muted tones: at the moment he was wearing a dark aubergine shirt, open at the neck, and black jeans that emphasized his height and his lean but well-developed physique.

He was also sweating heavily, his black hair plastered to his head, his pale face flushed, his breathing harsh and rapid. Plumes of condensation obscured his features.

"What's happened?" she asked in alarm, dragging him toward the front door. "Are you all right?"

"If you fear the beast," he said hoarsely, "you need not. It is quiet."

"Then where have you been?"

"Has Ryan spoken to you?"

She frowned at the non sequitur. "No. I tried to talk to him again after he refused to see Tashiro, but he wouldn't speak to me."

"Have *you* been aware of anything different within the past several hours?"

Mist scanned the area from the defunct factories and warehouses to the empty street and the area around the loft. "What are you getting at?"

He dropped the bag on the pavement. "I have seen a raven," he said.

"A raven?" she asked, trying to make sense of his statement. "I don't—"

Her tattoo nipped at her wrist, and suddenly his meaning became dreadfully clear.

"It rode on magic," Dainn said. "I felt it when I was downtown. It was moving east then, and one of Loki's Jotunar was pursuing it."

Mist struggled against the urge to sit down right on the icy sidewalk. "You followed it, too?"

"I tracked it on foot, but I did not see it or the Jotunn again. I was unable to determine where it was bound, so I came here to inform you."

"Odin's balls."

"Indeed. If our supposition is correct, Loki will understand its possible significance and attempt to obtain this bird as quickly as he can."

"Possible significance," she muttered. "That leaves a lot of wiggle room. Did you get any sense of where Loki might be?"

"No," Dainn said. "But . . ." He lifted his head, tilting it to the side and half closing his eyes. "I cannot be sure, but he may not be far away."

Curse it, Mist thought. "We're going to have to find this bird. Fast."

Dainn drew a small folding knife from his pants pocket, sliced the tip of his finger, and crouched, drawing bloody Rune-staves on the sidewalk with his fingertip.

"What in Hel are you doing?" Mist demanded, making a grab at his hand. "Using Blood-Runes when you're not sure you're—"

Dainn pulled his hand away. His blood froze almost as soon as it touched the ground. Slowly the staves began to shift shape, twisting into the image of a sinuous vine, complete with leaves of frost—elements of nature's life in the midst of snowy desolation. The vine curled around and around itself, forming a perfect bull's-eye.

"Anything?" Mist asked, crouching beside him.

The elf rocked back on his heels. "It is coming here."

"What?"

"I was remiss in not attempting this before. The Runes tell me that this loft is the bird's destination." He looked up. "It must be coming for *you*."

Mist didn't wait to ask questions. She raced into the loft, grabbed her cell phone and knife—her sword, Kettlingr, shrunk to a more convenient size—and ran outside.

"I'm calling Bryn," she said. "I didn't want her Einherjar to get involved in any real fighting so soon and without proper training, but if Loki already knows about the bird, I can't face him and his Jotunar alone."

"Even if Loki has located the raven," Dainn said, "fighting now would be most unwise."

"I'll only do it as a last resort. But if this bird has any importance at all and Loki gets it, he may force our hand."

"I am ready," Dainn said, getting to his feet.

"Forget it. This could all go to Hel pretty fast. You might be okay now, but we have no idea what you might do when things get hairy again."

His expression was as grim as she'd ever seen it. "Do you expect me to wait here and do nothing?"

"We can't leave the loft unguarded," she said, touching Bryn's name on her cell's contact list.

Dainn's eyes glittered in the shrouded moonlight. "Listen to me," he said. "If you meet Loki, remember that he almost certainly still believes you rely on Freya to work your magic. Since Freya is no longer among us, he will underestimate you."

"I'm not going to let him beat us, Dainn. Not even to keep him ignorant about what I can do on my own."

"Nevertheless," he said, "do not draw on the ancient power. If you—"

Abruptly he broke off, his gaze snapping up. Mist gasped as a wave of sheer magical awareness washed over her, accompanied by an aftershock of nausea.

The dark, cloud-swept sky seemed as empty as before, but she knew it *hadn't* been just a moment ago. She could still see the pale negative of a familiar image behind her eyelids.

"Did you feel that?" she asked, hardly aware that Bryn's cell had gone to voicemail.

"Yes."

"Why in Hel isn't Bryn picking up?" She rang again. Rick answered.

"Mist?" he said, his voice muffled with sleep. "Do you know what fuckin' time it is?"

"Rick, get Bryn."

"Oh. Uh, sorry about the language. I—"

"Right now, Rick. We have a situation."

There was pause. "Loki?"

"Maybe, but I can't explain right now. Ask Bryn to choose four or five Einherjar, the best fighters, and meet me at the loft ASAP." She hesitated. "This will be your trial by fire. If we do meet Loki, some of you may not get out of this alive. You can still change your mind."

"Give us five minutes."

He broke the connection, and Mist pocketed the phone. She belted Kettlingr on so hastily that she almost dropped it.

"There," Dainn said, pointing to the north.

Above them, banking against the chilly wind, flew a jet-black raven.

It circled closer, watching them. Around and around, ever earthward, voiceless as a shadow.

The roar of motorcycles interrupted the bird's aerial soliloquy. It darted upward again as Bryn, Rick, and three other Einherjar—Bunny, a bleached blonde with her hair cut in a ragged bob and her nose pierced with a small silver stud; Tennessee, lean and dark; and Edvard, a thick-set, brown-haired man who reminded Mist of a friendly bear—pulled up to the curb.

Bryn removed her helmet. "We're ready," she said, raising her voice over the idling engines. "Where are we going?"

"You see that bird?" Mist said, pointing up and to the north as Dainn had done.

"What is it? A crow?" Bryn kissed through her teeth. "Shit. It's a raven."

"We're going to follow it wherever it leads us. We may run into Loki along the way." She glanced at Dainn. He was staring, not at Bryn or Mist or even at the raven, but at Edvard.

She couldn't afford to take the time to ask him why. She ran to the side driveway, mounted the bar hopper she'd recently "borrowed" from an unsuspecting neighbor, released the clutch, and rolled out to the street.

Just as she was ready to join the others, she felt Dainn's gaze. She'd known him long enough to recognize the anguish behind his seemingly expressionless eyes.

But there was no more to be said. She accelerated north on Illinois, coaxing every last dash of speed out of the vehicle as the raven flew right above her.

8

___

Dainn remained where he was long after they had gone, waiting for the moment when he could be sure he was in no danger of destroying everything in his path.

It was only when his vision cleared that he saw that one man hadn't left with the others. He was broad-shouldered, muscular, and of average height. There was nothing particularly striking about his sunburned face and thick brown hair. His eyes were round and chocolate brown, nestled under heavy brows.

Nostrils flaring, Dainn took in the biker's scent. It was musky but not unpleasant, like earth and sun-warmed fur. And Dainn understood why instinct had focused attention on this one man.

He wasn't human.

The biker approached slowly—a wise decision on his part, Dainn thought—and stopped a good three yards away. "I hope I'm not bothering you," he said, keeping his arms at his sides.

Dainn stood very still. "Who are you?" he asked.

The man didn't offer his hand. "Edvard" he said. "I'm one of the Einherjar . . . but you know that."

"You are also a *berserkr.*"

"You're surprised."

"I was unaware that your kind still survived in Midgard."

"We've done a pretty good job of hiding ourselves. The way you have."

"What do *you* know about me?"

"I know you've been on Earth for a long time, and until all this happened you had to have kept a very low profile." He curled his fingers around the nape of his neck and stroked it nervously. "We've always known about elves, but I never thought I'd meet one. Especially not an elf who—"

"How did you recognize my nature?"

"I sensed it as soon as we showed up."

"How?" Dainn asked, slowly closing the distance between them.

Edvard retreated a step. "The same way I'd sense any other of my kind," he said.

"I am not your kind," Dainn said. He tried to clear his mind. "How many of you exist?"

"Enough to maintain stable populations," Edvard said, watching Dainn warily. "Some clans live on this continent, some in Europe, a few in other parts of the world. We're descendants of the Ulfhednar and Bjornhednar who fought in the ancient battles."

"How did you come to join Bryn?"

"She found me. I knew I was supposed to go with her, that something was happening that would affect me and my people."

"Does she know what you are?"

"Sure she does. Has since I joined her."

"Then why did she fail to inform Mist?"

"What makes you think she didn't?"

"She would have told me."

"Bryn knew I wouldn't be a danger to anyone, so she was probably just waiting for the right time." Edvard hunched his shoulders, giving his body a bearlike aspect. "Look, I'm not here to challenge you."

"Then why are you here?" Dainn asked.

"I heard you were pretty close to the edge."

"The edge of what?"

"Losing control."

Dainn breathed sharply through his nose. "This was Rick's assessment of our very brief disagreement?"

"I know what happened when that giant attacked Mist."

"Nothing happened."

"But it could have." Edvard hesitated. "Bear or wolf?"

"Neither," Dainn said bitterly. "No. Perhaps a little of both, but far stronger than either."

"And you've been fighting it. Fighting to hold it back."

Dainn clenched the muscles between his shoulder blades and released them, rolling his head to work the tension out of his neck. It did little good. "Your kind does not 'fight it'?" he asked.

"We're not ashamed of it, if that's what you mean." He seemed to realize he'd said something unwise, for he was quiet some time before he spoke again. "We learned to handle it a long time ago. Sometimes, when we're young, it takes a little work."

"I am not young, and you have no idea what I'm capable of." Dainn closed the space between them again. "You are committed to this cause for the sake of your people, are you not?"

"The result of this battle will affect the *berserkir* as much as anyone."

"Loki would be pleased to have you on his side."

"Look," Edvard said, a growl in his voice. "I think maybe I can help you. But if you keep cutting yourself off this way, it'll be as if you're working with Loki yourself."

It took great effort, but Dainn quelled his anger. "How can you help me?"

"I know strong emotion provokes your beast. It can happen that way with us, too. But when one of us can't quite manage the changes on our own, we have ways to calm it down. I can show you—"

"Thus far you have displayed nothing but profound ignorance," Dainn said, "and I am in no mood to deal with it."

Edvard dropped his gaze. "Obviously this isn't a good time. I thought since Mist left you behind, you'd want to—" He shook his head. "I guess I was wrong."

He turned to leave, but Dainn detained him with a hand on his arm. Edvard shuddered, and the corner of his lip lifted in an all-too-familiar warning. Dainn closed his eyes and let a little of the beast loose. He felt that almost addictive strength flow through him, opened his eyes and let the creature glare out at the *berserkr* with all its hate and savagery.

Visibly flinching, Edvard crouched low. "Okay," he whispered, not daring to move. "You've made your point."

Pushing the beast back down, Dainn released Edvard quickly. "What do you propose?" he asked, knowing himself for a fool. A desperate fool.

"We treat what you've got as a sickness," Edvard said, clearly relieved, "and we have a kind of cure that—"

"There is no cure."

"Then call it a palliative. A palliative that can help you keep your other side under better control."

"It is highly unlikely that any 'palliative' can make a difference."

Very carefully, Edvard reached inside his shirt and withdrew a small leather pouch. "How can you know if you don't try it?"

Dainn took in a deep breath. "What is it?" he asked.

"A kind of herbal compound. I didn't make it, but I always carry some of it with me."

"And you think I would sample this concoction without knowing anything about it?"

Edvard loosened the cord that held the pouch closed, dipped his finger inside and scooped out a small portion of the compound. He tapped the faintly dusty, green-and-brown mixture on his tongue.

"If it's poison, you'll know soon enough," he said.

"If it were poison, the effects might not be immediate."

"I'll still suffer those effects sooner or later. We can wait as long as you want. Unless you want to help Mist now."

He offered the pouch to Dainn. "Take it. Maybe if things get bad . . . well, you may decide to try it." Suddenly, he grinned. "If I'm not dead by then, of course."

Almost against his will, Dainn accepted the pouch. It was as light as a feather from Freya's Falcon Cloak.

"Thanks," Edvard said. "Thanks for considering what I've said. It's important to all of us."

"I make no promises," Dainn said, tucking the pouch inside his shirt. "Will you summon the other *berserkir* to fight for Mist?"

"I can only speak for my own clan. I'll send a report as soon as I understand what's going on well enough to explain it to them."

"If they are to be of any use, you must not wait too long."

"I know." He backed away. "I'll be going after Mist now, see if I can help. I'm a fighter, after all."

He returned to his motorcycle, his shoulders slightly tensed as if he expected Dainn to lope after him and tear his head off. In a few moments he was gone, leaving a thick trail of condensation behind him.

Loki had lost track of the raven by the time he reached Brannan Street. But once he crossed Bryant and passed under the James Lick Freeway, he knew that his Jotunar had found what he sought.

He sped up the quiet street, nearly hitting the giants on the sidewalk before he stomped on the brakes. They had formed a tight circle around a small figure, who held her arms over her head as if she expected to be gunned down in her tracks. Loki dismounted and walked at a casual pace toward the tableau, his gaze sweeping the sky once more for any sign of the bird.

Nothing. But if Haurr was right . . .

The mortal female was hardly impressive. Her black hair was loose and tangled and her face was flushed, as if she had been running. She wore a conservative gray suit, hardly appropriate to the weather, and her feet were bare. Her gaze darted from one Jotunn to the other with uncomprehending terror.

Loki attacked Hymir before the Jotunn could lift a hand in self-defense. The giant sprawled, and Loki spun to kick Grer's legs out from underneath him. Haurr backed away, utter confusion on his face. Loki ran at him and struck him hard across the jaw. The blow was powerful enough to knock the Jotunn unconscious.

Ide simply ran, instinct driving him away from a master who seemed to have lost his mind entirely. Hymir and Grer scrambled to their feet, taking off after their fellow Jotunn like the mortal dead fruitlessly fleeing Hel's long fingers.

Loki stared after them until they were well out of sight and then looked down at the girl, who gazed at him with wide, surprisingly pretty hazel eyes.

"Don't worry," Loki said, assuming his most sympathetic and worried expression. "They're gone." He held out a hand, but she shrank away.

"I saw them accost you," Loki said, dropping into a crouch. "Did they hurt you?"

"No," she whispered. "Where did you come from?"

"That doesn't matter now," he said gently. "I want to help."

"Thank you."

The look of hope on the girl's face told Loki that his natural charm and charisma were already beginning to have their usual effect. "This isn't an area where a young woman should be walking alone at night," he said. "Especially in this weather, and without shoes."

Her mouth curled in a reluctant, rueful smile. "That's obvious," she said.

Good, Loki thought. Her muscles were beginning to relax—not much, by any means, but enough that he thought she might soon begin to answer his questions without unnecessary prodding.

"You must be freezing," he said, beginning to remove his leather jacket. "Please, take this."

"I'm fine," she said, a violent shiver giving the lie to her words.

"Why *are* you here?" he asked with a very calculated frown of concern.

She looked down at the pavement. "It's . . . a little hard to explain."

"Take your time," he said. "I know you don't have any reason to trust me. But I really want to help."

It was obvious that she had many urgent questions of her own, but he concentrated on projecting warmth and unassailable honesty, softening his features, erasing the red penumbras from his irises.

"I was looking for my pet," she said suddenly, meeting his gaze again.

"Your pet?" he said, raising a brow. "A dog?"

She laughed, an edge of hysteria in her voice. "No," she said. "A bird."

"A bird? In the middle of the night?"

"Actually," she said, shifting her bare feet underneath her, "a parrot."

A parrot. Loki tamped down a stirring of anger. He could see no reason why this woman should in any way be connected with one of Odin's messengers, and now she spoke of tropical avians.

"What kind of parrot, Miss . . ."

She hesitated, clearly wondering if she ought to give her name to a complete stranger, albeit one who might have saved her from a most unpleasant fate.

"Anna," she said slowly. "Anna Stangeland."

Loki's heartbeat quickened. The name was Norwegian. "I am pleased to meet you, Ms. Stangeland," he said. "My name is Lukas."

"Lukas," she repeated. "He's an African Grey."

"Ah. I've heard they're quite intelligent."

"Very. But of course Orn isn't supposed to be out of my apartment. He escaped somehow, and I couldn't leave him out here alone. He could die of the cold."

Orn. "Eagle." Loki almost laughed aloud. If the bird was indeed one of Odin's, it could have the ability to assume a false appearance. The girl might well believe she was chasing after a parrot, and have no knowledge of its true nature.

But why was Odin's messenger—if that *was* the raven's purpose—be with a common mortal in the first place?

"How long have you had Orn, Ms. Stangeland?" he asked with an encouraging smile.

"He's . . . been in my family for decades. He came here with my parents and me when we moved to the U.S."

"From Norway?"

"How did you know?"

Ah, so very easy. "My surname is Landvik. My family immigrated from the Old Country as well." He smiled. "Quite a coincidence. A very lucky one."

Unease crept into her eyes. She scrambled to her feet, avoiding Loki's offered hand.

"I have to find him," she said, staring southward.

And what lay in the south? Loki thought. Or whom?

"He was going that way," she said in a distracted voice. "I think . . ." She massaged her temples. "I keep thinking he was trying to lead me somewhere."

"Did he perhaps . . . speak to you?"

"Yes," she murmured. "How did you know?"

"Merely a guess. What did he say?"

"A name. He was very—" Her delicate face screwed up in confusion. "Something else happened when we left. Someone was . . ."

She began to collapse, and Loki caught her. "Someone?" he prompted.

Her fingers clutched at his sleeve. "I know I sound crazy," she said, "but *they* were after us."

"Who?" he asked, cradling her close.

"I can't remember."

"That's all right. Now I want you to try very, very hard. Do you know anyone in this area?"

"No."

"Well then, perhaps I can help you look for your pet, and we can solve this mystery together."

"That would be very nice," she said, letting him support her as she straightened.

"Then you must take my jacket." He shrugged it off and settled it around her slender shoulders. She seemed to gain strength from its warmth and began to walk southeast on 4th.

"Wouldn't it be better to call a taxi?" Loki suggested, keeping pace. "Or, if you prefer, I have a car parked not far from here."

"I'm all right."

Loki's patience had begun to wear thin.

He should call the Jotunar again. In spite of the way he had treated them in order to win this mortal's trust, they would return because they had no choice. With a simple spell that wouldn't tax his strength, he summoned the Jotunar, who had been following at a little distance. They crept out of the shadows, regarding him like whipped curs begging forgiveness for some unknown infraction.

When Anna saw them, she all but fell into Loki's arms.

"They're back," she whispered. "The monsters."

Loki glanced at the approaching Jotunar. True, they were still larger than the average mortal, approaching seven feet even in their altered form, but there was nothing overly monstrous about this particular breed.

Did she sense something an ordinary mortal wouldn't?

"Never fear," he said. "I will protect you."

Just as suddenly as she had sought the shelter of his arms, she pushed away from him. "You *know* them," she said. "This was all a setup, wasn't it?"

Once again she surprised Loki. She'd gone from pliable cooperation to angry challenge in a matter of seconds.

"I don't know what you mean, Anna," he said.

"You want Orn!" she cried, staring at his face with undisguised terror.

This was the sign Loki had been looking for. The sign that she *did* know something vital about the bird, enough to want to shield it from any possible threat. Or from one who might take it from her.

Time for Bad Cop.

"Hymir," Loki said, "I think this young woman is confused. Why don't you help her."

He snatched his jacket off Anna's shoulders and pushed her into Hymir's arms. The giant wrapped his fingers around her throat. She gave a strangled cry as he lifted her off the ground.

"Be gentle, Hymir," Loki said. "We would not wish to damage her too badly." He looked at the girl. "Whom have you been sent to find?"

I don't . . . understand," she wheezed, gripping Hymir's thick wrists. Loki nodded, and Hymir lowered her back to the ground.

"Is Odin in communication with Midgard?"

She swallowed several times, coughing and shivering. "Odin?" she echoed. "Midgard? You mean like in the myths?"

Ah, Loki thought. Now they were beginning to get somewhere.

"This need not be unpleasant for you," he said. "Again, I ask you why the bird is here, and where he—"

"Boss!" Grer shouted. Loki followed his gaze. The raven was above them, circling and watching. Loki began to prepare another spell, but the raven shot southward again.

"There," Loki said between gritted teeth. "There is your bird, Anna. Not a parrot, as I believe you could clearly see."

"I . . . I still don't understand," she stammered, rubbing her reddened throat. "Orn . . ."

Once more, without warning, her demeanor utterly changed. Her eyes went blank, and when they cleared they had become more determined, more defiant, far more experienced than the eyes of any young mortal woman should be.

As if her body and mind were occupied by something—or someone—else.

"I know what you want," she said in flawless Norwegian. "But I won't help you. You can do whatever you want with me, and you will not learn a thing."

Loki frowned. It was clear from the focus of her gaze that she wasn't really addressing him at all. He reached out and sketched a

Bind-Rune on her forehead. The Runes glowed like neon lights on her skin.

Mortal, yes. But more than that. More than *one*.

He decided to take another chance.

"I know what you can endure," he said. "But even you can die, and death may not be easy after so many centuries."

"We always knew this day would come," she said, finally meeting his gaze. "But I face death without fear, something you and your honorless spear-pointers and gray-bellies could never understand."

He continued to follow her lead and his own instincts. "You know there are others who can be hurt if you refuse to speak."

"There is nothing I can do to help them."

Hymir reached for her again. The woman blinked several times as the Jotunn's hand began to close around her neck. Her face went white.

"No," she said, speaking in English again. "It isn't real."

Loki snapped his fingers, and Hymir let her go. "This is real enough," Loki said, breathing deeply as he drew the cold from the asphalt up around her legs like a frigid blanket. The street cracked, and the woman gasped in pain.

"Tell me, do you fear death now?" he asked. "I can freeze your heart in your chest where you stand."

"Oh, God," she whimpered. "Why?"

Did she remember nothing of what she had said mere seconds ago?

"Please," he said. "Call the bird. I will reward you handsomely."

Her teeth chattered. "This is a dream. None of it is real."

Loki nodded to Hymir again. The giant grabbed her by the collar of her blouse, and her feet broke free of the ice with the tinkle of shattering glass. At a brief word from Loki, Hymir dragged her toward a nearby storefront with a "for lease" sign in the window.

Grer kicked in the door, smashing the hinges, and Ide cleared a path for Hymir and the girl. Loki followed them into a space that had obviously once been some sort of gallery. Grer continued through a wide archway that opened into a back room and returned with a rickety chair, which he set down near Loki.

Loki took the seat, and Hymir pushed the young woman to her knees. Loki leaned down to stroke her cheek.

"Summon the bird," he said, "and I will let you live."

9

Dainn sat cross-legged on the scrap of dead lawn outside the laundry room door, the pouch cradled in his lap. He could feel the cats watching him from the window, their bright eyes intelligent and curious. Kirby would have followed him outside if Dainn had permitted it; Norwegian Forest Cats were well suited to cold climates.

But Lee and Kirby were strictly indoor pets. They could only observe as Dainn prepared himself to take a terrible chance.

A cure, Edvard had said. A cure for a disease. It was easy to think of the beast that way—as a parasite, growing like a cancer to invade every organ, every limb, intent on replacing his Alfar body with its own.

Dainn's fear for Mist had been feeding it ever since she'd left with the Einherjar. If he had been capable of thinking clearly, he might have given a little more thought to the risk of accepting the promises of a man he didn't know.

But Edvard had been correct. Mist needed him. Now, and after she returned . . . if he could only open his mind to her again, call upon all the ability he possessed to help her prepare.

Closing his eyes, he opened the drawstring to breathe in the earthy scent of crushed herbs and a dozen other unknown substances, spilling a little of it on his open palm. He brought his hand to his lips and let the compound melt on his tongue. A slow warmth spread from his mouth into his belly and through his bloodstream . . . a great, soothing sense of peace such as he hadn't experienced in a century.

He knew exactly when it began to attack the disease, dissolving the cancerous tissue until it had shrunk to no more than the creature it had been before Freya's mental touch had begun to weaken its cage. It growled and paced and snarled, but it was contained.

The influence of the beast was gone.

So simple, he thought. He was afraid to trust, afraid it couldn't last. But he was no longer at risk of flinging himself into a battle driven only by the indiscriminate and insatiable urge to kill. If there were side effects yet to come, he would gladly endure them in exchange for this miracle.

He rose slowly, lifting his head to scent the air. There would be snow again, but for now the sky was clear, revealing a rare glimpse of the few stars visible above the city. Across the street, lights still burned in the factory where the Einherjar had set up their camp; like him, they were waiting for Mist's and their comrades' return. Gabi and Ryan would likely be wide awake in their room, possessed by the same fears. Fears Dainn could do nothing to ameliorate.

But they would be safe. Safe because he could use his magic again to double the efficacy of Mist's wards, without fear of strengthening the beast.

He stretched his magical senses to their greatest extent, drawing the magic of the earth through the bare soles of his feet, imagining his own body as a great tree with roots deep in the rich soil and branches thick with emerald leaves.

A great, mewling howl rose up from inside the house, and the spell crumbled like desicated earth. Kirby had reared up against the kitchen window, his broad paws pressed to the glass, his mane a great ruff around his head. He cried again with greater urgency, and Lee echoed the howl from somewhere behind him.

Dropping the open pouch, Dainn ran into the loft. The cats raced ahead of him through the kitchen and toward the gym, where they stopped, fur all abristle. He opened the gym door.

The room was silent, empty, bereft of any sense of something amiss. Dainn moved cautiously, his gaze sweeping left to right as he crossed the rubber-tiled floor.

When he reached the other end of the gym, he realized what was wrong. He ran to the storage room and stopped at the door.

It was unlocked, the wards broken. The Jotunn lay where Dainn and Mist had left him, staring at the ceiling, unblinking, barely breathing. His already pale skin was nearly transparent.

Dainn knelt at the giant's side. He laid his hand over the Jotunn's forehead. It was as warm as a mortal's skin, a temperature no frost giant could endure for long.

Carefully Dainn removed the bandages. The wound was red and sere, a festering pit over his ribs.

"I am dying."

The Jotunn's voice caught Dainn unaware. He bent his head close to the giant's, certain the man didn't have the strength to do him harm.

"What is your name?" he asked.

"Svar— . . . Svardkell." The Jotunn coughed, spitting bloody froth. His pale eyes focused on Dainn, and he tried to rise.

Dainn eased him back down. "Save your strength," he said.

"Why?" The Jotunn tried to smile, displaying bloodstained teeth. "Am I . . . not your enemy?"

"You attacked Freya's daughter," Dainn said, sweeping all sympathy aside.

"I was not in my . . ." He sucked in a rattling breath. "Not in my right mind. I am not Loki's spy."

"Then what are you?"

"Loki knew . . . he forced me—" Svardkell jerked his head back and forth. "No time. So much to tell."

"Then speak."

"The boy must be protected."

"What boy?" Dainn said, leaning close again.

"You will know him. You, especially."

There was only one "boy" Dainn knew, and that was Ryan. "He is being protected," Dainn said. "How did you—"

"Tell her there are traitors," Svardkell interrupted, beginning to shiver uncontrollably.

The ghostly Freya's words still echoed in Dainn's mind. Bile rose into his throat.

Was he not a traitor himself?

"Who?" he demanded.

Svardkell began to choke on his own blood. Dainn spread his hands over the Jotunn's chest, trying to construct a healing spell with what little skill he had. It wasn't enough.

"Find the other fathers," Svardkell whispered.

"Fathers?" Dainn asked, giving up his attempts to ease the Jotunn's pain.

Svardkell met his gaze, and what Dainn saw left him stunned and shaken.

"You are—" he began.

"*Tell her,*" Svardkell said, gripping Dainn's arm with a last, desperate effort. "She must know."

"How many?" Dainn asked urgently. "Where are they? What does this—"

"Tell her not to fear . . . to become what she was."

"Svardkell," Dainn said, willing the Jotunn to stay alive. But the giant only gave a final sigh, and died.

Dainn closed the Jotunn's eyes with a pass of his hand and struggled to absorb the last few words Svardkell had spoken. If he guessed correctly, Freya had kept vital information from him. Information that might have great significance, and perhaps even explain why Mist was so much more than he had expected when he had first awakened her to her "duty."

But Svardkell had spoken of Mist becoming what she *was*. Mist had been many things: a common Valkyrie with no memory of her supposedly mortal parents; the guardian of Odin's Spear; Freya's daughter; a magic-wielder of great skill and impressive power.

Dainn rose to take another towel from the shelf and laid it over the Jotunn's face, moving slowly as he considered the possibilities. When Freya had contacted him in Midgard, He had learned that she intended to use her daughter as her vessel. But that decision had been made after the Dispersal, when Freya had been desperate to acquire a physical body capable of serving as her host in Midgard.

Was it possible, given the true nature of Mist's parentage, that the Lady had always expected her daughter to be more than a mere Valkyrie? Could she have had other plans for Mist before the Dispersal had forced her to make the brutal choice of her own survival over her daughter's? Had those plans been of such magnitude that Freya had kept them secret even from Dainn?

If so, she clearly wouldn't want Mist to discover the true circumstances of her birth, or what they might portend. She would have prevented Svardkell from approaching her daughter. Had the Jotunn hidden himself among Loki's spies in hopes of reaching Mist without Freya's knowledge?

"*Loki knew*," the Jotunar had said. Knew of his relationship to Mist? Or even more than that? Had he forced Svardkell to attack her?

Surely Laufeyson would find it amusing to send Mist's own father to harm her. But if he thought Svardkell might regain his senses long enough to tell Mist something that would help her understand herself, he would never have been so foolish.

Whatever Loki had thought or done, the ramifications of what Svardkell had revealed were staggering. The fact that the Jotunn knew of Ryan was puzzling in itself. And Mist would have to be told that her father—*one* of her fathers—had died because she had defended herself against a seeming enemy.

Taking a deep breath, Dainn whispered a few brief words in the elven tongue—words he hadn't heard spoken in centuries—and knelt to gather the body into his arms. Though he was even more anxious to set the wards and join Mist now, he had no intention of allowing her to witness the state of Svardkell's fatal injury or dispose of the body herself.

The house was still silent—as were the cats, who stood watching from the safety of the door to the hall. Dainn carried Svardkell out to the lawn, laid him down gently, and crouched over the Jotunn's body. He rested his palms on the brown, frozen grass.

The song of the earth seemed muted, more so than it had been only a short while before. When at last Dainn grasped the threads of life and began to weave them together with elvish Runes, they continued to slip out of his fingers as if they found his efforts somehow distasteful.

Dainn pushed his hair away from his face and frowned. He felt not the slightest trace of the beast, and he had worked such magic many times before. Once more he sang to the earth, and this time it responded. Thousands of tiny roots burst from beneath the soil, swaying gently as if no cold could touch them.

Working quickly, Dainn asked the roots to take what he offered. Each minuscule strand bent toward the Jotunn, prodding, pressing, until one by one they worked their way into the lifeless flesh. And fed, and thrived, and carried the body with them as they sank back under the soil.

Dainn got up, staring at the ground beneath his feet. He had done what was necessary. But there had been a strangeness to it he couldn't quite define, leaving a bitter taste in his mouth and an ache in his joints.

Brushing his palms against his pants, he went inside. He would look in on the young mortals, reassure them if necessary, and begin strengthening Mist's wards, weaving the subtle spells of nature among and around the unyielding elements of Mist's forge magic. If he worked efficiently, in ten minutes he should be finished and ready to go after Mist.

He stopped at the foot of the stairs. Ryan stood on the landing, clad in T-shirt and oversized jeans, his hair falling over his eyes.

"What's going on?" he asked.

Dainn hesitated for only a moment. "Loki is in the vicinity. Mist has gone after him with some of the Einherjar."

Ryan gripped the banister and closed his eyes. "I didn't know," he said. "No one told us."

"I am sorry," Dainn said. "There has been no time."

"But I didn't *see* it."

"You are not to blame," Dainn said, knowing better than to offer comfort. When the boy opened his eyes again, they were like cloudy glass orbs, utterly blind.

"Who died?" he whispered.

"One last chance," Loki said.

Anna only stared at him, her lips parted and her gaze blank. She almost looked, Loki thought sourly, as if she ought to be drooling.

Hymir raised a heavy brow. Loki waved his hand.

Dragging the woman to her feet, Hymir passed her to Grer and lifted his massive fist.

He never completed the strike. A jet-black arrow of feathers and fury dived through the open door and flew at Hymir, raking his face with razor-sharp talons. Hymir cried out and let the woman go, waving his hands to fend off the raven's attack.

"Orn!" Anna cried, beginning to rise.

"Get that cursed bird!" Loki shouted. Ide and Grer made a grab for it, ignoring the woman, and Loki began to gather his waning power. If he could slow the creature for a few vital seconds . . .

He had just begun the spell when another, distinctly human shape crashed through the window, shedding broken glass as she charged toward him with sword raised to strike.

Loki turned to face Mist, changing his spell to one of defense. The raven continued to attack each Jotunn in turn, preventing any of them from coming to Loki's aid.

Just as Mist's sword sliced down to cleave his flesh, Loki raised a ward between them. Her weapon struck the shield of transparent ice with the sound of a hundred mortal voices shrieking in pain.

Without hesitation, Freya's daughter skirted the shield and ran toward Anna, who had been bright enough to flee for the window. Loki raised his hands to gather the fragments of glass scattered over the ground and, sucking nearly all the scant warmth out of the Jotunar's bodies, hurled a spear of fire at the window.

Mist pulled Anna out of the way and jumped aside, but the flame fused the shards of glass and formed an opaque seal across the window frame, blocking Mist's escape. She pushed the young woman behind her and faced Loki again, looking past him at the Jotunar. They had been temporarily weakened by Loki's spell, their bodies so brittle that a precise blow at just the right spot might shatter them. But ice was their magical element, and Mist would know they'd soon be mobile again.

Of the raven there was no sign.

"Really, Mist," Loki said, careful not to give any indication that this fresh bout of magic had come very near to draining him of power completely. "So dramatic. It would seem you have been enjoying too many tales of heroes with extraordinary powers who rush in to save the day whenever the weak or innocent are in the clutches of a monstrous villain."

"At least one part of that conceit is true," she said. "You're pretty monstrous."

Loki laughed, but he found himself dangerously distracted. He had been eager enough to learn what might have changed with Mist since their battle and Freya's disappearance, but these were not the circumstances under which he would have preferred to test her.

She seemed no different to him than she'd been before: still straightforward and irreverent, tough and vulnerable, beautiful and utterly lacking in awareness of her beauty.

"That is all a matter of perspective," he said, discarding his brief fantasy of having both Mist and Dainn in his bed. At the same time. "I had not expected us to meet again quite so soon."

"I'll just bet you didn't," she said, baring her straight, white teeth in a grin.

"May I presume the raven brought you here?"

She didn't reply, but the answer was plain on her face. She'd never been any good at hiding her emotions, no matter how diligently she tried to maintain a stony expression.

Loki had always been of the philosophy that one should throw the maximum volume of rubbish against a wall and observe what clung to it.

"You didn't know about it before, did you?" he asked. "You didn't realize that Odin's messenger was here in Midgard, concealed as the pet of an ordinary mortal woman." He smiled. "Odd, that. Freya's daughter or not, you once served the All-father."

"I still do," she said, shifting her grip on her sword.

"Then you must find this situation most disturbing. Your slut of a mother said nothing before she disappeared, did she? Yet she was supposed to be the Aesir's only contact with this world." He examined a broken fingernail with disapproval. "Tell me . . . what did you and your mother discuss when you left my apartment?"

She frowned and Loki pressed on. "Surely you remember how delightful our party became after the Lady joined us? No?" He arched his brows in exaggerated dismay. "Perhaps you met Eric there?"

Loki recognized that only some supreme act of self-will kept Mist from charging him like a child with his first ax. He raised his finger to his lips before she could spit out an appropriate insult.

"What *do* you remember, little Valkyrie?" He asked. "Did you ever get the sense that perhaps you were being left out of the game?"

"If you think you won more than a single skirmish because Freya couldn't hold a physical shape—"

"*Did* I win?" Loki asked. "Of course, or Freya would be here, and I would not. But Odin's messenger shouldn't be here at all. Do you suppose that Odin has grown tired of Freya's failures and sent another ambassador in her place?"

Mist held admirably steadfast against his barrage of questions. "You have no idea what you're talking about," she said. "You didn't know about the raven, either, or you would have gone after it long ago."

"Oh, but I did expect a raven to turn up eventually. And here it is, just as predicted."

Anna pressed forward, her mouth open to speak, but Mist pushed her back again. "I don't believe you," she said.

"That is your privilege. I wonder . . . has it spoken to you?"

"Why? Did you expect a transcription?"

Which means no, Loki thought.

"It might amuse you to know that this woman you protect insists that our fine-feathered friend is a *parrot*," Loki said.

"Do you see me laughing?"

"We used to laugh together," Loki said gently. "Don't you remember?"

"It's not a time in my life I look back on with any fondness."

Loki clucked his tongue. "You'll give Anna a false impression of our relationship." He looked past Mist's shoulder. "Ah, Anna. We could have had a much more pleasant experience if you had only cooperated."

"*Stup ir*," Anna spat.

Loki ignored her. The recovering Jotunar began to stir behind him.

"You've come on a fruitless errand," Loki said, dropping his cordial tone. "The woman you protect she may be injured in a fight. Don't make me take her from you."

"Go ahead and try it."

"Your mother can do nothing to help you."

"Maybe I don't want her help."

"Perhaps that is wise, lover-of-mine. Either way, you are entirely on your own."

10

Mist weighed the odds as she waited for the right moment to call in the troops.

She could easily see that Laufeyson wasn't at his full strength, though he was preening and sneering and doing everything he could to hide that disadvantage from her. He was obviously trying to rattle her with his chatter about Freya and the fight in his apartment and how much she remembered.

And he was coming too close to succeeding. But she had one major advantage: he still seemed to believe she couldn't be a real threat to him without her mother's help.

"I'm not entirely alone," she said. "You have these Jotunar, but I also have *my* allies."

"I was informed about the arrival of the other Valkyrie bitch," he said, "but it seems she has come without her Treasure."

"What makes you think we need it?" Mist grinned at the Jotunar. "From the looks of these fools, all *we* need is a cereal box for a shield and a couple of toothpicks for swords and spears."

The biggest and obviously most dominant of the Jotunar growled and lunged toward her. Loki threw out an arm to hold the giant back.

"Is Dainn with you?" he asked.

"Right outside with the others."

She was lying, of course, but Loki didn't seem to know it. His eyes flared red with either rage or lust. Mist didn't want to know which.

"You should let him come in," Loki said. "I would like to apologize for my inconsiderate treatment of him when we last spent time together."

"I don't think Dainn has any interest in hearing your apologies."

"You might be surprised."

"You lie the way most people breathe. You're scared shitless, and you have reason to be."

It was always a safe bet that pricking at Loki's pride would make him reckless. He sent his Jotunar to attack.

They didn't get far. Bunny, Tennessee, and Rick rushed into the shop, slamming into the giants before they could reach Mist.

It was an unequal contest: even without magic, the giants were bigger and heavier than the Einherjar. Slender Bunny, in particular, was at a disadvantage.

Even so, the Jotunar hadn't yet recovered from the side effects of Loki's spells, and were moving at a slower pace. The Einherjar managed to dodge the worst of the blows, buying Mist a little more time.

She shoved Anna out the door, where Bryn grabbed her and hustled her out of the line of fire. Rick went flying, tossed across the room by the lead Jotunn. Another giant conjured on icicle as long and sharp as Gungnir and hurled it straight at Bunny.

It was Edvard who intercepted it—Edvard, one of the Einherjar she'd barely met, who suddenly seemed much larger and faster than he had been when Bryn and the others had gathered at the loft. She swung Kettlingr at the third Jotunn. The giant's fist, mailed in a thick glove of ice, hurtled toward her face. Tennessee caught the giant's arm and struggled to hold it back.

The raven streaked through the broken door and stabbed his beak into the giant's face just as the Jotunn prepared to smash Tennessee to a pulp. The giant knocked Tennessee away and snatched at the bird's wing. Blunt fingers slipped on midnight feathers and grasped at the raven's tail.

Loki, who had stood back during the fight, called up nearly invisible Merkstaves, strung them out as if he were spinning wool, and shaped a net just the right size and shape to catch and hold a large and powerful bird. Mist charged the giant who held the raven in his grip, cutting toward his legs. He leaped back and swung the raven toward Loki.

Mist knew she couldn't avoid using her magic now. The thrum of a motorcycle engine outside told her that Bryn was taking Anna to safety; all Mist had to do was save the raven and get the Einherjar out alive.

Her forge-magic had been less than cooperative when she'd used it against the Jotunn she'd left tied up at the loft, but she tried again, summoning Runes of fire and imagining Kettlingr as a hammer striking the anvil of the earth, cracking wood and concrete, sending jagged fragments flying up to fall again in a deadly hail that would strike her enemies down. She plunged the sword into the floor.

A great jolt nearly bounced her off her feet. The ground rippled. Loki's barrier of fused glass shattered, reduced to a pile of shards on the floor. Mist lost her balance and slammed against the wall. Her tattoo was burning like acid into her skin, ravens and wolves attacking with vicious teeth and beaks of iron.

The ground gave one final heave, and suddenly the world went utterly still. Rick and Tennessee lay on the floor, bloodied and breathing hard but still alive. Bunny, scratched but otherwise whole, was crouched in the doorway. There was no sign of Edvard, the raven, Loki, or the Jotunar.

The savage pain in Mist's wrist began to fade. She pushed away from the wall and yanked Kettlingr from the ground. It came out spotless, as if she had just honed and polished it to the finest sheen.

Gripping it in her right hand, she reached down to Rick with her left and hauled him to his feet. Tennessee groaned, tried to rise, and sank down again. Bunny knelt beside him.

"Are you all right?" Mist asked Tennessee.

"I think my leg's broke," he said, trying to smile. "But I'll live."

"Rick, Bunny," Mist said, "Can you take care of him? I've got to go after Loki."

"You can't," Bunny said, touching the spreading bruise on her cheek. "You look like you're about to fall over yourself."

"He may have taken the raven. I have to get it back."

"I saw it fly after Bryn and Anna. I think it's okay."

Mist fell back against the wall, wondering if she could even walk as far as the bikes haphazardly parked outside. She wasn't sure she could summon any more magic, not even the simplest protective spell.

Rick laughed. "Well," he said, rubbing his arm, "now I understand why you warned us when we got ourselves into this."

"Fuckin' right," Tennessee muttered through gritted teeth.

Bunny shook her head. "Never thought the bad guy could look so . . . so—"

"Normal?" Mist said. "Well, normal if you don't consider he's made himself into one of the most attractive men most mortals will ever see."

"Made himself? You mean that's a disguise?"

"No one knows what his true form is," Mist said.

"Damn," Rick said, shaking his head. "Where's Edvard?"

Mist recalled her impression of something large and brown. "I think he followed Loki," Tennessee said. "Shithead. He'll get himself killed."

But there was absolutely nothing Mist could do about it. Forcing herself to move, she broke a few long pieces off the shattered door and splinted Tennessee's leg. Bunny helped Rick maneuver Tennessee onto the back of Rick's bike, and Mist mounted Tennessee's motorcycle. After she'd started the engine, Rick pulled up beside her.

"Hey," he said through slightly swollen lips, "did *you* cause that earthquake?"

Mist cast him a startled glance. "I don't see how," she said. I didn't cause the other ones."

But she had to admit it was strange timing, and not only where the quake was concerned. She kept remembering Loki's words: *"This woman you protect insists that our fine-feathered friend is a parrot."*

An illusion, a false appearance of the kind both Loki—and Odin—were capable of? Who in Hel *was* Anna, and what could she possibly have to do with the All-father? Did Loki have some reason to suggest that Odin had sent a new ambassador in Freya's place?

The questions were piling up in Mist's brain faster than she could make sense of them. And she wondered just how much she was going to like the answers.

Dainn was struggling to find an appropriate response to Ryan's unexpected question when he heard a single motorcycle approaching from Twentieth Street.

"Stay where you are," he said. He ran to the front door and reached the street just as the vehicle rounded the corner, and he saw Bryn's distinctive winged helmet bent over the handlebars. A helmetless female passenger, her dark hair flying behind her, clung to the Valkyrie's waist. Bryn rolled to a stop at the curb.

"Where is Mist?" he asked.

"Okay, last time I checked," Bryn said, pulling off her helmet. "She was holding her own."

"And you *left* her?"

"Didn't have a choice." She gestured to her passenger, who climbed off, her legs nearly giving way beneath her. Bryn caught her and helped her stand.

"Anna," Bryn said. "The raven belongs to her."

As if it had heard her words, the bird dropped out of the sky and landed lightly on Anna's shoulder. It stared at Dainn so intently that he began to feel it knew him personally.

"Loki had her," Bryn continued. "Somehow I think it's pretty important to keep her and her pet out of his hands."

Her pet, Dainn thought. A raven with the scent of Odin all over him.

Odin, who had cursed Dainn as Huginn stabbed at Dainn's flesh.

"Why did Loki not kill her and take the bird?" Dainn asked, brutal in his fear for Mist.

"She and the raven have some kind of bond," Bryn said, hostility in her eyes. "And I don't think Orn would let anyone catch him, anyway."

"He wouldn't," Anna said.

"And now you're safe," Bryn said, taking the young woman's arm. "Let's get you inside and warmed up."

Gently guiding Anna toward the door, the Valkyrie passed by Dainn without a glance. He remained at the curb, listening, casting his senses wide for the sound of engines. The wind whipped his hair over his face, moaning and laughing.

After thirty endless minutes, the other motorcycles rounded the corner onto Illinois. Dainn watched their riders pull up around Bryn's vehicle: Tennessee, his leg splinted, perched behind Rick on his bike. Bunny.

And Mist.

Dainn's muscles unlocked. He waited while each of the Einherjar dismounted, removed their helmets, and walked or limped toward the door in silence. Rick supported Tennessee, who was obviously in considerable pain.

"Is everything all right?" Mist asked, stopping before Dainn.

"You defeated Loki," he said, his voice stretched thin by the wind.

"He ran." She rubbed her arms. "But it was close, Dainn. Very close."

If Mist had not been clear that there was to be nothing but friendship and alliance between them—if anything more had been possible—Dainn would have made an utter fool of himself.

But he stepped back, grateful that the beast was still quiescent in its cage. "Did you use the ancient magic?" he asked.

Her teeth began to chatter. "I . . . I'm not sure. But . . . if I did, nothing happened. No fugue state."

"And your tattoo? Did it trouble you again?"

"A little. Maybe it's really an earthquake detector." She gave a shaky laugh. "We saved Anna and the raven. That's all that matters."

"No," he said. "It is not."

"You shouldn't have worried about me. You've got enough—"

She swayed forward. Dainn caught her. She clung to him, her forehead resting against his chest. A light snow began to fall, finding its way under her collar and melting on her hair.

He rested his hand on the nape of her neck, aware that his pulse had risen to an unreasonable speed. Her fingers dug into his arms, an almost painful pressure he welcomed.

"I'm tired, Dainn," she said.

"I know." He smoothed her hair. "You need rest."

"You keep saying that."

"And still you refuse."

Mist looked up with an attempt at a smile. But it didn't last. She began to tremble. Her lips parted. She searched his eyes, looking for the vital thing, the monster, that stood between them.

"It's gone," she said, wonder in her voice. "How?"

He managed a smile of his own. "Not gone," he said. "Sleeping. Where is Edvard?"

Mist blinked. "He went after Loki. All we can do is hope he didn't do anything stupid." She pulled away and stood very straight, challenging her own weariness with her usual courage and stubborn will. "Right now, we have other priorities. We know Anna's connected to the raven and the raven to Odin, but not *how*. Or why the bird is here in the first place. I plan to talk to her first thing in the morning—" She laughed. "Hel, it's already morning. I hope she can handle all the questions I'm going to be asking. I have a feeling we're in for a few major surprises."

Surprises, Dainn thought grimly.

"There is something I must tell you," he said.

She met his gaze, and Dainn could see her bracing herself for bad news. "Go ahead," she said.

"The Jotunn is dead."

She swayed on her feet. "How?"

Dainn kept his hands to himself. "The cats led me to him," he said.

"You didn't answer my question. *I* killed him, didn't I?"

"You are not to blame."

"Was it the wound, or the spell?"

"The wound, I am certain. But you merely defended yourself." Dainn hesitated. "The giant spoke to me before he died."

Mist covered her eyes with her hands. "Did he say why he attacked us?"

"You could not have known, but—"

"Let me guess. He was never a spy for Loki, was he?"

"So he claimed."

"Then why *did* he attack?"

"He suggested that he was coerced. He was unable to elaborate."

"Was he working for someone else?" Mist asked, her words emerging in a rush. "Could have been spying for Freya, and Loki found out somehow? But why wouldn't she have warned you that she had her own Jotunn spies in Loki's camp?"

"We can only speculate," Dainn said, looking away. "I wish I could tell you more."

"It makes sense," she whispered. "I killed a giant who probably suffered from Loki's malice as much as anyone. If only I'd used more control—"

"You have no cause to berate yourself," Dainn said. "You were fighting for your life."

Mist swallowed. "What was his name?"

"He called himself Svardkell."

"Did he suffer?"

Dainn knew it was time to bend the truth. "I do not believe so," he said. "But before he died, he did convey a message. A warning. About protecting the boy, and watching for traitors."

"He didn't happen to say who they were?" she asked, bitterness creeping into her voice.

"Unfortunately, he did not. But the boy must be Ryan, and you are already protecting him."

"Do you think he meant that Loki is coming after Ryan now?"

"Clearly, we can take no chances," Dainn said. "Has Tashiro progressed in his plans for taking Ryan and Gabriella to safety?"

"He's working on it." She hesitated. "What about the body?"

"I took the liberty of giving it back to the earth."

"What?"

"You are exhausted. I thought it would be best that you not—"

"You were so sure that you have the beast under control well enough to risk using that level of magic again?" She glared at him. "You said it was sleeping. What's different now?"

"I found a . . . new technique to keep it at bay."

"What 'new technique'?"

"I found a certain key I had lost. It enabled me to put the beast back in its cage."

Her stare suggested that she wasn't sure she believed him. "Permanently?" she asked.

She had hit on the problem with the usual unerring precision. How could he know how long the herbal concoction would be effective? He had merely borrowed this control, not won it for himself.

"I cannot be sure," he admitted. "But I will know if the beast begins to escape again."

"Oh, Dainn." Her eyes glittered with moisture. "I wish you hadn't taken the risk, but I should be thanking you. I'm not sure I could have—" She broke off, clearly struggling against another open display of emotion. "I need to make sure Anna gets some rest," she said, abruptly changing the subject. "Let's go in."

Dainn remained behind, watching her walk toward the door and wondering how much more she could endure.

And wondering, too, what had become of Edvard. Had he gone

alone after Loki, believing that his nature would give him some advantage if and when he caught up with Laufeyson?

Or perhaps *he* was a traitor, and Dainn had yet to face the consequences of his decision to take the herb.

Bereft of answers, Dainn went inside, avoiding the others who had gathered in the living room. He found Ryan was still crouched by the banister on the second floor landing, seemingly unaware of the commotion.

"Who died?" Ryan asked, repeating his earlier question as if his conversation with Dainn had never been interrupted.

Dainn could think of no reason to keep the truth from him now. "The frost giant who attacked Mist," he said.

"Shit," Ryan muttered, dragging his hand through his unkempt hair. "This has never happened to me before."

Dainn sat on a step at the foot of the stairs. "What did you experience?" he asked gently.

"It was like someone . . . I mean, like someone's soul or something just kind of blinked out." He pressed the heel of his hand against the center of his forehead. "I think it could have been bad if it had lasted any longer."

"You felt drawn into this death?"

"Yeah." Ryan shivered. "I guess you could call it that."

Then the boy was lucky to be sane, Dainn thought with deep misgiving. He had heard of such experiences, but couldn't imagine how any sentient being could endure it.

"I am sorry," he said. "This sometimes happens among the Alfar, who bond closely in extended clans."

"But I'm not a giant."

Indeed he was not, Dainn thought. Why should Svardkell's death, in particular, affect the boy? Had the episode been provoked by Svardkell's relationship with Mist?

"Are you ill?" Dainn asked. "Shall I send for Eir?"

"No. Please, don't tell Mist or anyone else."

"If it should happen again—"

"I'll tell someone right away."

As he attempted to tell me before? Dainn thought. "Ryan," he said, "I know that we—"

"What's all the noise?" Gabi said, coming out onto the landing. She glared at Dainn. "What are you doing here? Where's Mist? What's happening?"

Dainn rose. "There has been a fight with Loki, and Mist has rescued a woman he attacked. One of us will explain the rest to you as soon as possible."

"Yeah," Gabi said. "The usual. Stay up here until someone comes, right?"

"Look after Ryan. He has not been well."

"I noticed. Nice that *you* did."

"I'm okay, Gab," Ryan said.

"Come down if he becomes ill in any way," Dainn said to the girl.

"Will do, *jefe*."

With a brief nod of acknowledgment, Dainn turned back for the living room. He still had to explain the most essential aspect of Svardkell's message to Mist when they could safely be alone and she could process the information. Only then might they properly consider why Ryan had been aware of Svardkell's demise.

As he paused in the hall, listening to the murmur of voices in the living room, Dainn was struck by the disturbing notion that it might be premature to send the young mortals away after all. And by the realization that if Odin had already become directly involved in the nascent war with Loki, Mist might no longer be in danger of losing herself to her mother's will.

If she was safe, Dainn thought, he might be spared the need to tell her just how far into the gutter the beast had dragged him.

11

Anna Stangeland sat in the oversized armchair by the fireplace, wearing a pair of Mist's jeans and a flannel shirt in place of the ruined suit. A handsome gray parrot perched on her shoulder and stared at Mist with a probing yellow gaze.

It was 10 a.m., and Mist could tell by the deep shadows under the young woman's eyes that she'd had little sleep over the eight or so hours since Mist had taken her from Loki. Now the young woman wore the stubborn, wary look of someone who wanted answers she wasn't sure she'd like.

Mist knew just how vulnerable an exhausted person could be. She remembered almost throwing herself into Dainn's arms. *Had* thrown herself, narrowly avoiding something much worse.

Or *would* it have been worse, if Dainn had really managed to . . . ?

"You don't have to be afraid, Anna," she said, forcing her thoughts back into more productive channels. "You're safe here."

"I'm not afraid," Anna said, lifting her chin.

"Good," Mist said, glancing at the parrot. "I have many questions for you. Very important ones having to do with what Orn really is, and your past with him. But maybe you have a few for me, first."

"A few?" Anna said with a faint laugh. "Considering that I hardly understand that anything that's happened, I don't even know where to begin."

"Why don't you tell me what you *do* understand," Mist said.

"I know that Orn has been nagging me to find someone called Mist. When he turned into a raven and started talking to me in a way he never had before, I just assumed I was losing my—" She broke off, flushing. "Orn saved me from a fire that was completely confined to my apartment, a fire no one else seemed to notice. He was leading me in this direction when three very large men and this guy—"

"Loki," Mist said.

"Yeah. He called himself Lukas Landvik. He tried to kidnap me and asked me questions about Orn and the Old Norse god Odin. Then I found myself stuck in the middle of a magical battle." She nodded. "Yes, I think that's about right."

This young woman really was remarkable, Mist thought. But she'd have to be . . . if, as she had claimed, the raven had been with her and her family since World War II.

Mist glanced toward the door. Bryn and Dainn were listening in, but she'd asked them to stay out in the hall so as not to overwhelm Anna or alarm Orn, who was obviously very protective of his—

What? Mist thought. Friend? Guardian? And why, if he was indeed what Mist, Dainn, and Loki suspected, had the raven hidden himself so long? Why was he so intent on reaching Mist now?

Loki had been right. Freya had never once mentioned even the possibility that Odin had any kind of presence in this world. Only *she* was supposed to be capable of communication between Midgard and Ginnungagap.

Had Odin sent another ambassador in her place?

But then surely the raven wouldn't have been silently waiting in Midgard all these decades.

Never believe anything Loki suggests, Mist thought. *Especially when he claims to have known the raven was coming.*

"You're right," she said to Anna. "Loki and I fought with magic. It was real, and Orn isn't an ordinary bird."

"And those men who captured me weren't men at all, were they?"

"No," Mist said. "They were frost giants."

Anna reached for the cooling cup of coffee on the side table. Only the slight trembling of her fingers gave any indication that she was still suffering the emotional aftereffects of her ordeal. "I know a little Norse mythology," she said. "Sometimes my grandmother and great-grandfather told me the old tales. Loki was responsible for starting the war between the gods and the giants, right? The one that was supposed to destroy everything before a new world rose out of the ashes."

"That's right," Mist said, relieved that she didn't have to cover the basics. "But Ragnarok, as it was foretold, never happened. Eight Homeworlds *were* destroyed, but Midgard survived." She hesitated, finding it difficult to explain the enormity of the threat to Anna's world.

"You need to understand," she said slowly, "that Loki plans to start that war all over again here in Midgard—Earth—and is gathering allies to fight the gods, led by Odin and Freya."

"Of course," Anna said, her hazel eyes almost fading into the shadows that framed them. "It all makes perfect sense."

"The Aesir are real, Anna. They're still alive, waiting for the chance to stop Loki. And Loki will do anything to stop *them*."

"Then where are they now? Why aren't they here?"

"They're . . . in a kind of otherworld, where they don't have physical bodies."

"But *Loki* is here."

Mist had no intent of explaining her past relationship with "Eric." "Yes," she said.

Compressing her lips, Anna began to stroke Orn again. "Loki wanted to know if Odin was in communication with Midgard, as if *I* would have any idea—"

"He knows you have some kind of close connection to Orn," Mist said. "The two ravens Huginn and Muninn were Odin's—"

"I know," Anna interrupted. "His advisors, and his messengers. Do you really think that's what Orn is?"

"We thought so as soon as he came to get us."

"And who are *you*, Mist? You're obviously not one of these goddesses . . . or are you?"

Mist wished she could laugh. "I'm a Valkyrie," she said. "Does that mean anything to you?"

"Do you still fly around picking soldiers off battlefields? Or just people with ravens?"

"Our job descriptions have changed a little over the centuries," Mist said dryly.

"But you came from Asgard, right? Why are *you* here?"

"Odin sent me to Midgard centuries ago, to protect something he wanted to keep out of the enemy's hands."

"You look as if you're in your late twenties," Anna said. "I guess you must have to invent new identities and move around so people didn't notice you weren't getting any older."

Sharp as Gungnir, Mist thought. "That's right," she said. "The name I go by now is Bjorgsen. Bryn is another one of us, and we're looking for the other ten Valkyrie who were also sent here by Odin. We're trying to hold out against Loki until the gods arrive."

Anna tried to sip her coffee. She couldn't quite hold the rim of the mug steady against her lips. "And he'll do anything to stop you," she said.

"Yes. But he's an egomaniac and a liar, and I don't believe he knew anything about Orn before he found you." Mist pushed loose tendrils of hair behind her ears. "Has anyone been following you, Anna?" she asked. "Anyone new come into your life since you arrived in San Francisco?"

"No." Anna set down her mug on the side table with great care. "No one."

"What about this fire no one else saw? How did it start?"

"I don't know. It wasn't natural, was it?"

"It sounds like magic," Mist said.

But whose? she thought. Evidently not Loki's. And aside from a few of his Jotunar, she couldn't think of anyone else who would have done it . . . except Vidarr and Vali, who would have approached Anna and Orn directly if they'd known about him. And Vali would simply have told Mist.

But if Orn had a message from Odin to impart, why would he come to Mist instead of Odin's sons? Because Freya had already paved the way?

"How did your family get Orn?" Mist asked, switching to a less troubling subject.

"My grandmother always had him," Anna said. "She never told anyone where he'd come from, but he was with her from the time of the war, when my great-grandfather adopted her."

"But your grandmother never mentioned anything unusual about him."

"Nothing. She gave Orn to me when she died. My parents immigrated to the United States when I was six. We lived in New York until they passed, and I stayed there until two weeks ago." She bit her lip. "I can't go back to my place, can I?"

"Not until we figure out what's happening. But I'll have someone go pick up some of your clothes and other necessities." Mist thought for a moment. "What made you move to San Francisco, Anna?"

The young woman frowned. "I . . . felt compelled to come here. I just didn't realize it until now." She paused. "Oh, my God. If Orn wanted me to find you so badly . . ."

He might have influenced Anna without her knowing it, Mist thought. Had Orn also caused the fire that had driven Anna from her apartment? Odin had been known to use illusion just as Loki did.

But if the bird was so formidable, why not simply save Anna from Loki?

"I have another question," Anna said, cutting across Mist's troubled thoughts. "When these gods show up, what's going to happen to Earth?"

Mist winced. She'd asked herself the same question at the very beginning, when Dainn had come to tell her that nothing would ever be the same again.

She'd never been happy with her own answers.

"The gods will prevent Loki from throwing all Midgard into chaos," she said.

"I see," Anna said. "But if they're existing in some kind of limbo, and the other worlds were destroyed, wouldn't they want to live here?"

"Everything is complicated right now," Mist said. "I won't lie to you. It's going to get a lot *more* complicated."

Anna touched her throat. Her movement briefly revealed a fine chain hung around her neck. "What are you planning to do with Orn?" she asked.

"Ask him to give us whatever information he has. Why he's here, and what he wants." Mist shifted on the couch, stretching her stiff, sore legs. "I forgot to ask . . . Can you take a break from your job? We can't have you going in to work, at least not for awhile."

"Then it's a good thing I don't have one yet," Anna said, "or I'd be out of one pretty fast. I'm in IT . . . a programmer analyst." She smiled wryly. "Maybe, with all your divine connections, you can help me find work when things go back to normal."

If *things go back to normal*, Mist thought. "I promise we'll do everything we can to help you," she said. "And I think that's enough for now. I hope you don't mind a half-finished room upstairs. We'll try to make it comfortable."

"I really have to stay here?" Anna asked with a touch of rebellion.

"You won't be safer anywhere else," Mist said.

"Not even if I left the city?"

"Without Orn? I don't think he'd like that."

Flapping his wings, Orn hopped from Anna's shoulder to her knee, shook out his feathers, and began to change. Gray plumage darkened to the color of onyx, and in a moment a raven was peering at Anna out of one clever black eye.

"Safe here," it croaked. "Trust."

Anna reached inside the collar of her shirt and clutched at the chain Mist had glimpsed earlier. The raven's head darted inside the collar and emerged with the chain in its beak, broken clasp dangling. The bird flew to Mist and dropped a small piece of stone into her hand.

The stone was irregularly shaped but flat, and on one side were engraved Rune-staves and the profile of a bird's head.

Mist's hand went numb, and she nearly dropped the pendant. "Where did you get this?" she asked Anna.

The young woman was clearly rattled. "My grandmother passed it to me along with Orn when she died," she said.

"What was your grandmother's name?"

"Rebekka. Rebekka Forren."

Rebekka.

Immediately Mist was swept back to that terrible day in 1942, the day when she had failed to protect her fellow Valkyrie and the innocent mortals under her care.

Bryn had fallen, presumed dead, and Horja had taken her Treasure, Freya's Falcon Cloak, along with the broken halves of Thor's "unbreakable" staff, Gridarvoll. A score of Jewish refugees fleeing the murderous Nazis had nearly made it to the border between Norway and Sweden.

Only one of them had survived—a nine-year-old girl, taken in and adopted by Mist's lover and fellow resistance fighter, Geir Forren.

Mist had never seen him or Rebekka again. She had left Norway behind, haunted by her failure. After the war, she'd tried to take up a new life alone. She had sent money anonymously to Geir and Rebekka for many years, though she knew Geir must have known where it came from. She'd wanted Rebekka to grow up without a constant reminder of the tragedy that had stolen all her kin and her childhood.

"What was your great-grandfather's name?" she asked thickly.

"Geir." Anna looked down at the carpet. "He stayed in Norway, but we . . . we were close."

Mist closed her eyes. She didn't want to imagine Geir as an old man, a man who must die like any other mortal. But he had succeeded in raising Rebekka and lived long enough to become a friend to Rebekka's granddaughter.

"Please give it back to me," Anna said, holding out her hand.

Mist opened her hand. She couldn't tell Anna that she had given the pendant to Rebekka when they had parted forever.

But she wondered if, and how, Orn was connected to the pendant. When Odin had given it to her just before he'd sent her and the other Valkyrie to Midgard, she had assumed it was only a token of his favor. She had worn the pendant for centuries before her work with the Norwegian Resistance, and she had never seen parrot *or* raven.

Slowly she passed the pendant back to Anna. The young woman tucked the broken chain and pendant in her jeans pocket.

"Come with me," Mist said, getting to her feet. "I'll show you your room."

"I saw that one of the men who helped rescue me and Orn was wounded . . ."

"If you're feeling guilty about that," Mist said, "you can stop. They volunteered."

Once Anna was safely ensconced in the half-finished room on the second floor, Mist went downstairs and found Dainn waiting alone in the kitchen.

"Where's Bryn?" she asked, rubbing her aching eyes.

"Your Sister said that she would speak to you of your interview with the young woman at a later time."

Mist had the sense that Dainn was deliberately avoiding her gaze. "What did *you* think?" she asked, plopping down into one of the kitchen chairs.

"That your judgment in this matter is sound."

Mist laughed. "'In this matter,' huh?"

Dainn shifted his weight. "Why is the name Rebekka Forren of such interest to you?"

Suddenly Mist didn't feel like laughing anymore. "What do you mean?" she asked.

"Clearly it evoked some strong emotion, as did the name of Rebekka's great-grandfather."

Mist sketched an invisible Rune on the table. Mannaz, the symbol of humanity and of the self. "They were part of my past. I never thought I'd see anyone connected to them again."

"These memories are painful?"

Erasing the Rune with a swipe of her hand, Mist shook her head. Dainn responded with a long silence that told her she didn't believe him.

"What is the significance of this pendant?" he finally asked.

"You saw it?"

"I was able to observe it, yes."

"I got it from Odin before we came to Midgard, and gave it to Anna's grandmother, Rebekka, during the Second World War."

"Indeed? Then your Rebekka would have been a child."

"I didn't know, then, that the pendant was anything more than a gift from Odin," she said. "Obviously I was wrong. I assume that the raven was somehow bound to it, and when I gave the pendant away, Odin's messenger went with it."

"Perhaps Orn was meant to be your guide."

"I never saw the raven in my life."

"And Anna implied that neither she nor her grandmother had ever seen anything but a parrot prior to her residence in this city," Dainn said. "Perhaps you were not meant to perceive the bird during your time in Norway."

Mist got up, opened the refrigerator door, and found a few cans of beer the Einherjar had left behind. She wondered if she was beginning to drink too much.

"Your guess is as good as mine," she said. "A lot of things might have turned out differently if I'd kept the pendant."

"What was done cannot be undone."

Mist closed the refrigerator door. "Thanks for another pithy bit of elven wisdom," she said. "I don't know what I'd do without them."

Dainn's lips thinned, but she could tell it wasn't because she'd angered him with her mockery. They'd been talking that way to each other ever since they'd met, and there was a kind of comforting rhythm about it.

Her next thought wasn't comforting at all.

"Loki's piss," she swore. "All this time, and I didn't think about what it would be like for you to face Odin's messenger after what the All-father did to you."

Dainn turned away. "That ceased to be of importance when I became Freya's ambassador on behalf of the Aesir."

"But you didn't deserve that punishment. Don't you feel anything?"

"No." His shoulders lifted and fell in a long, deep breath, and he turned toward her again." What will you tell Odin's sons, since they apparently have no knowledge of these events?" he asked.

Ashamed at her own relief, Mist sat down again. "Vali's been putting in his time at Asbrew, trying not to arouse Vidarr's suspicions about his working for me. But he'll obviously have to be told when he gets back."

"His reaction to learning about the raven will be interesting to observe."

"Yeah. But I want to keep Vidarr out of this as long as possible."

"Very wise," he said. "But are you certain Vali will agree to keep these events concealed from his brother?"

"I think so. I *hope* so." She speared her hands through her hair, too exhausted to care if Dainn saw just how vulnerable she was feeling. "Did I mention that Loki claimed he knew the raven was coming?"

"No, but I have no doubt that he was prevaricating."

"If by that you mean 'lying,' I agree."

Dainn took something out of the fridge and set it on the counter. "Did Loki say anything else of interest?"

His tone was off, Mist thought . . . too studied, as if he of all people had no real interest in Loki's "pronouncements."

"He asked after you," Mist said, suddenly angry with Dainn for no good reason. "He kept harping on what I remembered from our fight with him, and asked me if I felt left out of the game." She folded her arms across her chest. "I know I was in and out of that fugue state and didn't know everything that happened once Freya got there. Was there something important I missed that you didn't tell me about?"

Dainn moved to stand in the doorway to the laundry room, a few steps away from the lawn where he had given Svardkell to the earth. "Nothing," he said.

"Funny," Mist said. "Loki suggested that maybe Odin sent the raven in Freya's place because he wasn't happy with her. But obviously that isn't true, since Orn has been here far longer than Freya's been. And if Odin didn't need Freya to keep the lines of communication open, he'd have been a little more obvious about it, wouldn't he?"

"That would seem reasonable," Dainn murmured.

So many things *seemed* reasonable, Mist thought. Until they weren't.

"I guess it'll all become clear," Mist said. "But Loki isn't going to sit on his ass. He's going to come back for Orn."

"Yes," Dainn said. He squared his shoulders and strode to the counter, speaking in a rush. "And that is why we must find more allies. Loki attempted to kidnap Anna at the very borders of what would be considered your territory, and you will soon begin to lose your current followers to death and injury until none remain."

"Do you think I don't know that?" Mist asked, the muscles in her stomach beginning to tighten. "I *saw* the Einherjar fight Loki's Jotunar. But you said more allies would be coming . . ."

"I have also said that you would almost certainly need to use your glamour to obtain mortal warriors in sufficient quantities." A breath of cold air swept over Mist's shoulders as Dainn opened the refrigerator door, and plastic rustled. "You must abandon your inhibitions and fear of compelling others to protect their own world."

Stunned by Dainn's unexpected urgency, Mist stared at the sandwich Dainn had placed on the table in front of her. "My inhibitions—" she began.

"And you need not feel overly distressed," Dainn interrupted, pacing from one end of the kitchen to the other. "As Bryn felt the changes in Midgard, so will thousands of mortals, those you would call 'good.' They will be drawn to you because they possess an instinctive understanding of what Midgard faces, and what they will lose if we fail."

"The way they'll lose their right to choose their own destinies?" she demanded, shoving her chair back from the table.

"Their destinies have already been set for them." Dainn stopped abruptly, planted his hands on the table and leaned toward her, gazing into her eyes with an intensity more frightening than anything she'd seen in the beast's pitiless stare. "Think of Midgard's fate under Loki," he said, "of the chaos that will result, the ruination of this civilization as you know it. Is the salvation of this world worth the cost of a hundred free mortal wills? A thousand? Ten thousand?"

"Yes," Mist said, rising to face him, "how many *is* it worth? Not just minds, but lives? Even ten thousand mortals don't have much of a chance beating Loki and all the corruptible humans he'll be attracting to his ranks!"

"And now you have less than twenty." He stepped back, and Mist noticed that his hands were shaking. "You knew this time would come. You were given a responsibility to hold Midgard until the Aesir can fight for it. Allow those who can hear you feel that they come to one who will stop the destruction of everything they hold dear."

"Lie to them, you mean."

"You are the daughter of a goddess. You must now see yourself as one, and make others see it as well."

Mist fell back into her chair, silenced by his vehemence. He was right. She'd been putting off even thinking about it, and early this morning she'd had a very rude awakening.

But it wasn't quite as simple as Dainn made it out to be.

"The glamour is dangerous," she said, remembering what had happened when she'd used the magic to erase part of Koji Tashiro's memory. "I can't go throwing it around without understanding what I'm doing. And Freya isn't here to teach me."

"Freya must not—" Dainn broke off, drawing a sharp breath. "Freya cannot teach you what must come from within yourself."

"The ancient magic also comes from within me," Mist said, "but you don't think I'm capable of handling it."

"I will help you."

For a moment she didn't understand him. "You mean with the glamour? How?"

"I may be able to steady and support you. Lend you such strength as I can."

"Because the beast is gone? Are you that sure it's safe?"

"Perhaps if I test my magic under controlled conditions, I can be certain that my control over the beast is sound."

I hope you're right, Mist thought. *I hope by Ymir's Blood that you're right.*

"There is . . . one more thing," Dainn said softly.

Mist had no more strength left, mental or physical, to brace herself for another blow. "Make it quick," she said.

"The Jotunn—Svardkell—was your father."

12

If she hadn't already been sitting, Mist thought she might have fallen. The undigested contents of her stomach swelled up into her throat, nearly gagging her.

At once Dainn was kneeling beside her chair. "I am sorry," he said, his voice deeply contrite. "I should not have . . ."

"You were on a roll," she said. "Why stop?" She swallowed. "I'm all right."

Dainn stared at her, his dark eyes stricken with guilt.

"Give me the rest," she said, pointing to the chair on the other side of the table. "He told you his name. Did he say . . ."

"Nothing more than that," Dainn said quietly, rising to stand behind his chair.

Mist swiped at her eyes with the back of her hand, hoping without much confidence that Dainn didn't see. "You said there might have been some kind of spell on him. Could Loki have known who he was all along, and thought it would fun to have my own father attack me?"

"It would be . . . typical of him."

"And Freya never told me. I should have asked. I should have insisted—"

"When would that have been possible?" Dainn asked, resting his hands on the back of the chair. "You were unable to ask when she joined you against Loki, and even that was no true meeting." He hesitated. "I could have asked on your behalf. . . ."

"No. The fact is, I didn't really want to think about being half

Jotunn. They're the enemy, right? And I could never be sure if anyone I kill might be a relative." She shivered. "It looks as though I did, anyway. Was Svardkell watching me all this time? Waiting for a chance to reveal himself?"

"He didn't speak of it," Dainn said, his fingers tightening on the chair with such force that it creaked in protest. "But perhaps he was already coming to you when Loki caught him."

Mist stared at the sandwich without really seeing it. "Now I think I understand why Freya didn't give a curse about me in Asgard. She didn't care about Svardkell. I was just a mistake."

"No," Dainn said, avoiding her eyes. "It may seem an explanation for her neglect of you in Asgard, but you were no mistake."

"I guess I'll learn the truth if Freya returns." She looked at her watch. "If there's nothing else you need to tell me, I've got to call another council meeting."

"I should not have told you this now."

"But now I don't have time to think about it." She tried to smile. "I just wish I could have said good-bye. There are so many things—"

"I know."

She cleared her throat. "After the meeting," she said briskly, "you and I are going to do what you suggested and 'test' your magic. And I think I know how. Since Loki wasn't expecting Anna to turn up, we need to figure out what he was doing around here when it happened."

She was the woman in the photograph.

Anna sat on the bed, numb with the knowledge that the world she knew didn't exist. The shocks had come one after another, too quickly for her to absorb.

Mist Bjorgsen. Anna had seen the resemblance immediately— bright blond hair; strong, beautiful Scandinavian features; grave gray eyes. That aura of strength and purpose that had come through even in a black and white image taken over seventy years ago.

The same image that had haunted her dreams. A *Valkyrie*.

Lying back on the bed, Anna threw her arm over her eyes. What she wouldn't give to be back in her tiny studio in New York right now. How she wished that Mormor hadn't given her the pendant, that she didn't have to accept the fact that the woman who had saved her was not merely a descendant of the one in the picture, but the real thing. The woman great-grandfather Geir had loved and fought beside during the War.

A woman who had been alive since long before Geir was born.

Anna rolled onto her side and curled up her knees, torn between tears and laughter. The Valkyrie had reacted strongly when she'd seen the pendant, when she'd heard Rebekka's name, and again when Anna had spoken of Geir, though she was obviously trying not to show her emotions.

Had she known Rebekka? Oldefar had never said they'd met, just as he'd never said anything about specific missions he'd shared with Mist.

Had he realized what Mist was all along? Had she left him, all too aware that he must age and she would not?

No, Anna couldn't believe that Geir had recognized the truth. And if Rebekka had known Mist, she hadn't "revealed" it in Anna's dreams of the war and afterward. Anna knew that Orn had never spoken to Rebekka except as a parrot imitating human speech.

He had never told *her* to "find Mist."

Somewhere downstairs a phone rang, and Anna covered her ears. When she lost herself, she thought she *was* Rebekka. Or Helga. She saw herself in dark places, fighting for her life, mourning, sometimes suffering. She had seen the men in dark jodhpurs and closely fitted tunics with caps bearing a symbol of a double lightning bolt. She'd seen the bodies and blood in the snow. She could feel those cold eyes watching, the shadow-carved faces bent over hers, demanding answers. Just as Lukas—Loki—had done.

Anna drew the pendant from her pocket and rubbed the stone between her fingers. Loki hadn't noticed it . . . almost as if he wasn't *meant* to see it. But Orn had wanted Mist to see the stone. She, like Rebekka and Anna, must have some connection to it.

Glancing at Orn—who was now an ordinary African Grey, perched on the rather rickety metal headboard—Anna wondered why he had waited all these years to look for the Valkyrie. "*Odin sent me to Midgard centuries ago,*" Mist had said. Why would Orn suddenly decide to take action as a god's envoy?

And now that Orn and Anna were here, where he obviously wanted to be, why hadn't he said anything else?

What was he waiting for?

Anna began to rise from the bed, wondering if there was a tactic she'd missed in trying to make Orn talk. Dizziness washed over her, and she fell back with a thump. She felt the weight of her fears pushing her eyelids down, and her thoughts began to drift.

The snow fell heavily but gently as she and the others around her struggled to keep going, forging on to the Swedish border.

They would make it. Mist said so. Soon they would all be free.

"Hello," a man's deep voice said from behind the thick veil of snow.

She opened her eyes. The man immediately reminded her of a youthful Saint Nick, with his pleasant, slightly round and ruddy face, thick blond hair, and fuzzy, midlength beard over a broad chest and slightly protruding belly. His very broad shoulders and overall size told her that he was a strong man, in spite of his mild appearance.

Rolling over, she slid off the bed and scrambled into a crouch behind it. Orn squawked.

"Sorry if I startled you," Saint Nick, Jr. said in a deep, abashed voice. "I shouldn't have just walked into your room like this."

Anna poked her head up over the side of the bed, noted the open door, and rose.

"I couldn't exactly lock the door," she said, "since there wasn't any lock."

"Yeah," Junior said. He flashed her a hesitant smile. "I'm Vali.

Mist told me about you, so I thought I'd . . ." His face grew red. "I guess I should go."

Anna raised a hand to stop him, not completely sure if she was acting out of a sensible need to gather more information or just to prove she wasn't afraid.

"It's okay," she said, walking around the bed and extending her hand. "Anna Stangeland."

"Vali . . . uh . . ."

"Good to meet you, Vali," she said, deliberately holding the grip for a good five seconds, even though he could have broken every bone in her hand with the slightest pressure. He held it as gently as he would the leg of a sparrow.

"Good to meet *you*, Ms. Stangeland," he said. His smile was wide and open, his teeth very white and large as a horse's. "I'm the guy who works the computers around here, but I don't come up for air very often. I guess you're pretty much up to speed about what's going on."

"I wouldn't say that," Anna said, glancing at the sole chair near the wall. She doubted it would hold Vali, but she felt very uncomfortable bending her neck up far enough to see his face.

"Oh," he said, following her glance. "Uh, do you mind if I sit on the floor?"

"Be my guest," Anna said, moving closer to the door.

Vali lowered himself to the floor like an elephant trying to balance on a small rubber ball and sat cross-legged, still quite red in the face. She noted that he didn't so much as glance at Orn. If he knew about *her*, he had to know what Orn was supposed to be.

"Mist didn't mention you," she said, "but she seems to be pretty busy. And she wanted me to rest, so I assumed she'd fill me in on the details later."

"Yeah," Vali said, scratching his beard. "She has a lot on her shoulders."

"You and Mist are friends?" she asked.

"For a long time."

"Do you mind if I ask you a personal question?"

He blinked. "Uh, sure. What is it?"

"Are you immortal, too?"

"Oh. Well, as much as Mist is, I guess. I used to live in Asgard. I was—" He broke off, apparently deciding he didn't want to go into detail. "It's kind of complicated."

I've heard that before, Anna thought. "It's okay," she said. "I can only take in so much new information, anyway."

Vali sighed. "I'm sorry this has been so hard for you," he said. "I mean, finding out that all the stuff you thought were legends actually happened. Especially the *way* you found out, with Loki and all."

"I'm getting used to it," Anna lied.

"You must be a very brave lady."

Is he flirting with me? Anna thought. They'd only just met, and in spite of his boldness in entering her room he seemed far too . . . old fashioned, somehow, to think about a stranger that way. Especially not *her*.

"I'm not brave," she said evenly. "I got thrown into the deep end, and it was sink or swim."

Vali chuckled, though the sound was a little strained. "You're a good swimmer," he said.

"Passable," Anna said, "but—"

Suddenly Orn landed on her shoulder—all parrot, she thought with desperate relief—and regarded Vali with pointed curiosity.

"That's some bird," Vali said. "Can I touch him?"

"You never can tell with Orn," she said, "he might decide to bite you."

Vali reached out with a gentle hand and lightly stroked Orn's breast. Orn endured it, neither hostile nor welcoming.

"Has he said anything else yet?" Vali asked.

Anna had a pretty good idea that when Orn talked, Mist should be the first to hear about it.

"Not yet," she said.

An awkward silence fell between them. Just as Anna was feeling compelled to fill it, Vali brightened.

"I heard you're a programmer, too," he said. "Maybe you'd like me to show you what I'm doing to find Mist's Sisters. You know, the other Valkyrie."

Anna weighed the offer. She didn't by any means trust Vali, Mist's ally or not—he looked far too much like a frost giant—but this might be a chance to learn something from a completely different perspective.

"That sounds very nice," she said.

"Then I'll come up and get you when I have something interesting to show you, okay?" He practically bounced up from the ground, light as a child. "I hope . . ." His face grew serious. "I hope we can be friends, Ms. Stangeland. We're all going to be working together to save this world."

"I hope so, too," Anna said, standing away from the door.

With a strange little bow, Vali backed out of the room.

"What do you think, Orn?" she asked once Vali was gone. "You want me to trust Mist. Does that extend to him, too?"

Orn didn't answer. Anna drifted out the door and to the window on the other side of the empty space that made up most of the second floor. She'd been told that two teenagers occupied the other room, but she hadn't seen them yet. She was relieved that she hadn't needed to add still more people to her list of new—and very strange—acquaintances.

Orn flew off Anna's shoulder to land on the narrow sill, clinging like a gecko. The sky outside looked almost inviting with the early afternoon sunlight breaking through the clouds for what seemed like the first time in weeks. Anna's feet were itching for a walk . . . a regular, completely innocent walk, without the threat of giants or red-haired godlings getting in her way.

I won't be here forever, she reminded herself. "I guess you'll have bigger fish to fry than hanging around with me," she said to Orn wistfully. "You were never anyone's pet, were you?"

He craned his neck around to look at her. "You stay with *me*," he said in a perfectly clear if high-pitched voice.

Anna started. It wasn't just that he'd said it—it was the *way* he'd said it. Like a command. She would stay with *him*, not the other way around.

"Orn," she said quietly, "it's time to drop the act."

He croaked, shed his red and gray feathers, and studied her with ebony eyes. "You have purpose," he said. "Stay."

Purpose, Anna thought. When had she ever really had any purpose but going through the motions day after day, getting up and going to work and coming home and spending yet another quiet night with Orn and a glass of wine?

Was this what she'd been waiting for? A reason to live, to fight for something bigger than her very ordinary existence?

She met Orn's gaze as if she were facing Odin himself.

"I'll stay," she said. "As long as you need me."

"So what happens next?" Rick asked.

Mist glanced around the table at her council. Only Vali wasn't present; he'd shown up soon after Mist had taken Anna to her room, and she'd filled him in on her conversation with the young woman before he returned to his work with the computers.

Vali had been astonished by the whole situation, but he hadn't seemed angry. He was obviously puzzled by the fact that neither he nor his brother had known of the raven, but he'd agreed to keep the knowledge to himself and put off seeing Orn while Mist sorted things out with Anna.

"It all depends on Orn," she said, belatedly remembering Rick's question. She briefly and sketchily recounted the story of her and Bryn's work with the Norwegian Resistance during World War II— most of which the Einherjar already knew—the raven's likely connection to the pendant Mist had given to Rebekka, and what she knew of Anna's family and Orn's previous life with her and her grand-mother.

She left out the parts about her relationship with Geir and the massacre of those she had sworn to protect.

"There are good reasons why we think this could be Odin's mes-senger," Bryn said when Mist had finished. "The All-father could have sent this bird to keep an eye on Midgard as Huginn and Muninn did in Asgard."

"It's possible that Odin may have known at least part of what's been going on here ever since he and the other Aesir were flung into Gin-nungagap, even before Freya made contact with Dainn," Mist said. "We have no idea how much, but since Loki has—"

"Odin entrusted *you* with this pendant," Tennessee said, sitting in a chair with his splinted leg stretched out before him. "You gave it away. How does that fit in? What's the connection?"

"We don't know what Odin intended," Mist said, swallowing her guilt. "We don't know why Orn waited so long to find me after the war, or *how* he found me. If Freya had anything to do with it, she isn't around to tell us."

She glanced at Dainn, instinctively looking for support. As usual, he stood leaning against the wall, listening and observing but speak-ing very rarely. He had been even quieter than usual since their last conversation, and she knew something was eating at him. Not just the difficulty of having to reveal a painful truth to a friend, but some-thing very personal. Something he wouldn't share with her.

"We are still lacking vital information," he said, breaking his si-lence.

"And Orn isn't saying much," Mist said. "I don't think we should push him, or Anna. But we do need to protect them." She swept each face with her gaze. "I've already mentioned this before, but I can't emphasize strongly enough that no one outside this room is to know what's really going on."

"Loki knows Anna's here, right?" Bunny asked.

"He'll probably assume we'll keep her here. We can't send her anywhere else until we have concrete answers. Loki ran, so he must not think his magical energy is up to another try for Anna, at least not right away." She looked at Bryn. "We sent Vixen and Roadkill to check out Anna's apartment. There's some evidence that Jotunar have been searching it."

"But we were able to pick up some of Anna's belongings and make sure the landlady thinks she's coming back," Bryn said. "Her rent will be paid on time, as long as necessary."

Mist nodded, as if the gesture itself meant that everything was under control. "Keep your people on their toes," she said, "but no one is to engage with the enemy, or anyone who looks like an enemy, under any circumstance. The rule is return and report. Bryn will stay here to keep an eye on Anna while Dainn and I take care of some business. You all know to call me immediately if there's any suspicious activity near the loft."

"What about that giant you captured?" Rick asked.

"He's dead," Mist said flatly. "I doubt anything like that is going to happen again. One more thing . . . if any of you see Edvard, let me know."

"Got it," Bryn said, planting her hands on the tabletop as she stood. "It'll be another long day, Einherjar. Let's move."

"Thanks," Mist said as Bryn headed for the door. "I'll try to make sure you're not stuck doing this alone much longer."

Bryn flashed an enigmatic smile. "I know. Look, there's something I want you to see. Think you can spare a few minutes and come across the street?"

"Okay," Mist said. "Just give me a second."

Bryn left. Mist glanced at Dainn. "I'm going to give Tashiro another call," she said, "try to pin him down, and then see what Bryn wants to show me."

"She seems untroubled by Edvard's continued absence," Dainn said.

"I guess she knows him well enough not to be worried." Mist frowned. "Something bothering you about that? I didn't know you'd seen him except when Bryn brought the Einherjar to help me track the raven."

Dainn shrugged. "Merely curiosity."

Mist had good reason to doubt that kind of answer, but she let it pass. "I'll meet you in the driveway in about an hour," she said.

Once he was out of the room, she called Tashiro. He didn't pick up. She left a message and went out into the cold, her breath frosting the air like a Jotunn's spell.

It was snowing again, lightly, when she reached the factory. Inside the central open area, several of the Einherjar were clustered around a single motorcycle.

She recognized a few of the Einherjar, though she'd barely met them: Fatty, a small, thin man with a cherubic face; Headlights, tall and bespectacled; Harry Lime, a bald, heavyset man with striking green eyes; and Roadkill, unusually hairy and blessed with a very thick and very long black beard. Vixen was absent, as were Bryn and Rick, though Tennessee was leaning on a crutch against the nearest wall.

Bunny was just standing up, a polishing cloth in her hand. She stepped back to give Mist a clear view of the bike. "Do you know what this is?" she asked with a grin.

"It's a Valkyrie," Tennessee said, hopping to adjust his position. "Honda Interstate, 2001. One of the last off the line. Bryn did all the modifications and detailing, but she decided you should have it."

Mist flushed. "I can't—"

"Don't argue," Bunny said. "You know she won't let you refuse. She's out shopping for a new bike right now."

Bunny was right, Mist thought. Bryn wouldn't let her refuse. And it was a handsome machine, she had to admit, all chrome and purple and black. The modifications were subtle, which made it seem more practical than merely decorative.

"It's beautiful," she said.

"Come and take a look."

Almost as if she were approaching a dangerous wild animal, Mist circled the bike, examining the detail and discovering that it was still possible to take joy in pleasant surprises. Tonight she'd return the little bar hopper with a note and ten hundred-dollar bills in payment for the inconvenience she'd undoubtedly caused the owner.

"What you gonna call her?" Tennessee asked.

"Silfr," Mist said without hesitation. "That was the name of my mount when I . . . when I and Bryn and my Sisters were still in Asgard working for Odin."

"Hi-yo Silver," Fatty said. He winced at the disgusted looks the others shot in his direction. "Well, what d'ya expect?"

Mist laughed, cheered by the unexpected generosity of people she hadn't even known existed a few days ago. But then again, the real generosity lay in their willingness to give their lives to save Midgard.

"Thank you," she said.

"Thank Bryn," Bunny said. "You should go try it out."

"I will," Mist said. "In fact, I have a very specific trip in mind."

13

Loki was in a rather good mood, all things considered.

He kicked at the nearly fleshless corpse, listening to the hollow thump with a degree of satisfaction. Most of the remaining captains of crime, including the newest additions, were cowering in their chairs or against the walls, stark terror in their eyes.

"Perhaps I have not made myself clear," Loki said. "You are not only to accept my Jotunar, but follow their instructions exactly as I have presented them. This is not simply a matter of joining forces to increase profits. It is far greater than that . . . gentlemen."

"But my lord Loki," said Barker the outlaw biker, looking far less rebellious than he had several days ago, "we can give you what you want without them—" He shuddered. "Without the giants."

"You cannot give me what I want," Loki said. "And you will not get what *you* want without my help. I gave you a choice before, and I give you one last chance now." He nudged at the corpse again, drawing all eyes to his boot. "Leave, if you wish. Remove yourself from our association, but understand that those who are not my friends or loyal servants are my enemies."

Barker swallowed. A few who looked as if they might have spoken said nothing. Even the toughest, who still occasionally dared to give Loki lip and pretend to defy him, were not about to push him now.

Except one, the boy recently released from some prison in the southern part of the state—ostensibly Chavez's new lieutenant—who showed no evidence of having been reformed by his experience behind bars. Or by what he had just witnessed when Nacho Chávez had challenged Loki one too many times.

"I get that your hombres have some kind of powers," Ramón Garcia said from the back of the conference room, lifting his scarred, stubbled chin. "But it won't be so good if you try to push us out. We still got the numbers."

Stupidity and courage, Loki thought, so often went hand in hand. He was inclined to believe that this mortal's chief characteristic was the former.

"And *I* have the magic," Loki said. "But I would prefer not to 'push you out.' You have the operations already established, and the men to carry out our plans. You will simply have to trust me."

"I don't trust no one."

Loki sighed. "You are new here, my young friend," he said, "and so I will give you the benefit of the doubt this one time. I could easily see to it that you lose whatever status you have won during your brief stay in this city, and put you on your competitors' 'most wanted' list. But since you obviously have talent enough to reach the top of Chavez's chain of command so quickly, I will allow you to retain your turf. For the time being."

Ramón looked as if he would very much have liked to spit. Loki would have enjoyed roasting *him*, as well. But the boy had sense enough to hold his tongue, though his dark eyes were flat with anger.

"Excellent," Loki said, clapping his hands together. "You will each consult my Jotunar before any major operation or transaction. They will report your progress to me. Once I am certain you are competent enough to follow my advice, it may no longer be necessary to supervise you quite so closely."

Dead silence. Loki smiled jovially and indicated that his minions could leave.

They did, filing out without any of the usual jostling for preeminence. As far as Loki was concerned, they were all the same . . . tools, to be discarded once his Jotunar had taken over the criminal factions in San Francisco. Those who didn't resist their loss of power might be allowed to live, and of course Loki would still need flunkies to carry out the menial work.

Turning his back on the stragglers, Loki strode to his smaller private conference room where four of his Jotunar were waiting for his instructions. They snapped to attention as Loki entered the room.

"Our priority now," he said, taking his seat at the head of the table, "is to confirm that the bird is, indeed, Odin's messenger. I want every detail of the girl's past, from her childhood to the present."

"We've already searched her apartment," Hymir said.

"And found nothing. Question her associates and neighbors, but don't unduly harm them. I have no desire to attract the attention of the police . . . yet. You," he said, pointing to Grer, "dispose of the body in the main conference room. The rest of you go, now."

Hymir and the others bowed and turned to leave, moving with almost admirable haste for creatures of their size. They knew how badly they had failed their master. And what said master would do to them if they failed again.

Loki leaned back, fingers steepled under his chin, and pondered the events of the recent past. He had been right in believing that Danny's sketch of a raven was significant.

But how had Danny known?

That would be among the many questions he would ask the boy when he went downstairs. But an even more vital question remained unanswered: What did the raven's appearance portend, and what message did it have for Mist?

Surely if Odin had previously been capable of directly intervening, he would have revealed himself far sooner. And his messenger—if messenger it truly was—had hidden itself away for many decades . . . or so it would appear.

If its sudden arrival was directly related to Freya's unexplained absence, that turn of events was not the matter for mockery he had presented to Mist. It could mean that Freya had failed to contain the other Aesir, and Odin had discovered the scheme.

But Odin was not here *yet*, and the creature certainly seemed to lack any special power. There was still time to deal with the problem before things got out of hand. And now Loki would have help from an entirely new and very felicitous quarter.

Loki's thoughts turned to Mist, and he smiled, savoring his new knowledge. In spite of the raven's interest in her, the Valkyrie had evidently been ignorant of its purpose, or its origins. That ignorance had provided Loki with very useful information, and once he had obtained a few of Orn's feathers he'd had no qualms about letting Mist win the skirmish.

He had wondered how much Mist relied on her mother's influence to wield her magic, but now he had his answer. What she'd done in the abandoned storefront had been impressive, and it had felt distinctly unique to her in a way he had not expected.

He wasn't yet sure how to define it. Or properly counter it. If he hadn't felt several earthquakes before the battle, he might have suspected that Mist had caused the last one.

Still, there must be a flaw in that magic, one he could exploit. Surely she had not simply stumbled across these powers by herself— nor, considering her plans for Mist, would Freya have taught them to her. Dainn, however, might certainly have had some part in her magical development.

But Dainn still had many personal difficulties to distract him. Though Loki wasn't certain how much Mist knew about the beast or its true, physical form, she had left the elf behind when she'd come after Anna.

Had he told her what Freya meant to do with her, and she'd been too angry to accept his help? *Perhaps*, Loki mused, though his observers would have informed him if she'd severed ties with Dainn completely. Had she intended to protect him from Loki? Or was it the beast she feared loosing?

Give him back to me, Loki thought, *and I'll see that it never gives you another moment's trouble.*

Of course she'd never surrender Dainn to him. But Mist, like so

many others, tended to forget that Loki was perfectly capable of being very patient when it suited him. The elf had no way of knowing
it yet, but he had walked into a trap that would snap closed when he
least expected it.

In the end, Dainn would come to Loki of his own free will.

As if to shake off that very distracting subject, Loki spun his chair
in a circle. What interested him just as much as Dainn's predicament
and Mist's ignorance was Anna's changing behavior when he had
questioned her. At times she had cowered; at others she had been
bold and contemptuous.

She seemed to be two, perhaps even three different people. And
one, he believed, was a Valkyrie. The girl had used ancient Norse
insults such as "honorless spear-pointers and gray-bellies," which
few contemporary mortals would understand. And Mist had fought
beside at least two of her Sisters during the Second World War.

Anna was clearly not a Chooser of the Slain in her "normal" state.
Was it possible that some essence of one of the Valkyrie had entered
her, perhaps through Odin's messenger?

Loki brought his chair to a halt and got up. There was yet another
puzzle: where were Odin's sons in all of this? And what of the *berserkr* who had attempted to follow Loki? He had broken off the chase
the moment Loki had turned to confront him. Was he an isolated
creature, or one of many hidden away from mortalkind? And if there
were others, where would their interests lie?

Far more intrigued than irritated by the questions, Loki took the
elevator to his suite, continued to the walk-in closet of his bedroom,
and chanted the Runes to open the safe. Very carefully he drew out
the spell-bound box and cradled it in his hands.

The feathers were quite beautiful, he thought, streaked as they
were with tones of deep blue and purple and highlighted with silver.
But they were more than beautiful. They could be essential. And
Mist didn't know he had them.

His cell rang, jerking him back into the moment. He tucked the
box under his arm, closed the safe, and answered.

"You asked me to call, Mr. Landvik," Miss Jones said, her voice strained with long days and nights of fear.

"How is the boy?" Loki asked.

"Very well, sir." Her breathing was short and sharp. "Would you like me to get him ready?"

"I will be down momentarily."

Loki cut off the connection and took the elevator to the second floor. His programmers, hackers, and technicians were busy at their computers, but all work stopped when he entered the room.

"Mr. Landvik," the supervisor said, only slightly less nervous than Miss Jones had been.

"How are we progressing?" Loki asked, striding past the lanky mortal.

"We have a . . . few new leads, sir," the supervisor stammered as Loki stopped at the cubicle of one of the hackers, who swung his chair around and all but leaped out of it before Loki slammed him back down. He leaned over, narrowing his eyes as he examined the hacker's screen.

"Alert my assistants if you find anything at all," Loki said, straightening. "But don't waste my time."

Both the hacker and his boss nodded vigorously. Loki didn't bother to conceal his contempt. What did they say about not sending a boy to do a man's job? Or a mortal, a god's?

Unfortunately, he had acquired the best of what had been available to him at the time. He had already exhausted nearly all the funds he had acquired through magic. But his plans for the criminals under his control would bear fruit very soon, and Senator Briggs—the cringing object of Loki's recent game of blackmail—had certain illegitimate connections he was using to find and hire individuals to make up a new team of experts who would assure that Loki's business and personal investments became, and remained, highly profitable.

And then, of course, Loki had that valuable new source of intelligence. He expected to see results very soon.

Miss Jones, ensconced in her chair, jumped out of it when Loki walked into Danny's room. Loki knew she'd been awaiting punishment for permitting Danny to slip out of the building when Dainn had been so carefully observing it. Of course, she had no idea that Loki had arranged the "escape" himself.

Taking a seat beside the bed, Loki watched Danny rock in his usual way, ignoring his parent as if he were no more than a ghost. Loki opened the box and displayed the feathers to his son.

Danny's eyes focused on the feathers. He reached out, his fingers stopping just short of the glittering objects.

"You like them, don't you?" Loki crooned. "Can you guess what they are?"

The boy's eyes met his with complete comprehension.

"Do you remember the pretty picture you drew for me?" Loki put down the box and indicated that Miss Jones should bring the crude drawing of the raven to him. He showed it to Danny. "How did you know about this bird?" he asked. "Where did you see it?"

Danny shook his head. Loki curbed his impatience.

"Never mind that for now," he said. "Perhaps you knew the creature that wore these feathers is dangerous to your daddy, and to you. If we can take the bird and stop the lady who is keeping him, we won't have to worry anymore. And you can help me."

Danny's gaze fogged again. Loki was not displeased. He had engaged in such monologues many times, but Danny had seldom shown even this degree of interest. It seemed that his meeting with—

A shadow fell over Loki, and he swung around. Odin stood over him—Odin in all his glory, Gungnir clutched in one brawny hand, ready to strike.

"Kneel to me, Slanderer," the All-father thundered, "and I may bind you in the cave again instead of destroying you."

Loki sprang up, snapped the lid of the box shut, and snatched Danny off the bed. Shoving the boy behind him, he backed to the nearest wall, dropped the box, bit down hard on his wrist, and coated his fingers in his own blood. As Odin approached, his teeth white behind his beard, Loki drew Blood-Runes in great sweeping lines on the wall and chanted the most malevolent spell he had ever attempted. The Merkstaves twisted and writhed off the wall like the tentacles of a Lovecraftian monster.

Still Odin advanced, unfazed and smiling, severing the tentacles as if they were the plastic limbs of an ill-made toy. He reversed his spear and brought the shaft down hard across Loki's shoulder, the blow reverberating through Loki's bones and incapacitating him for a few desperate, vital seconds. The Merkstaves slid down the walls like liquid tar. Odin reversed the spear again, and instinctively Loki raised his arms to fend off the razor tip.

All at once Danny crawled out from behind him and grabbed the box Loki had dropped. The lid fell open and the feathers caught fire, sending up the acrid smell of incineration. In a moment they were mere silhouettes of ash in the scorched box.

Odin vanished.

Loki slid to the floor, nauseated with pain and the effort of using the Blood-Runes. The smears of blood remaining on the wall began to char like the feathers, turning black.

Utterly spent, Loki closed his eyes. It seemed that Odin, not merely his messenger, was in Midgard. He had escaped the bonds Freya had set on him and the other Aesir. He possessed Gungnir again because Mist, as his loyal Valkyrie, would be glad to give up her responsibility for the Spear. And Midgard.

Loki pushed himself to his feet again, bringing Danny with him. How could he have been so blind? How could have failed to sense the return of the All-father?

With a groan, Loki lowered himself to the bed, holding Danny close as if he, too, might suddenly vanish. His only comfort lay in the knowledge that Danny had determined how to use the raven's feathers against Odin. The mechanism was utterly foreign to Loki, and he would need to learn the secret of it quickly. And determine if the spell could be used a second time.

He lost his train of thought as Danny pulled away, slid off the bed, and walked the few feet to where Odin had been standing. He squatted to touch the ground, his face scrunched up in concentration.

Loki staggered over to join him, pain radiating from his broken clavicle with every step. Danny touched the carpet. A phantom rose out of it as Danny drew away, a ghost that rippled and wavered like elusive heat waves on a long desert road.

Odin. Half here, and half not. Danny chuckled, passed his hand through the image, and then made a fist. The ghost flickered out, no more real than an image on a movie screen.

Loki sank to his haunches in shock. Danny looked at him, and whatever bond they shared, so fragile and uncertain, came to life with shattering clarity.

Odin hadn't been here at all. Oh, he'd been real enough to break Loki's bones, a manifestation that could only have been created by a being of great power.

Like Danny.

Pain seared Loki's shoulder as he reached for the boy, and he dropped his arm. "Danny," he said. "Tell me what you did."

"I don't know," Danny said.

"*Why* did you do it?" Loki asked, touched by a fear even Odin could not incite. "Why send this vision to attack me?"

But the brief moment of communion was over. Danny had withdrawn into himself again, face blank, eyes unfocused. Loki knew from experience that it might take days for the child to respond again.

That was the least of Loki's concerns now. However he had achieved it, Danny's act suggested open hostility, though there had been no sign of any such emotion in Danny's behavior afterward . . . only curiosity and amusement, as if he'd just discovered how to make his first sand castle. Loki glanced at the drawings pinned to the wall. Odin wasn't among them, but if Danny had seen the raven, recreating Odin would pose no difficulty for the boy.

That still didn't explain his apparent use of the feathers. Had he been unable to control his power and unconsciously realized that he needed certain magical tokens to contain it?

So much depended on the extent of Danny's power and the origin of the manifestation. And his reason for using it against his parent.

Wincing in pain, Loki looked for Miss Jones. The mortal had squeezed herself into a corner with her arms wrapped around herself and tears streaming down her face.

"Get up," he said, his voice cracking with pain and anger. "Bathe Danny and put him to bed."

The woman looked from him to the blackened smears on the wall. "What . . . happened? Who was—"

"If I were to tell you, Miss Jones, I would have to kill you. Do as I say."

She dropped her hand from her mouth. "Yes, Mr. Landvik."

Doing his best not jar his broken bones, Loki retrieved the box Danny had dropped. Once he had assured himself that Miss Jones was carrying out his orders, he walked out of the room. The Jotunar guards stared at him, aware that something had happened but ignorant as to the nature of it. The effects of Danny's magic had clearly been confined to his room.

Loki almost forgot to step out of the elevator when it reached his private floor. His use of the Blood-Runes had slowed his healing, and he knew his shoulder would likely be stiff for a few days.

Fortunately, the exercise he had in mind would not require much use of it.

He called Nicholas and Scarlet to his bedroom. Dark-haired Nicholas, his personal assistant, wore a conservative suit, while blond Scarlet had poured herself into a tight leather skirt and spike heels. A zipper ran from waist to hem at the front. Loki knew from experience that she wore nothing but garters underneath.

Both mortals had ample reason to be grateful that he had taken them away from serving overpriced food to tight-fisted businessmen, and given them every luxury and pleasure they could imagine.

Including his own considerable erotic skills.

They were both sprawled across him, lost in an exhausted sleep, when his intercom buzzed. He shoved the mortals aside, grimaced at the pull on his shoulder, and threw his legs over the side of the bed. Since he had left strict instructions not to let any callers through except in case of emergency, he was very tempted to compose a spell that would teach his office administrator a lesson she wouldn't soon forget.

But when she announced the name of the caller, he didn't hesitate to take it. And when the call ended, Loki felt as if things were truly beginning to fall into place.

Perhaps, this time, he would not rely on a mortal or Jotunn to do a god's job. If he was not gone too long, this world he had carefully constructed was not likely to fall apart in his absence.

And Danny needed time. Time to wake up again, and understand.

"Mr. Landvik?" Nicholas called sleepily from the rumpled bed. His hair, long and black like Dainn's, fell enticingly over his pretty blue eyes. "You coming back to bed?"

"In a moment," Loki said.

Nicholas shook Scarlet, who groaned as her round, reddened bottom scraped against the sheets. "Ouch," she mumbled.

Turning his back on them, Loki went into the bathroom and splashed water over his face. He was reaching for a towel when the building shuddered and began to sway in the ungentle arms of an earthquake. Not a bad one, but after the others it would certainly attract the fearful interest of the city's mortal denizens.

Loki paused and listened until everything was still again. Strange. He might almost have thought the epicenter was here in this very building.

"Mr. Landvik?" Scarlet said, the sheets falling away from her full, delicious breasts as she sat up straight on the bed. "What happened?"

"Nothing at all, my dear." Loki smiled and joined her and Nicholas. "Believe me, *you* have nothing whatsoever to worry about."

14

———

Ryan helped Gabi the rest of the way through the window, taking a firm grasp on her arms and catching her as she tumbled to the floor. They were lucky that at least one of the windows opened; the rest were the kind that didn't. He still wasn't sure how Gabi got to the second floor without anyone seeing or hearing her.

"You okay?" he asked, pulling her to the rickety chair against the wall. "You were gone a long time. I was beginning to worry."

"It's only ten o'clock," she said, plopping down in the chair and scowling the way she tended to do when she was annoyed with his concern. "And anyways, I have some good news."

Ryan's heart sank. He knew the kinds of things Gabi considered "good news."

"Don't look at me like that," she said, rubbing her knee. "You're the one who always wanted to prove we could do something useful before they sent us away like a couple of snotty little kids."

Ryan sat on the floor beside Gabi's chair. "We already went through this, Gab. I told you—"

"I know, I know. You changed your mind. Ever since that last argument with Dainn, when you finally figured out you was getting nowhere with him, and there was no way they'd let us stay."

If only that were all there was to it, Ryan thought. If it were *just* what Dainn had said, like he didn't even care that Ryan had warned him about Mist being in trouble.

That still wasn't the worst. Feeling the giant dying . . . that had been bad, so bad that he'd felt he might die, too. But he couldn't seem to get anything right, now. He hadn't warned Mist and Dainn about the raven, or Anna, because had hadn't "seen" them.

Even when he saw something that really mattered, like the vision he'd had after Mist's fight with the giant—the terrible burning brilliance like an exploding sun, ripping everything apart—he hadn't been given the chance to tell Dainn and Mist the most important part: that they were at the heart of the holocaust.

Worse than that: they had *caused* it. He was sure now that they weren't what they seemed. And whatever that was, it terrified him. He didn't want to know how it ended. He wanted to pretend . . .

"You brought us here because you was so sure you had to be part of this," Gabi said, cutting across his thoughts. "At the beginning, I thought you was loco. But now I know we have to do *something*."

"And your way is running around trying to spy on the giants," he said bitterly. "We don't owe them anything, Gab. Let's just go."

She gave a dramatic sigh. "*Muchacho*, you can be such a pain in the ass. You *have* to go with Tashiro to make this work, just like we agreed."

"*You* agreed, Gabi," Ryan said, scrambling to his feet. "I never—"

"You find the money or whatever it is your aunt left you, and then we can help without letting them treat us like babies." She grinned. "Listen, I told you I had good news. I found my brother."

Ryan's heart froze. "You didn't go near him, did you?"

"Sure I did. He knew I was here in San Francisco when he got out of Lompoc. So he put out the word for me. I just let his homies find me. And you know what? He's working for Loki."

"Shit. How do you know that?"

"Some stuff he said about his boss. Look, I can learn a lot. I just hang out with them . . . you know Ramón won't make me do anything that could hurt me. He was a shitty brother, but I'm still *familia*, all he got left except our *abuelita*. So I can listen, and when I get the 411 I'll get it back to Mist. She'll have to respect us then, right?"

"*You're* the one who wants to prove something now," Ryan said, hugging himself. "Don't you understand, Gab? I just wanted to belong somewhere. I thought they needed me. I was stupid. If we—"

The seizure struck without warning, as they always did. Ryan went blind first, and then deaf, and he felt the jarring pain as he fell to the floor.

Then he was lost. And he saw himself with a woman whose form flickered from young to old and back again, leading him to the very brink of a crucible of flame, like the worst description of Hell, asking him to choose whether or not to let himself fall into the blazing pit. Terrible cries and howls of pain rose from the chasm. Gabi was reaching toward him, trying to hold him back, but he knew if he took her hand she would fall with him. Dainn and Mist stood on the other side of the pit, waiting for him to decide.

He could barely see Dainn's eyes, but he knew the elf's fate was in his hands. Dainn would die if he didn't figure out what it meant— the crucible and the fire and the threat to Gabi and those he had come to love.

"*Ryan.*"

The male voice was familiar, gentle and firm but definitely not Dainn's.

"Help him!" Gabi cried.

"Don't worry, Gabi. I think he's okay."

Ryan blinked, and his vision began to clear. Tashiro crouched over him, supporting Ryan's head between his hands. The tormented howling in his ears went silent, and the smell of burning faded.

"You're all right now," Tashiro said. "Are you able to sit up?"

Trying hard to make sense of words that buzzed inside his head like crazy flies, Ryan let Gabi and Tashiro help him into a sitting position. He squeezed his eyes shut, but he knew all too well that the terrible images were branded on his mind forever.

"Easy there," Tashiro said, holding Ryan upright.

"What are *you* doing here?" Gabi demanded. "Where's Mist?"

"Very busy," the lawyer said. "You know we've been working on getting Ryan his inheritance." He smiled at Ryan. "We're almost ready."

Gabi gave Ryan a hard stare, reminding him of their recent discussion. "When is he going?" she asked.

"Soon," Tashiro said. "I really tried to let you stay together, but it just didn't work out."

Ryan opened his mouth to speak, but Gabi was there first. "It's only for now, right?"

"Yes. There's more paperwork involved, and some legal issues to straighten out, but it shouldn't take me too much longer to take care of it."

"Then I can stay here with Mist while Ryan's away?"

"I'm sure we can arrange that," Tashiro said, looking at Gab with approval in his brown eyes.

Ryan shivered, overwhelmed again by the vision—Gabi reaching for him from the edge of the fiery pit, trying to save him, and how he knew that if she touched him she would fall, too.

He could never let that happen. God, if he could only go to Dainn and tell him, ask him to explain what it all meant.

But he couldn't, and he knew now that Gabi was right. If she stayed with him, something terrible might happen to her.

"You should rest," Tashiro said. "Gabi, will you help him?"

Ryan dodged her offered hand as he pushed himself to his feet. "I should go get ready," he mumbled.

"All you have is the stuff Mist gave us," Gabi said. "How long do you think it'll take you to pack?" She looked at Tashiro again. "You ain't leaving now, are you?"

"It could be any time," Tashiro said. "It wouldn't hurt to be ready. But you do need rest, Ryan. You can't risk another seizure." He rose. "Gabi, I'm going to see what I can do about letting you stay with Mist. Don't trouble her about any of this—she left it all in my hands, and she already has more problems than she can handle."

"You *know*?" Ryan asked, catching himself against the wall.

"About the gods and giants and monsters?" Tashiro said. "Mist told me some time ago, but we wanted to keep it between us for now."

"Dainn doesn't know she told you?"

"Not yet." He smiled wryly. "Dainn probably wouldn't like it. And it's better if we don't talk about it outside this room."

"Okay," Gabi said. "Ry, you're going to bed. I'll help you get ready later."

This time, Ryan let her help him into the room. She closed the door, and he sat down hard on the bed. Gabi sat beside him.

"Okay," she said, "what was it this time? What did you see?"

Her voice held an uncharacteristic note of fear, and he knew he couldn't let her wonder all the time she was alone. "I always knew this would be hard," he said. "I knew the big battle with Loki was going to . . . some people weren't going to make it."

"You saw *me* dying?" she whispered.

"Shit, no! But so much will depend . . ." He couldn't finish the sentence. "I just know it's right for us to stay apart for now."

"You're scaring me, Ry." She put her arm around his shoulder. "Maybe we *should* stay together. I've always taken care of us, haven't I?"

"You're braver than I ever could be, Gab."

"Not really," she said softly. "I wish I was."

It never did much good to argue with Gabriella, but now Ryan was more certain of his course than ever. "We'll follow your plan, Gab," he said. "It's the right thing to do."

"Yeah," Gabi said, scrunching up her face. "But one thing bugs me . . . why did Mist tell Tashiro what's really going on? I mean, she barely knows him, right?"

"I don't know," Ryan said, slumping over his folded arms. "I guess it would have happened sooner or later."

"Whatever," Gabi said, losing interest in the subject. "Just remember, if something big happens while you're gone, you'll tell me. Right?"

"I always do, don't I?" He fell back on the bed. Gabi rolled him onto his side and pulled the blankets over him, and he closed his eyes.

Let Gabi be safe, he prayed as he drifted into sleep. *Let them all be safe, and I'll do anything you want.*

The kids were sleeping when Mist went upstairs, both so dead to the world that they didn't move a muscle when she opened the bedroom door.

Of course, Mist thought, you could never really figure out what was going on in a teenager's head. Especially when you could barely remember being one yourself.

She went on to Anna's room, where she found the young woman sprawled across the bed in her borrowed clothes, also asleep. Mist was perfectly content to let her grab any peace she could get.

Orn, perched on the headboard in parrot shape, caught Mist's eye with a piercing stare and suddenly took wing, swooping down to hover before Mist like a hummingbird. His beak darted toward her belt, briefly touching Gungnir in its knife guise. Then he flew back to his perch and began to preen his glossy feathers.

Was he checking to see if she safely carried Odin's Treasure? If so, he seemed to be satisfied, and not in the least interested in engaging Mist further.

Leaving the bird to his stubborn silence, Mist joined Dainn in the driveway. Silfr stood proudly where Mist had left her, dusted with snow but still bright as a copper kettle. The elf was looking the bike over with a kind of remote curiosity.

He climbed onto the seat behind her, his arms clasped around her waist. The last time they'd done this, they were heading home from the battle with Loki at his former digs, Gungnir once again in their possession.

Now she and Dainn had something other than fighting in mind. Given the earthquakes, bad weather, and time of night—and in spite of the rapidly approaching holiday—traffic was light. The damage to the local streets and buildings didn't seem to have become much worse during the most recent quakes, including the one that had happened during Anna's rescue.

She and Dainn made good time north on Third. Dainn, his head lifted to scent the air, indicated that Mist should stop just as they reached Lefty O'Doul Bridge.

"He was here," Dainn said, dismounting and approaching the bridge. "He worked some powerful magic, but it was . . . interrupted."

"By Anna and Orn?"

"Very likely."

Mist joined him. "Trying to open a bridge to Ginnungagap in this spot makes sense, since they're supposed to be anchored to real physical structures in the city."

"Structures or elements that connect one thing with another," Dainn murmured. He walked halfway across the short span and stared down into the water below. The narrow inlet running beneath the bridge was black and cold and still, though the bay directly to the east was choppy.

Mist examined the bridge's girders. There was something unusual in their appearance, almost as if they had been covered with cobwebs of ice that had melted and left only a ghostly pattern behind them, crisscrossing the steel.

She touched the nearest girder. It was so cold that her hand nearly stuck to it, though she experienced no discomfort. She imagined that if she struck the steel hard enough, it might actually shatter.

"You guessed correctly," Dainn said as he returned to Mist. "He was attempting to open a bridge here."

"And he left so quickly that he didn't have time to clean up his mess," Mist said. "But he must have thought he had a good shot in this particular place. Why?"

"There is a certain energy here. Can you not feel it?"

"Yes. And Loki obviously considered it worth the risk to expend so much magic where we might discover him. Fortunately for us—"

A truck approached, honked briefly in warning, and rattled over the bridge as Dainn took Mist's arm and pulled her aside.

"Fortunately," Dainn continued for her, quickly releasing her arm, "he has also unwittingly done some of our work for us."

"You mean we could try to finish what he began?" Mist asked with a frown. "I don't think it's a good idea. I'm not sure I'm up to it yet, and if we're testing your magic against the beast, this is a pretty big leap for you."

"My magic appears to be functioning well enough, and I may be able to discover how far Loki progressed." His jaw set as he looked up at the top of the bridge. "There are no others here to be harmed if I should fail. If you will, watch for vehicles and ward them away before they approach the bridge."

"I still don't think it's a good idea," she said.

His expression remained impassive, but as always his eyes gave him away. "Perhaps it would be better if you return to the loft," he said.

"Forget it. If the beast does show up, I can probably calm it down."

He sighed, acknowledging his defeat, and stepped onto the bridge. Then, hesitantly at first, he began to chant the Elvish Galdr with his remarkable voice, singing Rune-spells that spiraled down from his spread hands to penetrate the earth. Mist felt the hair rise up all over her body, beginning to respond like the roots and seeds and dormant life under steel and concrete.

Then, without warning, the nascent spell collapsed. Dainn fell to his knees, his face bloodless in the moonlight.

Mist ran to his side. "Odin's balls. What just happened?"

"It failed," he said in a voice thick with shock.

"The spell failed?" she asked, kneeling beside him. "It felt like it was working to me."

"No." He struggled to his feet. "There was nothing behind it. A façade, no more."

He stumbled to the side of the bridge and gripped the railing until the bones in his hands seemed ready to burst through the skin. Mist was grateful that his rigid back discouraged her from touching him.

"So what went wrong?" she asked softly.

He shook his head.

"Maybe Loki set some kind of trap."

"I felt no such trap," Dainn said. "No wards of any kind."

Mist searched her mind, looking for a cause that didn't suggest some catastrophic turn of events.

"Is this some kind of . . . subconscious way of not tempting the beast?" she asked, snatching at a very "human" but perfectly logical explanation. "Maybe you're afraid you don't really have control after all. You're doing this to yourself."

Suddenly his hands let go their furious hold on the railing, and his shoulders relaxed. "Yes," he said, looking at her with embarrassing gratitude. "You must be right. I do not yet trust myself."

His relief was so palpable that Mist almost hugged him. She stopped herself just in time.

"Even Alfar need shrinks sometimes, I guess," she said with a witless attempt at humor. "But I don't think we have any mortal psychologists who know how to treat elvish psychoses." She glanced at her watch. "Let *me* try."

"No," Dainn said sharply, the color returning to his face. "You but recently fought Loki, and—"

"Let me give it one shot," she said. "There won't be a better opportunity. I won't touch the hard stuff, just basic Galdr. And maybe I can work in the Jotunn magic as well."

It was a lot of hot air on her part. She knew she wasn't at her best, and she was still dealing with the emotional fallout from Orn's appearance and her father's death at her own hands. Now she couldn't help but associate Jotunn magic with Svardkell's death.

But she'd always tried not to let her fear constrain her. She had to know if Loki had been on to something.

"I'm doing it," she said. She worked her fingers, numb not from the cold but with sheer terror. "If you think I'm getting in too deep, stop me."

She stared at the traceries of ice on the deck of the bridge and once again called upon winter's magic, constructing mental Runes, giving them form and shape by drawing on the cold in the air and from deep within her own body. She sang an unfamiliar song that came out of that same coldness inside her, made up of the whine of frigid wind and the crack of icicles.

The song shattered the Runes and sent the fragments flying across the bridge, where they clung to the remnants of Loki's magic. The sleet she had created flew straight between the bridge's supporting girders and splashed against some invisible barrier, like pebbles tossed on a piece of glass. She concentrated, altered her song and sent a hail of crystal arrows, each trailing a rope made of fused beads of ice, straight at the center of the barrier.

She wrapped the ends of the bead ropes around her wrists and skidded on the deck of the bridge as some force dragged her toward the barrier. Dainn caught her around the waist and held her steady.

"What is it?" he asked, his arms tightening hard enough to rob her of breath.

"Something's . . . on the other side," she gasped, hanging on to the spell as it reared and bucked in her grip like a stallion on the scent of a mare.

"Something, or someone?" Dainn asked. "Does it feel as if you have reached a bridge to Ginnungagap?"

She tried to ignore her intense and unwanted physical reaction to his touch. "Some*one*," she said between gritted teeth. "It's like I've caught a shark on the other end, and if I pull a little harder—"

"Stop!" he shouted. "Let it go!"

Mist relaxed her hold on the ropes. It was exactly like letting go of a fishing line, feeling the thing she'd caught plunge back into the ocean and beyond her reach.

Dizzy with the sudden release, Mist began to fall. Dainn eased her down to the deck.

"What *was* that?" she asked, wiping the chilled sweat from her forehead with her sleeve.

"Evidently Loki did achieve some measure of success," Dainn said, staring toward the center of the span with a grim set to his mouth. "And if he did, what you felt on the other side might very well have been his allies, attempting to cross over with the help of your magic."

"You mean if I'd pulled a little harder," she said, "the shark would have leaped right over the side of the boat."

"But they, unlike a shark out of water, would have a dangerous advantage," Dainn said. He rose and offered his hand to Mist. She grabbed it and clambered to her feet as a hard blast of bitter wind off the bay slammed into her. Dainn moved just enough to take the worst of it onto himself, though he knew as well as she did how unnecessary the gesture was.

She was too exhausted to protest his misplaced gallantry. "So now we know that reopening the bridges is possible without Freya," she said.

"And Loki will surely make another attempt as soon as he is capable of it," Dainn said. His hair came loose from its queue and flew around his face like raven's wings. "Unless he returns here, which is unlikely, we cannot hope to anticipate where he will try again."

"Then the bird had better give us something we can use," she said. "Loki's piss, sometimes I feel as if I'm on some über-god's giant chessboard, and I don't know if I'm a knight or a pawn."

15

The color drained from Dainn's face again. He looked away, at his feet, out toward the block waters of the Bay.

"You are not far wrong," he said, very quietly. "It *was* a game, when it began. A *Hnefatafl* game with rules that no longer apply."

She stared at him. "What in Hel are you talking about?"

"I told you before that Freya alone among the Aesir was able to reach Midgard with her mind, making use of her Seidr."

"I remember," she said. "You said that Odin and the other Aesir had to maintain the Asgardian Shadow-Realm while Freya dealt with Midgard. But that's changed, hasn't it? With Freya gone, and the raven—"

"Yes, much has changed," Dainn said, moving to the railing. "But when it began, in the Void, Freya and Loki struck a bargain. Loki had found the first bridge to Midgard, a physical means of reaching this world. He had also devised a corporeal body for himself, a feat not even the Aesir had managed to achieve. He was prepared to use this bridge well before the Aesir discovered his trick, but Freya caught him."

"I suppose," Mist said coldly, "that this is where I ask how she met him when the various Shadow-Realms were all separated from each other in the Void."

"Freya had found a means of traveling between the Realms. Her catching Loki was a stroke of good fortune. She was able to bargain with him, proposing a game in which she would represent the Aesir and he . . . himself and his allies."

"Why didn't she just try to stop him, or expose his plans to the Aesir?"

"Because there was little *they* could have done to stop him, and she and Loki both possessed the Eitr. If they had fought then . . ."

"Eitr," Mist said. "You never did explain it to me. Remember, I'm only an ignorant Valkyrie."

He didn't seem to hear her barb. "It is the very substance of the Void itself, of creation, matter that can poison or heal or destroy all life. Among the Aesir, only Freya and Loki possessed it."

"Why?"

"Freya never shared that information with me."

"Old times," Mist murmured. "So the Aesir thought a fight with Loki then could destroy all life, and there'd be nothing left to rule."

"And Loki wished to preserve his Eitr for another purpose, which was to deceive Freya and break the rules by opening a bridge, descending to Midgard before the game was to begin, and later transporting a number of his Jotunn followers while concealing himself and the giants from her awareness."

"You mean when he was playing boyfriend with me."

Dainn ignored her bitter words. "He did not seek the Treasures then because he knew such a search could expose him, and he hadn't enough Jotunar to risk sending them far from this city, the locus of the bridges."

"But he didn't waste his time, either," Mist said.

"No. We know now that he made contacts and laid out schemes he could set in motion when Freya would only have begun her own work in Midgard. He considered that advantage to be worth any penalties he might be required to pay later. When Freya joined you to fight him in his apartment, she knew what he had done and threatened him with her Eitr if he did not abide by the rules thereafter."

"I don't remember that," Mist murmured, recalling Loki's taunts when she and the Einherjar had rescued Anna. "What were these rules?"

"Loki was not to make use of the bridges until Freya could devise a physical body and send Alfar and Einherjar as a counter to Loki's Jotunar. Nothing but the ancient weapons were to be used, and wealth could only be acquired by mortal means. Mortal allies could be acquired in proportional numbers. No attempt would be made to find the Treasures until all had been laid out according to the agreement."

"Well, *that* didn't happen." Mist joined Dainn at the railing, clenching her hands around it. "Does Loki still have his Eitr?"

"Unlikely. Though I believe the game has ended in a way Freya and Loki never intended, she will still possess her Eitr if she returns."

If she returns, Mist thought. Since Orn's arrival, she found herself hoping that wasn't going to happen.

"What about the weapons?" she asked. "Are we going to be using machine guns now?"

"The use of such weapons is still *nidingsverk*, dishonorable."

"And Loki won't break that rule because . . . oh, yeah. Because he's afraid of bad luck. Forgive me if I find that hard to believe."

"Nevertheless, I think he will abide by that particular limitation."

Mist took a deep breath. "Why didn't you tell me about this game before?"

"There seemed no appropriate time. And the situation now seems moot, since Loki will see no reason to abide by the other rules."

"As I said, Loki never—"

Her cell phone, tucked in the pocket of her jacket, vibrated against her hip. She answered the call.

"Bryn?"

"Can you come back now?" Bryn's voice said. "Vali says has something important to show you, and it sounds pretty urgent. He won't tell me what it is. And Vidarr's here."

Loki's piss, Mist thought. "Okay. We'll be back in a few minutes."

She ended the call and looked at Dainn. "I know you heard that. Don't go picking a fight with Vid, even if the beast *is* under control."

"He is likely to be the one 'picking a fight,'" Dainn said.

"Look, I need to find out if he knows about Orn. Even if Vali didn't tell him, there's been a lot of magic flung around the city, and if Vid's bothered to remove his head from his ass for a few minutes once in a while, he might actually have noticed."

"Surely he would have evinced more curiosity about such use of magic before now."

"Vid's not the curious sort. You remember how he dismissed our concerns when he met you in Asbrew . . . I doubt he's much concerned with anything that doesn't portend a major battle. If he hasn't sensed that his father's messenger is here, he isn't likely to care if Loki and I squabble."

"Your 'squabbles' will not leave him untouched."

"Try to tell *him* that."

Silfr sped south on Third as another light snow began to fall. It was when they were within a quarter mile of the loft that Mist saw the shadow racing beside them. She glanced sideways, blinking the snowflakes from her eyes, and looked again.

A huge canine shape cloaked in heavy fur kept pace with Silfr, gaping mouth displaying white teeth dripping thick saliva, huge paws throwing up fountains of snow with every leap. It turned its head to stare at Mist, red eyes simmering with hatred. And triumph.

She gripped the brake, nearly sending the bike into a tailspin. But she caught herself, eased back into alignment and brought the bike to a stop in the middle of the street a few dozen yards from the loft. She almost threw Dainn from the seat as she leaped off, sang Kettlingr to its proper size, and swung around to face the Wolf.

"Mist?" Dainn said, moving up behind her. "What alarms you?"

"Don't you see it?" she asked, looking wildly in every direction.

"I saw nothing," he said. He sniffed the air. "I sense no threat to us."

Only a little while ago, Mist realized, she'd facetiously suggested that Dainn needed to see a shrink. Now she was wondering about herself. Hel, she'd wondered from the very first day of this convoluted mess.

"It was Fenrisulfr," she muttered.

"Loki's offspring?" Dainn said. "If *he* is here, then Loki has already—"

"He *wasn't* here," Mist said, lowering her sword. "Thanks for giving me the benefit of the doubt, but I guess I'm just seeing beasts everywhere I look." She glanced at Dainn with a grimace. "I shouldn't have said that."

"You cannot wound me with the truth," he said.

"Sometimes it's the truth that hurts the most."

Dainn's hand moved to touch her hair. "There are no easy answers, but—"

"Now isn't that sweet."

Vidarr's voice sent Mist leaping away from Dainn as if he'd tried to skewer her with the beast's six-inch claws. Vidarr strolled up to them, a mocking grin on his broad, bearded face.

"Catch you at a bad time?" he asked, looking from Mist to Dainn, who stared at Odin's son with cold, dangerous eyes.

"Dainn," Mist warned. She smiled at Vidarr. "Any time's a bad time when you show up, Vid. To what do we owe the pleasure?"

"Funny." Vidarr walked around Mist, deliberately shoving his way between her and Dainn. "So little gratitude for my help the other day. Weren't you supposed to return a piece of my property to me as soon as you got your boyfriend back?"

"I've been a little busy," Mist said, refusing to rise to his bait. "And it's still Odin's, not yours."

"I don't think its provenance had any place in our deal," he said. He glanced at Dainn. "You look a little surprised. Didn't she tell you that she agreed to give Gungnir to me in exchange for Loki's whereabouts, just so she could rescue you when you went after him?"

Mist felt Dainn's stare. "No," he said. "I never wanted nor expected her to come after me."

"Of course you expected it," Vidarr said, grabbing Mist's braid and giving it a sharp twist. "You expected her to pull your ass out of the fire, and she went after you like a bitch in heat."

Gods, no, Mist thought, jerking her sword up and carefully placing the tip against Vidarr's barrel chest. Dainn was about two seconds away from tackling him, and the result wouldn't be pretty, beast or not. Dainn was a Hel of a lot stronger than he looked at first glance.

She had no idea who would win.

"Dainn," she said, "can you go check up on our guests?"

There was no flicker of curiosity in Vidarr's eyes, nothing to indicate that he guessed that Odin's messenger was here in this very city and residing with someone he didn't much like. Subtlety wasn't exactly in his nature.

As for Dainn, he hadn't moved. Which was *exactly* in his nature.

"Dainn," she said.

Very slowly he backed away. Waves of heat rolled off of him, just about scalding enough to melt the snow for a few yards in every direction or keep the entire loft at a very comfortable temperature.

Not now, Dainn. Not now.

Vidarr glanced down at the tip of Mist's sword pressed against his sternum.

"Not a good idea," he said, pushing the blade aside with a Jotunn-sized hand. "You don't want another fight with me."

"That would give Loki the victory, wouldn't it?" Mist said. "Unless you lied to me when Loki grabbed you in Asbrew, and you're really his lackey."

This time Vidarr *did* surprise her. He didn't try to take her head off with his fist.

"If I was," he said, "you'd already be dead. After watching that lickspittle boyfriend of yours die. Slowly." He looked over Mist's shoulder at Dainn. "That may still happen if you don't hand Gungnir over to me. Now."

"And how do you plan to use it, Vidarr? All you can do is hold it for Odin, as I've been doing."

"But it is *my* right, as Odin's son. You befoul the Spear with your filthy woman's touch."

Dainn stalked forward again, head down. "You may try to kill me," he said, "or insult the Lady Mist again. Either way you are not likely to survive."

"I'll speak as I please, *nidingr*," Vidarr said. "Tell me . . . when you went to Loki, did he fuck you like he did in Asgard?"

A great shudder ran through Dainn's body, and he met Mist's gaze. "There is no danger," he said, as if only she could hear him.

"There never was," Vidarr said. He smiled at Mist. "Give it to me."

"I might," Mist said, "if you apologize to Dainn and asked very nicely."

"By all my father's kennings," Vidarr swore, all but spitting in her face, "I name you oath-breaker, *vagr*—"

"Hey, Mist!" Vali ran out onto the sidewalk, panting heavily, looking as excited as a bear with its face in a honeycomb. "I've got something! You need to come in and . . ."

He trailed off as he saw Vidarr. "*God kveld*, Brother," he said nervously. "I didn't know you were here."

"Didn't you, Brother?" Vidarr said, his voice dripping with scorn. "Come to save your lady love?"

"Go back in, Vali," Mist said. "I'll be with you shortly."

"No," Vidarr said. "I'd like to see this wonderful thing my brother's so eager to show you. And maybe you can show *me* where you're keeping my Spear."

Of one thing Mist was certain—she couldn't let Vidarr anywhere near Orn or Anna. And he wasn't going to just walk away.

"You can have Gungnir now," she said, "but you're not welcome in my house." She drew the camouflaged knife from its sheath on her belt and slapped it into Vidarr's hand.

Vidarr stared down at the knife. "The spell," he said.

She told him. His voice, unpleasant as it was, did the job, and in moments he held Gungnir's full length balanced in his hand.

"You've kept our bargain," he said. "Next time you come to me for help, you might have to give up something much more important to you."

"I'm not worried," she said, backing away. "If you're too stupid to know you're in this shit as deep as the rest of us, your help would be useless."

Vidarr reduced Gungnir and tucked the knife into his belt as if it were a switchblade he'd found lying on the street. "I think I'll just stand back and watch you, Freya, and Loki destroy each other," he said.

"And let Midgard fall into chaos?"

"Oh, I suspect my father will be along to stop the argument before it gets out of hand."

He was striding away before Mist could question him. *Did* he know about Orn, after all? If so, why hadn't he mentioned the bird, let alone demand to speak to it himself?

And he'd mentioned Freya, as well. Did he have some inside information she didn't?

Either way, she had to get Gungnir back, by fair means or foul. The time for honorable conduct—if there ever had been one—was long past, whatever Dainn had claimed.

Vali shuffled up beside her. "Sorry, Mist," he said. "I really didn't know he was here."

"You didn't happen to tell him about Anna, did you?" she asked, watching Vidarr climb into his massive SUV and drive off.

"No!" Vali said. "I know he's . . ." He sighed. "I'm sorry."

"It's not your fault that your brother is such a bastard. You're nothing like him."

"That is fortunate," Dainn said, "for all of us."

As if he'd been completely unaware of Dainn's presence, Vali glanced at the elf in confusion. "Shit," he said, taking in Dainn's grim expression.

"Exactly," Mist said. But she gave Dainn a quick nod of acknowledgment. She still wasn't happy about their conversation at the bridge, but he'd controlled the beast, even though he'd been pro-voked more than enough to give way to his more lethal half.

But he hadn't passed his "test." His *magic* hadn't worked, at least not at the bridge. Why had it failed so suddenly?

"Well," Vali said, "if you're ready, I'll show you what I've done." A grin broke out across his face. "I found two more of your Sisters."

Mist watched as Vali's fingers flew across the keyboard as he sum-moned up the list of names. A dozen were highlighted, and one of them had been marked out in red.

"Erin McLoughlin," she read aloud.

He stretched his legs out and crossed his arms with a slightly smug expression. "You know what McLoughlin means?" he asked.

"Viking," Dainn said behind her.

"Thanks," she said, covering her worry for him with a dash of sarcasm. She leaned over Vali's chair and examined the screen again. "Erin. Eir. If you're right, she didn't try very hard to disguise her real name."

"You didn't disguise yours at all," Vali pointed out, growing seri-ous again. "Neither did me and Vidarr. Unless she knew something we didn't, she had no reason to think she'd have to change it much."

"Point taken. How did you come by this information?"

"I had the computers sifting through reports of paranormal activi-ties, strange events, anything that might give us a clue about where we could start looking. My spell automatically eliminates anything that doesn't fit the parameters without any input from me."

"And you found . . ."

"Local myths about apple trees growing in the desert. No one re-ally admits believing the stories, of course, but it's sort of a folk tale in the area. So I did some more searching, and—"

"Where?" Mist interrupted.

Vali punched a key. "New Mexico. Somewhere north of a town called Gallup."

"Mysterious orchards where there shouldn't be enough water to keep even a sapling alive," she said, reading the report on his screen.

"Eir could not have chosen a better place to conceal the Apples of Idunn," Dainn said.

The Aesir's tickets to immortality, Mist thought, even if the gods had apparently managed to get by without the Apples since they'd landed in the Void. She was lucky Eir had chosen to settle in New Mexico; the Valkyrie's presumed location was only a couple of hours away by air.

And just as accessible to Loki as it was to her.

"Do you think Loki's caught on to this?" she asked Vali.

The big man's face fell. "That's the problem. I've had no trigger warnings, but those particular spells don't seem to be working as well as I'd expected. He must have some pretty good hackers working on his side."

"Then we must operate on the assumption that he might know," Dainn said.

"We *always* have to operate on that assumption," Mist said.

"What are you going to do?" Vali asked.

"Tell me about your other discovery," Mist said, "and we'll go from there."

"Italy. Small town just inland from the Adriatic coast." He handed her a printout. "It's got a convent of cloistered nuns called Monastero Santo Gaudentio."

"A convent?" Mist said with a brief laugh. "Are you saying that a servant of the so-called pagan god Odin is connected with a temple of the White Christ?"

"Seems to me a convent would be a good place to hide."

"Only nuns would live in such a place," Dainn said. "Servants may occasionally enter, but they would not remain there."

"A nun," Mist said with a snort. She searched the paper and read the name. "Sigrun?"

"She goes by the name Maria Simona," Vali said. "How I found her is kind of complicated, but if you want me to explain—"

"If any of us was going to turn out to be a nun, it would be Sigrun," Mist said, barely hearing Vali's words. "She was always the most . . . centered, I guess you'd say. An ascetic."

"You'd have to be, to live in a place like that," Vali said, patting his beer belly.

"She holds Gleipnir, does she not?" Dainn asked.

They looked at each other with complete understanding. Loki might want to get his hands on that even more than any of the other Treasures. The "unbreakable" chain had been used to bind Fenrisulfr, also called Fenrir, because the gods had feared what the Wolf could do: kill Odin, as prophecy foretold. And yet, for reasons of honor, they didn't dare kill *him*.

It went without saying that Loki hadn't been too thrilled about having one of his kin handled with such disrespect.

But Loki himself had been in a similar position just before the events of Ragnarok were supposed to occur. Events *he'd* set in motion. He'd never owned up to the legitimacy of his punishment, and he hadn't exactly forgiven the Aesir for that, either.

There wasn't a whole lot he *had* forgiven.

"Good work, Val," Mist said. "Take a long break. You've earned it."

"I'm on a roll," Vali said. "I think I'll keep going."

Mist nodded, grateful for his dedication, and gestured Dainn out of the room.

"This is going to be tricky," she said. "I can only get to one of these places at a time."

"I had assumed that I would go," Dainn said.

"We didn't get to find out if using magic would provoke the beast again."

"But I *was* able to give Svardkell's body back to the earth."

So now, Mist thought, he didn't think he needed another test. Right when she needed *him*.

"If Loki knows about these Valkyrie," Dainn said, predicting her next words, "he will focus on reaching them, not attacking here."

"He needs Orn," Mist said. "He can split his resources, and he has a lot more of them than we do. If you can work magic safely, you can still protect—"

"You don't have to worry," a woman's voice said.

Anna joined them, wearing only a fresh set of Mist's jeans, sneakers and a worn but comfortable T-shirt. Orn, in raven shape, perched on her shoulder.

"I'll be okay," she said. "Orn will protect me."

Mist looked at Orn. He was staring at Dainn with what she guessed was contempt . . . and a very personal dislike.

Orn must know about the curse, just as she'd feared—at least enough to hold some resentment toward Dainn, even though the All-father would have been well aware that Freya had called on Dainn to assist the Aesir in Midgard.

"Has he spoken?" Dainn asked, apparently unconscious of Orn's obsidian glare.

"Not since he said I was safe here," Anna said. "I just know he's not going to let anything happen to me."

"Like he didn't when Loki got you?" Mist asked, deliberately harsh.

Orn croaked, his crest rising. Mist didn't need an interpretation of *that* reaction.

"He came to find you, and you saved me," Anna said. "I know he won't let Loki get his hands on me again. And since your kids are here, they'll be safe, too."

Mist and Dainn exchanged glances. Anna seemed confident, but what if she was wrong? What if she was telling Mist what she wanted to hear?

"We have little choice but to accept Ms. Stangeland's judgment," Dainn said, speaking as if he and Mist were alone. "Your other options are few. Bryn has minimal magic, and the other Einherjar have none at all."

"What happens if Loki attacks you, and your magic does fail?"

"I ask you to trust me."

So once again the decision was hers. She closed her eyes, afraid for Dainn, afraid that Anna was wrong about Orn. She had to accept the judgment of a woman she barely knew, and to rely on a creature who remained silent when she most needed him to make his purpose clear.

"If you don't mind," Anna said, "I'll go inside now."

"You'll tell me if you change your mind about Orn."

Anna nodded and rushed off, Orn flapping his wings to keep his balance. Mist turned to Dainn again.

"Okay," she said. "Now all we have to figure out is which of us will go where, and then I'll have Vali get us the first available flights." She shook her head. "I still hate relying on Orn to protect the kids, too. I'll keep working on Tashiro until we're ready to leave."

"Let us hope your lawyer is more efficient than he has been thus far," Dainn said.

16

—————

"Maria Simona will see you now," the woman said in heavily accented English.

The sober nun, the "extern" who served as intermediary between the outside world and that of the monastery, slipped out of the waiting room. Dainn sat very straight in his hard chair and let the deep silence clear his thoughts.

The flight had been a long one, but Dainn had been grateful for the time to think. And prepare. For all he had assured Mist that he was in no danger of losing himself to the beast should he encounter Loki or his allies, he had no way to be sure.

All he had were the herbs, tucked in the inner pocket of his jacket. He still had no way of knowing how long the palliative would work, or if he was required to take regular doses. Edvard had never returned to answer his questions.

At least his magic had returned when he needed it. The Sisters of Santo Gaudentio met only with close family members once a month and never left the convent, so he had been compelled to use a small spell to obtain an interview with the nun who might once have been a Valkyrie.

He sensed the woman approaching and turned his attention to the plain, narrow door that led from the convent proper to the waiting room. She floated in, veiled from head to foot in her order's habit, only the round, pale center of her face visible. Even her hands were tucked into the folds of her robes. Her blue eyes met Dainn's, and he heard her sigh.

She knew what he was. As he knew *her*, even though he had never met her.

"I am Sister Maria Simona," she said in perfect British English.

Dainn rose. "Is that your only name, Sister?"

"I was born with another," she said, one brow twitching up ever so slightly. "I confess I did not anticipate an elf to show up at my door." She gestured. "Please, sit down, Mr. . . . ?"

"Dainn," he said, inclining his head. "I prefer to stand."

"Very well. Let us not waste time, since this interview must be short." She smiled slightly to ease the brusqueness of her words. "I am certain you have much to tell me, but this I know already. Midgard is in great peril, and you have come for something I have guarded for centuries."

"How did you come by this knowledge?" Dainn asked, watching her carefully.

"Naturally you are cautious," she said. "But I assure you, your enemies cannot enter this place. When one spends years in contemplative silence, one is open to the messages the world sends us. This world, and others."

"You knew the Aesir are alive?"

"No," Sigrun said, "but I am not surprised." She searched Dainn's face. "Where is she?"

"I do not understand you."

"But I understand *you*, I think. You struggle greatly with emotions you cannot master. A difficult situation for an elf. I am sorry."

"You need not be," he said, anger like a rope knotting around his heart.

"Forgive me," she said. "I do not mean to pass judgment." She smiled again. "In the most sacred tales of those with whom I spend my days, there is good and there is evil. It is quite simple. Only one side will triumph in the end. An angel with a flaming sword will fight the Dark One, with his hordes behind him."

"I know no 'angels,'" Dainn said. "And evil is not a useful concept among my kind. Have you then accepted the faith of the White Christ?"

The nun's face creased with amusement. "I am content here." She glanced at the unbroken wall behind Dainn as if she were looking out a window at the hills and fields beyond. "I was lonely in this world, and I saw much suffering and destruction I could not ease. A century ago, I sought and was granted sanctuary in this convent, thinking it would be for only a few days. But I found that the life suited me very well. I stayed. I became what you see now."

"Have your companions failed to notice that you have not aged?"

"My order considers it a gift from their god that I appear to remain young. Why should I disillusion them with stories they will not comprehend?" She displayed her callused hands as if letting Dainn see them was a precious gift. "I know you have come to recruit me to the coming battle. But I cannot go with you. All I can do is give you what you seek."

She reached down to her waist and untied the woolen belt that gave her habit its only shape, carefully removing the rosary from its hooks and laying it on the small table beside her chair.

"I have kept it hidden, as I was bid," she said. "It is yours now. Yours, and hers."

Dainn stared at the belt. It had become a slender silver chain, no wider than a bootlace, glowing with the magic of the Dvergar, the dwarves, who had forged it.

"Take it," Sigrun said. "And may you use it well for the sake of Midgard." She rose. "As much as I can do within these walls, I will do."

"Pray, Sister?" Dainn said, clenching his fist on the table.

"If you like." She hesitated. "You must have faith. Not in a god, or in the past. Have faith in this world and in the power her enemies have never been able to take from her."

"And in mortalkind?" he asked.

"In life, and in love," she said. "They always find a way."

Her words rang with the deep wisdom she had gained in her solitude and contemplation, the wisdom that had eluded Dainn in spite of all the centuries of searching. He wasn't prepared when she reached out and touched his forehead with her roughened fingertips.

"May you find your own peace, my brother," she murmured. And then she was walking away from him, passing through the door into the deepest silence Dainn had ever known in this world.

He took Gleipnir from the table, feeling its silky weight shift in his palm. Searing pain bit into his skin, and he dropped it onto the table.

Gleipnir had burned him, as the White Christ's symbols were said to burn his enemies. It sensed the beast in him—the creature that, like Fenrisulfr, was a threat to the Aesir and all who stood with them.

Ignoring the pain, Dainn picked it up again and let it fall into the small, warded box he had brought with him. Immediately it arranged itself into a tidy coil.

Dainn left the convent by the door that led into a tiny side courtyard. The temperate Mediterranean weather was a reminder that San Francisco, and California as a whole, seemed to be bearing the brunt of this unusual winter. Birds sang among the neat fields, which lay at the foot of the hill where the village and convent overlooked the countryside around it.

Dainn could feel the magic he understood—earth and grass and wood and all the living things that grew under and above it—seeping through the soles of his boots.

Kneeling under the shelter of a small grove of trees at the foot of the hill, Dainn laid his hands flat on the earth and closed his eyes. He attempted no magic. He had nearly five hours before he must reach the airport, and for a time—so brief a time—he could remember who he had been long ago.

❈

It was dawn when the cliff vanished.

Still groggy from another sleepless night, Mist tumbled out of the rented Jeep. There was a road where the end of the box canyon had been, the vestiges of the cliff barrier still floating around it.

Mist was sick to death of illusions. But this one might be keeping her Sister safe.

In the distance, tucked in a small, dry valley, stood a house. Mist could barely make it out in the dim light, but the road—lightly rutted with the tracks of a small truck—led straight to it.

Mist's neck began to prickle again, and she studied the landscape. It was as dry and forbidding as much of the desert she'd been searching since her plane had arrived in Albuquerque early that morning, but only over the last few miles had she begun to feel the strange magic.

If it were Eir's, she'd developed abilities she'd never possessed as a Valkyrie. There had always been rumors that she was, in fact, a goddess herself. But she'd never let on, and had seemed content with a Valkyrie life.

Unlike Mist.

Climbing back into the Jeep, Mist released the brake and continued along the road. But soon she found herself facing a completely different kind of barrier. Strange, ethereal voices, speaking in some ancient, unknown language, seemed to urge her to turn around and go back the way she'd come.

She did her best to ignore them as she lurched over the packed and corrugated dirt. When she looked in the rearview mirror, she saw that the road was blocked by another cliff exactly matching the one she had just passed through.

As she drove toward the house—a one-story adobe structure that seemed to blend in with the browns and reds and tans of the landscape surrounding it—Mist could see no trees at all, let alone divine apple trees. She could still feel watching eyes assessing her, weighing her nature and purpose.

But by the time she was within fifty yards of the building, the low red wall encircling the house shimmered, and suddenly there was an explosion of verdant life. Trees, a whole grove of them, with summer leaves instead of bare winter branches.

A woman was sitting on a bench in front of the house as Mist braked and turned off the engine. At first Mist didn't recognize her. She was thinner than Mist remembered, almost gaunt, her skin weathered and her light brown hair bleached nearly blond by the brilliant New Mexico sun. She wore an incongruous broad-brimmed straw hat, a jacket made from an Indian blanket, jeans, and scuffed boots. Lines carved by sun and wind bracketed her light brown eyes.

"Eir?" Mist said, walking around the jeep.

"Mist," the woman said, making no move to meet her. "How did you find me?"

"I had help," Mist said. "From someone on our side."

"Our side," Eir said. "Are there still sides?" She stroked the nearly shiny wood of the bench, worn smooth by years of constant use. "Why did you come here, Mist?"

Eir clearly had no knowledge of the Aesir's survival or Loki's arrival on Midgard. And her expression wasn't exactly welcoming. They had last seen each other in the early nineteenth century, when Eir had been working to help victims of the cholera pandemic in Europe.

Eir had nearly killed herself trying to save the dying, and she had suffered the trauma of a dedicated healer watching hundreds fall before she could so much as touch them. Mist had the feeling that Eir was perfectly content to live here in solitude, undisturbed.

"It'd be easier for me to explain if we got a little more comfortable," Mist said. "Can we go inside? I'm as thirsty as Yggdrasil."

Suddenly Eir sketched a Bind-Rune in the air, and Mist felt a blast of power, heat coursing through her like a fever.

She reached behind her for Kettlingr, her hands shaking with effort. She sang it to its full size, dragging it into a defensive position.

Abruptly the attack stopped. The heat burned away. Sweat beaded Mist's brow, drying rapidly in a wind hungry for moisture.

Shivering as if she had taken the fever on herself, Eir looked down at Kettlingr. "I remember that sword," she said. "And if you weren't who you say you are, you wouldn't have been able to withstand my spell."

"Why are you afraid?" Mist asked, all but jamming Kettlingr into its sheath. "Have you been attacked?"

"No," Eir said, rising a little unsteadily. "Old habits are hard to break. The locals seemed pretty sure of you, but I had to be certain." She smiled. "Come in, Sister."

"The locals?" Mist asked.

"Let's go inside, and I'll explain after you've told me why you're here."

The main room of the house was spare but comfortable, with a rounded fireplace built into the wall in one corner of the main room—its wide mouth sheltering low-burning flames—a set of chairs heaped with woven blankets and pillows, and a rough-hewn table.

"Coffee?" Eir offered. "Or would you prefer water? I suspect they kept you waiting out there some time."

"They?" Mist said, remembering the alien voices and the sense of watching eyes. "Didn't *you* dispel the illusion?"

"Oh, that wasn't me," Eir said, gesturing Mist to a chair. "This is *their* country, after all."

Before Mist could question her again, Eir walked out of the room through an arched doorway. Five minutes later she emerged with a glass of water and two steaming mugs of coffee balanced on a ceramic tray.

"Do you still take it black?" Eir said, setting one of the mugs in front of Mist.

"A lot has changed, but not that."

Eir sat down opposite Mist. "I have a feeling you're about to complicate my peaceful life," she said.

Mist sipped her coffee. "The trees?"

"Believe it or not, apple trees *do* grow in this state, though sometimes they don't bear when it's really cold. But of course mine are protected."

"And invisible," Mist said.

"Just a precaution. Not too many people find me out here. I go down to Gallup sometimes, but I don't think I've had more than one visitor in a decade."

Mist set down her mug. "It was legends about your trees that brought me here."

"Legends no one takes very seriously, fortunately for me." She cradled her hands around her mug as if she were cold, though her face was flushed. "Now you can tell me why you're here."

Mist leaned over the table. "I need you, Eir. You and all our Sisters."

Because of their shared past, Mist was able to tell the story in a little over an hour, leaving out certain personal details. Eir listened almost without interruption, solemn and growing more so by the minute.

"Now I begin to understand why the locals have become so restless lately," she said when Mist was finished. "I guess I must have sensed it, too, but I just couldn't believe anything could happen after all this time." She stared into her empty mug. "The Aesir alive. You, the daughter of Freya. Loki in Midgard, looking for us."

"So far," Mist said, "he hasn't had much success in that area. With all the irons he has in the fire, he's overextended himself, and you know how vain he is."

Eir rolled her eyes. "Thank the Norns I didn't have to deal with him much. But *you* have plenty of irons—or should I say swords—in the fire yourself. You can't find Freya, and you say your own magic is unpredictable, even if you've beaten Laufeyson more than once."

Mist considered, a little guiltily, how much she hadn't told Eir. "That's why we have to have the Treasures for the Aesir," she said. "Dainn's off to find Sigrun, and we've had hints that Rota may be coming to us."

"Five," Eir murmured. "And I'm not a fighter."

"We'll need healers as much as fighters before this is finished."

"But the girl, Gabriella. You said she appears to have abilities of some kind."

"They've hardly been tested yet," Mist said. "And her boon companion, Ryan, has equally unpredictable gifts that could put him in great danger." She met Eir's gaze. "Will you come?"

There was a long moment of charged silence. "Well," Eir said, gathering the mugs, "California has some pretty strict rules about bringing fruit and the like over the state line, at least the last time I was looking for somewhere to settle. But I won't have to bring the trees themselves. They'll all shrink back into seeds until I plant them again, and I have enough magic to conceal them." She looked around the house. "I'll be sorry to leave here. I've grown used to the high desert, the clean spareness of it. And I'll miss the locals. I think they'll miss me, too, even if I'm a guest in their country."

"You promised to tell me about these 'locals,'" Mist said.

"I have to get the trees ready," Eir said, getting up from the table, "and we'll have plenty of time to talk when we're on our way."

The scent came to Dainn before the sound of the heavy footsteps approaching his temporary sanctuary. He leaped to his feet.

There were only two of them, but they were formidable. As Dainn prepared himself, the Jotunar reached their full height and size, broad and muscular and capable of crushing a human skull with only the slightest pressure of one viselike fist. The grass withered under their feet, rimed with ice and turning brittle as ancient bones.

The small box resting inside Dainn's jacket grew warm, and

within it Gleipnir began to writhe like a serpent eager to strike. The beast, too, was stirring.

Dainn held it back. He would let the Jotunar move first, and respond accordingly—with the magic that hummed in the air all around him.

"Elf," one of the Jotunar said, with slightly less of the usual sneering and posturing. "I see you've already got what our lord sent us to find."

So they could feel Gleipnir, too, Dainn thought. He inclined his head. "I give credit to your master for discovering the Treasure's location. Or has he simply found a way to steal the information we have obtained?"

The second frost giant clucked his tongue. "There are no provisions against theft in this game, Alfr. And though you may think yourself better than the rest of us, you would slaughter everything in your path to gain your ends."

"Yes," Dainn said, preparing to bluff as much as necessary. "But I would prefer to let you leave alive."

The first Jotunn smiled with white, serrated teeth. "If the Sow's bitch hadn't saved you, Loki would have you in chains while he—"

"You are not the Slanderer," Dainn said, cold in every part of his body except where Gleipnir threatened to burn through the warded box and into his heart. "I have twice defeated your brothers. Three of them faced me and the Lady Mist with the arrogance so common to your breed, and there is nothing left of them now."

"Empty words," the second Jotunar said, though he looked a little less confident. "Give us Gleipnir, and we will take you back to Loki alive."

But the frost giant didn't wait for the answer he knew must be forthcoming. He sent a blast of ice-laden wind directly into Dainn's chest, knocking him backward. Slivers of ice struck Dainn's jacket but didn't penetrate it; the Jotunar were holding back. They wanted him in one piece.

Singing the Runes of growth and life, Dainn retreated to stand against the trunk of the tree and turned to place his hands against the bark. He heard the Jotunar lunging toward him and loosed the spell. Small branches and a whirlwind of leaves rained down on the giants, leaving them nearly buried and spitting twigs and curses.

But they were on their feet again within seconds. Dainn crouched to scoop up handfuls of earth and threw it directly in front of the charging Jotunar. The dirt swelled into a rampart, and the Jotunar slammed into it.

Before he could prepare the next spell, the box under his jacket grew unbearably hot, catching fire and burning its way through his jacket. Ash streamed from the charred fabric, and Gleipnir wriggled inside his shirt to lash at his skin.

He doubled over in pain, recovering just in time to rouse the worms and small insects sheltered under the soil. They swarmed over the Jotunar, who slapped at themselves and howled until their own bodies froze the creatures into tiny crystalline statues.

With a silent apology for the sacrifice he had demanded of them, Dainn caught his breath. Gleipnir had wound itself around his chest, binding his ribs so tightly that he could barely breathe.

Before the Jotunar could move again, he dodged behind the tree and set off at a pace only the swiftest Jotunar could ever hope to match.

But Gleipnir slowed him, and in a matter of minutes his lungs had constricted to the point where he could no longer breathe. He stopped, leaning over to brace his hands on his knees, and lost awareness for the few crucial moments that it took for the Jotunar to attack.

But these were not the same two giants. They were smaller, light and swift, and they took Dainn down before he could defend himself. He rolled out from under the one who had pinned him to the ground and grabbed another handful of earth.

He felt nothing. No life, no magic. It was only dirt he touched, dead to his senses.

Gleipnir. Gleipnir had stolen something more than his breath. He threw the dirt into the Jotunn's face and scrambled to his feet, panting for air. The big Jotunar had joined their smaller cousins, and the odds were deadly. Gleipnir could be killing him, and yet Dainn knew he had to survive long enough to deliver it to Mist.

Dainn closed his eyes and called on the beast. For once in his life, he prayed it would still be there.

He remembered little of what came after. His body moved with lethal precision, employing every martial art he had ever learned but backed with strength and endurance even his well-trained physique had never possessed.

Only the viciousness was missing, and he was able to keep a calm, cool head as the giants fell one by one, their ice and frost and bitter storm winds dashing against him without effect.

When it was over, there was a blackened circle of dead grass around him. The Jotunar lay insensible at the perimeter, injured but alive. Dainn called the beast home, and it slunk back to him without any resistance.

And the pain of Gleipnir was gone. It had coiled itself against his skin, but it no longer threatened to eat through his flesh. He could breathe freely again.

He left the giants where they lay. He knew they'd do no harm to the local populace; they would have to report back to Loki or face an even worse punishment than they'd suffer for their failure.

There was just enough time for him to catch a bus to the airport. The security machines were incapable of detecting Gleipnir, and he carried it aboard without difficulty.

As he sat in the window seat overlooking the ocean, he permitted himself to think of Mist. She would be back in San Francisco by now. He had no doubt that she had retrieved Eir and the Apples of Idunn. She would not allow herself to fail.

He leaned back in the seat and closed his eyes. He couldn't tell Mist the whole truth of *his* success until he fully grasped what had happened. He had been "tested" again, much more brutally than before, and it had been as if he'd returned to the years before Freya had called him, when centuries of discipline and training had finally conquered the thing inside him. He had borrowed the beast's strength but had never permitted it to possess his mind.

But he still didn't understand Gleipnir's effects on him, first burning into his flesh and seeming to impede his magic, and then—after he had restored the beast to its cage—turning quiescent and harmless.

The only thing he was certain of was that the herbs must have allowed him to keep the beast under control. What would happen if the concoction ran out?

"Would you like a drink, sir?" the Italian flight attendant asked. Dainn opened his eyes, and she favored him with a bright, curious smile.

"My thanks, but no," he said.

"You will let me know if you require anything," she said, her voice dropping to a purr.

"Yes."

She went on to the next passenger, and Dainn closed his eyes again. He wasn't Loki. He remained untempted by the interest with which mortal women, and sometimes men, favored him. The one he *did* want was not and had never been mortal.

And soon she would have no choice but to acknowledge it.

The sun was no more than a crimson streak on the western horizon, glowing coals of a dying fire that had never touched the cold. Mist imagined that feeble flame sinking behind the San Francisco skyline, plummeting into the frigid ocean, bubbling and steaming and vanishing into the unseasonable winter fog.

The rocks overlooking the arroyo that ran across the edge of Eir's property were cold as well, and the harsh wind sent red dust rolling along the bottom of the canyon like hands intent on stripping the earth to its bare bones. Mist almost thought she saw ghostly figures dancing along the dry streambed.

Eir came up behind Mist. "Ready," she said.

They walked down to the Jeep. Eir threw her duffle into the back and climbed into the passenger seat.

"The Apples?" Mist asked.

"Here," Eir said, withdrawing a small pouch from within her flannel shirt. "The seeds." She glanced toward the house. The trees were gone, vanished as if they had never been.

"Perhaps they will grow here again someday," Eir said with deep sadness. "When I return."

She didn't have to say what both of them were thinking: she might never come back at all.

"You look worried," Eir remarked as Mist took the driver's seat, staring at the road and the false rock face that seemed to block them in.

"I've been gone a day and a half," Mist said, "but San Francisco could be in rubble and I wouldn't know it."

"I think we'd have known somehow," Eir said. "Be glad Loki never showed up here. Though I think if he had, he would have found it difficult to get past my—"

Something yipped in the dark. Mist recognized the sound as the piercing cry of a coyote.

Eir held up her hand sharply. "Wait," she whispered. She climbed out of the Jeep and circled it slowly. "It might not be so easy to leave after all."

17

Mist joined her. "Loki?" she asked.

"Just stay very still," Eir said. She reached inside the pocket of her jeans and withdrew a handful of something that looked like a mixture of red dirt and acrid-smelling herbs. Lifting her hand, she opened her fingers and let the mixture fly away.

All at once she and Mist were not alone. Everywhere Mist looked figures appeared, outlined by the powder as it scattered against the wind. Mist could barely make them out, but some seemed to have the shape of lizards, some of rabbits, some of birds, and some vaguely humanoid—tall and thin, short and round. They were visible one moment and gone the next, as if they were made of air.

"Ordinarily I might say they were coming to bid me farewell," Eir said. "Sometimes I would give an Apple to the earth, and they would give me something precious in return. I have respected them, and they have helped me."

"Then these are 'the locals,'" Mist said warily.

"That's only what I call them. For the native peoples who lived and still live in this area, they have very special names. But I don't speak them aloud."

Native peoples, Mist thought. She knew next to nothing about the religious beliefs of the indigenous inhabitants of this land of stone and canyon and scrub, but what she saw now was no product of her imagination, no more so than Asgard and the Aesir were mere tales of primitive men huddled around a Northern fire.

"Until now," Mist said, rubbing windblown grit from her mouth, "I never even thought about how other spirits and gods might be affected by the war with Loki."

"Because you didn't care?" Eir asked, an unusually sharp note in her voice.

"Because I never met any during all my centuries in Midgard," Mist said. "I didn't realize that any of them had survived."

"They have here," Eir said. "But they have no desire to rule anything, only to guard this land." She pressed her fingers to her temples. "I'm trying to understand," she gasped, as if she were speaking to someone Mist couldn't hear.

The voice of the coyote rose again, eerily sustained.

"Is that one of the locals, too?" Mist asked, resting her hand on Kettlingr's grip.

"Coyote," she said. "Not *a* coyote, but *the*. One of the most powerful spirits. A trickster, like—"

Mist drew the knife. "Like Loki?" she asked.

"The difference is that the native peoples don't consider him evil," Eir said, dropping her hands. "He was here at the beginning of time, so he is wise. He can solve great problems and bring answers to the hardest questions." She smiled without humor. "It's just that you can't count on him."

"You can always count on Loki to do whatever benefits him, no matter who suffers," Mist said.

"But tricksters have always been essential to mankind," she said.

"Loki, essential?"

Eir seemed not to notice her sarcasm. "Perhaps, in some way, all such spirits are bound together."

"So is your Coyote joining up with Loki?" Mist said, grimly aware that things might be much worse than she'd assumed.

"I don't know," Eir said. She bent to lay her palm on the earth. "I can't believe—" She flinched.

"What's happening?" Mist demanded.

"Loki is here. He's trying . . . to—" She gasped. "There is a struggle going on. A terrible one."

"Will your locals help us?"

Eir straightened, blinking back tears. "It has never been the way of the spirits of this land to interfere in the doings of outsiders. But now one of them is under attack. And if they understand what may be at stake, everything that lives in this place—even the stones and the wind and the earth itself—will carry the message."

"Loki won't abide any competition. Even if they don't fight now, they'll have to sooner or later."

Eir didn't get a chance to answer. The coyote's howls and yips were closer than ever, just over a slight ridge a few hundred feet to the south. Mist could feel Loki now, but she was also aware of an emptiness where before there had been movement and life.

"Are your spirits still here?" she asked.

"They've gone, but whether it's to help Coyote or save themselves, I don't know."

Mist sang Kettlingr to its full size. She'd been ready to fight with every means open to her, but she could feel the wrongness of using Galdr and Rune-magic here. It would be like a introducing a lethal virus into a healthy body.

"Please, Mist," Eir said, "try not to disrupt the balance here more than you must."

Balance? Mist thought with an inward laugh. Loki had tipped the balance when he'd first invaded this world.

She stopped laughing when a coyote the size of a large wolf descended the ridge with teeth bared and hackles raised.

Loki, and not Loki. Mist understood now what Eir had meant about a struggle. Two beings were wrestling for control under the coyote's thick winter pelt.

And Loki was winning. There was an immense power in the spirit that Loki could draw on if he was victorious. He must have known about Coyote and planned to save his own magical strength for more vital battles to come.

If she managed to kill Loki after he gained complete control of his fellow trickster, Mist thought, Coyote could die as well.

"Listen to me!" Mist called out. "You spirits of this earth! Help me now, or I will have to bring my own magic into your country. Save your own, or watch him swallowed by one who will strike you down without mercy!"

Silence answered her, broken only by the coyote's yodel of amusement. Slitted eyes glowed red and green. The darkness turned bitter, the kind of cold that could only arise from one source.

Jotunar were coming.

"Spirits of this land!" Mist shouted, trying again. "I will bargain with you. Aid us now, and we will help you when you most need it!"

Eir moaned and sifted the earth through her fingers. She began to sing, a wild, strange song that caught the rhythm of ancient times. Ancient magic, very different from that of the Vanir, but just as potent.

"What do you want of us?" Mist asked the darkness.

This time there was an answer.

Save our Mother.

It was not quite a voice, but Mist heard it, or *them*. Heard the answer, but didn't understand.

What mother? Whose?

Without the slightest understanding of what she was agreeing to, Mist accepted the terms. The dark shapes of Jotunar were massing on the hill, frigid moonlight behind them. And Loki . . .

He grinned and sprang forward. Mist raised Kettlingr overhead and charged with her loudest battle cry.

It was very nearly her last. The ground began to give way under her feet, and instinctively she dropped and rolled, tossing Kettlingr aside so she wouldn't slice her own flesh. The coyote yelped as hundreds of the local spirits, not mere apparitions but very real, dragged and clawed at Loki-Coyote's paws, pulling him down as if the earth had become quicksand.

Loki-Coyote scrabbled for purchase on the crumbling edges of the pit. He pulled himself up and out, shaking off his attackers. Mist jumped to her feet, grabbed Kettlingr, and ran among the spirits, prepared to strike him down. He would not die permanently, but if she could just—

The wind shrieked, driving sand into her eyes and knocking her off her feet. Instinctively she reached for the ancient, elemental magic.

But this wind could not be harnessed. It sent her flying in one direction and Kettlingr in another, pinning her down as it spun around and around Loki and the spirits. She nearly choked on the dust as she tried to cover her eyes and mouth with her sleeve.

Silence came as suddenly as the storm. When Mist uncovered her eyes, there was no evidence that anything around her had ever been disturbed: no stone out of place, no grain of sand moved so much as a pin's width. The pit was gone. Nor was there a single sign of Jotunar.

The coyote shook out its coat, grinned at Mist—not Loki's grin, but not exactly friendly, either—and loped away.

"You shouldn't have done that," Eir said, coming up beside her. The healer's face was crusted with sand and dirt, and Mist imagined she looked no better. "They didn't mean to kill Loki, only send him away. And you could have done great damage to Coyote himself."

Mist looked for Kettlingr and slowly picked it up. "I knew that," she said. "I guess I lost my head."

"You never had much patience," Eir said. "I'm amazed you haven't already gotten yourself killed."

"I've change a little since you last saw me." Mist stared again at the hill where the Jotunar had been standing only a few minutes ago. "They got rid of the Jotunar too, apparently. But that doesn't mean the giants or Loki have gone very far."

"All this land will reject them now, as far as the wind can reach."

Mist knelt and, like Eir before, gathered soil in her hand. "I wonder if we can find allies like this in other lands."

"These spirits are not yet your allies," Eir said, wrapping her arms around her chest. "What did they say to you before they came to help?"

"They wanted me to save their mother."

"Their mother," Eir said. She touched her hair with a shaking hand, and a few bleached brown strands came away with her fingers.

"Do you know what it means?" Mist asked, feeling a jarring pain in her shoulder as she sheathed Kettlingr.

"I only know that many of the native peoples here consider Earth their mother."

"They want me to give them the Earth?"

"I have no more idea than you do. But you made them a promise, Mist, and it must not be taken lightly. Someday you must return and fulfill that promise."

"They'll have to take a number." She sighed. "Maybe Dainn can make it out. He's spent centuries wandering all over the world, and he's Alfar. He's likely to know as much about these kinds of earth-spirits as anyone."

"Asgard had its own, once," Eir said pensively. "I wonder what became of them."

"Maybe Dainn has a theory about that, too." Mist patted her jacket pocket with a scraped palm. "I don't suppose there's any cell reception out here? I booked a flight back to San Francisco for tonight, and we might be late."

"Tonight?" Eir said with a weary smile. "You must have been certain you'd find me."

Certain? Mist thought, stifling a laugh. How little Eir knew her.

"No reception," she confirmed, glaring at her phone. "The flight leaves at nine thirty from Albuquerque. If we hurry, we'll be at the loft before midnight."

They didn't see anything untoward during the drive back to Albuquerque—no sign of Loki or Jotunar or any other obvious danger. Mist didn't get even a single bar on her cell phone until they were within a few miles of Gallup. She spoke to Bryn—apparently Loki had been too busy in New Mexico to cause problems in California—and allowed herself to relax a little.

"Almost there," she told Eir as they approached Albuquerque on I-40. They hadn't spoken much, each occupied with her own thoughts, but Mist was wondering where Dainn was now. If everything had worked out as they'd planned, and considering the time zone difference, he should already be on his way back from Italy. He'd arrive in San Francisco at nearly the same time she and Eir did.

If everything had gone as they'd hoped. Loki had known about Eir. He might also have learned of Sigrun, and sent Jotunar to find her.

And that idiot elf hadn't called to update Bryn on the success or failure of his mission. He could just as easily be dead as on that plane. Sweet Baldr forgive Loki if he was, because *she* wouldn't.

Something dark and powerful and alien swelled inside her. Her own beast, clawing its way to consciousness at the thought of Dainn's death.

You'd better be alive, she told Dainn silently, *or I can't answer for the consequences.*

"We've found another one."

Loki paused in his pacing behind the row of cramped cubicles, turning to stare at the supervisor—the replacement for the first, who had very recently been "discharged" after failing in the simple tasks required of him. He and his workers hadn't actually found Sigrun and Eir; they'd merely been asked to research a few details, and they'd bungled even that.

"Without help?" Loki asked, scorn liberally slathering his words.

"Yes, sir. Just when I called you."

"Who?"

"Regin, sir."

Regin. *That* was better, Loki thought. Of all the Valkyrie he might take, she was one of those most valuable to him—the guardian of Mjollnir, Thor's hammer and one of the greatest of the Treasures.

Certainly more immediately valuable than the Apples would have been. Loki had to admit to himself that, once again, he had forgotten his priorities and lost his sense in a foolish bid to win even a small victory over Mist.

Humanity was beginning to rub off on him. Much more than he cared to be rubbed.

"Have you pinpointed the precise location?" he asked.

The supervisor showed Loki the data and ordered his underlings to continue their work, with bonuses promised for the successful, and something much less pleasant for the incompetent.

Like the Jotunar Loki had sent to Italy. Dainn had proven that he was still a force to be reckoned with . . . and that he was still very much in Mist's confidence.

New Mexico had been its own kind of fiasco. Loki's efforts to bind himself to the native trickster spirit and to absorb its powers had failed, and he hadn't anticipated the interference of the other local deities.

In fact, he hadn't even been aware that this Coyote existed until it had attacked him. It was part of a pantheon believed long extinct, like most of those others once worshipped in Midgard. Even before the Dispersal, Asgardians had accepted that these other "gods" were dead, lost, or weakened to the point of complete impotence.

Loki had had no reason to anticipate any local resistance, let alone guess that they would join forces with Mist.

Nevertheless, the encounter wasn't the complete disaster it might have been. He had learned something from Coyote that none of them—not Freya, not Mist, nor even Odin himself—could have anticipated. Something that might prove to be as great a weapon as Danny would become.

Perhaps that would compensate him in some small measure for his covert agent's apparently deliberate acts of disloyalty. Of course that agent's excuses had seemed almost reasonable on the surface, and had hinged upon the assumption that Loki and his Jotunar would have no difficulty in achieving victory over their respective opponents.

Loki scowled. He'd warned that particular individual to think more carefully about future mistakes, but there was no guarantee that it might not happen again before the current task was complete.

If Loki hadn't needed the agent's cooperation quite so much . . .

"Sir?" the supervisor said. "What are your orders?"

"Nicholas will inform you," Loki said. He returned to his suite, spoke briefly to his assistant, stretched out on the couch in his entertainment room, and turned on the 152-inch plasma TV. He flipped idly through the channels, pausing when he ran across local or global news of interest.

Others in his employ were tracking such data at every hour of the day or night, but he liked to keep his hand in. Especially when he personally identified world leaders, politicians, or entrepreneurs he might eventually lure—or coerce, or blackmail—into his fold. He never ceased enjoying the mental image of these powerful men crouched amid the rubble of their world, weeping in their sackcloth and ashes as they fully recognized all they had lost.

There was the matter of this African dictator, for instance. He might seem an obvious choice, but he would be of far less use to Loki than his terrified, starving people. They would certainly appreciate a friend who could channel both food and weapons directly into their hands without fear of confiscation by their corrupt government.

And then there were others like Senator Briggs, who attempted to assuage the fanatical hungers of his followers even as he used them to further his rise to power. He was gaining that power thanks to Loki, but his constituents had begun to believe that he and his fellow reactionaries were betraying their God-mandated principles.

Only a little prodding here and there would be needed to transform those constituents from slavish followers to disgruntled rebels. Remove all laws that restricted their ownership and use of weapons and give them a proper leader to focus their primitive fears, and they would turn not only against their enemies but against their own kind as well.

Loki's immediate followers would never have to pull a single trigger themselves.

Loki sat up and pulled a platinum cigarette lighter from his inner pocket, admiring his reflection in the bright metal. He'd bought it because it, like the television and his Goldstriker Diamond Edition iPhone, was an utterly frivolous luxury. He could summon his own flame with a snap of his finger any time he chose, but that was always too much a reminder of his father. It would be amusing to flash the lighter among envious mortals if he chose to take up smoking, perhaps as an alternative to drinking.

Dainn didn't *like* his drinking.

With a hiss of annoyance, Loki slumped back on the couch. He had suffered temporary setbacks, and he had learned from them. If he could obtain Mjollnir as well as Thor's glove, Jarngreipr, and his belt of power, Megingjord, he would have all three of the mightiest weapons the Aesir had ever possessed. And he knew what to do with them.

Loki's phone rang, playing the series of tones indicating that the call originated in the nursery. He listened to Miss Jones's brief report and went directly to the elevator.

New drawings, Miss Jones had said. Different from the others. Very different.

When Loki walked into Danny's room, he saw for himself. The image was strung around the room, paper taped to paper, and Danny was rocking.

So was the room, and everything around him.

Loki smiled. He knew now why the earthquakes had seemed to originate from this very building.

Because they had.

∞

Bryn met Mist and Eir at the curb as they climbed off Silfr and removed their helmets. After congratulating Mist on her victory and hugging Eir, Bryn gave Mist the best news she'd had since discovering Eir's location.

Dainn had called from Italy around noon that day. He was alive, and he had Gleipnir. Mist hadn't seen him at the airport, but she guessed he'd be arriving any time now.

She was also greatly relieved to hear that nothing had been seen or heard of Loki since New Mexico, though she would have been extremely surprised if he'd recovered enough to work any kind of mischief so soon. At least, not mischief of the magical kind.

There had also been no contact from Ginnungagap. Mist was relieved, given the business of Freya's "game" with Loki and her own certainty that more disagreeable surprises were in store.

Orn had maintained his stubborn silence. Mist wondered what in Hel he was waiting for.

Pushing her weariness aside, Mist escorted Eir across the street to the temporary quarters she'd share with Bryn. Though Tashiro still hadn't returned Mist's last call about taking the kids, she knew that the teenagers' room would soon be available for the healer, who was used to more quiet and solitude than staying with the Einherjar could afford.

By one a.m., Dainn still hadn't returned. Mist found a salad someone had left in the fridge and picked at it while she tried to keep herself awake. She rested her chin on her hand and felt her eyelids sagging. Her elbow began to slip, dragging her down to rest on the tabletop.

The quake struck so fast and hard that it set the very earth to rippling like the skin of a snake swallowing a rat. The chair skidded sideways, and Mist jumped off just as it slammed into the counter. She staggered into the hall, weaving her way toward the staircase.

This was the worst quake yet, she thought, no mere aftershock. She could hear car alarms from Third Street shrilling and the noise of metal striking metal as drivers lost control of their vehicles.

Anna was staggering down the stairs when Mist reached them. Orn, in parrot form, was hopping from one section of the banister to the next, squawking each time his feet clasped the wood. Eir was right behind them, her eyes wide in a heavily lined face.

"What are you doing here?" Mist shouted to her Sister as Anna reached the bottom.

"I was talking to Gabi about—" Eir broke off as the staircase swayed. "Where are Ryan and Gabi?"

"I fell asleep," Eir said, her voice rising in panic. "Aren't they down here?"

"I think they already got out!" Anna cried, reaching for the nearest wall.

Before Mist could respond, the entire staircase swung to one side, halfway breaking loose from the landing. Mist barely caught Eir as she tumbled off. It took another second for Mist to realize that the ceiling was just about ready to fall in on them.

If Anna was wrong about the kids . . .

"Get out!" she ordered Anna and Eir, preparing to climb up to the landing using any handhold she could find.

Something hit her in the face: not a physical blow, but a buffeting fist of magic. Her skin felt hot, as if she had suddenly developed a fever. She swayed, and someone caught her arm, dragging her toward the kitchen door.

Then she was running, stumbling beside the others, her senses clouded with sickness. She was dimly aware of a bird flying after them with raucous cries of alarm.

Her vision cleared a few moments later, and she found herself standing in the middle of Illinois Street. Eir, Anna, and a half dozen Einherjar were all staring around them with various expressions of shock, fear, and vigilance.

Mist started back for the loft. Rick struck her across the face.

Shaking with rage, she was about to return the favor when another wave pulsed under them, making the asphalt writhe as if it were made of some viscous fluid. Rick grabbed one of her arms, Eir the other.

"Let me go!" she screamed. "The kids—"

Her words were cut off by an explosive hiss, as if a boiler were about to burst. A hundred little hillocks pushed up from under the asphalt like miniature volcanoes ready to spew forth their full allotments of lava all at once. A single crack opened up in the street, running from one curb to the other.

The asphalt began to split apart, the crack expanding rapidly until it yawned into a chasm. Mist wrenched herself free and grabbed Anna, dragging her away from the edge. The others stumbled back from the widening gap, coughing at the burst of fumes that spurted out from within it.

The earth heaved again, and they all fell to their knees. Something rose out of the chasm, a ghostly shape with a long serpent's head and a mouthful of serrated teeth.

Mist's tattoo seemed to burst into flame. The agony was almost unbearable, but she forgot it when she realized exactly what she was seeing.

She drew her knife and sang Kettlingr to full size. Jormungandr, Loki's most terrible child, reared up like a cobra and hissed, nearly blowing Mist off her feet.

The World Serpent had risen.

18

Dainn sprinted south on Twentieth Street, his heart beating as violently as the earth was shaking, Gleipnir threatening to choke him with its furious response.

He dashed into the alley behind the loft, thinking only of Mist and the safety of her dependents. The door to the laundry room had swung open on creaking hinges, and as he approached it the cats streaked out into the small yard, fur on end and ears flat to their broad heads.

Dainn rushed through the laundry room and into the kitchen. Broken glasses and dishes littered the floor, and the table and chairs had slid across the linoleum to rest against the counter.

He paused long enough to take in the scents and sounds within the loft, realizing that Mist was not inside. He heard shocked cries from Illinois Street and the groan of asphalt being rent apart.

And he knew.

He turned for the hall and the front door, but another cry from the floor above brought to him a halt.

Ryan. And Gabi. They were still in the loft, alone, and he was the only one close enough to save them.

※

"Oh, shit."

Gabi grabbed Ryan's arm as the building began to shake, the windows rattling as if they would shatter into a million pieces any second. The entire loft groaned, and somewhere on the first floor something heavy fell, sending another shockwave racing across the floor.

Right away Ryan knew there was nothing Gabi could do to help him. He felt it coming. If he'd been paying attention, maybe this time he'd have had a little warning.

Vomit filled his throat, threatening to choke him as he fell to the floor and began to seize. Gabi fell to her knees beside him.

"You can't do this now, Ry!" she cried. "We have to get out of here!"

But it had already begun.

Dainn found Ryan lying on his back near one of the windows in the open area of the second floor, thrashing as helplessly and violently as the naked branches of a tree in a storm. Gabi knelt beside him, her hands poised above his chest. She jerked up her head as Dainn ran toward them, but she seemed unable to speak.

Dainn slid to a stop and dropped to his knees on the rippling floor, his hands pierced by the splinters he'd obtained climbing up to the second floor. His bare feet were bloody from stepping on glass, and Gleipnir burned under his shirt, thrashing at his skin.

He sent the pain beyond his mind's reach as the boy arched off the floor, his hands and feet drumming against the concrete. Froth bubbled from his lips, and his eyes were rolled back in his head.

From what he had learned during his centuries on Earth, Dainn knew he must prevent the young mortal from choking on his own vomit. But the floor hadn't stopped heaving and the boy continued to seize, making it nearly impossible for Dainn to help him in a way that wouldn't make matters worse.

The moment the young mortal's body stilled, Dainn pulled off his own shirt, ripped several strips from it, and gently rolled Ryan onto his side. While the quake violently resisted his efforts, he pried Ryan's mouth open and felt inside, clearing away the effluent as well as he could.

There was already blood in the foam on Ryan's lips, but no evidence that he had severely damaged his tongue. Dainn loosened the boy's collar, bundled the remains of his shirt, and pushed it under Ryan's head.

"Ryan," he said. "Can you hear me?"

The boy's wild, white eyes tried to focus on his, but another shock jolted the room and he seized again.

"Let me!" Gabi cried.

Before Dainn could intervene, she had placed both hands on Ryan's side. She closed her eyes, whispering a prayer in Spanish. Dainn could feel the foreign magic gather, buzzing in his bones, and a great anger began to rise in him, the very rage he had seemed to master so well in Italy.

The herb was no longer working.

Dainn grabbed Gabi's wrist and pushed her away. Her hands were already swelling, and soon the flesh would blister and weep clear fluids, the price of her *curandera* magic.

But she had not saved Ryan, and he could not help her.

Let me go.

Hatred. Fear. Lust. Jealousy. Desperation. The beast was awake. Awake and urging Dainn to set it free.

But it had never spoken to Dainn so clearly before. It was as if it had developed an intelligence it had not possessed in the past, a cunning beyond the capacity of a mere animal pacing in its all-too-fragile cage.

It was part of him, and yet, for the first time in his life, Dainn felt at its core a locus of magic and power he had never truly recognized for what it was. Magic of destruction, yes, but like a Rune-stave it could be reversed for a very different purpose.

If he could tap it . . . if he dared to risk everything . . . he might still have a chance to save Ryan.

"No," he said aloud, and reached for the pouch he had hung around his neck. It was no longer there.

You promised, the beast said. *You promised you would let me out. That we would be one.*

Dainn remembered that promise, given when he had been desperate to break the unconscious wards Mist had set around her own mind, the high mental walls that had prevented her from releasing her own magic.

But if he kept that promise . . .

Let me go, the beast said, *or he will die.*

Dainn let it come.

The beast swept through him with a scream of triumph, clawing at the inside of his skin and widening its jaws to swallow all that was Alfar, all that might be good in what he was. Dainn felt nothing but despair.

But desperation could serve more than one purpose. Dainn kept his own mind, as he had in Italy. He drew on the beast's primal strength, finding within himself the raw power he needed.

Ryan's heart was beating too fast, and his skin was white and bloodless. Dainn could feel death claiming the mortal, and the beast laughed.

He laid his palms on Ryan's chest, spreading his fingers as if he could take that heart, repair it, and return it without spilling a drop of blood. He sang the Runes, Runes that should not exist and had never been claimed by any elf or god, not even Odin. He felt Ryan's body relaxing, his heartbeat slowing, his chest filling with the air his frozen lungs had refused to take in.

The beast roared, and Dainn's hands were no longer a part of him. A second burst of savage strength seared him from elbow to fingertips.

Life. That was what the beast wanted. Not to give it, but to take, to drain the growing strength in Ryan's body and leave it an empty sack of skin.

Ryan thrashed onto his back, his eyes bulging. The earth shook again, but to Dainn the movement seemed to come from another world. Suddenly he was lost, struggling to remember who he was, to stop a thing he could no longer name.

Power. Blinding, unimaginable power. That was what *it* promised him. A nova exploded inside Dainn, remaking him, bringing a wholeness he had never known in all his years wandering Midgard. All the knowledge locked away inside him would be his again.

Nothing would be able to stop him. Even Loki would fall at his feet. Loki, treacherous Freya, all the Aesir who would make this world their battlefield.

You can save Midgard, the beast whispered. *All you need do is give me this one, insignificant life.*

One small mortal life. One strike and he would have what he craved. He would be a god. Every door would be open to him forever.

Mist would be his.

Her image filled him: the stubborn set of her jaw, the thick, golden hair pulled tight away from her face in a severe warrior's style, her unflinching gaze, the curve of her lips when she was at peace.

Yours, the beast said. *Yours*.

Then the Valkyrie spoke a single word within his mind, drowning out the beast's heady, vicious promises.

Dainn. And as her voice filled him, Gleipnir released its hold and coiled around his neck, no longer burning but warming him with Mist's phantom touch.

It was enough. He threw himself back and away from Ryan, twisting his body as if he were literally casting off an animal bent on severing his spine and tearing out his throat. He struck the ground hard. His leg almost snapped under him, but he rolled over, pulled his knees against his chest and tucked his head between his shoulders.

The beast came at him, but the battle was not in the physical plane. He couldn't see what he was fighting; it moved in a dark mist, feinting, withdrawing, striving to devour what remained of Dainn's will. Again the beast tried to push him toward Ryan, whispering promises even as it battered at his mind with its evil. Dainn resisted, locking his muscles until they screamed for release.

But the beast was clever. Suddenly it changed tactics, telling Dainn what he most wanted to hear.

I will let him go, it said. *But there will be another sacrifice.*

You may take me, Dainn said, *if we go to some distant place where no mortal can be harmed.*

And where is the pleasure in that? the beast mocked him. *Do you not remember the joys of destruction?*

Dainn did remember, and it was agony. *There are ways of killing without taking innocent lives.*

A compromise? The beast asked. *Perhaps you speak of destroying evil men, those you judge deserve to die. But it may be you will grow to love the killing in itself, as I do, and the nature of the life you take will no longer matter.*

Leaning over, Dainn retched. He saw himself as the beast saw him. As he truly was.

Do with this mortal child as you will, the beast said. *But when you call me again, we will become what we were meant to be.*

All at once the beast was gone, leaving Dainn as small and powerless as one of the tiny, winged fairies of distorted legend. His mind was sluggish, as if every synapse in his brain had been short-circuited by the beast's immense and terrifying strength.

But he knew what he had to do. He released his rigid hold on his body and pushed to his knees. He found a shard of glass on the floor, cut his wrist and crawled toward Ryan.

"No!" Gabi yelled. "Stay away from him!"

"It's all right," Dainn said, holding her terrified gaze. She made an attempt to move between him and Ryan, but when he touched her arm she scooted away.

Dainn painted the Rune-staves in his own blood across Ryan's shirt and forehead, where the boy's sweat streaked and obscured them. Ryan gasped. His eyes snapped open. He blinked, his fingers bent as if to clutch the floor.

"Ryan!" Gabi cried. "Are you all—"

The building shuddered again, and Dainn knew he had no time to wait for Ryan to recover. "Gabi," he shouted, "the window!"

He swept the boy up in his arms and sprinted across the floor. He set Ryan down in front of the window and gestured for Gabi to support the boy while he punched the glass with his elbow. The already weakened glass shattered, and Dainn found enough strength for a spell that sent the jagged pieces still set in the frame flying to the ground below.

"You can't!" Gabi shouted.

Dainn grabbed both teenagers, one under each arm, and leaped out the window. He hit the ground hard, glass slicing his feet, rolling just enough to keep both Gabi and Ryan from striking earth and glass along with him. Then he jumped up and, still carrying the young mortals under his arms like unwieldy parcels, ran into the alley.

He emerged on Twentieth and fell to his knees in the center of the street. He released Gabi and eased Ryan down to the asphalt. The earth was still trembling like a traitor facing the headsman's ax. A mélange of scents and sounds assaulted him, and he remembered what he'd felt before he had gone to find the young mortals.

"What?" Ryan murmured, his eyes bloodshot and his skin still white as the snow that had begun swirling out of the black sky. "Where am I?"

"Gabi," Dainn said, "stay here with Ryan."

He sprinted around the corner onto Illinois and skidded to a stop.

What he found was worse than he had imagined. The creature towering above Mist was nearly the size of the loft—a miniature version of the immense, world-spanning serpent that claimed Loki as its father. Dainn saw immediately that the evil thing was only half in this world, both literally and figuratively, its lower section still hidden within the crack in the asphalt. Its skin was almost translucent, like a blurred negative image in an old-style photograph. Dagger teeth filled its open maw like enormous sickles.

An image, a ghost of itself, strong enough to make the entire city shake.

Mist was facing the thing alone, Kettlingr poised to strike, as a number of the Einherjar raced around the immense creature, waving and shouting in an attempt to attract its attention. Anna and Eir stood well off to the side, the raven croaking and flying close circles around them. Bryn was nowhere to be seen.

Mist's exhausted face told Dainn what he already knew: she had little hope of harming the World Serpent with the sword she carried, no matter how skillfully she wielded it. He had no idea if she had resorted to magic when she'd gone to find Eir, but considering the way she had driven herself and how little time had passed since she had fought for Anna, she could not yet have regained sufficient strength to face such an enemy with the Galdr alone.

Desperation would drive her to acts of thoughtless courage and sacrifice. Dainn understood with terrible certainty what would happen if she were forced to use the ancient magic now. She would face not the risk of Freya's possession, but the prospect of losing her identity entirely, or even destroying herself.

As if she had sensed his presence, Mist glanced Dainn's way, and he saw the question in her eyes.

She *needed* the beast. She had no idea what had happened since he'd left for Italy. But she feared for him as he feared for her—feared what he would lose if the monster came again and he could no longer control it.

Now he knew that the beast had never really left him. It was poised to attack, waiting for Dainn's final surrender.

It still wanted its sacrifice.

You will harm no one I value, Dainn told it silently.

It spoke no words, but he felt its mocking reply. He recognized the cruel joke it played on him: when he needed it most, it refused to come.

He ran toward Mist and Jormungandr, preparing to use what remained of his Alfar strength, physical and magical, to protect her. But her gaze stopped him, and he saw in her eyes the acknowledgment of his failure, the realization that she could expect no help from him.

"Get Anna away!" she shouted. "Make sure Eir is safe!"

The great Serpent swung its head toward Dainn. And laughed.

Bryn hadn't returned. The Einherjar were next to useless, no matter how much they'd willingly risk to help Mist, and neither Eir nor Anna was a fighter. Vali seemed to have vanished as well. And Dainn couldn't—or wouldn't—call on his darker half to help her.

She hated herself for even thinking of asking him. But she hated *him* just as much.

This isn't like being threatened by Vidarr or attacked by frost giants, she reminded herself. She didn't know what had happened in Italy. Maybe he was simply afraid that he might attack his friends instead of the enemy looming over her. And still it felt like a betrayal, as if he had turned coward on her.

All the contradictory thoughts and emotions washed through her in an instant, and then she was watching Dainn half-drag Anna and Eir toward Twentieth, where they would be out of Jormungandr's sight. Eir tried to resist, but Dainn didn't let her go.

The Serpent hissed again, rising as tall as the roof of the loft. Mist was barely ready when the Serpent's wedge-shaped head plunged toward her. She braced herself and slashed upward, catching the Serpent's lower jaw and cutting across as if she could severe its arteries with one stroke.

But the creature had no real blood, and the white ichor that pumped through its body congealed as soon as it fell to the asphalt. It shook its head violently and retreated a little, swaying from side to side and eyeing Mist with the black pits that served as its eyes.

Hoping to catch the Serpent off guard again, Mist charged, determined to strike a more telling blow. The creature reared up again, twisting around to snap at her head. Mist jumped back, her blade dripping with ichor, just before the immense jaws could crush her skull.

"Mist!" someone called behind her.

She half turned to find Gabi just behind her, a switchblade in her hand. Vali was running toward them from gods-knew-where. And Edvard, who had disappeared during Anna's rescue, was also approaching at speed, loping more like an animal than a man.

"Go!" Mist yelled at Gabi, her heart jamming under her ribs as she realized that the teenagers had escaped the loft unharmed. "Edvard, take Gabi to Dainn!"

"I'll take her!" Vali said, reaching for the girl.

"You can't make me leave!" Gabi cried, trying to jerk free of Vali's grip.

The last thing Mist wanted to do was injure the girl, but a few bruises were not as bad as the hundreds of lacerations and broken bones she'd suffer if the Serpent got her in its jaws. She slapped Gabi hard across the face. Gabi stumbled backward with a look of shock and confusion. The knife fell from her slack hand.

"Get her out of here!" Mist shouted.

Vali retreated, pulling Gabi in the direction Dainn had gone. Finished licking its wounds, the Serpent began to weave, feinting first to the left and then to the right but never quite coming within reach of Mist's sword. It almost seemed to be afraid.

If Jormungandr wouldn't attack when it seemed to have every advantage, her sword alone must be doing real damage.

Or, she thought, the Serpent was holding back for another reason, and it had to be a very bad one. For her and those under her so-called protection.

She looked quickly over her shoulder. The Einherjar had paused to catch their breaths, their faces ashen with fear and exhaustion. One had broken away and was running full-tilt toward the Einherjar's camp, presumably to fetch more help. Unless something had gone terribly wrong, Gabi, Eir, and Anna were safe now.

As if it had sensed her thoughts, Jormungandr tilted its head toward Twentieth Street. No amount of sword-waving or shouting on Mist's part could regain its attention.

She had run out of choices. It had to be magic. And she was fully prepared to use any and all varieties to stop the monster.

Holding Kettlingr in a guard position, she called once again on the spells native to her Jotunn father, drawing down handfuls of lightly falling snow out of the sky, gathering them in her left fist, binding each snowflake to the next and shaping a ball with packed layers of ice that expanded around her hand, extruding spikes until the whole construction became like the head of a giant medieval mace.

When Jormungandr finally struck, she swept both hands up simultaneously, the left with the mace and the right with the sword. The mace struck the Serpent's jaw while the sword cut across its chest. But the blade lodged in the creature's bones, and Kettlingr was jerked from her hand.

Before Jormungandr could recover from the mace's impact, Mist snatched more snow and ice out of the air and built a shield, plank by frigid plank, butting them together and sealing them with Rune-reinforced ice as strong as steel. She shaped a boss out of iron-Runes and constructed a grip to hold the shield to her chest.

Jormungandr shook his head, sending long threads of pale spittle flying across Mist's arms and face. Wherever it struck, the sputum ate into her flesh like the poison it was. She called on her anger and disgust to strengthen and expand the shield until it was large enough to cover her whole body and yet light enough so that she could easily maneuver it.

With a wail of rage, the Serpent plunged toward her. Its head crashed against the shield and it screamed, the vibrations of its unearthly voice ripping along Mist's nerves like the blade of a saw on chalkboard. She staggered, her energy beginning to fail her.

"Mist!" Dainn shouted.

She didn't dare turn, but instinct told her when to reach out and snatch Gleipnir from the air. It lashed at her skin, and she remembered when she'd told Dainn that she and the other Valkyrie weren't permitted to use the Treasures.

But the risk had to be taken. She coiled the Chain into a whip and snapped it at Jormungandr. It lengthened to accommodate her intent, but its end fell to the ground before it made contact with the Serpent's scales. As the creature coiled its body upon itself, poised for an attack Mist knew she would likely not survive, she yanked Gleipnir back and prepared to run.

Before she could retreat more than a few steps, she felt a blast of furnace heat from the chasm. Forge heat. She darted toward the Serpent, dived under its neck, and tossed one end of Gleipnir into the fissure. Fire coated the Chain's surface, and she hurled it upward.

The fire struck and opened a blackness in Jormungandr's skin. It bellowed again, flinging its head forward and back. Gleipnir dropped to the asphalt, limp and still.

Mist knew she'd used up all her resources except one.

"Mist!"

She turned to see Eir dashing toward her from the corner of Twentieth and Illinois. Eir, who was no warrior.

Yelling at the top of her voice, Mist struck at the black wound in Jormungandr's flesh. With a squeal of outraged pain, the creature flung itself back and down, withdrawing into the crack in the earth. The ground trembled again and then went still, leaving behind it a profound silence.

Mist retreated, set Kettlingr down carefully, and bent over, resting her hands on her knees and breathing hot air into her lungs. A bitterly cold pool of water covered the area where she'd worked her last magic, fire melting all the snow for yards around. She didn't for one minute believe that Jormungandr was defeated, but at least it had withdrawn.

For now.

Straightening again, she blinked the sweat from her eyes and watched Eir approach with the mortals who had attempted—and failed—to distract Jormungandr.

"You shouldn't be here," she rasped.

Eir stared at the chasm and shivered. "It's not really gone, is it? Where did it come from?"

"It's Loki's child. What do you think?" She caught at Eir's arm and jerked her head toward the loft. "Did you keep me from going after the kids with some kind of anti-healing magic?"

"The fever," Eir said. "Yes." She muffled a cough. "It was the only way to stop you. There is so much more at stake than the lives of those two children."

"You're a healer, and you can talk like that?"

"I have spoken with Gabi. They know they might die like any of us."

"Maybe I'm not ready to sacrifice—"

The earth shook again, and a fresh crack formed in the street. A ghostly shape shot out of it like a geyser, flinging a shower of broken concrete from its body. Jormungandr's wound had healed, and it seemed possessed by new strength and purpose.

But it wasn't Mist the Serpent was after now. Gabi had returned and was standing in front of the monster with an expression of angry defiance.

Immediately Mist snatched Kettlingr from the pavement and ran toward Jormungandr. She wasn't fast enough. The creature shot down toward Gabi, and caught her up, swinging its head skyward as if it would swallow her whole.

Gabi screamed, jabbing her knife into the creature's jaws again and again. Mist realized then that she couldn't send Eir away. She needed someone else with magic, no matter how limited it might be.

"Eir!" she yelled.

The healer rushed to her side and raised her hands. She spoke without making a sound, her lips moving, her palms filling with water drawn up from the asphalt at her feet.

Mist almost lost her footing as the water turned blood-red and the force of the Rune-spell caught her in its wake. Laguz, the Rune of Water, the source of cleansing, life, and healing, but reversed: madness, withering, sickness.

The water streaming from Eir's hands struck Jormungandr just behind his jaw. He screamed again, shaking ichor and pus from a weeping burn that covered the side of his neck. His skin began to tighten around his huge skull, sinking inward and buckling around his eyes.

Eir cried out and dropped to her knees, cupping her hands in the water and splashing her face. It was a mask of pain and horror, ravaged, little more a thin sheet of flesh over bone, eyes sunk so deep that Mist could not even see their color. Her hair was as lifeless as straw, and some of it had fallen out. It was as if she had been subjected to a deadly blast of radiation.

But Mist couldn't help her now. In spite of Jormungandr's injuries, he still had Gabi. The teenager was still alive; no blood, or anything *like* blood, suggested that she'd been hurt. But she was no longer a solid figure struggling in the Serpent's jaws. She and her knife had become as ghostly as the thing that held her, her screams now silent as if her voice had drained away with her substance.

Swinging Kettlingr, Mist sliced into Jormungandr's side again. It flinched but didn't release its prey.

"Take me!" she shouted. "I'm the one you want!"

The Serpent ignored her. Mist closed her eyes and sang, trying to summon Runes she was no longer clearheaded enough to understand. She swung Kettlingr again and again, all to no effect.

The Serpent lifted its head and tilted it back like a boa constrictor ready to ingest a mouse. And then, without warning, a huge brown animal charged directly at it, batting at its flesh with paws the size of dinner plates.

The bear reared up on his hind legs and roared, revealing sharp yellow fangs and scythelike claws. He raked Jormungandr's side until the Serpent, never loosening its grip on Gabi's body, slammed one of its massive coils against the animal.

With an almost human yelp of pain, the bear tumbled onto his back. As he struggled to rise again, something almost too fast to be seen darted behind the Serpent—

And ran right *through* it.

19

Stretching its jaws wide, the Serpent released Gabi. Mist barely had time to drop Kettlingr and catch the girl, who fell like a dead weight into her arms. Jormungandr made a choking sound and thrashed from side to side, focused on something far more deadly to it than Mist could ever be.

There was a shadow in the Serpent's gut. A larger-than-human shadow, heaving like an enormous parasite. An enemy *inside* Jormungandr.

Mist had no time to make sense of what was happening. "You!" she shouted to the disorganized Einherjar. "Roadkill, Rick, Bunny, Vixen—get Eir and come with me!"

Mist headed for the street corner at a dead run and turned sharply onto Twentieth. She found Ryan kneeling on the sidewalk, clearly in a state of shock. No one was with him—not Vali, who had failed to protect Gabi, nor Dainn, who would surely have seen the teenager when he'd taken Anna away from the fight.

"Ryan," she said, easing Gabi to the ground. "Are you hurt?"

He stared at her blankly. Mist saw that there were smears of blood all over his shirt, but the garment itself was in one piece, and Mist couldn't detect any injuries. It was as if it wasn't Ryan's blood at all.

"Did you see Anna and Dainn?" Mist asked, kneeling beside him. "Where's Vali? He was supposed to—" Ryan slumped, and she held him up. "Can you hear me?"

But he wasn't listening, and he obviously wasn't capable of answering. She glanced at Gabi, whose skin was more gray than brown. Her breathing was labored. Mist took her wrist, frantically counting her pulse.

A moment later Bunny, Rick, and the other two Einherjar arrived, Eir slumped between them. They helped the Valkyrie sit and stepped back. Mist moved to crouch beside her.

"What can I do?" she asked.

"I'm . . . all right," Eir said. "This will pass. Take care of the others."

Hating the necessity of leaving Eir or the kids in such a state of suffering and uncertainty, Mist looked west toward Third Street and the chaos the latest quake had created. Local residents were still running back and forth on the sidewalk and street, helping the injured, working to get stalled or damaged vehicles off the road or simply weeping in shock.

There was no sign that the mortals there—or even her closest neighbors—were aware of the battle that had just taken place. It was as if she and Jormungandr had been fighting in some vast invisible bubble.

She turned back to the Einherjar. "You two," she said to Bunny and Roadkill, "I want you to get the kids and Eir away from here. If Ryan seems hurt or Gabi doesn't improve, get help, even if you have to flag down an ambulance. We'll deal with the repercussions later. Rick and Vixen, you look for Anna and Dainn. He's got to have taken her somewhere he thinks is safe."

The earth heaved again, and there were more screams from the direction of Third Street. Mist spun and raced back to Jormungandr, snatching up Kettlingr as the Serpent coiled around and around on itself, attacking its own body. With increasing desperation it ripped at its underbelly, tearing off chunks of what passed for flesh. Ichor flowed, but still the monster bit and tore, striving to reach the shadow writhing and clawing under its skin.

The shadow reached up, part of it seeming to flow toward the Serpent's head, balling in its throat like a fist made of smoke. Jormungandr gagged, trying to expel its tormentor. Its efforts were futile. As if it realized it could not destroy the thing inside it without destroying itself, it shrieked loudly enough to rattle the loft's already-rattled windows and fell back into the chasm, moving so fast that it had disappeared before Mist could blink.

The crack began to close over it, but something prevented the edges from coming together.

That something was Dainn, covered in ichor and struggling to pull himself out. Mist dropped Kettlingr again and ran to grab his hand. It slipped out of her grasp, and Dainn fell farther into the chasm.

With a last burst of strength, Mist clutched his right wrist in both hands. The bear appeared out of nowhere and seized Dainn's shoulder in his jaws. Together they hauled the elf out of the pit. As soon as he was free the gap closed, becoming a thick black line in the pavement with hairline fractures radiating in all directions.

Dainn lay on his stomach, barely breathing. His chest, legs, arms, and feet were a bloody mess. Mist rolled him over and wiped his face with her hand. He coughed and expelled a stream of ichor.

"Dainn!" she said.

He opened his eyes. They were empty. Soulless.

"Jesus," Edvard said.

Mist turned to stare at the biker, who was crouched exactly where the bear had been.

"*Berserkr*," she hissed. "Why didn't you tell me before? Why didn't Bryn?"

"Never had the chance," Edvard said. "Did he do what it just looked like he did?"

"He's the only one who can tell us." She shook the elf lightly. "Dainn!"

Still nothing. Mist slapped his cheek, not nearly so gently. "Wherever you are right now," she said, "you have to come out. We need you." *I need you.*

Life came slowly back into Dainn's eyes. He rolled onto his side, curling up in a fetal position. Mist laid her hand on his shoulder, careful not to touch the abrasions where Edvard's teeth had marked his skin.

And to think, Mist thought with brutal self-disgust, that she had briefly considered the possibility that he had turned coward.

"That was you inside the Serpent, wasn't it?" she asked. "How? What did you do to it?"

"It will not be back," he whispered. "What of Gabi?"

"Safe," she said. "Dainn, where is Anna?"

He coughed once more, deep and racking. She steadied him as he struggled to his knees. "I left her with the young mortals . . . and Vali," he said.

"Vali and Anna are missing."

"He must have . . . taken her to safety when I returned."

"And left the kids?"

Dainn looked at her as if he were blind. "I am sorry I couldn't help you before."

"Curse it, Dainn, what did Vali say when you left him and the others?"

"I could not call the beast," he said, as if he still hadn't heard her question.

"You can explain that later," she said. "Right now we have to—"

"You do not understand. The beast *did* come, when I found Gabi and Ryan in the loft."

"You saved them?"

Dainn breathed in a lungful of air and released it slowly. "I could barely master it then, but when I most needed it, it defied me." A tear leaked from the corner of his eye. "What control I had is gone. The beast has become . . . greater than before."

"It's okay," Mist said, feeling her own self-control beginning to crumble. "You didn't hurt anyone. All I want you to do now is tell me what happened to Anna and Vali. What's the last thing you remember before you came back and attacked Jormungandr?"

"I . . . don't know."

She released him. "We have to find them." Her heart stopped. "Odin's bloody eye, this whole attack might have been a feint on Loki's part so he'd have a chance to take Anna and Orn. I didn't think he was capable—" She broke off and glanced at Edvard. "I'll need you to track Anna, and Vali if he's with her." She turned back to Dainn. "Can you help?"

"No," he said hoarsely. "No."

"Dainn, we can't let Loki—"

"Don't you understand?" Dainn said, his gaze suddenly clear, his lips curling back from his teeth like a cornered tiger's. "It is not Loki you must fear now. The beast defied me to prove its power. It wants blood. It will take whatever I cannot prevent it from taking. You, Anna, . . . the children." He bent over, spitting red-flecked foam.

Mist dug her fingers into his arms, no longer caring if she hurt him. "I won't let it. I'll help you. If I'm with you, we—"

He lunged at her so suddenly that she fell back, instinctively raising her fists to defend herself. Edvard grabbed Dainn and pulled him down again. The elf slapped the biker aside, sending him rolling across the street.

"Dainn!" Mist shouted, looking for Kettlingr.

"This thing inside me demands a sacrifice," Dainn snarled. "It will use me until it has what it wants."

"You're talking crazy. I don't—"

All the blood vessels in Dainn's eyes seemed to burst at once, flooding his sclerae with red. "I almost killed Ryan when I found him and Gabi in the loft."

"The blood on his shirt . . . Hodr's tears, what did you do to him?"

"It wasn't his blood."

"Then you—we—can still stop this thing!"

He laughed, a terrible grating sound no elven voice should be capable of making. The transformation happened so quickly that Mist had no time to imagine, let alone prepare.

The thing rising before her was neither bear nor wolf. It reared up to a full eight feet, triangular ears pressed flat to its round skull, muzzle pulled back from far too many needle-sharp teeth.

It was the thing she had seen before in Dainn's mind, but a thousand times more terrible.

"Now, you see," Dainn rumbled, the words barely comprehensible.

Mist recoiled. She felt horror, and shock, and rage that he had never told her.

But she didn't let him see her emotions. He was trying to prove he couldn't be saved, that this beast—this real, physical, deadly creature— couldn't be stopped.

She couldn't let him believe it.

"Dainn," she said softly. "This isn't you."

"It is," Edvard said, moving up behind Dainn. And he, too, changed, into a bear as big as the largest Kodiak, rising to stand only a few inches shorter than Dainn's beast. Dainn swung around, and the two creatures faced each other, assessing strength and weight with savage intelligence.

Mist didn't have the leisure to ask Edvard what in Hel *he* knew about it. "Is this what you showed Loki when you went to kill him?" she asked Dainn, stepping quickly around his massive body to separate him from the *berserkr*. "Did he see this before, in Asgard?"

It seemed impossible that there should be anything left of the elf in the beast, but when he looked down at her she saw Dainn's agony, his desperate need to be free. He lifted one powerful arm and tapped his temple with a curved claw.

Did he mean Loki had only seen a beast of the mind, as she had before? Was *this* the part of Odin's curse Dainn had been so intent on hiding from her?

Carefully she reached out to touch the dark fur. Edvard tried to get in her way, but she pushed him aside as if he were a three-week old cub.

"It's all right, Dainn," she said, stroking the surprisingly soft coat. "You could kill me now, if this creature was really in control. But it isn't. And it never will be, if I have anything to say about it."

With a howl of some indescribable emotion, Dainn broke free. He dropped to his haunches, supporting his upper body on his forelegs, and shuddered violently.

Then he was Dainn again, Dainn as she had always known

him—a little more like the ragged indigent she had found in Golden Gate Park than the one in the aubergine shirt. His hair was still a mass of tangled black, there was a gauntness to his face, and his eyes were couched in deep shadow.

He remained still, head down, breathing harshly. Mist knelt beside him.

"Dainn," she said, holding out her hand.

Scrambling away, he kept his eyes averted. "I cannot help you. Protect the young mortals, and find Anna. Keep them out of Loki's hands."

"I'll go when you promise me you'll stay right here and wait for me to come back."

Edvard came to stand next to her. "I'll watch him," he murmured.

Mist blinked, suddenly aware that she'd never seen the *berserkr* change back again. She jumped up and grabbed the biker's collar.

"I don't know exactly what you have to do with all this," she said, "but you're going to have one Hel of a lot of explaining to do." She released him. "Until then, I still need you to track for us."

"At least let me speak to Dainn before we go."

"So the two of you can—"

"It's all right," Dainn said, lifting his head. "I . . . will not hurt him. And I wish to speak to him."

Mist studied Dainn, noting with relief that he had lost a little of that wild look. In fact, he was beginning to sound rational again.

Thank the Norns.

"Okay," Mist said. "Edvard, I'm trusting Dainn right now. Don't take too long, or I'll come looking. Meet me at the factory in ten minutes." She bent to touch Dainn's matted hair. "I'll never abandon you to the beast, Dainn. Believe that."

She glanced at Edvard one last time, and then reluctantly turned away.

"Mist," Dainn said. His voice was almost normal now, but his tone . . .

"What is it?" she asked, her relief evaporating.

"The Serpent . . . it wasn't entirely real."

"Not real?" She crouched beside him again. "Dainn, after what you've just been through . . ."

"I am not delusional," Dainn said. He sat up, meeting her gaze as if they were back in the loft's kitchen engaged in some debate or other. "This may well be the phenomenon we witnessed when we saw Freya in the loft."

"You mean the Freya who blasted us around the kitchen like the Serpent tried to eat Gabi?" she asked, falling back on the old, sarcastic banter.

"Yes," Dainn said. "Manifestations of some kind, able to cause hurt but not entirely of this world."

"I don't think I understand. Are you saying these are ghosts, and that Freya is dead?"

"No. I believed they were sent to us."

"Sent?"

"That is all I can surmise at the moment," Dainn said. "My mind is not . . . functioning as well as it might."

Mist almost laughed. "Okay. But I can't imagine who would—" She broke off. "If you're suggesting Loki did this . . . Jormungandr is Loki's son, and Freya is his enemy. It doesn't make sense. Has he become this powerful? And why—" She stopped again. "Curse it, we don't have time for this now. You'll need to tell me everything you know when I get back."

"I know little," Dainn said quietly. "But what I believe, I will tell you."

And that, Mist thought, was the best either one of them could do for now, even if Dainn's theory suggested that even a *real* Jormungandr might not be the worst problem they could face.

With a another brief nod at Edvard, she went looking for kettlingr, wiped the blade clean on the tail of her shirt, and sang it small again. Gleipnir lay where she had left it—nothing but a cord now, dull and limp. She wondered if it would take vengeance on her for attempting to use it.

She went looking for Kettlingr, wiped the blade clean on the tail of her shirt, and sang it small again. Gleipnir lay where she had left it—nothing but a cord now, dull and limp. She wondered if it would take vengeance on her for attempting to use it.

Let the punishment fall on me, she thought. *The others are innocent.*

But she knew cursed well that innocence was long a thing of the past.

◑◐

Dainn had Edvard by the throat the moment Mist was out of sight.

"Is this what you intended?" he growled, dangling the *berserkr* a foot off the pavement. "Did you know the herb would fail?"

Edvard grabbed Dainn's wrists, struggling to pull them away from his neck. "No," he rasped. "I didn't . . . I never said—"

Letting him down slowly, Dainn released him. "You said if the problem got 'too bad,' I should take the powder. That it would help."

"Are you saying it didn't?" Edvard said, rubbing his neck. "Not at all?"

Dainn swung away from Edvard, walked toward the sealed crack in the street and measured its length with his footsteps. "In the loft, when the beast returned," he said, "I couldn't find the pouch."

"Then you don't know if it wouldn't have stopped the beast again," Edvard said, his voice still raspy. "I never said it would get rid of the problem permanently."

"Perhaps I should have ingested the full contents of the pouch when I had the chance."

"That could have killed you. Or kept you from . . . doing whatever it is you did to Jormungandr."

Dainn stalked back toward the *berserkr*, beginning to understand. "You had no idea how I might respond to this mixture, did you? Was it a test? An experiment?"

"No. You've got it all wrong." Edvard raised his hands palm out. "I may still be able to help you. No one could understand this better than I can."

"I saw your bear. It was nothing."

"But not even Mist knows what it's like. She never actually saw it before, did she? I saw her face when you changed."

Dainn shivered at the memory. He should have shown her long ago, when he might have done it in a way she could understand. Yes, she had accepted him. But she couldn't conceal her immediate, visceral reaction of horror and shock.

Now it was too late. No matter what she might say about standing by him, never abandoning him . . .

"We can find the dosage that'll work for you," Edvard said, "at least to keep your beast under control when you need its abilities. If you can find balance—"

"There is no *balance* for this world or anyone who lives in it," Dainn said with contempt. "I lost the pouch during the earthquake, but it must be somewhere in the loft. I will return it to you."

"No. There's still a chance that the herbs might be the only thing that stand between you and killing someone you love."

Raising his hands, Dainn studied the long fingers, remembering claws that could tear a Jotunn's head from his body without the slightest effort. The herbs *had* worked, for a time. Maybe that would be enough when the beast was ready to claim its sacrifice.

"I trust you to keep what you have seen to yourself," he said.

"*I'm* trusting you not to hurt my friends," Edvard said, his jaw hardening.

"Don't get in my way, Edvard," Dainn said softly. "I cannot be sure what will happen if you do."

"I have a pretty good idea," Edvard said. He dropped his gaze, a predator of lesser rank acknowledging the greater strength of a rival. "I have to go. Think about what I said. There may still be a way out for you."

Dainn laughed.

20

They were all around her, staring down at her bed, dark uniforms with glittering lightning symbols on their collars, guns at their hips, cold ruthlessness in their eyes.

"Come, now," said the one sitting next to her bed. "This is unnecessary. We wish only that you ask the creature to speak."

"I . . ." She swallowed, her mouth so dry that words were almost impossible, tearing at the inside of her throat. "I can't control him. *He* has to decide—"

"Here," the man said, holding her head up and lifting a glass of water to her lips. "We know he is not entirely a free agent, Fräulein." He set the glass down and eased her head back to the mattress. "He looks to you for guidance, and we must have the message he carries. What he knows of the objects."

"So you can . . ." She squeezed her eyes shut. "Where is he?"

The man raised his hand, and an underling brought Orn in a cage barely large enough for him to fit in, let alone move. He croaked piteously, his black eye fixing on her as if she were his only hope of salvation.

She couldn't even save herself.

"Orn," she whispered. "Don't. Whatever they do to me, don't say anything."

A broad, hard hand slammed into her face. Blood spurted from her nose and her head rang as Orn screamed in rage, sounds no raven should be capable of making.

"We have been too careful," another voice said somewhere in the glare of lights above her head. "The bird clearly cares what happens to her. There is only one way to compel its cooperation."

She never heard the other man's answer. Ungentle hands pulled her up, slung her sideways, carried her out of the room with her feet dragging behind her. Orn banged around inside the cage, shrieking words the men didn't understand.

"Orn," she whispered as the men hurled her into a darker, colder, fouler room than the one before. "No matter what they do, don't say anything. Don't—"

Another fist struck her, and she spun into darkness.

Anna moaned. Someone held her head and put a glass to her lips. She jerked away, letting the water splash all over her chest and the sheets and the hand that held the glass.

"I'm . . . I'm sorry," Vali stammered, pulling back. "It's just that you've been having these nightmares, and I thought—"

"Get away from me," Anna said. She heaved herself up on her elbows, blinking to clear her vision. This wasn't the same cell or the same bed. The room was small and undecorated, but it was clean and warm and dry. The bed was a real bed, not a sagging cot with a dirty mattress like a board.

She was in Vidarr and Vali's flat above Asbrew. She was wearing the same clothes she'd had on when Vali had brought her here, and she felt as if she had been in a state of limbo, neither awake nor asleep, for days.

"I'm really sorry," Vali said again, dropping his head between his shoulders. "Vid . . . well, he said it was only right that we should hear what Orn had to say,"

"You tricked me," she said, scooting away from him. "First you introduce yourself as a fellow programmer, Mist's good friend, without bothering to let me in on the fact that you're one of Odin's sons.

Then you go all gallant and pretend to protect us from the snake. And lead us right into a trap."

"I didn't want . . . I really didn't . . ." He sighed. "Vid's my brother, and he has his reasons."

"Reasons." She pressed her back to the wall. "I know Orn had plenty of chances to escape before we got here. How did you stop him? Some kind of magic?"

"He wouldn't leave you."

"He would if he thought he could go for help again. But your brother did something to him, didn't he? His own father's messenger, who obviously didn't want to see him?"

Vali looked away, but Anna had already slipped into the horrible memory of when she'd first recognized Vidarr, the son of Odin.

Not because she'd ever seen him before. Not in *this* life, anyway. Either Rebekka or Helga or both had met Vidarr under very different and terrifying circumstances. Or perhaps not so different, after all.

He wouldn't know *her*, of course. Not Anna Stangeland. But he was very close to getting what he'd always wanted.

Anna shivered and took a deep breath to steady herself. "So, is your fine brother working with that red-haired creep?" she asked.

Horror contorted Vali's face, almost comical in its extremity. "By my father's beard, no! They're enemies. Loki's everyone's enemy."

"But that snake was Loki's son." She stared into his face, daring him to deny it. "Very convenient for you and your brother."

"Loki wants to destroy Odin. Vid just wants to communicate with our father."

"Who hasn't looked for you in all these years. He went to Mist instead. Why *is* that?"

With a miserable shrug, Vali rose. "You must be hungry. I'll get you something to eat."

"What time is it? How long have I been here?"

"It's only a little after dawn."

"Did your brother make me sleep?"

"I'll get you breakfast," Vali said, nearly running for the door.

She slid off the bed. "Help us get out of here, Vali. I believe you're a good man. I know that Vidarr hates Mist, and I don't think he has the welfare of this world at heart."

Vali's jaw hardened. "You don't know him. You don't know anything, and I can't help you."

He walked out the door, nearly slamming it behind him. Anna ran after him and checked the doorknob. Locked, of course. In addition to a small bathroom, her prison had an additional locked door and a single small window, but it had been boarded up, and she wouldn't leave Orn even if it wasn't.

Mist will come after me, she thought. But surely, once she realized Anna was gone, she'd go after Loki.

Would she be wrong?

Still woozy from whatever she'd been given to make her sleep, Anna went into the bathroom, pretending she didn't see the hollow-eyed reflection in the mirror, and splashed water on her face. She couldn't use her feminine "wiles"—if she'd ever had any—to get Vidarr off his guard. But she couldn't believe that Vali knew what Vidarr had been up to nearly seventy years ago.

She had to keep working on him. Carefully. Even if she had to play damsel in distress, a ploy she thought he might actually respond to.

But to get him to betray his brother . . .

She returned to the bed and sat down, trying to calm herself. When the bedroom door opened again, she was ready.

Vidarr sat at the bar, watching Anna as Vali led her from the back room into the small dining area parallel to the bar. He wore jeans, a belt with a buckle engraved with some kind of Rune symbol, and an open-necked corduroy shirt. The pendant hung around his neck. For a moment, all Anna could see was a black uniform and the paired lightning bolts on its collar. She barely managed to keep her feet.

Orn perched on Vidarr's gloved wrist, the raven's legs bound by jesses like those of a hunting falcon's. Vid held his arm away from his body, and when Anna saw nearly healed lacerations on Vidarr's face she knew that Orn had made a couple of effective stabs at him.

"Good for you," she said aloud.

Orn knew who she was talking to. "Anna," he said. "Okay?"

"I'm fine, Orn." She stared at Vidarr. "If you've hurt him . . ."

"*Hurt* him?" Vidarr said with a decidedly unpleasant smile. "He's my father's messenger, an extension of Odin himself. I would no sooner harm him than I would the All-father."

"But he doesn't want to talk to you, does he?"

Vidarr was clearly not about to let her see if she'd stuck a blow, though his cold eyes were expressive enough. "Let's have a chat, the four of us. We might find a solution to our problem."

"*Your* problem. Kidnapping and threats aren't a very good way to gain cooperation." She held out her hand. "Let me have Orn."

After staring at her for a good long while, Vidarr released the jesses. Immediately Orn flew to her and rubbed his beak against her hair.

Feeling stronger already, Anna obeyed Vidarr's gesture and sat at one of the cramped tables. The worn surface was covered with stains from hundreds of glasses, and smears she didn't want to think about.

"Quite an appropriate hall for the son of Odin," she said.

Ignoring her quip, Vidarr moved behind the counter and poured himself a drink, while Vali brought a sandwich to her table and perched on a barstool.

"Like to get started early, do you?" she asked Vidarr, amazed at her own temerity.

"I'm sorry how this went down," Vidarr said, his hand tightening around his glass, "but Mist should have come to me in the beginning." He took a long swallow of whiskey. "She was Odin's Valkyrie, not his daughter. She had no right to take the bird from me."

"She didn't, and you know it," Anna said, trying not to stare at the sandwich.

"Mist could have *forced* Orn to come to her," he snapped.

"Oh? You admit she's stronger than you?" Anna shook her head. "No, Orn chose without any influence from anyone, least of all me. And if he trusted you, he'd have told you whatever it is you want to know." She met his gaze. "What is that, anyway?"

Orn cackled. "Power," he said.

"Tell him to speak to *me*," Vidarr said, "and I'll let you go."

"Give me my pendant."

"I don't think so," Vidarr said. He touched the stone hanging around his neck. "The raven has to stay with it, doesn't he? Like he stayed with you and your family since your great-grandmother got it from Mist."

There were two ways he could have known that, Anna thought. Either he'd figured it out during the Second World War, or someone had reported Anna's first discussion with Mist.

She stared at Vali, who refused to meet her gaze. Anna knew that the situation might be even worse than she'd guessed.

And it wasn't going to get any better soon. She had to buy time.

"Orn," she said, "do you have a message from Odin?"

"Oh, yes," Orn said, cocking his head in Vidarr's direction. "You are not the one. You are not the one."

The voice startled Anna. It didn't seem to belong to the raven at all. It clearly startled Vidarr as well. He charged around the counter and stood before Anna's table, towering over her and Orn.

"Which are you?" he demanded. "Huginn, or Muninn?"

"Memory," the bird said. "Memory of you."

For the first time, fear passed over Vidarr's face. "You do not speak for Odin," he said, planting his fists on the table. "Who is controlling you?"

Orn croaked a laugh.

"I'll get it out of you," Vidarr said, "even if I have to mark your friend's pretty face."

With a sweep of black wings, Orn flung himself at Vidarr. Vidarr batted him aside, and Orn went spinning to the ground. Anna sprang out of her chair, but Vidarr held her back with the tip of one finger. She could the feel the pressure bruising her chest.

"I'll do it," Vidarr said, addressing the raven as he hopped to his feet. Anna forgot her own pain as she noticed that Orn was favoring his left leg and listing to one side, his feathers all askew.

"You've hurt him," she said, pushing at Vidarr. "You said you'd never . . . Damn you, let me—"

Vidarr struck her. The blow numbed her entire face, and her teeth cut into her lips and the inside of her mouth.

"Vid!" Vali yelled.

But her head was ringing, and she barely heard him. Dragging one wing, Orn hopped to the table and half jumped, half flew to the chair.

"I will tell," he said. "I will tell."

"Orn . . ." Anna mumbled through rapidly swelling lips. "Don't—"

"Vali, take care of the bitch," Vidarr said. "I'll question the bird back in the office."

"Vid—"

"Remember, you fucked up. You couldn't even finish the second part of the job. Do what I tell you, and maybe I can fix it."

Heaving himself up from his chair, Vali all but crept to Anna's table. He took her arm to help her up.

"What second part?" she whispered. "Vali—"

But he swept her up in his arms, carried her through the back rooms and up the stairs. Anna caught one last glimpse of Orn before they passed out of sight and Vali took her into the bedroom. He didn't try to apologize as he laid her down, but in a moment he returned with a washcloth soaked in warm water.

He bathed her face, despite her efforts to turn away, and then retreated with his chair to the far side of the room. He knew she wouldn't accept anything else from him, not even the food and water or the shower she so desperately craved.

Maybe they'd try to force her to eat and drink later. Maybe they'd do worse. But she'd survived before, when Loki had tried to make her talk. And even before that, in the memories. Even torture hadn't broken her then, and it wouldn't this time, either.

There was always a way.

It was soon very clear that neither Vali nor Anna was anywhere in the vicinity of the loft. Bryn had returned with the Einherjar who had been running patrols, assuring Mist that they'd come back as soon as they had found a way around the stalled traffic and blocked streets. But neither she, Mist, Edvard, nor the Einherjar could find a single trace, magical or otherwise, of the people they hunted.

The loft had suffered considerable damage, as had the buildings to either side, but the factory seemed to be structurally sound. Mist's thorough physical and magical search in the area failed to turn up any sign of Kirby and Lee. She could only hope that, since the cats had had the sense to escape when she hadn't been able to help them, they'd eventually return.

Afterward, Mist saw to it that Eir, Gabi, and Ryan were put to bed until they were fit to be questioned. Gabi was still a little gray, and her hands were swollen. But Eir was far worse off. Mist considered risking an ambulance, but it didn't seem likely that one would come when there were probably hundreds of injuries much more severe demanding their attention.

"Rick told me that Jormungandr was only about the size of the loft," Bryn said, continuing the council's discussion in what passed as the Einherjar's living room. "He was tiny compared to what he should be."

"You call that tiny?" Bunny asked with a grimace.

"How did Loki get him here?" Bryn asked. "The bridges are still closed, assuming the World Serpent was in the Void with the rest of that asshole's kids."

"We don't think it was the real Jormungandr," Mist said, choosing her words with care. "Not completely real, anyway."

"Real enough to kill people," Rick said, "and make the whole city shake."

"Gabi isn't dead, is she?" Mist reminded him.

"I know Loki's good at illusions," Bryn said, "but from everything you've been telling us, he's not anywhere strong enough to do something like this."

Mist had already made the decision not to talk about the appearance of Freya's "ghost," or share most of what she and Dainn had discussed about either apparition. "We can only speculate at this point," she said. "But assuming Loki managed it, Vali's and Anna's disappearance happened while we were fighting the Serpent."

"Loki thought he could get to Anna while we were busy with Jormungandr," Bryn said. "Hurting us was only a side benefit."

"He was going to come after them again sooner or later," Mist said. "It ended up being sooner, and in a way I never would have suspected. I should have been prepared."

"No one could have expected *this*," Bryn said, gesturing broadly to encompass the large room and everything beyond it.

"But I'm responsible," Mist said, her throat tightening with misery. "Maybe not for what happened to the city, but it shouldn't have been so easy for him to kidnap Anna and Orn."

"And it was probably even easier than he thought," Rick said. "Where's Dainn? He was the one you originally sent to watch Anna, right?"

His voice was heavy with suspicion, and suddenly all eyes were on Mist. She took a deep breath.

"Since I sent you all to look for Vali and Anna when they first disappeared," she said, "you weren't here to see the end of the fight."

Praise the Norns, she thought, that no one *else* had, except Edvard. And he'd keep his mouth shut.

"Dainn helped me kick Jormungandr back to wherever he came from," she said. "He assumed Vali was looking after Anna when he joined me."

"What if *Vali* betrayed us?" Bryn asked.

21

The room fell silent. No one wanted to believe it, least of all Mist. At first she'd wondered if Vali had told Vidarr about Orn, and let his elder brother persuade him to kidnap Anna when the opportunity presented itself. That was bad enough.

But that meant Vali had to have been on the alert for a chance to take Anna every moment since he'd learned about her and Orn . . . unless he already knew the attack was coming.

Now she was forced to consider the very real possibility that her initial fears might be true. Had Vali and Vidarr carefully planned this entire event right under Mist's nose? Why in sweet Baldr's name would the brothers ally with their father's deadly enemy?

"I don't know," Mist said. "Even if Vali has been involved with Loki in some way, he may have been forced into it. And if Vidarr has some idea of keeping Orn away from Loki, he's more stupid than I thought. We may have time to get Anna and Orn back before Loki takes them, assuming we're right about any of this in the first place." She rose from the single battered couch, eager to get away from the worried stares. "I want to thank all of you for your courage in distracting the Serpent. We'll meet again before we take any further action. Resume the patrols, and stay on the alert. If the ground cracks open anywhere else . . ."

There were nervous laughs and snorts and assorted grumbles as the Einherjar scattered to resume their business.

Since Dainn had left the area of the loft after Edvard had joined the searchers, and Mist didn't yet have the heart—or the courage—to face him again, she set aside her worry for him and entered the makeshift infirmary in one of the larger offices opening onto the factory floor.

In spite of her weakness, Eir was speaking quietly with Gabi and Ryan. Mist nodded to her, pretending not to see her ravaged face, and sat down a little distance from the layered sheets and blankets that served as the ward's temporary bedding.

"You're lucky you're not badly hurt," she said to Gabi. "What you did was very stupid."

Gabi didn't have the grace to look ashamed. "I had to do *something*," she said. "I couldn't help Ryan, and—"

"I have your knife," Mist said ,"and you're not going to try something like this again. In fact, you won't get the chance. I expect Mr. Tashiro to call any time now."

Muttering in Spanish under her breath, Gabi glanced quickly at Ryan. Mist moved to the young man's side. He wasn't up to much protesting when she peeled back his bloody shirt, though he squirmed and blushed.

Dainn had been right, Mist thought as she examined his chest. It wasn't Ryan's blood.

But Dainn had said the beast had tried to kill Ryan. For the second time. At least the first time, he'd still looked like an elf.

How in Hel was she going to deal with that thing she'd seen him become? How could she possibly fulfill her promise to help him?

"Ryan," she said, covering him with a blanket, "Do you know what happened to you?"

"No," the young man said, too quickly.

"You do remember that you had another seizure?"

"It was—" Gabi began. A quick glare from Mist silenced her.

Scrubbing at his eyes, Ryan shook his head. "I sort of remember Dainn carrying me." His voice tightened with frustration. "I didn't *see*."

"It's okay, Ryan," she said, trying to soothe his obvious shame.

"When we first met, you spoke of *'things rising up.'* Well, you were right. Jormungandr certainly did that."

"I'm sorry," Ryan stammered. "I think I was about to die. Dainn saved me. He painted some kind of . . . Runes on me with his own blood to keep me alive."

So Dainn had supposedly almost killed the kid, only to save his life. Elf fighting beast. And winning.

"Is Dainn . . . is he all right?" Ryan asked, smearing the tears across his face.

"Yes," Mist said a little thickly. "He helped stop Jormungandr."

"It really *was* one of Loki's kids?" Gabi asked. "How did it get here?"

"That's what we plan to find out. And we'll get Anna back."

Gabi's eyes began to close, though she fought to stay awake. It didn't work out that way. Soon both she and Ryan were sleeping again, and Eir, who had earlier assured Mist that both teenagers were recovering from their ordeal, lay down herself.

Mist left the infirmary to find Bryn waiting for her. Rick, looking befuddled, stood at her shoulder.

"You found Anna?" Mist asked.

"Almost as good." Bryn gestured behind her. A slightly rounded, red-haired woman with generous breasts and hips sashayed up behind them.

"Rota!" Mist said.

"Hello, my most upstanding of Sisters," Rota said, winking as broadly as a barmaid.

"Vali"—Mist gritted her teeth—"Vali said he thought you'd contacted us."

"I do think my little communiqué was rather clever, don't you?"

"It was," Mist admitted. She embraced Rota and stepped back to look her over. "You're—"

"No need to be delicate," Rota said, peering at Mist from beneath full lashes. "I've gained a bit of weight here and there, but it hasn't exactly hurt me with the mortal males." She smoothed her very tight pencil skirt. "In fact, I'd say it's improved my . . . selection."

"Same old Rota," Bryn said.

"You did interrupt a promising affair," Rota said. "I had very mixed emotions when I learned you'd put out feelers to find us."

"You knew we were looking for the others?" Mist asked.

"I have my own very reliable sources," Rota said. "Don't worry, no one else knows about them. Certainly not Loki. And he would never have found me." She ran a manicured hand through her artful tousle of fiery curls. "I've been going by the name 'Rita' in Brazil. Rita Hayworth."

"Oh, sweet Frigga," Bryn said, rolling her eyes.

"You won't have much time for exploring your love life here," Mist said brusquely. "You might have noticed that we've had a bit of trouble."

"Yes," Rota said, her smile fading. "Quite a mess out there. I see I have a lot of catching up to do."

"Bryn can fill you in on most of it," Mist said. "We've got several crises going on at once, and it's hard to decide which one is the worst." She searched Rota's eyes. "Do you have it?"

"But of course." Rota reached into her shoulder bag and withdrew a single velvet glove. "I have two, and I wear them quite often. But this is the important one." She laid the glove in Mist's hand. "Jarn-greipr . . . in the flesh, so to speak."

Jarngreipr, one of the three Treasures belonging to Thor. Without Thor's hammer Mjollnir, it wasn't of much use, since its function was to allow the Thunder God to control his weapon and catch it again, no matter how far it flew.

Mist could hardly believe the flimsy thing was really a metal gauntlet twice its apparent size. "You keep it," she said, giving it back. "There's really no safe place to hold it just yet. Eir has hidden the seeds of the Apples and—" She broke off, not quite ready to admit her failure with Gungnir. Or with its owner's sons.

"Eir is here?" Rota asked.

"In the infirmary. She's had a rough time of it."

"But the others . . ." Rota glanced at Bryn. "Freya's Cloak?"

"Another long story," Mist said. "Let's just say that the Cloak was given to Horja along with Gridarvoll, and they're probably well concealed somewhere pretty far away from here. We've been working to find them and the others."

"So has Loki, I presume," Rota said. "Has he had any success?"

Mist suppressed a crazy laugh. "Not that kind. Not that we know of, anyway. There's a lot of very complicated stuff you'll need to understand."

"Hmmm," Rota said, glancing around the factory. "You've been living a very Spartan existence, I see. I don't suppose you have a room for me?"

"If you'll stay in a hotel a couple of nights, I hope to have more accommodations lined up very soon."

"Then I shall make arrangements," Rota said. "For now, I'd just like somewhere to change my clothes." She smiled over her shoulder at Rick. "You wouldn't mind getting my luggage, would you?"

The biker raced off to do her bidding, and all Mist could think was that Rota should have been Freya's daughter. She'd been *born* with her glamour, minus the magic. And she had no scruples about putting it to use.

Just like Loki.

"What really happened with Dainn?" Bryn asked when they were alone.

"I told you before. He helped me stop Jormungandr."

"You said he left Anna with Vali so he could fight beside you, but no one seems to know exactly what he did. And now he's missing."

"Not missing," Mist said, struggling to keep her voice level. "He needed to rest afterward, that's all."

"But not in the loft," Bryn said, her bright eyes very grave.

Mist sidestepped the subject. "Why didn't you tell me about Edvard?" she asked.

"Why didn't you mention who Dainn really was?"

Here it comes, Mist thought. She couldn't get out of it now.

"How did you find out?" she asked.

"I didn't recognize him when we first arrived. But after I got to thinking, I remembered where I'd seen him. I was with Odin's guard when he showed up to warn the All-father about Loki's plans for attack. I knew what he'd done." She turned her head aside as if she would spit. "Why Freya chose *him* . . ."

"But she did, and Odin must have known about it. At least now I understand why Rick doesn't like Dainn. You've got a loyal lieutenant."

"Yeah," Bryn muttered.

"And you're still loyal to the Aesir. So Rick won't provoke Dainn, will he?"

"Not if Rick wants to live. I also know about Odin's curse."

But you don't know the half of it, Mist thought. "Let me deal with that," she said. "He may have come to me on Freya's behalf, but Freya isn't here, and his problems are my responsibility."

"Is that all?" Bryn asked, ruffling her short hair with a callused hand. "I think he's a lot more than just a 'problem' to you."

"If I felt anything else, it would be irrelevant to our fight."

"Would it, Mist?" Bryn asked, searching her face. "Would it really?"

"Drop it, Bryn. What about Edvard?"

Bryn shoved her hands in her pockets. "I didn't think it would be an issue until we actually got to the real fighting." She paused. "I understand he helped you."

"He did. I presume that none of your other Einherjar is concealing some kind of hidden talent?"

"Not to my knowledge."

"Then we're done here. You have work to do, and so do I."

Her face creasing into a complex expression of anger, hurt, and defiance, Bryn backed away.

Smoothing her half-undone braid, Mist wondered if Bryn's

resentment of Dainn would become a problem. If Dainn really had lost control of the beast again, it was all but certain.

Mist had seldom seen Dainn so still. He was like one of those people who used to stand on street corners pretending to be a mannequin, refusing to move even if an observer did something outrageous like kiss or tickle them.

Once, Dainn's kiss had awakened her. The gods knew what would happen if she ever tried it with *him*.

Of course that wasn't going to happen. She tried to put off the inevitable by looking up at the sky.

For once the morning was clear, typical of the kind of winter day San Francisco had known as recently as two years ago. The clouds had temporarily vanished, though the air remained crisp and the wind still cut through Mist's jacket.

But a day of storms would have been more appropriate for this meeting in the park, the little rectangle of frost-damaged trees and lawn that served as the neighborhood's outdoor gathering place. No one else chose to brave the slush that covered the grass and dripped from tree branches, not after the chaos of the past few hours.

At least, according the news, the city's infrastructure was stable, even if half the roads were closed, holiday shopping had been severely disrupted, and plenty of cars had joined together in unholy union.

As long as Jormungandr stayed in his hole, San Francisco would recover soon enough. Until the war really began.

Mist forced herself to look down and face what she'd come here to do.

"Dainn," she said.

He snapped out of his silent meditation and looked at her. His eyes were normal now, the correct color and shape and expression, if you could call grim desolation an expression. He approached her slowly, head slightly down, walking as if he was afraid any rapid or sudden movement might awaken the beast again.

"It would have been better if you had stayed away," he said.

"Did you really think I would?" She sighed. "It's time for you to come home."

"You have not come to your senses?"

"I haven't changed my mind, if that's what you mean. Maybe you shocked me a little, but I got over it."

He looked above her head at something she didn't think she wanted to see "And will you forgive my failure to tell you about my true nature?"

"I'll have to think about that one," she said with a forced smile.

The muscles in Dainn's jaw flexed. "A long time ago," he said, "when I first came to Midgard, the physical beast you saw did not exist. It was only a thing of the mind, as I told you in the beginning. But the first time I was threatened with physical harm by a mortal, it appeared. And it killed. It killed more than once before I found a way to begin fighting it."

"And you managed to hold on to it," she said, "until Freya came for you. And you met me."

He continued to gaze at the sky as if he might fly up like Orn and simply disappear. "I learned long ago that magic of any real significance strengthened the creature, and so I avoided it. Strong emotion was also a dangerous catalyst. I lived in isolation, century upon century.

"But a time came when I succumbed to temptation, and I worked a few small spells. I began to lose mastery of the beast soon after. The cage was no longer as strong as it had been, and I spent every waking moment attempting to reinforce it. But when the Lady entered my mind, it was weakened yet again."

"Did she know it was more than a beast of the mind?"

"Yes. She believed she could cure me."

"But you told me she couldn't."

"Freya said . . ." Dainn took a deep breath and exhaled slowly. "She said she couldn't help me until her full power was established in Midgard."

Mist wondered if Freya had dangled that hope in front of Dainn the entire time since she'd called him to be her messenger in Midgard. He would have done—*would* do almost anything to rid himself of what he despised above everything but Loki, the one who had ultimately brought the curse upon him.

No wonder he had been so intent on making Mist cooperate when they had first met.

"When I was condemned," he said, as if he and Mist had joined minds again and he had heard her thoughts, "she stood between me and Odin's full wrath."

But his voice was dull, and Mist knew he wished Freya had left him to die.

In that moment, Mist almost hated the Lady.

"It's all right, Dainn," she said, clenching her fists at her sides. "We can still figure this out."

"As we did before you saw what I really am?"

Mist refused to be drawn into that same argument again. "I might remind you that you saved us from Jormungandr," she said. "You choked it, tore at it from within. It didn't know how to fight you. And you rescued Gabi and Ryan from the loft."

"You forget that I almost—"

"But you didn't hurt Ryan, did you? I know you used some kind of Blood-Runes to heal him."

"I was fighting the beast. The rest is unclear."

"But you were *fighting* it." She gathered her thoughts. "I saw you cast Blood-Runes when you tried to find out if Loki was near the loft," she said. "And I used them against Hrimgrimir. But they're not for healing."

"I understood only that they were necessary to save Ryan's life."

"That tells me nothing. Dainn, you *have* to remember."

"I have no answer!"

Though she'd faced the full power of Dainn's true beast only hours before, the agony in his voice made her flinch. He wasn't going to tell her a cursed thing more, and she knew it. Maybe if she let him talk to Ryan . . .

No. She couldn't put either one of them through that. Not now, or anytime soon.

"Then maybe you can explain what's been going on with you and Edvard," she said quietly.

Dainn released his breath, and the muscles in his jaw relaxed. "He sensed what I was and came to see me, claiming that he knew I was"—Dainn laughed briefly—"having difficulties, and that he could help."

"Help how?"

"With methods his people use to regulate the behavior of their animal natures."

"Then when you referred to 'new techniques' before we took Anna from Loki, you were talking about something he showed you?"

"Obviously, it failed."

Mist kicked at a mushy combination of rotted leaves, dirt, and melted snow with the toe of her boot. "Edvard hasn't been seen since I asked him where you'd gone after we returned from searching for Anna," she said.

Dainn opened his mouth to speak, but only turned away.

"What?" Mist asked.

"It no longer matters," he said. "I was, as always, a fool."

"Do you think Edvard intended to hurt you in some way?"

"Unless he works for our enemy, I cannot fathom a good motive for his behavior."

Mist pushed her hands into her pockets. "Bryn knows who you are, Dainn. And I didn't tell her. She recognized you from Asgard."

"Ah," Dainn said, his tone flat. "And does she know the rest?"

"She knows the nature of the curse, but not what you can become. She and Rick won't cause any trouble."

"Perhaps it would be better if someone you trust is prepared to . . . deal with me should I prevent you from doing what is necessary."

"What in Hel are you talking about? Dainn, you have to go on as if you can beat this thing. If I thought you'd really stay this way, I'd kill you myself."

"May I take you at your word?"

Her heart stopped and then broke into a lurching rhythm that made her ribs ache. "Are you asking me to kill you if you—"

"I told you of the sacrifice the beast demands of me," Dainn said. "I believe that sacrifice will be someone to whom I have an emotional attachment. You will know what must be done if the time comes. You will show no mercy if I lose myself."

Almost against her will she moved close to him, so close that she only had to tilt her head back an inch to look into his eyes. "It won't come to that," she said. "I can see you want to run, but you won't, because you know you could still hurt innocents wherever you go. I'll keep you here even if I have to tie you up every time you even come close to letting go."

"And how will you manage that?" he said, cruel amusement in his voice.

As drained and discouraged as she was, she wove a cable of steel Rune-staves and cast it around him. Even without the power of the beast's shape, Dainn snapped the bonds as if they were made of frayed ribbon or rotted twine.

"You see?" he said, backing away quickly. "Even you cannot hold me. But perhaps you have access to something that can."

"Loki's piss, what is it?"

His gaze grew distant again. "Only three things might bind me," he said slowly. "My own will, which has failed me; death; or the roots of a mountain."

Mist knew he was quoting what they said of Gleipnir: that it had been forged by the dwarves out of the sound of a cat's footfalls, the beard of a woman, the roots of a mountain, the sinews of a bear, the breath of a fish, and the spittle of a bird.

"You can't be serious," she said.

"I carried it back from Italy," he said. "It had . . . certain effects on me that suggest it may be of use against the beast."

"What effects?" she demanded, her heart picking up speed.

"It attempted to bind me."

"By itself?"

"I am Fenrisulfr's mirror image." he said. "It was forged to hold him when no other binding could."

"You're nothing like Loki's wolf-child," she said, furious again. "And Fenrir *did* break Gleipnir in the end."

"Nevertheless, it—"

"You said it 'attempted' to bind you. That means it didn't succeed. None of the Treasures work for anyone but the Aesir, not without terrible consequences." She gathered her courage and, for the first time, told him the ugly story of what had happened during World War II, when she had dared to use Gungnir against Nazi pursuers.

"While I was busy fighting a few soldiers," she said, "almost the entire group of refugees I, Bryn, and Horja were escorting was massacred."

"And you blamed yourself," Dainn said with unexpected warmth. "It explains so much."

Mist's eyes burned, and she looked away. "I urged Bryn to use the Falcon Cloak, and she died for it."

"You *thought* her dead, yet she is alive. What were the consequences of attempting to use Gleipnir against Jormungandr?"

"Maybe it's that Anna is gone, and—"

"Don't be foolish," he said harshly. "Anna is gone because I trusted Vali."

"That doesn't mean—"

"If you truly wish me to remain here, we must attempt it."

"I told you I *wanted* you here, you thick-headed elf. But if this idea of yours backfires, *you* could be the one hurt."

Dainn crouched, running his hand over the dead grass. "You *did* use Gungnir again," he said. "When we fought Loki in his apartment."

"What?"

"You were in possession of it when you entered the fugue state. You threw it at Loki. He barely escaped death."

She took a few agitated steps away from him, ran her hand over her hair, and swung to face him again. "Freya was with me part of the time. It could have been *her* presence that made it work."

"You have won two subsequent battles virtually alone, with no loss of human life and only a few injuries among your followers."

"You'd call what happened to Ryan and Gabi minor? And what about Eir, who used a corruption of her healing magic to help me, and now looks as if a single snowflake could kill her?"

He rose and strode to a nearby tree, gazing up into its bare branches, stroking its scarred bark. Mist felt the power of life in Dainn's hand as if were her body he was touching.

"Gleipnir," he said, curling his fingers into the bark as if he would tear it off.

"All right!" she snapped. "We'll try it. But *if* it works, I won't chain you up like a junkyard dog. When you're with me, you can be free."

"You have quickly tired of my company in the past," Dainn said, the faintest trace of humor in his voice.

"You can be a big pain at times, but I've survived somehow." She hesitated. "You know you won't be able to fight at my side."

"But if I am bound, perhaps I can assist you in retrieving Anna and Orn without putting you at risk."

"You're crazy, you know."

Dainn's fingertips grazed her chin. The contact lasted no more than a second, so light she could barely feel it. But when she met his gaze, what she saw in his eyes was worse than anything that had come before.

Hope. Hope of a life in which he could harm no one because it would be spent in perpetual bondage.

"I'll go back to the loft," she said, pretending that Dainn's offer hadn't torn her apart. "I'll expect you back by nightfall."

22

Ryan was halfway up Twentieth when Dainn saw him.

The teenager froze, his eyes widening in panic. It was still midday, hardly a time for him to be leaving the loft clandestinely with his backpack over his shoulder and a furtive look on his face.

And yet Dainn knew that was precisely what Ryan was doing.

He approached the young mortal cautiously. "Should you be out, Ryan?" he asked. "Surely you have not fully recovered."

Ryan nearly flinched, but quickly caught himself. "I'm fine," he whispered. "I just wanted to, you know, get away for a little . . ."

He trailed off, but Dainn knew he was lying. "I have much to apologize for," he said, keeping his distance. "Yet I cannot expect you to accept my regrets."

"If you mean what happened in the loft," Ryan said, "It's okay. Gabi told me what I couldn't remember."

"It is not 'okay.' You have had little but trouble from me since you came to Mist. But soon I will be unable to harm you, even if the beast escapes my will again."

"Are you going away?" Ryan asked, a note of distress in his voice.

"There is another possible method of containing it, and I have every hope that it will—"

"I'm not afraid of you. I never have been." Ryan's gaze flickered behind him in the direction of the loft. "You saved my life."

His trust struck Dainn like a hail of Jotunn ice. "Then why are you leaving now?" he asked. "Is it because of the Jotunn's death, or have you had another vision?"

"Nothing like that," Ryan said. "But I have to go."

"You will soon have the freedom and wealth to live as you choose," Dainn said. "Leaving before the arrangements have been completed can only endanger your life further."

"I'm no good to anyone the way I am now."

"No one expects anything more of you."

"Maybe you won't *mean* to. But we all know it's not working. I can't help anyone."

"Ryan," Dainn said, dropping into a crouch, "Even if this were true, there is no reason that you must leave today."

"Please don't make me explain. I can't." Ryan's eyes grew moist. "I'm asking you not to tell anyone until I'm really gone. I don't want you to follow me. There's just . . . something I have to do."

Dainn nodded. He knew he ought to take the boy back, but he knew just as clearly that he would not. Ryan had more than earned the right to make his own choices, even if they were foolish and dangerous ones. He was no longer a child.

"You have left Gabi behind?" he asked

"She needs to stay here." He swallowed. "I've left a note. Please, just let me go."

Dainn stepped aside, leaving Ryan's path toward Third Street unimpeded. "If you need us, call. We will come. Or Mist will, if I cannot."

"I know." Ryan smiled. "You take care of yourself, too."

And then he was striding away, clearly afraid and yet determined to meet whatever destiny he meant to pursue.

He was so much stronger than Dainn had ever been.

Kneeling in the melting snow, Dainn closed his eyes. He had finally admitted the extent of his shame to Mist in the park, the way in which he had failed to control the beast in the years long before Freya had touched his mind. He had made himself vulnerable, opened up to her more fully than he had ever done before.

And yet, once again—when he should have warned her of the Lady's many deceptions, both past and potential—he had turned coward. Too much a coward to be honest with the woman who had stood beside him, supported him, determined to help him when he so little deserved it.

When first he had learned of Orn's appearance, part of him had believed it signaled the end of Freya's influence in Midgard, and over Mist. Now that Orn was taken and the bird had proved to be so much less than they had anticipated, he no longer dared harbor such hopes.

But now there was another chance. Two chances, either of which might serve his purpose, and possibly save Mist. He knew his magic functioned, if irregularly, and it was possible that he could still aid Mist in developing and controlling her magic so that she could obtain her mortal army and bar Freya from threatening her mind. As long as Gleipnir kept him bound, he need not fear loosing the beast by calling on abilities that could help her master her untapped power.

If that was not sufficient, and Freya *did* return, there was still another way. A way the beast's ever-growing strength might at last make possible. And Mist need never know that all he was, elf and beast, was built on lies.

He opened his eyes and looked toward Third. Ryan was standing on the corner with a man whose body was nearly obscured by the falling snow. Before he could make out the man's face, the other was suddenly gone. And so was Ryan.

Dainn started after them, but with each step toward Third his pace slowed. He had to trust that Ryan knew what he was doing, and that this was not a return to his former life as what mortals so crudely called a "rent-boy."

Ryan knew far too much now. He could not go back.

None of them could.

The boy didn't respond.

Loki leaned back in his chair, allowing his anger to flow through him and dissipate with a hiss of steam that fogged the small bedroom. Oh, Danny had done exactly as Loki had wished, manifesting the image he had drawn on fifty separate sheets of paper tacked to the walls of his room. An image he had turned into a weapon at Loki's behest. It had barely been necessary to coax him; he had known what Loki wanted and simply followed his instructions without question or hesitation, like a well-programmed computer.

But now Danny didn't rock, or make repetitive gestures, or behave in any of the ways he had always done when he was farthest from the world. Even Miss Jones couldn't account for his utter stillness.

Loki could. He'd demanded too much. Just because Danny could create stunningly effective "ghosts"—apparitions that could be brought to life at some distance and were capable of doing great damage— didn't mean he had endless supplies of power. Or the disposition to continue furthering Loki's plans merely to please a parent he barely noticed.

What he had done with Odin's manifestation was proof enough of that. Perhaps he was not so unlike Loki as he had always seemed. Perhaps a beast lay in wait behind Danny's blank-slate eyes. And since the other beast was still at large . . .

Loki let the chair slam back to the floor. Miss Jones gasped. "Get Danny ready, Miss Jones," Loki said, straightening his suit as he rose. "We are going for a walk."

Ten minutes later the nurse had Danny dressed and in his stroller, one made especially for an older child. Danny was thoroughly warded against the day's chill, though the afternoon had been clear and the temperature a few degrees above the recent average. Most of the sidewalks and streets were still slick with ice, and the aftereffects of the earthquake were visible everywhere. Tow-trucks and public works vehicles far outnumbered private automobiles and taxis, which were hopelessly jammed together as their drivers negotiated obstacles ranging from traffic cones to impressive holes in the streets.

Nevertheless, the life of the city continued, and intrepid mortals always found ways of acquiring what they needed. Or wanted.

Loki found the walk quite pleasant. He wore a very casual, ready-to-wear suit that had cost a mere $7,000, a green scarf that perfectly matched his eyes tucked ascot-style under the lapels, and an open overcoat he didn't need but which beautifully completed the effect he wished to create. He wore his classic fur felt fedora at a rakish angle, but he could have worn rags and the attention he received would have been no less appreciative.

The only thing to ruin the effect was that the cane he carried was not Gungnir. And that should also be restored to him very soon.

A number of attractive women, and more than a few men, paused to coo over Danny, only to realize he was not a "proper" child at all. Those who revealed their consternation tended to take rather bad falls on the sidewalk as they walked away, or find themselves with uncontrollable failures of their digestive tracts.

They would not mock *his* son.

He smiled, signaled to the limousine that had been following at a discreet distance—finding its way through stalled traffic with an ease that would have astonished any observant mortal—and instructed the driver to take them to the modest neighborhood known as Dogpatch. The driver let them off at the small park, with its ragged deciduous trees and few battered pines. Miss Jones, bundled to unrecognizability under her down coat, adjusted Danny's blankets and fussed at his cap before preceding Loki toward Twentieth Street.

It took a little effort, but since Danny had been almost entirely responsible for the attack on Mist's headquarters, Loki still had enough magical energy to shroud himself, Miss Jones, and Danny in a spell that made them seem quite ordinary to the mortals Mist had set to watching for enemies. The first Loki encountered was a large man with a scruffy beard worthy of a Jotunn. Loki simply made him look the other way.

When he, Miss Jones, and Danny turned onto Twentieth Street, Loki quickly spotted two more of Mist's "Einherjar" patrolling the area on foot. They ignored him. At the corner of Illinois Street he met Mist's newest acquisition, the voluptuous Rota, dressed in black leather that was highly suggestive of dominatrix sensibilities. She was walking toward a red Jaguar parked at the curb when she noticed him. She paused for a moment, frowned . . .

And looked right through him.

He admired her full, swaying posterior as she continued toward the car, and then led Miss Jones and Danny back to Twentieth. It was only a matter of minutes before Dainn arrived.

There was no doubt as to what was on the elf's mind. He charged toward Loki, head down, black hair flying behind him, half beast even before the transformation began.

"Calm yourself," Loki said. "I am not here to squabble, my Dainn. Only to talk."

With obvious effort, Dainn slowed and stopped, keeping two yards' distance between them. "Where is Anna?" he demanded, his breath rasping in his throat.

"That is hardly a proper greeting for a friend," Loki said. "We have plenty of time to discuss your current predicament."

"Friend," Dainn spat.

"Of course. Mist is still alive, is she not?"

To his surprise, Dainn remained perfectly still. His dark gaze pierced Loki's with open hatred and then flickered to Miss Jones in consternation.

"Ah, you have met before," Loki said, knowing very well that they had.

"Are you a prisoner?" Dainn asked the nurse.

Miss Jones shook her head. "No, sir."

Loki smiled approvingly. It was a measure of Miss Jones's earnest desire not to be punished that she had learned to be extremely convincing.

"The boy," Dainn said, his gaze dropping to Danny's nearly invisible face. "Is he safe, Miss Jones?"

"Yes, Mr. Alfgrim," the woman murmured. "Safe as houses."

"Thank you." The elf's hard eyes met Loki's again. "You could not have killed Mist," he said, as if there had been no interruption in their conversation. "She defeated your monster."

"No," Loki said, "not if my observers are to be believed. Mist's forces were disorganized and supremely ineffective, but you"—he clucked in admiration—"*you* did something quite remarkable."

"Mist did more than—"

Loki raised his hand. "Do you really seek to convince me that she is an amazing adept capable of single-handedly routing such a creature? Because then I would be forced to consider her a truly worthy enemy, and that might be extremely dangerous for our Valkyrie princess."

The elf trembled with the effort to hold himself in check, fully aware of the game Loki was playing. And that there was no way for him to win.

"Are you here to gloat over what you have done to this city?" he asked.

"It wasn't *my* doing," Loki said.

Dainn laughed.

"No, truly. As admirable a feat as it was, the serpent's appearance at Mist's loft was not my work."

"It was Jormungandr. You are responsible."

Loki strolled around Dainn, his hands behind his back. "And how can I possibly summon Jormungandr, when all the bridges are closed?"

The outlines of Dainn's body seemed to quiver like a dancer caught in a strobe light. "You know it was only a manifestation."

"Only? Quite an effective one, then. My kudos to its creator."

"Where are Anna and the raven?" Dainn demanded.

"Do you truly suppose I would tell you if I had such information, my handsome elf?"

"You don't have them," Dainn said, his eyes narrowing.

"Don't I?"

"I know you too well."

"If only you did."

"What is your purpose here?"

"Why, to inquire after your health, and to congratulate you. And to reassure myself that your friendship with Mist has not been . . . shall we say, 'strained' by recent events."

Dainn clearly understood his meaning. "Did you expect her to reject me?" he asked.

"Not really. She is made of stern stuff, our girl. But I know that seeing you that way was a blow to her. She knows you deceived her, and you could not expect your relationship to remain what it was."

"There was never any relationship to damage."

Loki rocked on his heels. "Still such a poor liar. Tell me, how did she handle Svardkell?"

Dainn's fingers curled into claws. "You knew who he was," the elf accused. "You sent him to Mist deliberately, and set a spell on him to attack her."

"Yes, I have been aware of his identity for some time. I allowed him to continue his charade out of curiosity. He refused to admit he was working for Freya, or explain why he had hidden himself among the Jotunar I brought from Ginnungagap. Remarkably sturdy, that one." Loki tilted his hat a fraction of an inch. "As I never permitted him access to any information he could turn against me, I thought Mist might like to meet her father."

"How did you discover that Svardkell was Mist's sire?"

"I kept myself informed about Freya's lovers in Asgard, even those she preferred to keep confidential. Of course I always knew that Mist was Freya's daughter, and it amused me to discover which of her many inamorati had planted the seed."

"What else did you know of him?"

"Why this interest, my Dainn?" Loki asked, suffering a rare moment of disquiet. "Surely you and he had little time to become acquainted."

"Your spies must have told you that he wasn't dead when Mist defeated him. Either your spell or your calculations must have gone awry."

"How long did he remain alive before Mist was forced to kill him?"

Dainn gave himself away with the slightest twitch at the corner of one eye. "He spoke to her before he died," he said.

"Of his undying paternal devotion?"

"About how you made him attack her. You failed to make certain that she would take the whole blame upon herself."

"And yet she *does* blame herself, does she not? Even if she despises her Jotunn blood, she never knew a father's love."

"Surely you could have found a better way of using the relationship to your advantage?"

"I could hardly expect you to believe any false intelligence I might force him to impart."

Dainn studied him intently, and Loki realized that the elf knew Svardkell was not supposed to have spoken at all.

"What is it, Laufeyson?" Dainn asked, taking a step toward Loki. "What more did you know about the Jotunn?"

There was some puzzle here, Loki thought. A dangerous one.

"I truly do not understand you," he said.

"Then perhaps I can improve your comprehension." Dainn bared his teeth and moved toward Loki with a predator's lethal grace.

Loki raised his hand. The still-unhealed scar of their Blood-oath stopped the elf as surely as a rampart of ice eight feet thick.

"Perhaps our original agreement is no longer in effect," Loki said, "but you cannot deny that something still binds us. You will not harm me today."

The elf shuddered violently. "Do not expect that to protect you forever."

A charged silence hung between them—charged with more, Loki knew, than simple hate.

"In that case," Loki said, "might I ask a question before I die?"

"Only one, Slanderer?"

In spite of himself, Loki felt a stab of anger at the insult. "I only mean to compliment you on your success in preventing Freya from seizing Mist's soul after she left our little party the other night. How did you achieve it?"

An expression of genuine confusion crossed Dainn's face before he took himself in hand again. "Mist was never in any danger."

"Oh, but I think she was. Freya nearly had her. But sometime between her departure and your return to Mist's loft, the Lady vanished and Mist was herself again."

"Freya was weak."

"Ah." He smiled. "I don't think that was the case at all. I think you did effect the separation, and you don't know quite how you did it. And I believe you still haven't told Mist of your part in the Lady's thwarted scheme."

Dainn had never done a better job at trying to conceal his emotions, and he failed utterly. The muscles in his jaw flexed, and the pulse beat hard at the base of his throat.

"Well," Loki said, "perhaps Freya won't return. Perhaps her services are no longer required, and Odin will pop up at any moment to take the reins."

"But you don't believe that," Dainn said, his voice hardly more than a rasp.

"If matters were so simple," Loki said, "it would never have been a game worth playing. Let us say that I believe the All-father would already be here if matters in the Shadow-Realm are as Freya described them to you. Perhaps Odin is inconveniently . . . tied up."

Dainn stared into Loki's eyes. "What is your meaning?"

"Only that things are not always what they seem, and Freya is a very good liar. But you know that, my Dainn. And now I would very much like to return to a more agreeable subject." He nodded to Miss Jones, who had remained as frozen as one of the snowmen some ambitious children had built in the park. "I hope, my dear elf, that you will allow me to make known to you my pride and joy."

Miss Jones bent to fold Danny's blankets away from his face.

Dainn's reaction was all Loki could have wished for. The ferocity drained out of his face, and looked up at Loki with growing realization in his eyes.

"Who is this boy?" he asked.

"Why, I believe you met my son when you came to stare at my house, but so uncharitably neglected to call on me."

"Your *son*?" Dainn whispered.

"Why does that surprise you? I have proven myself fully capable of producing a wide variety of offspring. Not all my children are monsters." He gazed tenderly down at Danny's glassy eyes. "Perhaps you have forgotten Narfi, whose entrails were used to bind me under the serpent when the Aesir saw fit to torment me for centuries on end."

"You deserved torments only the Christian's Yahweh could devise."

"I am not here to argue," Loki said mildly, refusing to let his pleasure be dampened. "You are clearly not as shocked as you pretend to be. Perhaps you guessed at the truth when you met Danny before?"

Dainn sank to his knees before the stroller, his eyes intent on Danny's face. Danny showed no sign of recognition.

"What did you do to him?" the elf asked.

"He was born as you see, and I have taken good care of him."

"Born in the Void?"

"Where else?"

Dainn reached out as if he would touch the boy, but quickly withdrew his hand. "This is not a child of the Jotunn woman Angrboda," he said.

"You know that that good lady and I haven't dallied for a long while now," Loki said. "And Sigyn—" He shrugged. "She was never worthy of me."

"The one who bore him must have had many virtues unworthy of you."

"Oh, she does, I assure you."

"If I had the means—" Dainn began.

"To take him away from me? Perhaps you would rather return with me and have a proper visit. Miss Jones said he did seem rather fond of you on that previous occasion." Loki reached out, brushing his fingertips across Dainn's face. "My poor Dainn. You have chosen Mist over Freya—even over Midgard—and yet you are still so far from finding the peace I know you seek. I once offered you the chance to join me in defeating Freya and keeping Mist safe from all harm. I offer that chance one last time."

23

Dainn jerked his head away. "What did the mortal genius Einstein say of insanity?" he asked. "That it consists of doing the same thing again and again and expecting different results."

Loki sighed. "Sometimes I can make no sense of you, my Dainn. I still hold every obvious advantage, and several more of which you are entirely unaware. I am very close to opening a bridge to the Void. I have resources on this mortal plain you will not be able to match in a year."

"The Aesir—"

"Are not here. Where are Mist's mortal allies? Those pathetic bikers? Three Valkyrie? What of the Treasures?"

"Where are yours?"

"They will come to me, like everything else. You clearly have no idea how you kept Freya from claiming Mist, and you have no confidence that you can protect her if the Lady returns. What more can you do for her?"

"I can die for her."

"And that is why I am so fond of you. That stubborn, blind nobility, fatally flawed though it may be." He smiled. "When it comes to surrender, as it must, you know what will incline me toward mercy."

Dainn turned his back and began to walk away.

"Dainn!" Loki called after him. "Don't make the mistake of telling Mist of our conversation. Those who have seen me will not remember, and I would hate to see our Valkyrie act on another dangerous impulse."

Moving faster than any earthbound creature had a right to, Dainn rounded the corner.

"I think Danny's cold, Mr. Landvik," Miss Jones said in a surprisingly firm voice.

"We won't keep him out any longer," Loki said. "My business here is done." Loki bent to kiss his son's pale forehead. "Twice," he murmured, straightening again. "The third time will be the charm. And then, my son, all will be as we wish."

The boy tilted his head and gazed directly into Loki's eyes. "Brother," he said.

Jerking back, Loki nearly stumbled. He glared at Miss Jones, who quickly glanced away, and then looked at his son again.

"Yes," he said. "You brought your brother here, and did a very fine job of it, too."

"Brother," Danny repeated, more insistently. The ground quivered ever so slightly beneath Loki's feet.

"Hush," Loki said. "I cannot reach your real brother yet."

"*Brother.*"

"You shall have all your siblings with you soon," Loki said. "Angrboda's children. They will all love and care for you, as I do."

Danny shook his head. "Not *them.*"

Kneeling beside the stroller, Loki took the boy's cold hand. Suddenly he understood.

"Sleipnir," he said.

Sleipnir the eight-legged, swiftest and best of all horses. And Sleipnir—Odin's mount, given by Loki to the All-father—was one of the Treasures sent to Midgard, hidden away like the others. He had never been Loki's top priority, but now . . .

"Ride," Danny said. "Sleipnir."

"I understand," Loki said. "But I will need your help to find him, my son. And then you shall ride him, just as you wish."

Danny's eyes dulled and then closed. Loki stepped away to allow Miss Jones to cover him again, swallowing his frustration. He snapped his fingers, and the limousine pulled around the corner.

As soon as he had returned to his headquarters, he'd set his programmers and technicians—and other allies—to searching out every conceivable location where an eight-legged horse might lose himself. Even if he had been concealed as an ordinary equine, Sleipnir would outshine others of his breed as Brisingamen did all the mortals' gold.

To family reunions, Loki thought as he poured a drink from the limousine's minibar.

He had just arrived at his apartments when Nicholas appeared with very good news.

Regin had been taken. She was being held in the block of cells Loki had appointed for the Valkyrie he captured, and was awaiting interrogation. Her Treasure, Mjollnir, was under guard by ten of Loki's best Jotunar. And if Loki's formerly incompetent ally were to be believed, he'd soon have a peculiar young woman and a raven ensconced in cells beside hers.

And a willing captive in his bed.

Dainn was sitting in the middle of the living room floor as Mist had seen him do many times since his first day at the loft—eyes closed, legs crossed, hands resting palm-up on his knees in a perfect imitation of the stereotypical New Age practitioner of Eastern meditation techniques.

But she could see by the tension in his body that he was far from a state of peaceful detachment.

Was it possible he already knew?

Hel, she thought, what he was facing now was bad enough without adding to his burden. But it had to be done.

She looked carefully around the room, noting the cracks in the walls, the broken furniture, everything that had prevented them from moving back in. The wooden staircase was only half attached to the second-floor landing. But this room, at least, was temporarily inhabitable, and she had to hide what she was doing from Bryn and the others.

She sat on the listing couch, resting her elbows on her knees. "I didn't intend to be gone so long," she said. "Are you all right?"

He opened his eyes. "Yes," he said. "But *you* clearly are not."

"Ryan has left us."

Dainn's muscled tensed as if he would jump to his feet, and Mist knew it had come as much as a shock to him as it had to her when Eir and Gabi had told her.

"Don't bother," she said. "He's long gone."

"And Gabriella?"

"Gabi is still here. She said he left her a note saying that he had to go and couldn't explain why, or where. He wanted her to stay behind so she could learn from Eir." Mist stared down at her boots, stained two inches up from the sole by mud, crusted snow and water. "He asked Gabi not to tell us until he had a chance to get away, and no one saw him leave."

"I am sorry to hear it," Dainn said, his voice a near-whisper. "Once could infer that his choice to leave was due to my mistakes."

"Oh, sure," she said, her own heart swimming with guilt. "*Everything's* your fault."

"Forgive me," Dainn murmured, as if he we apologizing for every sin in the world. "What more did Gabi say?"

"Not much. She was crying too hard."

"But she has made no effort to go after him?"

"No. At least Eir's with her." Mist leaned back, briefly closing her eyes. "That's the one good thing. They've hit it off, and Gabi seems to take some comfort from that." *Even though Eir would have let Gabi and Ryan die to save me*, she thought.

"You have informed Tashiro?"

"I contacted him as soon as I could after the battle, but he's apparently been held up by the street blockages and traffic."

"So he has finally responded to your many queries."

She tried to ignore his taunt. "I've asked him to send people out to look for Ryan, but we can't stop everything to search for a teenager who doesn't want to be found. At least Tashiro's arranged it so that Gabi can stay here as long as she wants to."

"Then there is nothing more you can do. We know Loki has never shown interest in Ryan since Hrimgrimir came for him. And if Loki's agents have been watching him, they will have observed that he has been of very little use to us."

The words were blunt and callous, and Mist wanted to deny them. But he was right. She was secretly glad that she had one less mortal to worry about.

Even though she was going to miss the Hel out of the poor kid.

Another thing she was going to miss was watching Dainn walk around like a free elf instead of a mad animal. She cleared her throat. "You should know that we'll be going to Asbrew as soon as it's dark. We're guessing that Loki doesn't have possession of Orn yet. I have a feeling we'd know if he did."

"Let me accompany you. If we succeed with Gleipnir—"

"That's the thing, Dainn," she said. "I want you to stay here. You'll use the beast if you think I'm in danger, and this way we can make sure the Chain holds you." She met his gaze. "I think I'm a match for Vidarr, at least."

"He will be prepared for you," Dainn said after a long hesitation.

"I'm not going to take any stupid chances. I promise that if we need you, I'll come back and get you myself."

He stared at her for a good while, searching her face. "I hold you to that promise, Mist," he said.

Convincing him had been much easier than she had expected. Almost too easy. But she sure as Hel wasn't going to argue with him.

"We should continue," Dainn said. "I am ready."

Forcing her body to move, Mist retrieved the Chain from the warded safe in her bedroom. It was limp and lifeless until she brought it into the living room, where it began to lash from side to side in the snakelike manner she'd seen before.

It *knew* Dainn was dangerous. She hated it.

"I'm sorry," she said.

Dainn shook his head, dismissing her apology. "The legs should not be necessary," he said, as if the limbs didn't really belong to him. "The wrists, ankles and neck should be sufficient."

Mist knelt beside him. "I can't do this," she said. "I can't treat you like—"

"I would not accept this from anyone but you."

"Then let's get it over with," she said, swallowing the foul taste in her mouth as she got to her feet. Gleipnir seemed to vibrate, eager to do its work.

Dainn unfolded himself and rose. Mist's fingers shook as he held out his hands and she looped the Chain around his wrists. Gleipnir lengthened to accommodate her as she wound it around his waist and chest, giving him just enough room to move his arms in front of his body.

Her hands, however, didn't want to accommodate her, especially when she realized what the Chain was doing to him. He was nearly successful in hiding it, but she'd learned to read the small changes in his body—the tic at the corner of his eye, the way small muscles jumped like the skin of a horse tormented by flies, the almost inaudible hitch of his breath.

"It's hurting you," she said.

"No," he said. "Continue."

Spitting out a long stream of curses, she wrapped the Chain around his neck. She remained close to him when she finished, feeling his breath on her skin as he fought to control his pain.

"I wish it were me," she whispered. "I wish I could—"

"This is how it must be."

"If Freya comes back . . ."

"We cannot rely on her."

She reached out to cradle his face between her hands. "This won't be forever."

"It is forever we fight for."

She let him go. "Do you need anything? Water? Something to eat? Ibuprofen?"

His laughter sounded genuine. "I doubt that will be effective," he said. He lowered himself to the floor, leaning his back against the armchair. "If you have no need of me now, I will rest."

"We should get you to your room. The bed's still in one piece, anyway." Before he could protest, she moved to stand behind him, grabbed him under the arms and lifted him to his feet. It always surprised her how solid he was in spite of his leanness.

"I can walk," he chided her, pulling free. But he was unsteady enough that Mist had to support him most of the way. He fell onto the bed before she could ease him down, rolling to the side in one motion. His skin was bone-white except for the red marks where the Chain touched his flesh.

"Go," he said roughly. "I will be well enough."

Everything inside her urged Mist to sit beside him, stroke his damp hair away from his face, murmur words of comfort as if he were a child. But he wouldn't welcome it. And she . . .

She would forget all the hard facts she had struggled to learn. Again.

"Your hands are free," she said, moving his phone from the bed table to the mattress. "You can still call me."

"I will," he said, meeting her eyes, "if you do not keep me informed of your progress."

"I'll remember the warning. Get some rest."

There was nothing else she could think to say, except to remind him that he had nothing to be ashamed of. And that she would be perfectly safe.

He'd never believe a word of it.

"We're working on it," the voice on the other end whispered.

Loki regarded the cell phone with disgust. *And they call* me *the Deceiver,* he thought.

This one, he thought, was going to be far more trouble than he was worth. When it was finished, he would meet with an accident . . . one not necessarily worthy of a son of Odin.

"You had best hurry," Loki said. "I expect interference, and if I don't have what I want very soon, I will have no choice but to personally see that you keep your end of our agreement. And that, I assure you, would not go well for you."

"*I'll make sure it gets done.*"

"Are you prepared to defend yourselves?"

"*I'm not stupid. We'll be ready.*"

Both are highly dubious statements, Loki thought as he closed the connection. But even if his allies failed again, Loki knew it was only a matter of days, likely hours. The connection between elf and boy was unmistakable. Like an electric current, that connection must be closed.

Half the streets were blocked off, and though much of the rubble had been cleared away, plenty of windows were broken and pavement cracked. Public employees had been out in record numbers, inspecting and cleaning and supervising.

Now it was late, and only the usual dealers and panhandlers were on the street. Mist saw no point in trying to conceal the approach of a dozen bikers. If it came to a fight—and she expected one—she planned to throw up a ward to keep mortals from seeing it, though she hoped she wouldn't be forced to maintain it too long. She'd need all her energy if things went south.

Now she, her Sisters, and Bryn's hand-picked Einherjar stood across the street from Asbrew, noting the interesting fact that Vidarr and Vali had made no attempt to protect the bar—at least not to the degree that Mist couldn't easily penetrate.

"He must have magical defenses somewhere," Mist said.

"You said Vidarr had let himself go," Rota said, "that his magic is rusty."

"Loki would never leave Orn and Anna with him if he couldn't handle them. If he's holding them here against their wills, he has to be powerful enough to keep them and fight for them."

"*If* they're still here," Rick muttered.

No one spoke. After a time, Bryn said, "Do you really want to talk to them first?" she asked.

"We can't do anything else until we know Anna and Orn are safe."

"They've turned against everything they were in Asgard," Rota said. "They won't listen to you."

"Better trying to talk than—"

Mist broke off, stunned by an overwhelming sense of disaster.

And it wasn't coming from Asbrew. She felt as if live wires were wrapping themselves around her neck and arms and chest, squeezing, burning, destroying her mind and body.

Dainn.

"I have to go back," she gasped, spinning Silfr around.

"Go back?" Bryn said, catching at her arm. "Why?"

"I can't explain right now."

"Is it Dainn?"

When Mist didn't answer, Bryn asked, "Is that why you didn't bring him tonight?"

"Look, all you need to do is watch. Vid is going to wait for us to make the first move."

"You'll risk this operation for a traitor?"

"I'm not going to argue with you, Bryn. I'll be back in ten minutes."

"Wouldn't make a move without you," Rota said with a grin. "I, for one, am not ready to die just yet."

Dainn rolled off the bed, instantly awake. Gleipnir clawed at his bare arms and neck and chest, hurling him onto his back before he could catch his balance.

The call was steady, like an alarm that would not be silenced. It pulled on him, on his soul, as nothing and no one had ever done before. Powerful as Gleipnir itself, it wound itself around his limbs and his body and pierced his skull, like a dog's whistle pitched too high for mortal ears to perceive.

He stumbled out of bed and staggered toward the door, his palm flaring with excruciating pain. Awkwardly he turned his right hand up. The half-healed wound, the twin of Loki's, was throbbing as if it were about to burst open.

Had Loki planted some spell in his blood when they'd made the blood-oath? Had he activated it somehow when he'd brought the boy, Danny, to—

The pain flared again, and Dainn slammed his body against the wall. The explosion of agony almost sent him to his knees, and the call broke off cleanly, like the snap of a dry twig under a heavy boot.

He got to his feet and returned to the bed, leaving spatters of blood behind him with every step. His cell phone buzzed, vibrating on the scarred wood of the bed table. He recognized the number and put it on speaker, leaving a smear of blood on the screen.

"Dainn?"

His lips curled in an instinctive snarl. "Traitor," he whispered.

"I never wanted to do it. Vidarr said he'd kill her and take Orn if I didn't—"

"You're working with Loki." Dainn swallowed the metallic taste of blood. "Have you and Vidarr—"

"I can't talk about it now. Vidarr's out. I'll make sure you can get in and take Anna with you."

"Mist has gone to Asbrew. Deliver them to her, and perhaps she will forgive you."

"She was here, but she's gone. I can't give Anna up to the others." Vali took an audible breath. *"Look, I know about your other half—the whole thing, fur and all. If you come, I can tell Vidarr you attacked me, and if you make it look good he and Loki will believe me."*

Dainn cut the connection and clenched his fingers over his crimson palm. He knew it had to be a trap. Loki's trap.

But if he could spare Mist the risk of death, or worse . . .

He looked down at his bound wrists. He had compared himself to Fenrisulfr, who had been unable to break free until the days just before the Last Battle.

But he was not Fenrisulfr.

He bent to grip the magical Chain in his teeth, groaning deep in his chest at the fresh shock of pain as it burned his mouth and tongue. Gleipnir writhed as he ripped it apart, freeing his wrists, and tore it away from his arms and neck. It fell on the bed, and, as he watched, the various parts slithered toward each other and joined into one seamless whole. He half expected it to leap at him, determined to overcome his rebellion, but it lay quiescent on the bedspread, as dry and dull as a strip of uncured hide.

The damaged loft was empty. Gabi and Eir slept across the street, and the Einherjar left behind were holding themselves ready for another attack. Dainn pulled open the bed table drawer with his left hand and grabbed the pouch of herbs he'd found lying just outside the laundry room door after his last discussion with Edvard.

For all he knew, the stuff might kill him the next time he attempted to use it. And that might not be such a bad thing. He pushed the pouch into the waistband of his pants, slipped through the front door, and stepped outside.

In spite of the streetlights on Third, the snow fell so heavily that visibility had been reduced to no more than a few dozen yards. Dainn burst into a run, his bare feet setting the steady pace he could maintain for hours. Rising wind tossed his hair into his face as he ran north and west along deserted streets.

His wound ceased to bleed when less than five minutes had passed.

24

It was the overwhelming sense of magic that ended the interrogation, a pressure that seemed to squeeze all the air out of Loki's lungs. In the cell, the Valkyrie Regin huddled in the corner, her lips swollen and her dark blond hair tangled like a rat's nest around her face.

She was a very lucky woman. Loki grunted to the Jotunar waiting outside and strode through the two sets of heavy doors that separated his "dungeon" from the other half of the basement.

He found Danny's six guards cowering against the wall in the corridor leading to Danny's room, staring at the door. Burning yellow light seeped out from underneath, fanning across the floor in pulsing waves.

Shouting a spell that flung the giants to the floor like pigeons diving into invisible glass, Loki pushed the door open.

Danny's small form, perched on the bed, was surrounded by a brilliant luminescence—a halo that sketched a wide circle on the wall behind him as if someone had pointed a large and powerful flashlight at the pale blue surface. Miss Jones stood at the foot of the bed as if mesmerized, her brown skin bleached to the color of aged oak.

Loki threw up his hand to block the intense light and approached the bed. As his eyes adjusted, he saw what the light had concealed.

A portal. Not a bridge to Ginnungagap as he had hoped, a passage mottled blue and black with the Void's chaotic energy. This one was gold and green, and it opened to another land. Another place in Midgard—a vision of endless grassland, hills, and a distant herd of horses set against a backdrop of vivid sunlight.

Loki moved closer to the wall and reached out to touch it. His hand seemed to catch fire, and then it was on the other side, bathed by the cold of open steppes in winter.

One of the horses lifted its head. Loki took another step. A bitter wind caught him across the face, and intense pain bit into his wrist. He snatched it back, his feet once again firmly planted on the floor of Danny's room.

And none too soon. The moment he stepped away from the wall, the portal began to contract. It shrank with considerable speed until the view of the other side vanished and the circle of light was a mere pinprick.

Danny walked across the bed, his body perfectly balanced, and touched the wall. The pinprick closed, and nothing remained but paint and plaster.

The boy turned to Loki and smiled, the sweet and innocent smile that concealed so much power.

"My brother," he said.

Sleipnir, Loki thought. Sleipnir was somewhere on that plain, almost within reach.

"Hurry," Vali whispered, opening the side door with a furtive glance toward the street. None of the Valkyrie or Einherjar, watching Asbrew from the front entrance, had seen Dainn slip behind the building and into the side alley, wreathed in falling snow and a touch of cautious elven magic.

"Come on," Vali said, grabbing Dainn's arm as he stepped into the short corridor leading to the back office. "Vidarr's still gone. We have time—" He stared from Dainn's hand to the burns on his torso and hastily released him.

"Let me see Anna and the bird," Dainn said. "I have no reason to trust you, and if you've set a trap for me, I will act accordingly."

"I know. She's right in here."

He opened the door at the end of the corridor. Anna was sitting at Vidarr's scarred desk, half hidden behind the computer and a high stack of paper trays. She looked up, her eyes bleary with exhaustion. Several bruises marred her delicate skin.

"Dainn?" she said in a barely audible voice.

"Are you well?" Dainn asked, approaching the table.

She straightened. "They haven't hurt me, but Orn—"

"Orn's with Vidarr," Vali said.

Dainn glanced at Vali, his heartbeat thudding in his throat. "You led me to believe Anna and Orn were together."

"Would you have refused to come if you knew it was just Anna?"

"You lied." Dainn circled behind Anna, never taking his eyes from Vali's face.

"Orn," Anna moaned, sinking her head into her hands.

Vali moved closer to the desk, spreading his hands. "Please believe me, Anna. I didn't want this to happen."

"We can retrieve the raven later," Dainn said to Anna. "We must go."

"Do you really think it matters what happens to me?"

Dainn took Anna's arm and gently pulled her to her feet. "We must go."

"But you just got here!" a deep voice said behind them.

Vidarr strolled into the room, releasing the Rune-ward that had disguised his presence from Dainn's senses. Dainn looked at Vali, and Odin's younger son backed away as far away as he could without leaving the room.

"After all these centuries," Vidarr said, "after all you've suffered, you still trust those who have already betrayed you."

"I never trusted Vali," Dainn said calmly, concealing his despair.

"Where is Orn?" Anna cried, trying to pull herself free of Dainn's grip. "What have you done with him?"

"Oh, he's safe," Vidarr said. "We still have a lot to talk about." He looked Dainn up and down. "You didn't tell Mist you were coming, did you? Think you could spare her the danger of facing me?"

Dainn pushed Anna behind him. "The Lady Mist doesn't need my protection, least of all from you."

"No. She understands how weak you are, like a dog on a chain." Vidarr checked his watch. "Oh, yes, I know all about it, that thing you become." He gaze lingered on Dainn's burns. "My observers tell me that she left here not long ago. Why? Going to check up on you?"

"*Your* observers," Dainn asked, "or Loki's? How long have you been serving him?"

Vidarr's forced good humor vanished. "I only took the bitch because I wanted a little chat with my father's messenger. Now that I have what I—"

"What would Odin not freely give his own son?"

"Orn didn't tell you anything!" Anna shouted at Vidarr. "You were there during the war, looking for the pendant because you believed you could control Orn if you had it. But it isn't working for you, is it?"

For a moment Odin's son looked genuinely surprised, touching his neck with his thick, half-Jotunn fingers. "The messenger should have to come to me in the first place!"

"Liar!" Anna shouted. "You were ready to kill to get that pendant, and the Treasures. You tortured—"

Abruptly she went limp, and Dainn barely caught her before she hit the floor. Vidarr shook his head.

"She's insane. Why the raven chose her as his companion I'll never understand." He grinned. "She's of no further use to me now, but I still intend to make you pay for her, Dainn. Oh, yes."

"Why did you have Vali bring me here?"

"Because maybe we can work out a deal. Maybe."

"If you mean a deal with Loki, you are the one who is mad."

"I don't make deals for the Slanderer," Vidarr snarled, balling his substantial fists.

"Then what do you want?"

"Your surrender for the girl's release."

"But not to deliver me to Loki?"

"I've been thinking about killing you for a long time. Slowly. Because what my father did to you wasn't enough."

"You clearly have no idea what was done to me."

Vidarr grunted. "I remember when you showed up at Valhalla, all mysterious and powerful. My father took to you right away. But you wouldn't tell anyone where you came from. You put Odin under some kind of spell." He thumped his chest with his fist. "*I* used to be his closest advisor—closer than Thor or Mimir. And then you just stepped in and pushed me out."

"That was never my intention," Dainn said, frozen in the grip of uncertain memory. "I did not know where I had come from. Not then, and not now."

"But you were everything the noblest of elves should be," Vidarr said. "Detached but generous, cool but compassionate, always believing you could be objective because you were never quite one of us. Believing you could stop a war prophecy had foretold centuries before you showed up." He barked a laugh. "You thought you could *reason* with Loki. Instead, you let him seduce you. You robbed us all of our honor. You prevented the rebirth of the world, the new paradise."

"And *you*," Dainn said, "so inappropriately named the Silent One, were to rule over that 'paradise' after Ragnarok. Is that what most infuriates you, Lord Vidarr? That you find yourself a bartender on a world of mortal inferiors, when you should be a king?"

"I *will* kill you, you cursed—"

"You will not. Whatever has driven you to work with Loki, you intend to give me to him. I only wonder what you receive in turn, *hraumi*."

Vidarr's face turned crimson at the insult. "Loki will never get the better of me, no matter what tricks he plays."

"Do you truly believe you can ally with him and then betray him?"

Dainn was prepared when Vidarr swung at him, and leaned sideways just enough to avoid the blow while keeping a tight rein on the beast. Vidarr lost his balance and stumbled forward, righted himself quickly and turned again.

"Your behavior is not wise," Dainn said softly.

"You won't let it loose," Vidarr rasped, "because the thing inside you is the only part of you that isn't soft, and you piss yourself whenever it gets too strong."

"And what will make *you* piss yourself, Vidarr Odin's-forgotten-son? Mist facing you in honorable battle?"

Vidarr charged. Dainn swept Anna up in his arms and danced aside. Vidarr spun with surprising grace and stood with his feet planted apart and his head sunk between his shoulders. Anna began to stir in Dainn's arms, and he shifted his grip, prepared to push her behind him as soon as she could stand again.

"Look at you," Vidarr sneered, circling Dainn slowly. "A *nidingr* like you has no honor. You disobeyed Mist by coming here, didn't you? You *knew* you'd probably be betrayed, but you'll give yourself up because you keep making mistakes that are slowly robbing her of everything you want for her." He grinned. "I think you *want* to die, Lord Elf, because staying alive is too hard for a spear-pointer like you."

Dainn held Vidarr's stare. "Permit the girl to leave, and I won't fight. But Loki must have no part of it."

"Oh, he won't," Vidarr said, cracking his knuckles.

"Vidarr—" Vali began.

"Shut up," Vidarr snapped. "You take the girl to the door, and when I've finished you can let her go."

"No," Dainn said, distantly aware that his palm had opened again and was dripping blood on the floor. "You will give your oath as Odin's son and heir to release the young lady without hindrance by you, your brother, or any of your followers. We will go to a public place, where you will call to inform Mist of Anna's location, and then I will surrender myself to you."

"That's quite a mouthful of conditions," Vidarr said. "But I don't have to agree to any of them. I have every advantage."

"Except one," Dainn said. "You assume I won't release the beast because I fear it too much." He lifted his burned wrists. "You are wrong."

"I know you won't risk the girl," Vidarr said. "Let her leave with Vali, and I'll give you a clean death."

Suddenly Gungnir was in Vidarr's hand, gleaming with purpose.

"No!" Anna cried, freeing herself from Dainn's hold. She spun to face Vali. "You son of a—"

"Silence!" Vidarr roared. He aimed the Spear at Dainn. "Mist ain't gonna win this one."

"You sure about that?" Mist asked, striding into the room. She glanced at Vali dismissively and turned her gaze on Vidarr. "You didn't really think I'd wait around for you to kill either one of them, did you?"

With a grunt of rage, Vidarr hurled Gungnir at her. Dainn tried to step into its path, but he found himself frozen. His paralysis only lasted for a few seconds, but when he could move again Mist was still there, unharmed, and Gungnir was stuck in the door exactly as it had been at the end of Mist's first battle with Loki in Asbrew.

"You've made a mistake," Mist said. "Vali warned me what you were up to. I already had plans in place to stop you. Dainn was just a distraction."

Dainn stared at her, trying to make sense of her words. Was it really possible that she'd known he would break Gleipnir and come after Anna?

"I've been working magic centuries before you were born," Vidarr said. "Do you really think you can match me?"

"I saw you surrender to Loki," she said, tearing Gungnir from the door as if the wood were as flimsy as paper.

"I never—"

"You couldn't even use your own father's weapon," she said, balancing the Spear in one hand. "I don't understand how you ever thought you could get away with this." She smiled. "Let Dainn and Anna go, give me the bird, and we'll pretend this never happened."

"Give it your best shot, bitch."

She nodded to Dainn. "Take Anna outside."

Dainn's vision blurred as if he had received a powerful blow to the head. Vali was gone. The air grew thick with magic.

"Anna," he said. "Come."

She blinked at him with a dazed expression, leaned on his arm, and let him lead her out of the room. The cold night air slapped his face, and he shielded Anna from the bitter chill as best he could. A dozen Einherjar were visible beyond the mouth of the alley, their motorcycles sending clouds of condensation that thickened the air like heavy fog. Dainn considered leaving Anna with them and surrendering to his overwhelming desire to join Mist in her fight.

But she would win without him. She was Vidarr's equal, half Jotunn and half divine. And more.

She *must* win.

"What's going on?" Anna whispered. "Isn't Mist—?"

"Wait," he told her.

No more than a few minutes passed before Mist walked out of Asbrew, Gungnir dangling from one hand like a walking stick.

"Well," she said, "that's that." She grinned at Dainn. "You didn't actually think I wouldn't figure out what you were up to?"

"Where's Orn?" Anna asked, searching Mist's face with a look of bewilderment.

"Apparently he's escaped," Mist said. "He took the pendant with him."

"He wouldn't leave without telling me!"

"Oh, I'm sure you can lure him back," Mist said. "He wouldn't really want to see you hurt, after all."

Dainn tried to focus. There was something wrong in Mist's voice, in her manner. An overconfidence, a carelessness utterly unlike her.

And no anger at him for escaping, only a jovial camaraderie he would never have expected.

"Vidarr?" he asked her.

"Oh, he'll be incapacitated for a while. No real harm done." Mist gestured behind her, and Dainn followed her glance. Five of the Einherjar, including Bunny and Rick, stood at the mouth of the side alley. "Anna, go with Bunny. Dainn, I'd like to have a few words with you. In private."

Now it comes, Dainn thought. But Mist's smile didn't fade once they were alone. She dragged him toward her by the nape of his neck and kissed him without inhibition, nearly biting into his lip.

He broke free, staggering backward. The Einherjar in the alley—no longer mortal, but shapeshifting Jotunar—had slipped by Dainn and were dragging Anna behind the building. Mist seemed to melt and reformed into someone equally beautiful and utterly familiar.

"Surprise," Loki said. He slid his hand down Dainn's arm, and Dainn was frozen again. "I should have known Vidarr wouldn't play ball. Vali, at least, had the good sense to warn me of his brother's intentions."

"Then I was right," Dainn said, barely able to move his lips. "This was a trap for me."

"Hmmm." Loki cocked his head. "I'll give Vidarr this much. He did a good job of keeping you distracted." He turned Dainn's bloody hand palm-up. "Now, how did that happen? Let me help you." He produced a strip of ice-woven fabric out of the air and wound it around Dainn's palm.

"Where is Mist?" Dainn growled. In spite of Loki's spell, the beast was rising in his blood, unrestrained and ready to kill.

"I wouldn't do that, my Dainn," Loki said softly. "You might—"

"Papa," a high voice said from the street.

Danny was standing barefoot on the slushy sidewalk, wearing only pajamas printed with prancing horses. The snow swirled about the boy like protective wings. He stared unblinkingly at Loki with a little pout of disapproval.

"I don't like this," he said.

"Danny!" Loki snapped, dragging Dainn toward the boy. "I told you—"

Danny turned around and ran into the street. The roar of a motorcycle engine drowned out Loki's shout, and he and Dainn arrived at the sidewalk just as Mist rode into the alley, forcing them to stumble out of the way. There was a squeal of tires, and moments later Mist returned with Anna on the back of her bike and the shapeshifting Jotunar barreling after her.

The true Einherjar in the street rode to meet the giants as Mist raced past them. The bikers ran down two of the enemy and gunned their engines, speeding after Mist.

She cast one final glance over her shoulder, her gaze meeting Dainn's. He could feel the unspoken message, a brief touch of minds, the sorrow of a final parting.

He had made his choice in breaking Gleipnir and ignoring Mist's orders that he not go to Asbrew. She must realize now that he was too dangerous to remain with the allies, and that his life and freedom were not worth the cost she might have to pay.

And perhaps she hoped that this time—if he found his wits and courage—he might do Loki some damage from within.

"Ah," Loki said, scowling at the mangled Jotunar whose blood was freezing even as it spilled onto the asphalt. "A pity about Anna, but I'll find the raven. With your help."

"That is unlikely," Dainn said, his mouth as dry as Ymir's bones.

"Oh, I think it's very likely I'll be able to persuade you," Loki said. He looked beyond the dying Jotunar to the other giants, who had formed an outward-facing circle like musk oxen protecting their young. Loki pushed Dainn ahead of him as he went to join them.

"No!" Danny cried, squirming through the wall of giants. He ran straight to Dainn and took his hand.

Everything vanished.

25

———

Dainn doubled over, barely retaining the contents of his stomach. Danny clung to his hand, looking straight ahead and clearly not in the least disturbed by the sudden shift from one location to another.

The *boy* had done it. Loki's son.

Lifting his head slowly, Dainn followed Danny's gaze. Lefty O'Doul Bridge looked almost exactly as it had the last time he and Mist had examined it, save that all signs of Loki's magic had vanished, to the eye and to every magical sense.

And the first light of dawn was tinting the sky. When he and Danny had "left" Asbrew, it had been closer to 2 a.m.

Where in slavering Fenrir's name had they been for six hours?

Dainn knelt to meet the child's eyes. "Why did you bring me here?" he asked.

"Family," the boy said, gazing at the bridge with rapt attention.

"Where, Danny?" Dainn asked, touching the boy's surprisingly warm cheek. "What family?"

The boy smiled with an almost mischievous delight. Loki's smile, when he had decided to be charming.

"My brother," he said, turning to point at the bridge.

That was when Dainn fully realized that the boy was in no way the seemingly helpless, mentally challenged child Loki had presented before. Loki clearly hadn't expected his son to help Dainn escape. And Dainn had no explanation.

But he did know that Danny had more than one brother, as well as a half-sister. One of those brothers in ghostly form had attacked the loft and provided the means for Vali to take Anna and Orn.

"Is he here?" Dainn asked urgently, remembering how Loki had denied being responsible for the phantom serpent's appearance.

Was it possible . . .

"You have to help," Danny insisted.

"Help how?" Dainn asked, instinctively putting his arms around Danny to protect him from the cold he apparently didn't feel.

Protect *him*. Svardkell's final words. "Protect the boy."

The blood drained out of Dainn's face. He had assumed that boy to be Ryan. But now he knew he had been wrong.

Danny squirmed out of Dainn's arms and pulled hard on his hand. The boy was remarkably strong, and Dainn took an involuntary step forward. He scooped Danny up into his arms and broke into a jog, heading south toward the loft.

"Dainn!"

Loki's voice, the tingling sensation of magic at Dainn's back, magic ready to strike. He found himself coming to a sudden halt, compelled to return to the bridge.

"Put him down," Loki said, "and bring him to me."

Dainn searched for his enemy. Loki stood several yards away from the bridge, apparently bereft of his usual Jotunn escort. But Dainn knew they were there, as surely as he knew the boy was in danger.

"Bring him to me," Loki repeated, ice and fire crackling in the air around him.

Danny clung to Dainn's hand with that surprising, tenacious strength and shook his head. "No," said.

"What do you want with him?" Dainn shouted against the wind.

"He *is* my son," Loki said, his red hair whipping across his face, green eyes dancing with satisfaction. "I don't want him running about all over a dangerous city. Of course you are welcome to join us."

Dainn felt a blast of heat on his face and pushed Danny behind him again just as the middle of the bridge caught fire.

It was clearly none of Loki's doing. Laufeyson leaped back, as startled as Dainn. The fire expanded into a ring and suddenly cooled to a golden green, the center framing a tinted, semi-transparent surface like a stained-glass window.

Through the glass Dainn could make out a flat plain rolling ahead of them where the rest of the bridge should be—a dry, moonlit steppe scattered with thin patches of snow and broken only by low shrubs and the occasional scrubby tree. Hills rose in the distance, and shapes moved closer to the portal—long-legged horses cropping at winter grasses.

It was not a bridge to Ginnungagap, but it was very real. Danny squirmed loose of Dainn's hold, ran pell-mell at the opening and vanished through it. Jotunar lumbered after him while Loki lifted his hands and began to chant.

The giants never made it through. They struck the "glass" through which the boy had passed, pain and astonishment on their faces. Loki dropped his hands and ran toward the portal.

Dainn hesitated. A part of him believed that Danny would want him to follow, would have left the way open for him. But if he had guessed incorrectly . . .

The motorcycle leaped toward Dainn like a snow leopard, the woman astride it as fierce and bright as one of the White Christ's avenging angels.

"Get on!" Mist yelled just as Loki spun around to face them. Dainn swung up behind her as she gunned the engine, clutched the accelerator, twisted it hard, and barreled through the portal.

Silfr's wheels skidded on mud slick with recent snow. Mist braked both front and back, spinning in a circle as she tried to avoid the boy who had run ahead of them.

"The portal is closing," Dainn said behind her, his arms still tight around her waist.

Mist looked back, her vision quickly adjusting to the surrounding darkness. The portal, previously a ring of pulsing green and gold, was now a strange, glassy distortion in the air, seemingly opaque but with the unfamiliar landscape visible around it as if it were suspended just above the ground.

"Do you think Loki can get through that thing?" she asked.

"I do not know who or what controls it," Dainn said, uncertainty in his voice, "but I do not believe so."

And how many times has Dainn been wrong? Mist asked herself. She waited for Dainn to dismount and then did so herself. A chill gust of wind sweeping across the plain caught her loose hair, flinging it across her face and into her mouth.

"Are you all right?" she asked Dainn, pulling strands away from her lips.

"Yes," he said. His bare feet slid on brittle grass, and Mist thought he was focusing just a little too much attention on catching his balance. The ragged ends of a loose, blood-soaked bandage fluttered around his right hand. When he looked up, he saw her staring and attempted to hide the injured hand behind his back.

Mist moved to grab it, unwound what remained of the bandage— soaked through with Loki's magic as well as Dainn's blood—and held his hand palm-up between her own. The scar she'd noticed before was red and angry, tracing a swollen path across his skin.

She didn't have to ask if it hurt.

"What happened?" she demanded. "I returned to the loft and found blood everywhere."

"I apologize for any damage," Dainn said, pulling his hand free of hers. "Why did you go back to the loft?"

"I felt—" She broke off, not yet prepared to discuss the sense of disaster that had sent her speeding back to the loft . . . the certainty that Dainn was in desperate trouble. He'd been in plenty of trouble other times, but this profound awareness—this *connection*—was something new, stronger than anything that had come before.

"How did you get free of Gleipnir?" she countered.

"That is how I reinjured my hand," he said in a perfectly calm and reasonable voice, as if he snapped unbreakable magic chains every day. "The Chain could not hold me."

"So this puts us back at square one," she said wearily.

"You might have been rid of me had you not returned to Abrew."

"Rid of you?" she asked. "Because Vidarr might have killed you?" She looked up at the incredible display of stars. "I think *he* would be the one pushing up the daisies."

"I thought you meant to save Anna and Orn."

"That was my intention," she said. "I was pretty pissed off when I found you'd left the loft. I just about gave up on you. But the idea of leaving you with Loki . . ." She hunched her shoulders. "The idea of letting you run loose where I couldn't keep an eye on you just seemed too dangerous."

Dainn looked away quickly. "So you returned to Asbrew, and I was no longer there."

"I thought Loki had taken you back to his headquarters, but once I tried out a couple of basic tracking spells I realized Laufeyson had left Asbrew without you. I went looking, figuring you'd escaped, and there seemed to be some kind of blockage every time I got near this area." She rubbed a smudge of muddy slush from her chin. "I'd never run across anything like it before. I don't think I would have found you if not for this." She jerked up her wrist to display the tattoo. "It nearly burned my hand right off again."

"But it aided you this time."

"Yes. And at that point, it suddenly became a game of hot-warm-cold. It still took me hours to find you." She looked for the child, who was walking toward a herd of horses, eight or nine of them watching his approach with pricked ears. "Who is he, and why is he with you?"

"The boy . . . transported me from Asbrew," Dainn said. "We only just arrived."

"Six hours after you left?" She did a double take, staring at the boy again as if she'd only just seen him. "Wait. You mean he tele-ported you or something? Who in Hel *is* this kid?"

Dainn flinched, a small muscle jumping under the skin of his cheek. "It is complicated," he said. "He—"

Before he could finish, the boy, chortling with laughter, led the horses toward her and Dainn, the animals flaring their nostrils and twitching their elegant ears forward and back. The mare in the lead bobbed her head in a friendly gesture, and the gelding right behind her nickered a greeting.

They encircled Dainn and Mist, bumping and prodding at their heads, necks, shoulders, and arms, lipping at loose hair. Dainn stroked their powerful necks, whispering endearments in the tongue of the Alfar.

One of the horses poked its head over Dainn's and thrust its muzzle right into Mist's face. She jerked her head aside, not because she didn't like horses but because she wasn't in the mood to get a mouth-and nose-full of slobber in her face.

"This sure as Hel isn't Ginnungagap," she said. "Where are we?"

"Somewhere else in Midgard, I believe," Dainn said.

"I'd never have guessed." She examined Danny more carefully. "Did he also—"

"I can confirm that Vali is a traitor," Dainn said suddenly, cutting her off. "He promised to help me retrieve Anna and return her to you. Of course I realized it might be a trap, and so it was."

"Anna told us. Vidarr was in on it, just as we suspected."

"Yes. He was clearly working with Loki in spite of his former protestations to the contrary, but it was his intent to kill me rather than turn me over to Laufeyson. Loki, however, was alerted by Vali, who apparently knows which wolf not to tease."

"Did you happen to find out why Vid and Vali went over to Loki in the first place?"

"I believe Vali is acting more out of fear than any desire for power, which is surely what Vidarr hoped to gain by working with the Slanderer."

"Then he's as stupid as I always thought he was. But Vali . . . why would he tell us where to find Sigrun and Eir if he was going to be-tray us and give Loki the same information?"

"Perhaps," Dainn said slowly, "he is not yet sure where his true loyalties lie."

Mist refused to hope that Vali was playing some kind of deeper game against Loki. That kind of subtlety wasn't in his nature. "Vidarr won't have that problem," she said. "Where is he now?"

"I doubt Loki killed him, which can only mean that Laufeyson still has use for him."

"Good luck to him," Mist said. "At least now Anna's safe. But Orn—"

"Loki claimed that he had flown away with the pendant," Dainn said.

"When Loki was pretending to look like me."

"You saw?"

"Anna told me. That was a nice trick. How long did you believe it?"

"Not long."

"But long enough." She locked her fists behind her back, remem-bering that the nasty desire to taunt Dainn over his inability to see through Loki's illusions was only a result of her own frustration. And maybe something even more shameful. "Do you think he was telling the truth?"

Dainn hesitated. "I do not believe he has Orn. And if Orn is free, surely he will return to Anna."

"Will he?" Mist grunted as the affectionate horse bumped her chin, nearly breaking one of her teeth. "I still don't know why the Hel he came to me in the first place." She stared hard into Dainn's eyes. "Again, who is this kid? Why did he transport you, and how did this . . . portal appear right in the middle of Lefty O'Doul?"

"As you said, this"—he gestured toward the small distortion hang-ing in the air—"is not a bridge between worlds. It is clearly meant to connect one part of Midgard to another."

"So how did it happen to appear?"

He looked at the laughing boy with an odd tenderness in his expression. "I believe that Danny was responsible."

"*Danny?*"

He explained Loki's "visit" to the loft in a few terse sentences. Mist knew he was doing his usual job of concealing something important, something he didn't want her to know. She hadn't thought she could get much angrier.

She'd been mistaken.

"Loki came to the loft," she said, "and you didn't bother telling me?"

"Calling your attention to Loki's visit would have resulted in a battle you could ill afford so soon after the last, and you know what might happen if I felt compelled to attack him. He seemed quite intent on claiming he had nothing to do with Jormungandr's actions."

"And you actually believed him?"

"I—" He broke off, and then rushed ahead. "I am certain that it is this child, not Loki, who sent Jormungandr, and perhaps the manifestation of Freya at the loft. Not because he wished to cause harm to us, but because he was led to these acts without understanding what he did."

"*This* kid?"

"Even so."

"Led to them? By Loki?"

"Yes. Because Danny is Loki's son."

"I have to find Orn," Anna said, feeling as if the factory walls were closing in around her.

Bryn and Rota, who had been watching her for the past couple of hours as if she were a piece of precious crystal a stray breeze might shatter, shook their heads in near unison.

"You have to sit tight," Rota said soothingly, primping her endless tumble of red locks . "We don't know where to look for him yet, but you can be sure Mist'll put everything into it."

"Loki made himself look like Mist so he could get to Dainn," Anna said, "but he didn't seem worried about Orn at all. What if he already knows where Orn is?"

"Maybe he just wasn't interested," Rota said. "It's not as if Orn has told Mist anything useful, if you'll forgive my frankness."

"He might have decided the raven's no threat to him," Bryn added.

"No threat to him?" Anna said, trying to think with her head instead of her heart. "Orn's tied up in everything that's happened. I told you that Vidarr made some kind of bargain with Loki so he could get Orn and Loki could have Dainn. But once Loki had Dainn, he'd never just let Vidarr keep Odin's messenger."

"Sit down and drink your coffee," Bryn said. "This isn't helping."

Anna sat at one of the card tables the Jotunar had set up, taking the cooling mug between her hands and gripping it until her fingers ached. "Maybe Orn escaped while Vidarr was with Dainn and me, or he was already gone, and Vidarr was bluffing all along."

"Just so he could kill Dainn?" Bryn said with a snort. "What in Hel was he thinking?"

"I don't know," Anna said. "We don't even know if he's alive or dead."

"Or if Dainn is, for that matter," Rota said.

Anna almost spit out her coffee. "Why has Mist been gone so long? If she thinks Loki has Dainn, she—"

"Might do something stupid," Rota said, her full lips pursed. "In fact, we think she already has."

"So why aren't you trying to help her?"

"We would, if we knew where to look," Bryn said. "After we brought you home, Mist went back to Asbrew. She told us not to follow her, but we did anyway. We tried getting into the bar, but the door was warded. If we hadn't found Vali outside—"

"You found Vali?" Anna asked. "He didn't go with Loki?"

"We don't know. He got away before we could grab him, but he told us that Loki didn't take Dainn. The elf just . . . disappeared with some little kid."

Anna had learned not to be surprised by anything her semi-divine protectors told her. "Did Mist *see* this happen?" she asked.

"We don't know that, either. Rota and a couple of my people checked out Loki's headquarters. If Mist had been around, we'd have picked up some magical trace. It's as if she just disappeared, too—bike and all."

"That doesn't mean we stopped looking," Rota said. "But I don't think Mist wanted us to find her. And believe me, she can make sure we don't."

"And what do we do while she's gone?" Anna demanded. She pushed her chair back. "I'm not just going to sit here and—"

"You can't fight," Bryn interrupted. "If Loki gets you, he'll have a weapon to use against Orn."

"If Loki thinks he can get Orn back through me," Anna said, sinking back into her chair, "then maybe my being *here* means Orn will return to Mist."

"Good reason not to go haring off now," Rota said. "She knows what she's—"

She broke off. There were noises from the direction of Illinois, and Bryn shot to her feet.

"Stay with her, Rota," she said. "Some of my people are out there, but it sounds like a pretty big commotion."

Anna shifted in her seat and strained to hear. Rota was listening, too, and not paying very much attention to her mortal charge. With a casual sweep of her arm, Anna pushed the mug to the floor, where it broke into chunks and splash coffee all over the concrete floor.

Rota jumped up, surprisingly strong curses coming out of her sensuous mouth as she noticed the dark liquid splashed on her red leather spike-heeled boots.

"I'm sorry!" Anna said. "I'll get a mop right away."

While Rota was using a paper towel to clean her boots, Anna slipped out through the factory's side door and sprinted toward Illinois.

And came to a startled halt.

The reason for the "commotion" was very clear. There were perhaps two dozen people standing in the street . . . strangers, some clearly bewildered, some curious, others determined. Anna saw uniforms of several kinds, suits, casual clothing on men and women alike, and she knew they were all supposed to be here.

Mist's mortal allies, finally come at last. And Anna had a feeling that they were going to be plunged into a boiling cauldron before they'd even felt the steam.

Nothing Dainn had said of the boy's appearance at Loki's headquarters, and again at the loft, had prepared Mist for this.

"You're telling me that Loki has a kid no one ever knew about?" she asked. "Or is he one of the others hiding in a human child's shape?"

"I have no doubt whatsoever that he is what he appears to be," Dainn said. "At first, I believed he was subject to what mortals call autism, or some similar condition. He could hardly speak when I first met him, and showed little interest in the world around him. I have since realized that he possesses abilities that may even exceed his father's."

"No kidding," Mist said. A hard gust of wind, unhindered by any obstacle on the nearly featureless plain, knocked her against one of the overaffectionate horses, and she took a moment to sort her questions into some semblance of order. "If Loki wasn't ready to provoke another fight when he met you at the loft, why was he so intent on showing the kid to you? Wouldn't that be a huge disadvantage to him, if you guessed how powerful the boy—Danny—really is?"

"He could honestly claim that he had not used Jormungandr to attack us, because that was the literal truth. I have no doubt that he enjoyed the game."

"And why would he send a manifestation of Freya?"

"Perhaps to sow distrust between us, or to make us believe Freya had returned."

"And *this* could be a trap. The boy could summon another monster and try to kill us right here."

The beast flared in Dainn's eyes. "Danny is an innocent, free of Loki's taint."

"Like Jormungandr? Like Fenrir?" She held Dainn's gaze, wondering why he had reacted so strongly to her suggestion. "If Danny did send the Serpent, or whatever it was, at Loki's behest, it doesn't matter if he knows what he's doing or not. Loki is using him to attack us, and it's working all too well."

"I can only assure you that this boy is bereft of the evil qualities to be found in Loki's surviving offspring," Dainn said, the threat in his eyes replaced by entreaty. Mist didn't know which was worse.

"Loki claimed the boy was born in the Void," Dainn went on. "Time in Ginnungagap is not measured as it is here, so it is difficult to determine Danny's true age. But he is, in every way, still very much a child."

"Loki didn't happen to mention the mother, did he?"

"He avoided the subject entirely."

"But *you're* not related to the kid. Why is he so interested in you? Why rescue you from his own father and make this portal to help you escape?"

"I do not understand his apparent affection for me," Dainn murmured, pausing to watch the boy wander fearlessly among the horses as they drifted away. "When I found him outside Loki's headquarters, he came to me without hesitation, as if he sought my help. Perhaps a part of him realizes that Loki's actions are wrong."

"And it never occurred to you that Loki set it up that way?"

"It had. But I now believe that Danny was the boy that Svardkell meant for us to protect. To save."

It was difficult for Mist to hear her father's name without grief. "From *Loki*?"

"Yes. Not only for our sake or his, but for a much greater purpose."

"To keep Loki from using him as a weapon?"

"Svardkell never had a chance to make his meaning clear, or explain how he knew these things. I can only tell you what I believe to be true."

Dainn turned, walked toward the horses, and, stopping very close to Danny, reached out as if to touch the boy's soft ginger hair. There was real affection in the gesture, a kind of tenderness that almost took Mist's breath away.

Mist watched them, wondering what she was missing. There obviously was *some* kind of bond between them, a bond that superseded the boy's connection to his lying bastard of a father. And if he was powerful enough to sense the beast under Dainn's skin, he clearly wasn't afraid. Quite the opposite.

As she jogged to catch up with Dainn, the horses turned about as one, facing away from their two-legged guests. The moonlight glistened on something behind the horses, a shape moving more swiftly than the fastest thoroughbred. Its coat bore a metallic sheen halfway between gold and silver, and its mane and tail were so long they nearly brushed the earth.

Like courtiers in the presence of their king, the horses bowed their heads. The stallion slowed to a prance, his muscles rippling under glossy skin, his proud neck arched like a swan's.

And he danced on eight hooves, as graceful as a spider spinning its web.

"Sleipnir," Mist whispered.

26

The house was very old, very grand, and very ugly. And probably haunted.

"This is it?" Ryan asked Tashiro.

They stood on a hill in Benicia overlooking the Carquinez Strait, with San Francisco out of sight behind brown hills that should have been green from mild winter rains. There were large, dead-looking brown shrubs all around the house, a couple of tall bare trees, a wide porch with a swinging chair, and multi-paned windows under a ga-bled roof. The door looked as if it hadn't been occupied in twenty years.

He hadn't seen *this* coming. Not even a little of it. When he'd unexpectedly met Koji on Third Street, he hadn't been prepared.

But he'd come anyway, though he still didn't know why Tashiro had kept all this from Mist.

"Shit," he muttered. "I thought my aunt was rich."

"She is," Tashiro said, not even bothering to look at him. "Just not in the way you expected."

"You mean you lied to me and Gabi," Ryan said.

"I agreed to bring you here," Tashiro said. "Now my work is done."

"What the hell is that supposed to mean? You think I'm going to *stay* here?"

"You'll be taken care of," Tashiro said, no warmth in his voice at all. He set off at a fast walk toward the rickety garden gate—if you could *call* it a garden—and on to the curved driveway beyond.

"Hey!" Ryan shouted, beginning to follow. "You can't just—"

He froze. The door to the haunted house was starting to open, creaking and groaning on ancient hinges.

A woman walked out onto the porch. She looked like a bag lady to Ryan, all dressed in layers and layers of clothes that didn't match, shirts on top of shirts and layers of skirts that fell almost to her ankles. She wore about a dozen necklaces and jangly bracelets hanging from her wrists, and a scarf wound around her head.

No, not a bag lady, Ryan thought. A gypsy, like the fortune-tellers he'd seen in old movies. She had all kinds of pouches attached to her colorful woven belt, and other stuff Ryan couldn't identify stuck in her clothes.

"I am no ghost," the woman said, stepping with surprising agility down from the porch. "Nor am I precisely your aunt. I had expected Mr. Tashiro"—she nodded in the direction the lawyer had gone—"to do a better job of arranging matters, but it appears he was not able to perform his work to my expectations. That, alas, is only further indication of my waning abilities." She smiled warmly. "Fortunately, you are where you are meant to be."

"Who are you?" Ryan asked, noticing for the first time that her eyes were such a pale blue as to look almost white. "What do you want?"

"You have nothing to fear from me," the gypsy woman said. "My ability to act upon this world is scanty indeed. That is one reason I need you, Ryan Starling." She spread her hands to indicate the property. "Your inheritance is so much more than this. More than can become clear to you until you begin to learn what I will teach you."

"What are you talking about?" Ryan asked, backing away.

"My name is Mother Skye," she said. "And I will teach you how to become all you are meant to be."

Crying out with joy, Danny ran straight into Sleipnir's chest and embraced the broad neck. Odin's mount snorted into Danny's hair, blowing it every which way. The animal's startling blue eyes examined Dainn over the boy's shoulder.

"This is my brother!" Danny said, beaming as he turned to Dainn. "Can I play with him now?"

Mist found herself gaping in astonishment. Dainn sat on the short grass, looking as dazed as she felt.

"He spoke of his brother on the other side," he said. "He wanted my help. But I did not realize . . ."

"Sleipnir," Mist repeated, joining him on the ground. "The Slipper. The only decent child Loki ever had."

"And one of Odin's Treasures," Dainn said. "Danny has led us to him."

"I still don't understand what in Hel's going on. Why would he do that?"

"I have no idea."

They both looked back at the portal while Sleipnir bounced around Danny like a rowdy puppy, his eight legs working in perfect unison.

"Okay," Mist said, expelling her breath. "Let's say this is some kind of—gift—from Danny to you, for some incomprehensible reason. We both know that Loki's waiting on the other side, ready to grab whoever goes back. We have to get the kid and Sleipnir to San Francisco without returning the way we came."

"If we are where I believe we may be, it will be difficult to transport the horse by conventional means. But Danny—"

The boy looked around as if he'd heard his name.

"Danny," Dainn said, beckoning as he got to his feet.

Leading the eight-legged steed with a hand on the stallion's shoulder, Danny ran to the elf and grinned up at him expectantly.

Sleipnir nudged Danny gently out of the way and paced up to Dainn, his ears telegraphing a certain ambivalence that only a fool could mistake. Dainn bowed.

"Well met, Bearer of Odin," he said in the Old Tongue.

Sleipnir snorted and backed away until he was beside Danny again. Dainn dropped to his knees and extended his arms. Danny ran into them as if he'd known Dainn all his life.

"Danny," Dainn said, "Has Sleipnir spoken to you?"

"How do you know he—" Mist began.

"I could hear them," Dainn said, impatience in his voice. "Danny?"

The boy nodded gravely. "He doesn't like Loki."

"Does he know why he was sent here?"

"Yes. He wants to come with us."

"Good. Can you take us back the same way you brought us here, but perhaps in a different place where Loki can't find us?"

Grasping Dainn's hand, Danny held on until the elf got to his feet. The lead mare of the watching herd trotted back to the elf and bumped his chest with the full force of her considerable weight.

Dainn's expression changed. Without hesitation, he leaped nimbly onto her back. All at once Danny was atop Sleipnir, and Dainn was holding his uninjured hand down to Mist. She grabbed it and settled on the mare's bare back behind him.

She'd spent plenty of time on horseback over the centuries in Midgard, and even longer before the Last Battle as a Valkyrie in Asgard. But Dainn was an elf, who could become one with the natural world.

This was not a cold city of steel and concrete. Here his feet touched the grass, and the air he breathed was almost clean. He was part of the mare, not a trace of the beast left in him. The taut muscles of his waist flexed under Mist's arms, and his hair whipped behind his head like the horse's flaxen mane.

Mist spat a few black strands out of her mouth, her throat tight with unexpected emotion. She pressed her face into the warm skin of Dainn's back, smelling him, hearing the steady rush of the breath in his lungs, feeling the rhythmic bunch and release of muscle under her cheek. For one terrifying moment she wished it would never end.

The mare jumped, knocking Mist out of her dream. She straightened, pulling her hands away from Dainn's waist and balancing herself with her legs gripping the mare's loins. A woman on a fine white gelding was riding bareback to meet them, her hands resting loosely on her mount's withers. Her hair was as white as her horse's—not merely blond, but silver—wrapped around her head in two thick braids. Her face was strong, what mortals had once called "handsome," and the body under her rough winter clothing was wiry and lean.

She lifted one hand in greeting as Sleipnir pranced up beside Dainn's mare, lifting one leg after another in a fine display any Lipizzaner would envy.

"Show-off," the woman said in the Old Tongue. She studied Mist with watchful eyes. "It's about time you came," she said in accented English. "Spider hasn't given me a moment's peace with all his dancing and bugling."

Mist slid off the mare's back. "Hild," she said, hardly surprised at all. "You expected us?"

"We expected *someone*. Sleipnir didn't see fit to share his secrets."

Odin's balls, Mist thought. Now horses were predicting the future.

"I have a lot to tell you," she said.

Hild nodded. She looked toward Dainn, who had dismounted as the other horses milled around them. "Alfr," she said. "*That* I didn't expect."

"Lady Hild," Dainn said, inclining his head.

"Do I look like a lady?" Hild asked with a touch of sarcasm. "I was just a mortal once, like Mist."

Mist glanced away, far from prepared to tell her Sister that she wasn't some mortal lord's daughter after all.

"Is there a place we can talk?" she asked.

"My cottage." Hild looked at Danny, and then at Dainn and Mist again. "This is no ordinary lad," she said with a lift of one silver brow. "Yours?"

Dainn flushed, and Mist bit her lip. It occurred to her that Hild might be assuming that Danny was *their* son.

"No," Mist said. "It's . . . complicated."

"Danny, can you tell us if anyone tries to come through the portal?" Dainn asked.

Plucking at Sleipnir's large ears, Danny nodded. "They can't get in," he said.

"It seems you do, indeed, have much to tell me," Hild said. "Come into the house for a hot drink and fresh bread. I must become used to the idea that the quiet years I've spent here are coming to an end."

The child had deceived him, and Loki could only count himself a fool. A fool for believing Danny might help him bring Dainn back peacefully. A fool for allowing himself to hope that the boy was finally and consciously acting upon his parent's desires.

He'd been a fool too often of late. But then he'd had no idea that Danny could teleport, let alone carry Dainn with him such a distance. He had never guessed that Danny would even have *thought* to do so.

It seemed quite appropriate, however, that Danny had chosen the physical bridge where Loki had failed to open the metaphysical one—even though the portal was not truly a bridge at all, and led only to some other location in Midgard.

A location the boy had accessed from his own room.

Banking his rage, Loki strengthened his spell to ward off local traffic and approached the portal again, his Jotunar bumbling along behind him in an overly eager attempt to placate their master. He could see a sliver of light on the other side of the glassy surface, but it was as if he were looking through the wrong end of a telescope. Every attempt he had made to widen the portal had failed.

But he *had* been able to determine that Danny had found Sleipnir, and that he was evidently in no hurry to return. The boy seemed to have focused all his loyalty on the elf for the time being . . . a circumstance Loki would have used to his advantage if he'd had both Dainn and the child in his hands.

He hadn't expected Mist to find them first and pass through the portal herself.

Loki rubbed his hands together vigorously. It was time to try the spell he had been withholding until all others had failed.

Closing his eyes, he called up the Runes and Merkstaves. He didn't require the use of his own blood, the most powerful basis for any spell. He had something better.

Dainn's blood, soaked into the portion of the bandage Loki had torn from the elf's hand just before he'd escaped. Loki held the scrap of stained cloth between his hands, pressing his own scar into the fabric and drawing Dainn's blood out of it, letting the very atoms pass into his skin. The absorption brought on a kind of ecstasy that set Loki's heart to racing and filled his skull with brilliant light.

When his own hands were painted red, he dropped the cloth and walked onto the bridge, just short of the portal. He had already frozen the tiny aperture open with a remora's mouth of jagged ice, and the glazed surface reflected his distorted image as he drew the Runestaves with Dainn's blood. He chanted a summoning spell as each stave flowed into the next, melting ice and blood comingled. He pulled, and the Runes stretched from the portal's perimeter to his palms, gripping his scar as he became the puppet master. He tugged again, and blood began to run along the length of the strands.

He knew when he almost had it. He felt Dainn, and the boy, beginning to respond. But then the threads snapped, and something appeared almost directly over his head, a whirling cloud, a ragged tear in the air that opened onto an impenetrable darkness.

The sheer power of it revealed its nature instantly, and Loki laughed. He didn't know if the bridge to Ginnungagap was entirely the result of his own spell, or if Danny had unwittingly weakened the barriers between Midgard and the Void when he had created the portal.

It didn't matter now. Loki had what he'd been searching for since the bridges had closed.

"Grer," he said.

The Jotunn joined him immediately, snapping to attention.

"You will set all your men to guarding me, and give ground to no one. Do you understand?"

"Yes, Lord Loki."

As the Jotunar gathered into a protective cordon around him, Loki chanted the spells that effectively severed his awareness of his own body so that all his attention would be focused on the rift above him. He left only his autonomic nervous system functioning at full strength and locked his muscles so he would remain in place when he lost all sense of the mortal world. A heavy, snow-laced fog settled around him, so dense that he could see nothing beyond his hand before his face.

Every particle of his being, his magic, his mind fixed on the bridge to the Void. All the gray fog disappeared as if sucked into a vacuum, and Loki could see what lay beyond the rift: glittering walls, crystal furnishings, an immense hearth where flames crackled without melting even a drop of the icy hearth that cradled it. All was white, frigid familiarity.

Home. The palace Loki had hacked out of Ginnungagap, the place he hated, where his army awaited his summoning.

And they *were* waiting. A pair of Jotunar—one large and far from beautiful and one of the more refined type, not too dissimilar to an elf in his attractiveness—appeared in the room on the other side. They stared at Loki, mouths agape, as if they had never anticipated that their waiting might not be in vain.

Dimly aware that the Jotunar around him had gathered close to keep him from collapsing, Loki began to feel his body again. He held himself erect with sheer strength of will and built a path of ice that arched up to the rift, connecting Midgard and Ginnungagap.

"My lord!" the more attractive of the giants said, walking toward him down the shimmering path. Loki recognized him: Amgerd, a Jotunn of no great distinction who, nevertheless, was quite possibly more valuable to Loki than the pathetic creatures he still had left to him in Midgard.

The other giant, whose name Loki didn't remember, had the sense to wipe the stupid shock from his face. He bowed deeply. "I am Suttungr, my lord. We have been awaiting your summons." He glanced over his shoulder at the ice palace, already crowded with frost giants reacting with varying degrees of surprise, calculation, and glee in anticipation of battle.

And of possession of the world they had been promised.

"Is everything prepared?" Loki asked.

"We have never ceased our vigilance," Suttungr said. "We can move within an hour of your command."

One hundred Jotunar had been in Loki's original plan for the second crossing, since holding the bridge open for the first four dozen giants had been far from easy. But as he was nearly certain that this bridge was at least partly of Danny's inadvertent creation, he intended to get as many through as possible before it vanished.

"Assemble two hundred Jotunar," he said. "Have them assume mortal form. And do it quietly."

Suttungr raced back over the bridge. Amgerd remained with Loki, looking around in some confusion. "My lord," he said, "whom are we to fight? Where are our enemies?"

If Loki had not already been weary of berating his underlings, he might have lost his temper. "You will learn soon enough," he said. "Has anything changed in Ginnungagap since I last contacted you?"

"We can see little, my lord," the Jotunn said, "but our watchers believe that there has been conflict among the Aesir . . . a struggle for power that may have weakened them."

A struggle for power. Loki felt a jolt of shock, though he was not truly shocked at all. Only a handful of his Jotunar knew the truth of his original bargain with Freya. If his watchers in Jotunheim's

Shadow-Realm had noticed any activity at all, then at least some of the Aesir must have awakened.

Now it was clear why Freya had remained away from Midgard, and why Odin's messenger had suddenly arrived to work its own kind of pointless mischief. He had almost certainly thrown off the deep sleep Freya had imposed upon him and the other gods with her glamour and witch-magic. He had discovered her treachery. She might very well be struggling merely to survive, even if the Eitr was sufficient to preserve her from the worst of Odin's wrath.

But Odin had himself had neither arrived in Midgard nor achieved anything of significance with a certain truant, ebon-feathered ambassador.

And that, Loki thought, meant exactly nothing. The game had ended, but nothing else had changed. Freya might no longer be a consideration, but eventually Odin or one of the others *would* devise proper bodies and pass through the Void to challenge him.

Fortunately, he still had Danny. Or would, when he was finished here.

Loki looked beyond the mass of apparently human bodies beginning to crowd the other end of the bridge. "Where is Fenrisulfr?" he asked.

"Quarreling," Amgerd said, his voice low and cautious; he well knew the uneasy and contentious relationship between Loki and his eldest son.

"Naturally," Loki said with disgust. "With Hel?"

"Hel broods over the loss of her hall and so many of her subjects. Shall I summon them?"

"Fenrir only. Now, go."

Amgerd turned and ran up the bridge, dodging the Jotunar descending from the palace.

Keeping a close eye on the portal below the bridge, Loki waited impatiently for the Jotunar to arrive. They were a motley crew, for no two giants looked the same. They were tall and thin, or short and stout; ugly or handsome, bearded or clean-shaven; skilled in magic or only in battle. A few were even *ividyur*, giantesses, as ready for war as the males.

All were armed with weapons shaped from the very substance of the Void, but as solid as any forged in Midgard—axes and swords, daggers and clubs and the rare bow none but another Jotunn—or the most powerful Aesir—could draw.

The bridge was beginning to grow unstable when the group was fully assembled, large portions of the ice-ramp melting away. Amgerd had still not returned with Fenrir. Suttungr stood before the rest, his club on his shoulder, his beard flowing nearly to his waist.

"What is your command, my lord Loki?" he asked.

Loki watched the bridge disappear completely, the rent in the sky vanishing as if it had never been, and turned his attention to the portal. It had begun to crack open, the aperture gradually widening as if a blowtorch had been rigorously applied to thin, cloudy plastic.

This was not Danny's work, Loki thought. Nor was it *his*. Something—or someone—else was involved.

"Scatter and hide yourselves," he said to his warriors. The veil of heavy snow he had manifested throughout the area was beginning to thin, and Loki could not allow any unexpected observers now that dawn was soon to break.

Weak as he was, he called up a spell drawn from the very heart of his nature—the foremost of Jotunar, equal to the Aesir in every way. He knelt and placed his palm flat on the ground.

Creeping like some foul sludge, the blood still remaining on his palm began to spread, forming a thin layer of ice so transparent that it could scarcely be seen by mortal eyes. It radiated outward with increasing speed, covering the steel bridge on which he crouched; the streets to either side; the withered grass of the nearby park; the parking lots to the west; north and south along Third Street as far as the eye could see.

Black ice. Ice so treacherous that no mortal could walk upon it, no vehicle gain purchase. By the time he was finished, most of the Jotunar had found concealment. There were few places to hide, but no one would get close enough to see them until they attacked.

"You and the others wait here," he said to Grer and his other personal guards. "I don't care if you must watch an hour or a week. You will inform me immediately when the aperture is wide enough for a Jotunn or mortal to pass through. Do you understand?"

"Yes, my lord."

Moving easily over the treacherous ice, Loki walked away from Lefty O'Doul Bridge and called for his chauffeur. As he climbed into the back seat, he glanced at his palm. The wound was only a faint scar now, as if it had been made many years before.

Loki knew it wasn't really closed at all. And never would be.

27

Mist let off a string of expletives so inventive that Dainn was almost tempted to ask her where she had learned them. But under the circumstances, such a question would not be wise.

Not only because of her foul mood, but because he had been less than well during many of the long hours that he and Mist had remained with Danny, Hild, and Sleipnir on the steppes. The sickness had come on suddenly, when his wound had begun bleeding afresh and left him nearly prostrate with pain.

He had not understood the reason for the wound's reopening when he had left the loft, and he understood it no better now. Fortunately, he had been able to hide his illness from Mist and replace Loki's bandage with cloths he'd discovered in Hild's cottage.

But he had found it increasingly difficult to communicate clearly with Danny. And until this moment, there had been no change in the portal whatsoever.

Now its "seal" was dissolving. Danny seemed oblivious in his play with Sleipnir, though Hild had emerged from the cottage and stood behind Mist, muttering softly in Russian as the moon broke through a haze of low-lying clouds.

She, too, found a number of interesting curses with which to regale her companions. "*Blin!* Did the boy—"

"He had nothing to do with this," Dainn said, getting to his feet. "Perhaps the portal was never meant to last so long."

Or Loki has found a way to open it. He left Mist with Hild and walked toward Sleipnir, doing his best to conceal his unsteady galt. He touched Danny's dangling foot.

"Danny," he said gently.

The boy's eyes were almost glazed, as if he had drifted into another world: seemingly unaware of his surroundings, unresponsive, gently rocking on Sleipnir's back while the horse endured with infinite patience.

Dainn understood immediately that the boy would be of no help. A fresh stab of pain in Dainn's palm nearly sent him to his knees. He heard Mist's footfalls behind him and quickly concealed his hand again.

Is he all right?" she asked, nodding toward Danny.

"I doubt he will be able to help us," Dainn said. "If we wish to escape Loki, we must ask Sleipnir if he will bear us away from this place."

"Bear us away? You don't mean—" Her eyes widened as she looked from Dainn to Sleipnir's eight powerful legs.

This spider could fly.

She turned and strode across the brittle grass to rejoin her Sister. They engaged in a brief conversation, and then both returned to Dainn.

"He hasn't flown since I brought him to Midgard," Hild said with her usual terseness. "I don't know if he'd be willing."

"Can you find out?" Mist asked.

With a brief frown at Dainn, Hild cupped Sleipnir's velvet muzzle in her hand and spoke to him softly. He stared at her without recognition.

Hild dropped her hand. "Either he isn't listening, or he can't hear me," she said. "*You* try it, Alfr. You're the ones who are supposed to breed the finest horses in the Nine Homeworlds . . . or did."

Odin's mount bobbed his head up and down several times and snorted forcefully, slewing his head around to stare at Dainn.

Slowly Dainn moved to place his unbloodied hand on Sleipnir's neck. The horse hopped backward, half rearing, and snapped at

Dainn's fingers. Passive and oblivious, Danny clung to the Slipper's back like a monkey.

"There is your answer," Hild said.

Dainn stared at his hand, stunned by Sleipnir's hostility. "He will bear Danny away," he said, "but not the rest of us."

"Then let him take the kid to safety," Mist said, "and we'll get ready to fight."

"No!" Danny cried. Sleipnir tossed his head, snorting and squealing, but Danny slid from his back and stood as straight as the boldest warrior. "I want to stay," he said. "With you."

"And *there's* your answer," Mist said. "The most important thing is to protect the boy." She met Dainn's gaze. "We're going to need the beast."

"No," Dainn said, panic seething in his chest. "If I lose control, and hurt Danny—"

"You won't."

Dainn touched the bulge of the pouch under his waistband. He still had the herbs, but he had no desire to trust their efficacy again. "What will *you* do?" he asked, already knowing the answer.

"Call on every ounce of ability I have." She shivered. "Loki's not going to back down this time. It's going to be all-out war. If I can make the ancient magic work for me, I'm going to use it."

Tell her, Dainn thought. *Tell her what you should have told her a dozen times before.*

But Freya wasn't here. There was still no sign that she would ever return.

And he had not forgotten Loki's offer. "Listen to me," he said. "Perhaps if I meet Loki before he passes through the portal—"

"And what? Give yourself up to save us?" She laughed. "There's something I think you're forgetting. No matter how much he wants you, he's going to want his son more. And he's not going to stop."

"Nevertheless, I can try," he said.

"And I can slug you before you take one step toward the portal."

They gazed at each other, and Dainn was lost. He understood

nothing but that this Valkyrie and this child were more precious to him than all the mortal lives in Midgard combined. He would extinguish the universe to save them.

But he could not stop Mist from stopping him.

"If you find yourself beginning to lose awareness of who you are," he said, "you must promise to resist it. Resist it with all your strength, or I may be compelled to take extreme measures to bring you back."

"Narfi's entrails, I don't like it any more than you do."

"I will do everything I can," he said. "Mist."

Her eyes were suspiciously bright. "What now?"

"Do not forget your promise."

"What promise?"

"To end my life, should I become too dangerous."

"I never made any such—"

"Must I beg?"

"No." She turned her face away, one hand raised to silence him. "I promise."

Hesitantly, as if she were a skittish mare that might startle at too swift a touch, he brushed her shoulder with his fingertips.

"I am sorry for the many times I have deceived you," he said. "But I was never anything but your friend." He bowed his head. "It has been my honor to serve you, Lady Mist, and to fight by your side, even if I have frequently . . ." He smiled, ever so slightly. "Even if I have as often complicated your mission as assisted in it."

"Shut up," she said, smearing the tears across her face with her fist. "Just shut up. We're not dead yet."

He looked away, giving her time to gather herself. After a while he heard her take another deep breath and knew the crisis was over.

"Hild," she said, "stay with Sleipnir and Danny. We'll do our best not to let Loki get anywhere near you. You're the last line of defense. Get them away if it starts to look bad."

Hild nodded, put her hand on Sleipnir's nose, and led the horse and Danny toward the cottage. As they were disappearing behind it,

Danny looked up, his face alight as if he had seen a shower of meteors illuminate the endless sky.

Dainn followed his gaze. He saw nothing, but he felt it: a weight above their heads, a storm about to break in a cloudless heaven.

He had never actually seen a bridge from the Void, and he well knew that there were only a handful of beings capable of opening a passage to and from Ginnungagap.

But no bridge should appear in this place, so far from the city where all the others were said to converge.

I am mistaken, he thought. *As in so much else.*

"Wake up," Mist said, barely touching his shoulder. "I'm going to need all your senses in working order."

Lying beside Mist just on the other side of a low hill facing the portal, Dainn caught the pungent smell of Jotunar riding on the chill breeze of a Russian dawn. Sunset had fallen over San Francisco, and the aperture had grown so wide that he knew it couldn't be much more than a few moments before the enemy broke through.

He glanced up. The storm he had felt overhead had neither dissipated nor expanded. The silence was absolute; not even the small nocturnal creatures who still braved the cold of winter dared stir.

The first Jotunn to enter the portal changed from an average, bearded man to an eight-foot-tall giant just as he stepped over the threshold, swinging his ax at Mist's head as she ran to meet him. Kettlingr's blade struck the ax like hammer striking anvil, and Dainn loosed the beast.

At first it refused to respond. As other Jotunar poured through the widening gap—carrying flails and axes and impossibly heavy swords, knives and clubs—a blast of bitter, ice-laden wind entered with them, freezing everything in its path and sealing Mist's and Dainn's feet to the ground. An *ividja*, a Jotunn woman, slipped under Mist's guard and struck her in the belly with her club.

Nothing more was required to fully awaken the beast than Dainn's sudden rage. His feet were no longer those of an elf, his vision no longer Alfar, his mind no longer completely rational. He slapped at the giantess with a massive paw, knocking her aside like so much chaff. One by one he ripped at the Jotunar who attempted to pass through, only half aware of Mist working free of the ice and blasting the giants with all the Galdr at her command.

Then the storm overhead broke, and something floated down from the sky: a figure, gold-limned, in elf's wool and leather—a woman the beast did not recognize but knew as he knew his own ravaged soul. She wore an Alfar body, borrowed or stolen, and when she alighted on the earth she looked straight at Dainn.

Instinctively he turned toward her, lowered his head between his shoulders and started in her direction. Mist's hand clamped on his heavily furred foreleg.

"Dainn!" she shouted. "I can't do this alone!"

He swung back toward her, struggling to find the means of speech. *Now* he must warn her, but no words would come.

Mist glanced over her shoulder, and a look of perplexity crossed her face. Blinding brilliance exploded inside Dainn's skull, and then she was fighting again in a way elf-Dainn recognized all too well: her face taking on a strange, ethereal glow, her magic sweeping up rocks from the soil to batter her enemies, flinging needles of ice back into their faces, blinding them with shafts of morning sunlight that transformed into spears of flame.

She was truly a goddess now, and she wielded the ancient, elemental magic as easily as she might toss a handful of dust into the air. But the female elf was striding toward her, and she had a terrible power of her own.

Power to take Mist—mind and body and soul.

Before Dainn could put himself between goddess and goddess, the flow of Jotunar through the portal stopped abruptly, and he could hear a new battle outside, in the part of Midgard the giants had left behind—cries and shouts and the clanging of steel, screams of pain and grunts of men and Jotunar succumbing to death. He smelled the new arrivals: Rota and Bryn, nearly all the Einherjar, a dozen mortals he failed to recognize.

Mist forced her way through the shredded margins of the portal, Kettlingr in one hand while the fingers of the other sketched Runes in the air, calling up a wind that would sweep all before it.

So, the elf-woman said. *It has come to this.*

The voice was inside his head, as it had been in the beginning. The voice he hated.

Dainn snarled, his massive heart pumping great quantities of blood into his limbs, all his will and his senses bent on killing. The power was within *him*, too. He could destroy her, now. Destroy her, before she could . . .

But suddenly Sleipnir was hurtling toward him, Danny perched on his back. As Odin's mount came to a stop, Danny slid to the ground and faced Dainn with confusion on his innocent face.

Kill him.

Dainn roared, clawing at his own head.

The boy is too powerful, the voice said with a gentleness that grotesquely contradicted her words. *He will destroy us all.*

Dainn dropped to all fours, losing even his ability to stand.

I can save you. This will be your last act at my command. Then you will be free.

The voice compressed his brain into a fist that held nothing of love in it, nothing of gentleness or compassion. But there was another voice inside him, one he knew as well as his own beating heart.

Take him, and we will be one.

The sacrifice, he thought with his last scraps of rationality. He scored deep ruts into the earth with his claws, struggling against his darkest self. He took a single step toward Danny, and then another. He broke into a run, charging toward the boy with no will to stop.

Danny stared up at him as he reared and swung his foreleg back, ready to rend the child in half.

"No," Danny said.

The spell shattered. Dainn cast out Freya's voice as he would expel rotten food from his body, and in moments he was an elf once more, his fingers scrabbling at the waistband of his pants, withdrawing the pouch, lifting it to his lips.

The herb fell into his open mouth, bitter as defeat. He swallowed it, felt it shock his entire system, burn into his blood, turn his limbs to rubber. He fell, utterly helpless, scarcely able to see Sleipnir kneel to let Danny climb up on his back, wheel about, and return the way they had come.

Dainn lay on his stomach, tears leaking from his eyes. He snatched handfuls of dry grass in his hands, searching for the life that pulsed underneath. He felt nothing. The earth and all it nurtured was as dead to him as hope itself.

He heard Mist run up behind him, pause, fling another deadly spell at those who pursued her, come to a sudden stop. Even now, deaf and blind as he was to the world, he could feel her mingled horror and grief. She was utterly unaware of the goddess so nearby.

"You were going to kill him," she said, anguish in her voice. "Sweet Baldr. You tried to . . ."

Dainn curled into himself, his head pressed to the earth. "End it now," he begged.

For an eternal moment all Dainn heard was the battle beyond the portal. Then he felt the chill of sharp metal against the back of his neck, requiring only a hard push to drive it through his spine.

Abruptly Mist withdrew the sword. "You stopped yourself again," she said. "You changed back."

How could he tell her it was none of his doing? That the beast had gone with the last of the herb, along with his magic?

He could not. But he could still protect the Valkyrie he served. Freya had shielded herself from her daughter's sight, and Mist was still in the greatest danger of her long life.

"Go," he said hoarsely. "The beast is gone. I . . . cannot harm Danny now." He pressed his face into the silent earth. "Your allies fight and die as we speak. Hold the Jotunar at the portal. It is our only hope . . . for his continued safety."

Mist was far too much a leader to allow her emotions to cloud her reason when the survival of her own people was at stake. She crouched beside him and dropped her plain knife on the ground near his hand.

"If you're wrong about the beast, try to slow it down. I told you I'd help you fight it, and I will." She got to her feet. "Just hold on."

Then she was running back for the portal, and Freya was suddenly standing above Dainn, black elven hair flowing gently about her face. The empty pouch dangled from her fingers.

"Very touching," she said. "My brave daughter has developed a strong affection for you, has she not? One might even say love, if she were capable of making such a mistake again. As *you* have." Her eyes glittered with spite. "I told you to prepare her. You did far more than that."

Dainn climbed to his knees, looking the way Mist had gone. She had vanished, and there was no one left fighting at the portal. He and Freya were alone.

"I did nothing but allow your daughter to recognize her potential," he said.

"You drove me out."

Laughter tore at his throat. "Have I so much power?"

"A kiss," she said. "How appropriate. How bold, how very clever of you to use my own ways against me." Her long shadow fell over him as she moved closer. "I admit that I was mistaken in believing that your desire to rid yourself of your beast would outweigh any unlikely attraction you might feel for a woman as blunt and unrefined as my daughter. But she was repulsed by your touch, as she is repulsed by this thing you have become."

"Yes," Dainn said, lifting his head. "But my method was successful."

"And yet here I stand." She glanced up at the bridge he had so foolishly ignored, the strangely localized storm that circled round and round in a clear morning sky. "A little trouble delayed me in the

Shadow-Realm," she said, "but it is over, and I will claim what is mine."

Dainn braced his arms and pushed himself to his feet. "And I," he said, "will stop you."

"How?" She dropped the empty pouch in front of him. "This substance seems to have robbed you of your one reliable weapon. Unless, of course . . ." She leaned close, her eyes heavy-lidded, full lips parted. "Unless you wish to try your 'method' on me again."

"I would not find it pleasant."

Her flawless face darkened. "Nor effective. You have lost more than your savagery, have you not?" She brushed the pad of her thumb across his lower lip. "An elf who loses his magic is no better than a beast."

The crushing weight of Dainn's loss was as nothing to his fear for Mist. And Danny.

"You can no longer protect my daughter, and that torments you, does it not?" Freya asked. She waved toward the portal, through which Dainn could still hear the clash of metal and cries of pain. "I know you wish to die. I shall grant your wish if you tell me who created this portal. Was it the boy?"

"Why do you want him dead?"

The Lady buffeted Dainn with a wave of lust that fogged his mind and hardened his body. "What does he mean to *you*?"

"Why . . . do you fear him?" Dainn gasped, fighting the helpless desire to tell her everything Danny had taught him.

She pushed Dainn to his knees. "He is Loki's son. But you know that, do you not?"

"I . . . took him from the Slanderer."

"And you let him live? Have you no comprehension of what he can do to this world and every one of us?"

"How is he more dangerous than his father?"

She flicked her fingers, and Dainn dropped to his belly. "Tell me where he is," she said.

"Gone."

"There is a bond between you. You can find him."

Find him, Dainn thought. His magic was gone, like the beast, but perhaps . . .

Run, he thought, flinging his thoughts outward, envisioning light like rays of the sun warming Danny's face, penetrating his strange, innocent, precious mind. *Save yourself.*

Freya swayed. "Be silent!" she screamed, pressing her fingers to her temples.

Dainn writhed on the ground, distantly aware that Freya was shaking uncontrollably, her features frozen in an expression of shock and terror.

But her moment of vulnerability was brief. She lifted her hands and assaulted Dainn with her glamour, turning him into another kind of beast.

"You long for death," she said, "but I will not kill you. I will find the boy, and destroy him. You may wander this world as you did before, knowing that those you love are lost to you forever. And I shall make quite sure that Mist believes you have betrayed her before I finish with her." She turned her back on him. "Now I must join my daughter. I would not wish her to suffer an injury before I claim her."

Dainn struggled to rise, to reach her, to kill her, to love her. Sex and death became one, spinning in an obscene dance, pulling his mind and soul and body apart like some medieval device of torture. He bit down on his tongue, driving the crippling lust away with pain.

"Freya," he called, spitting blood into the grass. "What was the trouble in the Shadow-Realm? Have you . . . quarreled with the All-Father?"

"Odin?" She turned toward him quickly, as if she was eager to refute him. "No. Our enemies, the Jotunar—"

"Why is the bridge here, Lady?" he said, feeling Freya's spell begin to lose its grip. "Why not in the city where your enemy waits? Is it because you did not create it at all?" He struggled to his knees again. "I think you have lost control, and that makes you desperate. You are terrified."

She strode back to him, struck him down, and clenched her fingers as the full force of her glamour tightened around his groin like a vise of white-hot barbs.

"I have changed my mind," she said, breathing fast. "When I am finished, I will return in Mist's body and kill the boy before your eyes."

She strode toward the portal, nothing of seduction in the jerky movements of her body. She paused by Mist's forgotten motorcycle and steered it toward the portal.

Dainn rolled onto his back. The pain receded. The rent in the sky from which the Lady had emerged remained open, and from it descended a path of silver mist, a surface that appeared as slick as ice and nearly as transparent.

Two, six, a dozen lean and graceful figures, some bearing Void-forced daggers and slender blades, descended along the path—Alfar, a full four dozen males and females racing toward the portal. Jotunar spilled through from the other side.

The Alfar stopped as one, drawing upon the flora and fauna rife in the grasslands to build their spells. In soft, taunting voices they lured the Jotunar onto the steppe where their power was greatest, weaving grass into nets, shaping dirt into smothering shrouds, raising small earthly creatures to climb and crawl over the Jotunar in a frenzy of frantic motion.

The giants began to retreat. As they scattered, Dainn glimpsed Freya passing through the portal, the elves at her heels.

But not all of them had gone.

Dainn had just managed to rise when three Alfar raced past him, running in the direction Sleipnir had taken Danny with the speed and agility of cheetahs on the hunt.

Gathering his uncertain strength, Dainn pursued them. As he approached Hild's cottage, he saw with a sinking heart that neither

Hild, Sleipnir, nor Danny had fled. Hild faced one of the Alfar with a long knife in her hand. Sleipnir—Danny astride and clinging to his mane—had risen on all four hind legs and was beating another elf back, while the third Alfr circled boy and horse, his voice rising in a spell-chant.

The circling Alfr saw Dainn, and their gazes locked. The elf broke away from the others and charged, a curved dagger gripped in his hand. He leaped, twisting lithely in midair, and came down with the dagger's point aimed at Dainn's neck.

28

Contorting his own body to avoid the blow, Dainn rolled and found his feet again before the elf could regain his balance. The elf dropped the dagger and raised his hands to call up a binding spell.

A single scream froze them both. The first of the Alfar had Danny in his arms, and the boy was fighting as if Dainn's beast had possessed him. Hild lay dazed on the ground, but Sleipnir had already put paid to the second elf.

Dainn wasted no more time. He attacked his distracted opponent, making use of his centuries of training, toughness he had developed over years of wandering Midgard and subjecting himself to every challenge, physical and mental, that could strengthen his control over the beast. He brought the other elf down and crouched over him, his arm across the Alfr's neck.

But the one who held Danny, now limp in his arms, was already running back toward the portal.

"Sleipnir!" Hild shouted. She scrambled to her feet, leaped onto the horse's back, and rode off in pursuit.

"You," Dainn's captive whispered in the elvish dialect of the Old Tongue. His eyes were filled with hate. "Faith-breaker. Coward."

Dainn made no effort to deny it. "The Alfar are no harmers of children. Why do you attempt to take the boy?"

"Loki's child." The Alfr tried and failed to spit. "The one who will destroy us all."

"Is that what the Lady told you?" Dainn said, bearing down

harder on his opponent's throat. "How will he carry out this destruction, and why?"

The Alfr coughed. "It is enough that the Lady knows of the danger."

"Why didn't you kill him, then, as she commanded *me* to do? Can it be that you did not fully trust Freya's claims?"

"We—"

"I, too, trusted her. Once." Dainn took the leap. "What has Freya done to the other Aesir?"

The elf stared at him as if he'd spoken gibberish. "The other Aesir . . . sleep to conserve their strength until Freya has cleared the path."

"Do they sleep, or are they gone?"

"I do not understand you."

"Would you serve Freya before your own people? What if you must choose between one and the other?"

"I would . . . serve us all by killing you." Suddenly there was an unelvish madness in his eyes, and he seized Dainn's wrist, gripping so hard that Dainn's bones ground together. His eyes widened.

"Gone," he said. "You have nothing." He heaved himself over, throwing off Dainn's restraining arm. Dainn lunged after him, struck his opponent's neck with the side of his hand and heard bone snap. The elf tore at the earth with clawed fingers, but the light was already fading from his eyes.

Dainn concealed his grief. "I am sorry," he said. "Is there anything you would have said to those you leave behind?"

The elf's fingers slackened. "She will destroy you."

"Perhaps. But I will do everything within my meager power to protect her daughter from her twisted schemes, whatever they may be, and fight to my last breath to see that the boy never becomes Loki's tool."

The elf sighed. "My name is . . . Skolmr. Farewell."

And then he died, having given the gift of his name. Dainn had no time to sing the song of passage and wish Skolmr a swift return to the earth. He got to his feet and ran toward the portal and San Francisco.

They fought side by side: the Einherjar; the mortals who had appeared so abruptly at the loft; the Alfar who had burst through the portal with the elf-woman who led them; Mist's two Sisters with knives and swords forged in Mist's own shop.

None of them was truly ready, especially not the mortals whose fighting skills wildly varied so widely. But Mist was. She drove Dainn from her thoughts as three of Loki's new Jotunar barreled toward her, axes as sharp as Hild's tongue, clubs as big as a man's torso.

The black ice underfoot made even the most careful movement treacherous, and it gave the Jotunar a fearsome advantage. Mist held her hands palm-up and began to prepare as Rota and one of the Einherjar, Fatty, tried to slow the Jotunar, Rota with her sword and the mortal with a heavy length of rebar.

Fatty slammed it down on one Jotunn's shoulder and went flying, swept aside by the giant's casual gesture. Rota managed to land a substantial blow on the ax-wielder's arm before she slipped to one knee on the ice and the Jotunar resumed their charge.

"Mist!" Rota cried.

Mist didn't look up. Wolves and ravens raced around her wrist, trailing agony. She called the forge-Runes, set them alight like coals in a hearth and cupped them in her free hand, holding steady as they burned her flesh. Just as the Jotunar came near enough to strike, she let them fall.

Molten fire raced away from the ice melting under her boots, reaching the first Jotunn's feet as he raised his club to strike. He shrieked as the searing heat enveloped his boot and climbed up his leg.

The other two Jotunar stopped for a moment, staring at their bellowing comrade, and then came at Mist. She caught one ax on Kettlingr's blade, ducked aside as the second Jotunn swung for her head, and skipped away just as the fire turned the ice underneath to boiling water.

The Jotunn tottered and fell, screaming as the water soaked through his breeches and scalded flesh. The third stepped back, his gaze snapping up to something behind Mist.

She had Kettlingr ready and another spell on her tongue when the two Jotunar behind her struck, but even the simplest Galdr required more than a few seconds to effect. She felt the breeze of an ax blade whistle past her ear, nearly severing it, before she realized why the Jotunn had missed.

The elf-woman who led the Alfar had plunged a slender but deadly spear through the giant's neck, and he was already dying. His companion had turned and was staring at the Alfr as if mesmerized by her striking beauty.

She grinned at Mist over the dying Jotunn and then looked up into the second giant's eyes. Abruptly he fell to his knees, and one of the male Alfar plunged another narrow blade into his neck.

Mist felt the battle fever fade from her mind and looked around. Two score Jotunar were scattered over the ice, many dead but with only the smallest wounds on their bodies—as if they, like the Jotunn the elf-woman had killed, had simply knelt and allowed themselves to be destroyed.

But there were a dozen desperate battles still being waged, mortals injured or dead, Bryn and Rota trying to protect them as they fought for their own lives. The Alfar were valiant, but they were vastly outnumbered by the Jotunar who survived.

Flexing her aching hand on Kettlingr's grip, Mist drew a deep breath and imagined the carnage necessary to win this fight. She could not be everywhere, and none of her Sisters had any magic of real worth in a battle. The Alfar were hamstrung by the asphalt and concrete and steel all around them, and by their lack of true connection to this world . . . the connection Dainn had developed over centuries of living in Midgard. Many of them would die, and so would most of the new mortal allies and Einherjar.

The ancient magic was at the tip of Mist's fingers. She had felt it come to her at the portal like an eager hound, taking her hand gently in its powerful jaws and showing her how easy it was to kill. She had used the magic only briefly then, but she had not known that a bridge to the Jotunn Shadow-Realm had opened in San Francisco.

Now, as her rage and desperation grew, the hound took her hand again and clamped its teeth into her flesh, drawing blood, filling her with rage and the knowledge of what she was.

Freya's daughter. Half-Jotunn. And more than either.

"Yes," the elf-woman said, gliding on silent feet to stand at Mist's side. "I feel it in you, Valkyrie." She swept the battlefield with her gaze. "Our people are failing. We cannot win without your help." Dark eyes met Mist's. "If you have the means, I beg you to make use of it now."

Mist didn't pause to wonder how the elf had sensed her power or knew that it could bring victory. She set Kettlingr gently on a dry patch of asphalt and opened herself to the world, to the elements, to sun and air and flame and earth. She felt the frigid wind off the bay and pulled it to her with hands bathed in the very essence of magic, drew heat from the silent factories and warehouses and other buildings around them, blinding light from the cloud-wreathed sun, ice from the surface of the ground on every side.

"*Yes,*" a gentle voice said, only half-heard. "*Take it in. Let it fill you. Discard everything that can distract you from what must be.*"

Drifting into a dream, Mist absorbed it all into herself, fed it with fear for her allies and hatred for her enemies.

And the indisputable knowledge that at last she would become what she was meant to be.

"*Let go.*"

Mist did. She spun the wind between her hands until it formed a weapon of whirling air like a tornado condensed to the width of a throwing spear, and added heat that burst into flame as it touched the whirlwind. A simple thought, and the wind-spear split into a dozen copies of itself, and then two dozen, each exactly like the next. Each capable of killing a Jotunn with one blow.

All she had to do now was let them fly.

The world went dark, blinding her. She held the spears frozen in midair. An unfamiliar weight pressed against her mind, and suddenly there was only warmth, bathing her very being in gentle breezes and honey and the scent of primroses.

"Freya," Mist whispered.

"*Yes*," her mother whispered. "*Join me. Fight with me. Let go.*"

The portal appeared unstable, shimmering in and out of focus as if it was about to close at last. Dainn squeezed through the opening and crouched unnoticed in the center of Lefty O'Doul Bridge as the fight raged at the east end of the short span. All around them, a dark skin of ice covered the ground as far as he could see.

There was no sign of Danny or the elf who had taken him. Dainn saw nothing of Sleipnir and Hild, who had pursued elf and boy. All was chaos, blood, and battle, mortals Dainn didn't recognize standing with Alfar and Valkyrie against dozens of well-armed Jotunar, far more than Loki had brought from Ginnungagap before the bridges had closed. It was a storm that no ordinary mortal could see, but that the soul of Midgard must feel down to its very heart.

And there was an eye to the storm. Mist stood at the center with narrow, sharp-tipped spears of wind and flame hovering above her upraised hands. Her hair whipped about her face in spite of the strange stillness that surrounded her.

The ancient magic. It sang loudly enough to deafen any but mortal ears, yet none of the Alfar seemed to notice. Only the woman who stood beside Mist . . .

Without a moment's hesitation, Dainn raced across the bridge and plunged in among clashing weapons and struggling bodies, dodging those already fallen on the ice. He shouted, his voice lost among the cries and groans.

But Mist heard. She looked in his direction. The elf beside her leaned close, whispering in her ear. The wind-spears rose as one and separated to form a halo around both women, pointing outward. One spear was aimed directly at Dainn.

"Mist!" Dainn cried, sliding to one knee.

Freya turned and smiled at him. The spear hurtled toward him, unstoppable. Dainn closed his eyes and reached out with his mind, knowing he could not succeed. The battle seemed to stop, every weapon stilled, every voice silenced.

Hot wind blasted his hair away from his face as the spear dissolved mere inches from hitting its mark. He opened his eyes. Mist had collapsed, but Bryn was already with her, shouting for help.

The Lady's elven face was a mask, coldly beautiful, revealing nothing of her rage. But when she looked at Dainn again, he knew she would kill him, even if she were forced to do it before her daughter's very eyes.

And if she killed him, he could never save Danny. Never warn Mist that what had nearly happened on this strange field of battle would happen again.

Where is the boy? he asked, sending his thoughts to the goddess he had betrayed.

Only desperation had driven him to hope she would hear and answer, but it seemed that desperation was enough.

Loki's child? she asked, reaching out with her glamour to bind his will. *He is dead.*

Dainn knew it would be easy for her to lie, even within his mind. But the shock choked him, stole the strength from his limbs, the breath from his lungs. She could take him now without the slightest effort.

"Get up."

Dainn lifted his head. An elf-lord stood over him, hand extended. Freya's spell shattered.

"Those who took the boy were not mine," the Alfr said. "And they never returned here."

Grasping the strong, slender hand, Dainn scrambled to his feet.

Freya still stared at him, waiting for him to put himself in her power again. He would never reach Mist's side, not without magic or beast to aid him.

"Tell her," he begged the elf-lord. "Tell Mist that Freya cannot be trusted."

"I will do what I can." The Alfr glanced over his shoulder. "Go!"

Dainn turned and ran, his feet finding purchase on the treacherous ice. He heard the battle resume behind him, certain now that it would be won by the allies. Freya would make it happen, though she would lose any second chance at Mist in order to achieve victory.

But she would have been too careful to let Mist sense what she had almost done to her daughter. She would make every effort to appear the loving mother come at last to save Midgard. She would either convince Mist that Dainn was dead or poison the Valkyrie against him, whispering lies and half-truths—yes, and some truths as well—to convince her daughter that he had never been anything but a traitor. Not only to Mist and Freya, but to all Midgard as well.

Mist would fight the poison, but Dainn could not wait to see if she succeeded. The elf-lord had given him fresh hope. If the Alfar kidnapper had never returned to Freya, there was still a chance . . .

"If you are looking for the boy," a Jotunn voice said as Dainn cleared the outer edge of the battle, "you will find him with Lord Loki. He is eager to discuss his son's future with you."

Freya gazed at her daughter with the greatest sympathy, her legendary hair black instead of gold, her eyes deepest blue rather than azure.

But, Mist thought, she still wore a face and body worthy of a goddess . . . a body that Freya had apparently "borrowed" from one of the Alfar in Ginnungagap just before she had returned to Midgard with a handful of the allies she had promised.

The lingering shock of her mother's sudden appearance did nothing for Mist's grim mood as she and the goddess walked among the injured and dead, Jotunn and Alfr and mortal, scattered over the ice that glazed the asphalt and the steel of Lefty O'Doul bridge. Frozen blue and red blood smeared the transparent layer, rapidly vanishing under a thickening quilt of snow.

"We are fortunate that so few were lost," Freya murmured. "I am sorry that certain difficulties delayed my return."

Mist clenched her fists, reminding herself that Freya was partially responsible for that bitter victory. Not that Mist didn't loathe her mother's primary method of fighting, which depended heavily on the glamour Freya wielded so proficiently. Glamour that shocked Jotunar into lustful insensibility so that they could easily be dispatched by her elven followers.

It was all too easy to forget that Freya had once been a goddess of battle, the reason she had claimed half the dead the Valkyrie brought from mortal battlefields to Asgard.

But she had abandoned that martial aspect long before Mist had come to Valhalla. Or so Mist had believed. Now she was having difficulty imagining that there could have been anything good in her joining with Freya when they'd fought Loki "together" in his apartment. So much of her memory of that night remained a blank, and somehow Dainn had never gotten around to filling it in for her.

Dainn.

Mist stopped, letting Freya walk ahead of her. The Lady hadn't once mentioned the elf. She had described the position of the bridge she had opened on the steppes, and it would have been close to the place where Mist had left him.

Could Freya have passed him without seeing him? If she had, then why hadn't she inquired about him even once since she and the Alfar had burst through the portal?

In spite of the way she had treated Dainn—and Mist was convinced that she'd treated him very badly indeed—he'd still been her envoy to Midgard, and to her daughter. She wouldn't simply abandon him and then pretend he didn't exist.

Mist glanced over her shoulder at Lefty O'Doul Bridge. The

portal seemed to be closed, or as good as. She hadn't even noticed it happening. She'd have to find a way of opening it again, and not only for Dainn's sake. Hild and Sleipnir were still on the other side, along with Danny; Mist hoped he'd found his way back to Hild, and that they'd stayed well away from the portal until the battle was over.

At least she knew that Loki, in his usual heroic fashion, hadn't gone anywhere near it. She had to assume that all of them were safe, and that Dainn was holding the beast in check until she could get back to him.

She could never forget the look on his face when he realized what he'd nearly done to the very child he'd been trying to protect. He would take the knife she'd left and run it through his own heart before he'd risk it again.

Don't think about it, she told herself. *Not yet.*

Forcing her leaden feet to move again, she went to visit the new mortal "recruits"—men and women she had met only in the course of the battle—silently huddled together with dazed, bloody faces. Guilt seized her by the throat, cutting off her breath as she caught sight of Rota moving among the injured, her round face unusually grim and her fashionable clothes torn and blotched with vomit and blood.

Several of the more ambulatory Einherjar were helping her and one of the other recruits bind wounds and offer comfort as best they could. No ambulances would arrive, sirens wailing, to carry the casualties to proper beds, and Eir—left back at the factory with Anna, Gabi, and a handful of guards—could be of little help in her present condition.

But even amid so much suffering, Mist found that she could still feel worse than she already did. Bryn, tears streaming over her cheeks, was kneeling beside Bunny's body where it had been laid beside three of the other Einherjar.

Mist swayed, struck by a sudden weakness that reminded her of the moment just after Freya's arrival. It had been as if the ancient magic had suddenly become too much for her, and when she'd come back to herself she'd felt drained of strength, barely capable of staying on her feet.

"Daughter," Freya said, suddenly beside Mist again with arms extended to offer support. "Are you not well?"

Not well? Mist thought, straightening without the Lady's help. *Look around you, Mother.*

"Of course," Freya said. "Your distress naturally weakens you." She laid her long-fingered, delicate hand on Mist's torn sleeve. The touch was a caress, filled with affection and warmth, the kind that might pass between a real mother and daughter.

Mist wasn't buying it. Her bitterness wouldn't let her.

"This is not the reunion I would have hoped for," Freya said, compassion throbbing in her golden voice. "How I wish I could have returned more quickly."

Mist had a vague memory of Freya explaining what she had been doing since she'd disappeared, why the bridge had opened on the steppes instead of in San Francisco—something about Mist's presence there anchoring the Midgardian end of it—and how she'd come to be wearing an elven body instead of the one she had intended to build for herself. None of the reasons seemed to matter now.

"I know the weight you have carried upon your shoulders," Freya said when Mist remained silent. "I can only say that I hope to make amends for our estrangement in the past."

"You're the goddess," Mist said, holding still so that Freya wouldn't tighten her grip. "I wouldn't think you'd have to make amends for anything."

Freya smiled. "You have all the spirit I could ever have desired. And the skill, the ability to lead others beyond what I expected."

"Is that ability necessary now that you're here to pick up the reins?"

"Oh, my child. You know I am not here to take your place. When we work as one, Loki cannot stand."

She sounds like Loki herself, Mist thought. Except Loki wouldn't try to compliment her before claiming that victory was already in his pocket.

"Won't we need the other Aesir to make sure of that?" Mist asked.

"It will be all right," Freya said, her hand slipping from Mist's shoulder. She smiled, and such light and love flowed out from her that she caught every eye capable of sight and turned each snowflake to crystalline gold. Hearts were eased, and hope blew across the battlefield like a soft spring breeze. Even the ice under the Lady's feet seemed to glow from within, as if whole fields of primroses might break through to burst into bloom beneath her soft elven boots.

Though she resisted the pull of her mother's magic, Mist found a little of her guilt and sorrow beginning to ease. Freya was right. In the end, everything would work out. They would win.

She turned toward Lefty O'Doul and the portal, feeling oddly light on her feet.

"Mist," Freya called after her. "Where are you going?"

"I have to get the others," she said without stopping.

Suddenly Freya was beside her. "You may leave that up to my Alfar. They will make certain that no danger remains on the other side."

"What danger?" Mist asked. "All the Jotunar are dead." She continued to the very threshold of the portal. It had widened again, and the aperture was just big enough for her to climb through.

"Stop!" Freya demanded. "You *will* hear me, Daughter."

Mist turned, trying to make sense of Freya's sudden anger. "I need to go before it's too late," she said slowly.

"Lady," a musical male voice said from behind Freya, "if you will permit me, I will see to it."

"No," Mist said, absurdly seeing herself as Dorothy in *The Wizard of Oz*, struggling to reach the Emerald City while the wicked witch's poppies dragged her down into sleep.

"Go to your people," Freya said. "We will deal with Dainn."

"But he needs my help."

"Harald will see to it," the Lady said coldly.

Mist stared at the elf. "Do you know who he is?" she asked.

"The Lady has explained," Harald said with a bow. He started toward the portal. It had begun to shrink again, the margin darker and more rigid than before.

Mist grabbed Harald's arm. "He won't trust anyone but me," she said.

"Daughter."

The poppies twisted around Mist's ankles, binding her to icy asphalt where no flower could grow. Freya sighed.

"I saw Dainn," she said. "You must not go to him."

"Why not?" Mist asked, wondering how slender flower stems could be so strong.

"The elf you knew is dead."

Somehow, the flowers held Mist on her feet. "No," she said. "I would . . ."

"There is nothing left of what he was." She approached Mist slowly, holding out her arms. "He has gone beyond the reach of sanity or any cure."

Mist remembered to breath. "He isn't dead. He isn't *dead.*"

"Death is not the worst fate that can befall man, elf or god."

Mist found that her head was filled with stars and silk and the scent of a thousand primroses, and there was almost no room left for questions. "I don't understand," she whispered. "Why didn't you help him?"

"I have not been blind, even in the Shadow-Realm. And I have seen him as he truly is—traitor to the Aesir, Loki's pawn, uncontrollable monster. I mistakenly believed he was capable of serving me, but his insanity had gone too far." She bowed her head. "On the other side—"

Mist's stomach heaved. "What did you see . . . on the other side?" she asked.

"You know, Daughter," Freya said gently.

29

Danny, Mist thought, her legs beginning to buckle. *Dainn killed—*

Her knees struck the ground before her thoughts could reach their terrible conclusion, and the poppies flattened under her weight. They withered and died, red petals turning black against the ice.

All at once her mind was clear again. She lowered her head, took a deep breath, and got to her feet.

"What did you see?" she demanded, holding her mother's gaze.

Freya lowered her arms and took a step back. "What did *you* see, Daughter?" she asked. "Why did you leave him behind when you returned to this mortal city?"

"To help Hild and Sleipnir," she said, not caring whether or not Freya believed her.

"And why did they require his help, if all the enemy are dead?"

Don't talk about Danny, Mist thought, hearing the command as if it had come from somewhere outside herself. And she realized that she'd never once spoken his name to Freya aloud, even when she'd briefly told the Lady about finding Hild and Sleipnir on the steppes. Not once had she explained how she and Dainn had found the portal, though she had never noticed her own omission. And Freya had never asked her how it had come to exist, though the Lady had to know that neither Mist nor Dainn could have created it.

If she assumed that Loki had found a shortcut to Sleipnir's hiding place, wouldn't she ask why he was so conspicuously absent?

Would she know that Loki had a son who appeared so human, and yet harbored such astonishing power? And if she *did* know, what would she do if she had such a child in her grasp?

Svardkell—Mist's father, and once Freya's mate—had warned Dainn to "protect the boy." Dainn had believed that boy to be Danny, and Mist knew he was right.

But Svardkell had not mentioned Freya. He had not asked Mist to approach her mother for help in protecting one who was important enough to die for.

Maybe he'd known Freya too well. Maybe he knew that her love wasn't gentle and kind, but ruthless and cruel.

She'd do anything to win this war, Mist thought. *But I won't.*

"I know what Dainn is," Mist said. "*Everything* he is. I'm not giving up on him. You can either accept that, or—"

"I can't find him anywhere," Harald said.

The elf approached Mist from the portal, and she realized that she had never even noticed his absence.

He had been to the steppes. And now his long face was grave, his eyes apologetic as they met Mist's.

"I am sorry, my lady," he said. "He is gone."

Mist closed her eyes, shutting out the elf, Freya, all the terrible things that had happened in the last several days. She felt as if the beast had raked its claws across her chest, cutting through flesh and ribs and grasping her heart in its massive paw.

Dainn had made his decision. She'd asked him to wait for her, but he'd taken the choice out of her hands and removed himself from the equation.

"Mist!"

She opened her eyes at the sound of Hild's voice. The Valkyrie was leading Sleipnir through the portal, which had abruptly expanded again to allow the big horse's passage. As soon as they were through, the aperture snapped back to its ever-shrinking diameter like an overstretched rubber band.

Hild paused to look over the carnage, only the hard set of her lips betraying her emotions. Her gaze fell on Freya without recognition.

"Hild!" Mist said, running to grasp her Sister's rough hands. She nodded to Odin's mount, wishing she could read his thoughts, and lowered her voice. "Listen to me, but answer quietly. Where is Danny?"

With a slight frown and a searching look, Hild matched Mist's low tone. "He isn't here?"

"No. And he was riding Sleipnir the last time I saw him."

Hild muttered a curse in some obscure Russian dialect. "Spider rode off with him before I could stop them, and when they came back to the cottage three Jotunar attacked us. Jotunar disguised as Alfar. One of them carried Danny off. Spider and I went after them, but we were—"

"You can explain later," Mist said, cutting her off. "Did you see him at all after that?"

Hild shook her head. "I didn't see Dainn, either," she said. "Has something—"

"The situation is complicated, and I'd rather we speak in private." She glanced at Freya, who seemed completely absorbed in her conversation with Harald. "I'm going to need your help cleaning up here and getting these people off the street."

"So many," Hild murmured.

"New recruits came in while I was gone. Innocent mortals died today."

"And Alfar, I see. What do you want me to do?"

"Help us with the survivors. Ask Rota and Bryn what needs to be done."

"It will be good to see them again. What of Sleipnir?"

"We have a good-sized abandoned factory and warehouse we're using for a temporary shelter. There's plenty of room there until we find a safer place to keep him. And Hild, say nothing of Danny. Not to anyone."

To Mist's vast relief, Hild didn't ask for her reasons. The pale-haired Valkyrie nodded and led Sleipnir onto the street. The horse stepped lightly on the ice, his nostrils flaring and head bobbing at the familiar smells and sights of battle. He looked once at Freya, his ears lying flat against his head.

Mist turned back to the Lady, not much caring if her divine mother had been offended at being ignored. "You got your wish," she said. "Dainn isn't coming back."

"It was never my wish," Freya said with an expression of profound sorrow. "He served me well."

And you promised him things you could never give him, Mist thought. *You made him what he is as much as Odin ever did.*

"It's done," Mist said. "What can you do to help us now?"

The Lady should have been angry at Mist's brusque tone, but she only nodded her head with all evident grace. "I can bring comfort to the living," she said. Her eyes welled with tears. "I truly grieve for you, my daughter. But we do what is best for Midgard. For these mortals who are so willing to die for you."

Not for me, Mist thought. *Never for me.*

"I hope you don't require my followers to kowtow to you the way Loki expects his to do," she said.

"I require no deference," Freya said. "Only respect. When, of course, you have properly introduced me."

"Do you intend to stick with that body?"

"It cannot contain my magic indefinitely, but it will give me time to build another shape more appropriate."

They parted, Mist slowly going numb as she tried to make her mind function a little longer.

Dainn was gone, but she had to find Danny. If a Jotunn disguised as an Alfar had run off with the boy, he could already be back with Loki. In fact, Mist was willing to bet on it.

Oh, Loki hadn't won completely, Mist reminded herself. He'd managed to open a bridge to the Shadow-Realm of Jotunheim while Mist, Dainn, and Danny were on the steppes, and that meant he could probably do it again, but he'd lost Jotunar, including many of his new warriors. He didn't have Dainn. And he'd have to reckon with Freya, after all.

But if he could make Danny do what he wanted, Mist thought, it was going to get very ugly very fast. Much uglier than anything they'd witnessed on this modest field of battle.

Who would protect Danny then?

Mist found the will to exchange a few words of encouragement with her Sisters and the Einherjar as they prepared to escort the Alfar and mortal recruits back to the factories. The snow-laden air was oppressive, the mist of condensation obscuring everyone's faces as the uninjured carried the casualties on foot or, for those able to ride, on the Einherjar's bikes.

It was not an easy journey. The Alfar warded the procession from mortal sight and worked with the humans as they had during the battle, though the two groups hardly spoke to each other. As they moved away, Mist began to clean up the mess still left on the ice, though her magic was more than a little shaky after the energy she'd expended. She was amazed she could use it at all.

She was too weary to be surprised when Freya and Lord Konur, leader of the Alfar, remained to help her. Amongst the three of them, they managed to clear away all traces of the battle. Only Loki's black ice remained, beyond their combined abilities to remove.

It was only then that Mist realized that Silfr was standing off to one side of the bridge, as bright as if it had never seen mud and ice and the soil of another country.

She didn't have the heart to ride it back to the loft.

Hardly able to walk, Mist staggered after her ravaged army. She'd taken no more than few steps when the elf-lord took her arm and refused to let go until she accepted his support. She looked over her shoulder once to see Freya gazing at the portal as it finally vanished.

∞

Loki was patient. He watched on his monitor as the Sow's child and her followers gathered up their dead and injured. Even Freya, easily recognizable in spite of her elven disguise, assisted Mist in cleaning up the battle site and disposing of the Jotunn bodies. He was pleased to see that none of them could remove the ice.

Everything was going his way. Well, he admitted to himself, *nearly* everything. His losses had been modest, considering Mist's and Freya's combined talents, and though both the bridges and the portal had closed, he would be able to move his warriors more widely around the city even before he brought more across from the Void.

The one fly in the ointment was Freya's return. And there were positive aspects to her reappearance that might outweigh the negatives.

Loki drained his glass of plain orange juice and set it down, rather pleased with himself for taking it straight. Of course Orn really had escaped, just as Loki had told Dainn and the others when he had taken Mist's shape. Vidarr's astonishing stupidity was responsible for that.

But unless the raven, intelligent though it seemed, had far more autonomy than it had thus far displayed, its behavior dovetailed very nicely with Loki's theory that Odin had awakened and staged a brief uprising—the "struggle for power" his Jotunar had sensed in Ginnungagap. The bird had disappeared when Freya had neutralized Odin again, though Loki doubted that Freya had found a way to make the All-father's condition permanent.

In any case, the bird's loss seemed of little importance, though Loki would have his people on the lookout for it. He didn't like leaving loose ends.

There would be a few less such open questions by dawn. Freya had rejected Dainn and given him up as lost, a perfectly sane reaction given that she'd have discovered very quickly that he had betrayed her in favor of her daughter. Loki was rather surprised that she hadn't tried to kill him.

"Tried" being the operative word. Loki doubted she could even come close unless she used the Eitr, and he suspected she'd needed that to put down Odin's "uprising."

Perhaps she guessed, or sensed, more about Dainn than he'd believed.

And what, Loki wondered, must Mist be thinking now? She'd also lost Dainn, and she could blame at least part of that on the child she had tried to help "save." She must know that Danny was Loki's son. Dainn would not have kept that from her once he had enlisted her help in protecting the boy. And she would know how powerful Danny was, the feats of which he was capable, the ruination he could bring down on her and her allies.

If Freya had seen Danny on the other side of the portal—which, given Loki's somewhat spotty intelligence of the events on the steppes, was quite possible—she would surely try to convince Mist that the child must be destroyed for the sake of Midgard.

Without Dainn's influence and appeal to her sentimentality, would Mist agree? Even if it meant saving this world?

Loki shook his head with a soft laugh. No, not Mist. Such a suggestion from her mother might actually backfire on Freya. And the Lady was certainly intelligent enough to realize it . . . if she understood her daughter at all.

But Dainn evidently hadn't told Mist of Freya's intentions for her, thwarted though they had been for the time being. And once the Lady discovered what had really become of her former servant, she would do her best to make Mist believe that the elf had deceived and forsaken them both.

Returning his attention to the monitors, Loki changed the image to a view of Danny's room. If the boy seemed to have reverted to his usual state, silent and staring and rhythmically rocking to music only he could hear, Loki knew that relapse was illusory.

Danny *was* different now. Dainn had awakened him, just as Loki had hoped.

"Sir."

Nicholas approached Loki's desk with a respectful bow. "The limousine is approaching the building."

"Excellent," Loki said. He exchanged his clothing with a sweep of his hand, donning casual but impeccably tailored attire that perfectly suited his form and face, and walked into his private sitting room. Scarlet was waiting with a tray of drinks.

Loki waved it away. "Not now," he said. "But I may call for refreshments when my guest arrives. Tell Nicholas to make him feel welcome."

Scarlet walked away, gracefully balanced on her spike-heeled pumps. Loki sprawled on the couch, observing Dainn's approach on his tablet. Even on the small screen he could see how haggard the elf had become, how weary, how utterly defeated.

He was not coming to fight. There was no evidence that the beast rode on his shoulder. Surely he realized that he was as hopelessly out of his depth now as when he had come to kill Loki after Hrimgrimir's ill-fated attack on the loft.

The elf's tender, all-too-fragile heart would make him helpless, especially when he had nothing else to live for.

Or die for.

Loki's heart began to beat a little more quickly, a sensation he found quite pleasant under the circumstances.

"Sir," Nicholas said from the doorway, "he's here."

"Send him in," Loki said. "Alone."

Nicholas nodded and backed out the door. A moment later Dainn walked in, still half-dressed and barefoot, his once-sleek hair a mass of tangles laced with bits of dead grass and leaves, his eyes bloodshot and his lips cracked. He still moved with elven grace, panther-sleek, and even now he was the most beautiful creature Loki had ever beheld in any of the Nine Homeworlds.

Dainn stopped just inside the doorway and turned a hollow gaze on Loki. "Where is the boy?" he asked.

"His nurse will bring him up presently," Loki said, stretching his arm along the back of the couch. "Why don't you make yourself comfortable?"

Dainn turned to leave the room.

"Wait," Loki said. "You *did* come to see him, I presume? You *are* concerned for his welfare, after all you have attempted to do for him?" He patted the couch beside him. "I think you'll want to hear what I have to say."

"Nothing you have to say interests me," Dainn said in a voice as barren as the steppes. But he didn't walk away. He simply stood, lost to himself, bereft of something essential he had possessed in full measure the last time he and Loki had met near the loft. Something Loki felt as a void as deep and vast as Ginnungagap.

Dainn had lost his magic.

For one of the few times in his life, Loki was in no mood to gloat. He felt nothing but a kind of shock dangerously close to pity. For an elf, to be stripped of magic was not merely to lose the use of spells and the ability to shape the natural world. It was a severance from all that made Alfar what they were, from the life of nature that flowed through them wherever they walked.

For Dainn, it must be like being blind and deaf and crippled all at once, stumbling through a world stripped of meaning or context.

Perhaps it was even worse than the beast.

"Nicholas!" Loki snapped.

The young man appeared instantly behind Dainn.

"Help Lord Dainn to the couch and tell Scarlet to fetch blankets and water."

Nicholas took Dainn's arm gently and steered him toward the couch. At first Dainn resisted, his muscles tensing, his lip beginning to curl as if the beast were about to awaken. Loki had already prepared a spell to counter any attack, and he gathered it around him now.

But there was no change. Dainn let himself be guided to the couch, sat stiffly as far from Loki as possible, and stared at the opposite wall. When Scarlet arrived with the requested items, Nicholas settled one of the blankets around Dainn's shoulders as she offered the bottle. Dainn ignored them both.

"Drink," Loki said.

Dainn turned his face aside, but his body rebelled against his mind and he drank the bottle dry in less than a minute. Loki gestured for another bottle, but this time Dainn refused to be coaxed.

"Let me see me the boy," he said.

"I show you kindness," Loki said, getting to his feet, "and yet you never see fit to show *me* the slightest gratitude."

Dainn's laugh was no more than a hoarse bark. "You do nothing out of kindness, Laufeyson," he said.

His words stung, though they should have meant nothing to Loki at all. "One might say I do nothing out of cruelty, either, but I can be very cruel." Loki resumed his seat and snapped his fingers again. Scarlet hurried away and returned with the tray she had offered Loki earlier.

"Magnier Grande Champagne Cognac, 1893," Loki said, as Scarlet poured with her usual expertise. He picked up one of the glasses and sipped, closing his eyes as the smooth liquor spilled into his mouth. "I strongly advise you to try it."

Dainn only stared at him, his hatred beating against Loki like a dozen Jotunn clubs. "You drink too much," he said.

"So you are concerned for *my* welfare as well. As I am with yours." Loki set the half-empty glass on the side table and settled back into the cushions. "It's not only the magic that's gone, is it?"

The elf went very still, but there was no surprise in his expression.

"The beast is gone, too," Loki continued, leaning closer to Dainn. "You lost them both somewhere on the steppes. How did it happen? Did Freya have something to do with it?" He smiled. "Of course I recognized the Lady when she arrived in San Francisco, in spite of her inadequate disguise. I would have liked to have seen how she managed to open a bridge on the other side of the portal, given the distance from this fair city."

"Even you are not omniscient, Scar-lip."

Loki tutted. "I have never cared for that appellation." He waved his hand. "No matter.. We will speak of these matters later. You need rest and time to recover."

"Danny opened both bridges and portal," Dainn said abruptly.

If Dainn had expected that to come as a surprise to Loki, he was to be sorely disappointed. "I was there when the portal appeared," Loki said, "as you may have cause to remember. And it had occurred to me that Danny might have had some influence on my ability to open a bridge on this side without the usual preparation." Loki picked up his glass again. "But you said 'bridges.' Do you believe that Danny also assisted Freya and the Alfar, his parent's enemies? Or did you urge him to do it?"

"I did not."

"Curious," Loki said, leaning back to display his unconcern. "We will have to look into the matter. But in his defense, Danny is still unaware of what he does much of the time."

"He created the portal to escape from *you*."

"Or to retrieve Sleipnir, in whom he had expressed considerable interest. Or perhaps, most of all, to save you."

"He believed I could help him."

"And you did. You wanted to protect him from me, from all danger. Why, my Dainn? Why are you so devoted to a child you have met only three times, and he to you? Why does Mist feel bound to follow your lead in 'protecting' my son?"

Dainn's legs tensed, and he began to rise. He never made it to his feet. Nicholas stepped in to ease him down before he could fall.

"Go," Loki said to the mortals. "Both of you."

Scarlet and Nicholas hurried out. Dainn bowed his head, his eyes tightly closed.

"Mist bears many heavy burdens," Loki said, "but Danny, like you, is no longer one of them. Our Valkyrie will have enough to deal with, considering her mother's plans for her. Which, once again, you failed to warn her about. Just as you failed to do more than temporarily separate them after our little contretemps at my former apartment."

"She is too strong for Freya now," Dainn whispered. "She cast the Lady out during the battle."

"Is that what you observed," Loki said, "or are you merely guessing because Mist is still with us?" Loki shrugged. "Perhaps Mist has the means to resist, but that is no longer your concern. You can never return to her again. You have nothing to give her—no magic, not even the dubious advantage of an uncontrollable beast to fight her enemies. Once Freya turns her against you, she'll have wished you dead a hundred times over."

Dainn was on him in an instant, but Loki was ready. He pressed his left palm on Dainn's chest, froze the top layer of his skin—temporarily paralyzing the elf—and pushed him to the floor. Dainn lay still as Loki rose to stand over him. Loki reached down, offering his hand.

Shaking off his paralysis, Dainn rolled to the side and pushed himself to his knees. His face was gray. "Would you let me go if I chose to leave now?" he asked.

"But would you?" Loki crouched beside him. "In all our time together, I have only once seen you so helpless. I could do anything to you now, and you would not be able to prevent it."

Dainn looked into Loki's eyes. "Then do what you will," he said.

"I want you willing, my Dainn." He ran his finger down the elf's cheek. "Your compassion is your weakness. You will never leave the boy with me." He dropped his hand. "You have already changed him. Perhaps you can help him understand what he is, and then *he* can choose whether or not to do my will."

"You would never give him the choice." Dainn almost smiled. "Even though you forced him to send manifestations against us, you can't control him."

"But he will be quite safe with you," Loki said, getting to his feet. "Your instincts have been correct, my Dainn."

"The instincts that tell me that your son will never be like you?"

"*My* son?" Loki stroked Dainn's hair as if the elf were a favorite pet. "Not mine. Ours."

30

Loki sighed with real regret as Dainn's expression altered from one of hatred to disbelief and horror. It was not the reaction he would have wished for, but it was what he'd expected.

"Perhaps now you'd like that drink," he said, strolling back to the end table.

Dainn rose awkwardly, listed to one side, and found support against the wall. "It isn't possible," he whispered.

"How is it impossible?" Loki asked, pouring two glasses of Cognac. "We were together a more than sufficient time."

"I don't believe you."

"But you do, because it all makes sense now, doesn't it? Your obvious feelings for him, and his for you." He pressed the keypad on the wall next to the bedroom door, engaging the intercom. "Nicholas," he said. "Call Miss Jones. She is to bring the boy."

As usual, Nicholas was laudably quick to obey. Five minutes later, during which time Dainn remained absolutely still, Miss Jones walked into the room, her fingers clutched tightly around Danny's hand.

"Miss Jones," Loki said. "Please let Dainn see the child."

The nurse spoke softly to Danny and led him closer to Dainn. The elf continued to stare out the window.

"Look at him," Loki said. "His hair is mine, to be sure. But his face, I think, is almost entirely yours. And his eyes . . ." He nodded to Miss Jones, who lifted Danny up in her arms. "Do you notice how dark they are? Elven-dark, the color of a twilit sky."

"This is some illusion," Dainn said, briefly glancing at Danny before returning his attention to the cityscape outside. "A trick, typical of your—"

"Papa?"

Dainn started and looked down again. Danny's gaze was fixed with perfect awareness on his father's face.

"Oh, my God," Miss Jones whispered.

Slipping his hand from the nurse's, Danny held it out to Dainn.

"Papa," he said again.

Slowly Dainn sank to his knees. "Danny?" he said.

Loki smiled. "I thought he ought to have a name similar to his father's," he said. "Of course he will carry my name, Lokason, as I carry my mother's, but you have some claim on him. If you choose to accept it."

"You have coached him," Dainn said hoarsely. "You have lied to him."

"Look inside yourself," Loki said. "Tell me he is not your flesh and blood."

Watching intently, Loki recognized the precise moment when Dainn believed. "When?" he asked.

"Do you remember how you hesitated when you almost killed me just before the Last Battle?" Loki smiled sadly. "I can see you do. He was already growing in my belly. You sensed it even then, and you could not harm our child."

What was left of the color in Dainn's face seemed to drain away all at once. Slowly he closed his arms around the boy, and Danny buried his face against the elf's shoulder.

Dainn looked up at Loki with that fierce hatred he no longer had the ability to back up with anything but words. "I will not let you keep this child," he said.

"Already the devoted father," Loki said, swallowing his jealousy. "Though I think I posited that you won't leave him alone with me, and you have no means of taking him away."

With a very unelvish grunt of sheer misery, Dainn pulled Danny closer and cradled the back of the boy's head as if he could literally pull the boy into himself. "Why?" he asked. "Why tell me now, and not when you brought him to me at the loft?"

"I wanted this revelation to come at a time when your only choice would be to stay with me. You have no other options, my Dainn."

Dainn pressed his face into Danny's hair. Loki saw the surrender in the lines of his lithe body and in the angle of his head, heard it in the shortness of his breath and the pounding of his heart.

The elf—*Loki's* elf—knew he was trapped.

"You have other children to serve you," he said, his desperation almost tugging at Loki's heart. "Fenrisulfr and Hel and the real Jormungandr—"

"None of them have half the ability this child does. After so many centuries, I have finally begun to recognize his full potential. The potential you and I have bequeathed him, and something greater." He inclined his head. "Yes, even I am compelled to admit it."

"I will not let you use him as a tool to summon monsters."

"So you refuse to help me?" Loki glanced at the side table and regarded his nearly empty glass with regret. "It would be a great pity if our son were to suffer permanent damage because of my clumsy efforts to gain his cooperation."

"You are the basest creature that ever sprang from Ymir's armpits."

"Oh, my tender feelings," Loki said, pressing his hand over his heart. "I know you too well, Dainn. I said you might have some influence with me where our son is concerned. I will still have my victory, but the manner in which I make use of Danny's talents is 'up for grabs,' as they say. *Par exemple*, there is no reason he cannot help me obtain the other Treasures by reasonably peaceful means. But again, that is up to you." He waved his hand. "Miss Jones."

The nurse approached Danny and held out her arms. Dainn let the boy go, despair on his face. Danny turned to his nurse, gazed at her with a frown, and then looked at Loki. The very air began to tremble, and something huge and shadowy appeared between them.

It had the shape of Dainn's beast, but ghostly, as if only half of it existed in this world.

"Stop, Danny," Loki said. "Stop at once."

The shape wavered and then became solid again. It opened its mouth to expose rows of razor teeth.

"Danny," Dainn said quietly.

The boy stopped, turning to look over his shoulder at Dainn. The phantom beast vanished.

"He took that from your mind," Loki said, trembling with anger and shock. "Control your thoughts, my Dainn, or we shall quarrel. And I generally win my quarrels."

But Dainn's attention had turned back to Danny. "It's all right," he said, somehow managing a smile that was halfway convincing. "Go with Miss Jones."

Danny cast another long, all-too-aware look at Loki, took his nurse's hand, and walked out of the room. Loki exhaled and sank back onto the couch. He knew Dainn had seen him at a disadvantage, and he was furious.

But he still held all the cards. Every one that mattered.

"There is one more question I did want to pursue before you go to your rest," he said. "A rather important one. Did Freya see Danny?"

Loki was aware that Dainn was carefully weighing his answer, afraid he might lose some illusory advantage. But instinct saved him.

"She saw both of us," he said, his voice breaking oddly. "She knows who he is. She would have killed him."

"Yes. And thus you can shed any remaining loyalty you might believe you owe to the Lady. And to Mist, should she choose to turn against—"

"Mist defended him," Dainn said, though he nearly choked on the words.

"Ah. A pity she isn't on our side, then. It would be very awkward for you if you should ever have to choose between her life and our son's." Loki rose, standing toe to toe with Dainn, and curled his hand around the nape of Dainn's neck under the midnight fall of hair.

"You will have a very comfortable life here, I assure you," he said. "I will not expect you to encourage Danny to work any direct harm on those for whom you have developed affection. But there are other things I *will* expect."

He ground his mouth against Dainn's. Dainn jerked back and dragged the back of his hand across his lips. Loki raised his fist, preparing to strike, and dropped it again.

"Not an auspicious beginning to our new domestic life together," he said. "I shall give you one more chance to walk away. But you will never see our son again."

Dainn stared into Loki's eyes. "If I stay, you will let me see Mist one last time."

"Why?" Loki said mockingly. "Perhaps so that you can give her a belated warning about Freya's intentions—a warning she is unlikely to believe once she learns you've come to me? Or, like any proper star-crossed lover, will you simply confess your deep and abiding devotion to Freya's daughter, in spite of every barrier that stands between you?" He shook his head pityingly. "Do you think anything will change?"

"I will stay only on that condition."

"I know you bluff, my Dainn, but I will permit it. On *my* condition that you tell her nothing of what has passed between us or anything else you think you know of my plans."

"I agree."

"And I accept. But the next time I choose to bestow my affections on you, I expect you to be a little more cooperative."

Dainn laughed. It was not a sound of defiance; he had accepted his defeat. Still, Loki knew whatever he did to the elf, he would never break him.

But he would certainly try.

It took nearly six hours to get all the wounded back to the factory and arrange proper bedding for the new mortal arrivals. Freya set a kind of anti-glamour ward around the entire region of the loft, repelling trespassers or those who might show the slightest interest in what went on behind it. Though in the past Mist had done a fairly decent job of deflecting the attention of the mortals who lived near the loft and encouraging them to avoid the area of Twentieth and Illinois, she was reluctantly glad to have more powerful magic at work.

Even though she couldn't make herself trust her mother farther than she could toss Thor's Hammer.

While Eir, still very weak, did her best to work with the wounded— Gabi beside her, observing her techniques—Rota stayed with the new recruits and Bryn resumed regular patrols with the uninjured Einherjar. Mist dealt with the Alfar, who were understandably disoriented, standoffish, and insistent upon dealing with their own dead and making their separate camp on one of the abandoned factory parking lots. They were stoic in the wake of their sacrifices, and Mist found that she couldn't look at a single elvish face without thinking of Dainn.

It was worst with Lord Konur, the Alfr who had unexpectedly offered her support after Harald's return with the news of Dainn's disappearance. He looked nothing like Dainn, and was no more related to him than any of the Alfar, but Mist was drawn to him for reasons she couldn't explain. And in spite of his elvish pride, he was surprisingly kind, respectfully and formally acknowledging Freya's daughter as if she were his undoubted superior.

Mist didn't believe it for a moment, and the Alfar would obey Freya in any case. But it was a relief to know she'd have their leader on her side.

Before she had a chance to visit the new arrivals, who had suffered higher losses than any of the other fighters, she found Koji Tashiro's Prius parked on the curb outside the loft.

"I'm sorry I didn't get here sooner," Tashiro said, concern in his voice as she met him near the door. "I've had people out looking for Ryan just as you asked, but—"

"Do you have any idea where he's gone?" Mist asked, planting herself between him and the loft.

"I personally went to Benicia to see if he'd learned about his aunt's house and gone there. There was no trace of him." He hesitated, his gaze flickering away from hers almost as if he was hiding something.

As Dainn had so often done, she thought bitterly. But Tashiro wasn't Dainn, and he had no reason to lie.

"We won't stop the search," Tashiro continued, meeting her eyes again, "and I'll expand beyond the city if we don't locate him in the next few days."

If he even should *be found,* Mist thought. He'd never have left Gabi if he hadn't had a powerful reason to do so. Without the constant pressure of exposure to magic and the looming threat to Midgard, he might revert to a "normal" teenager again.

Except he'd never been a normal teenager. The visions had always been with him.

At least he doesn't know that Dainn—

"I really am sorry," Tashiro said, cutting into her thoughts. "I hope you can forgive me."

"I'll think about it."

The silence that followed was long and awkward, but Tashiro couldn't be suppressed for long. He scanned the area of the loft.

"Pretty quiet around here," he said.

"I haven't been out and about much lately," Mist lied. "What's it like out there?"

"That weird black ice is finally melting," he said, "but now that it's snowing again it's going to be bad. I wouldn't go driving around any more than necessary. What about the loft?"

"Some structural damage. We're working on it."

Tashiro nodded and glanced across the street. Mist knew that the wards would make it difficult for him to focus on the factory and the area around it, and his gaze quickly slipped away to focus on the bike parked at the curb near his car.

"Nice pair of wheels," he said. "Yours?"

Mist had forgotten that someone had fetched the bike from Lefty O'Doul Bridge and brought it back before some lucky thief got around to stealing it. She didn't think she would have cared.

"A gift," she said brusquely.

"From your cousin? He's usually around to meet me as soon as I show up."

"He had to go."

She couldn't miss the highly inappropriate satisfaction in the lawyer's eyes. She'd told Dainn that she thought he might be trusted with the truth, but if they were going to work together—assuming he believed and was willing to get involved—she was going to have to put a stop to his obviously amorous intentions. It wasn't just the glamour now, and she didn't have room in her heart for him or any-one else.

"It's a beautiful machine," he went on, as if he'd never introduced the subject of her "cousin." "I admit I'm a little envious."

"You can always trade in your car."

"I'm too used to it now." His dark eyes grew serious. "I'm becom-ing used to a lot of things I never thought I'd want."

Mist folded her arms across her chest. "Excuse me?"

"Never mind." He ran his hand through his hair. "I should get back to the search. You *do* forgive me?"

"Yeah." She sighed. "This isn't your fault. It's mine, for not keep-ing a better eye on Ryan."

"Then you'll let me come inside next time?"

"If the loft is fixed by then."

He offered his hand. She took it, and he cupped hers between both of his in a gesture more intimate than a friendly good-bye.

Mist carefully pried her hand loose. He turned on his heel and strode back to the Prius, banging the door as he climbed in. Mist felt a frisson of regret and then set it aside, thinking again of the people under her care. She walked across the street to look for Anna.

She'd barely spoken to the young woman since her return from the battleground. Vali's computer gear had been moved to the main factory, and Mist found Anna busy at one of the stations, staring at the largest monitor as she clicked away at the keyboard. Mist's inquiries as to her state of mind were met with absent nods and distracted reassurances. Like Gabi, she'd found something important to distract her from her grief and sense of loss.

When Mist had finally introduced both young women to the Lady—omitting any mention of Orn—Freya had barely acknowledged them. She had no interest in day-to-day operations, or in the mortals who handled them.

She also seemed uninterested in learning about Vidarr or Vali, though Dainn had informed her of their presence in Midgard soon after he'd met Mist. The Lady seemed to think them irrelevant, and since both men had vanished Mist saw no point in making an issue of their treachery.

Nor had she mentioned Danny. She still felt that strong sense of inhibition, an instinctive desire to keep his name out of their conversations. She was all but certain that the boy was back with Loki, and there was nothing she could do about that for the time being.

And then there was Svardkell, who had given his life to warn Mist of traitors, a warning Mist had utterly failed to heed. Freya had said nothing of him. Either she had never known that he, too, had been in Midgard, or she simply didn't care. And since the things he had said—the words Dainn had relayed to Mist—were on subjects Mist had no desire to share with her mother, she tried to set aside her need to know more about the Jotunn Freya had loved. For a time.

After she'd seen Anna, Mist checked in on the infirmary and sent Eir to bed. The healer was looking much better, though she had just spent hours working with injured fighters, and Mist wondered if the very act of healing had offset the consequences of using her powers in battle.

Gabi had been kept busy watching Eir and helping the Valkyrie with small tasks such as cleaning and bandaging minor abrasions. She had dealt surprisingly well with the horror of seeing so many injured and dead.

"I wish I could have fought, too," Gabi said as Mist finally chivvied her and Eir out of the infirmary to the sleeping area.

"You remember what happened last time," Mist said. "Healers aren't supposed to fight. You *do* want to be a healer, don't you?"

Gabi subsided with a grumble. "Do you think Ryan's all right?" she asked plaintively.

"I know he is," Mist said, stroking a dark lock of hair away from Gabi's face. "You know he'll be back when he's done whatever he needs to do. Now go with Eir."

Mist watched the two healers, young and old, walk stiffly to their beds, Eir to a cot and the girl to a bedroll. She returned to the infirmary to look over the wounded, most of whom were in a twilight sleep induced by one of Eir's spells. The dead were awaiting a final service, which Bryn had arranged for that evening. Bunny's death had hit the hardest. But some of the fallen had barely known what they were fighting for.

Hardening her will against the pull of grief, Mist continued on to the adjoining area where the relatively whole recruits had been given beds and food and minor medical attention. Most of the mortals were sleeping, though they needed no spells to provide incentive.

One man was awake: a somewhat grizzled but well-conditioned African American man in his forties whom Mist recognized at once as ex-military. A nasty cut crossed his cheek, half-hidden under a bandage. One of Mist's swords lay on the floor beside him.

He rose quickly from his inadequate bed of a single thin blanket, and Mist saw his arm twitch as he moved to salute her. Fortunately, he didn't.

"Taylor, ma'am," he said, his posture as straight as Odin's Spear. "Captain, United States Marine Corps."

"At ease, Captain," she said, flushing. "My name is Mist. I am the . . ." She trailed off, suddenly unsure how to define herself to a man like this.

"I know, ma'am," the captain said. "The Einherjar informed us. You're the general of this outfit, and the daughter of the goddess Freya."

"You know more than I expected of someone who just arrived," she said. "But then I didn't expect any of you to become part of this so quickly." Another wave of guilt caught her flailing in the deep end. "But I have to know: did you come here willingly?"

Taylor held her gaze with the directness of man well accustomed to facing fear. "I'm not sure I understand, ma'am, but I've been having dreams for a long time. When I heard the call . . ."

The call. Mist looked away, afraid Taylor would see her distress. The only "call" she knew of was the glamour Dainn had so recently urged her to make use of, the inherited ability that would supposedly bring all the mortal allies they needed.

But she *hadn't* used it. Not consciously.

Taylor cleared his throat. "Did I say something wrong, ma'am?" he asked.

"Not at all, Captain." She smiled at him, and he smiled back, creased skin pulling at the bandage. She found herself prepared to trust this man she'd only just met. Norns grant that her instincts were correct this time.

"What did you dream about?" she asked.

"The world coming to an end," he said, his smile fading. "I spoke to some of the others before the fight." He gestured toward the newcomers. "It's been different for everyone. But we all came because we knew we had to fight for Earth against something pretty bad. I guess we have a better idea what that is now."

"It shouldn't have been this way," Mist said. "I should have been here to meet you. I would have told you not to become involved in a battle you weren't ready for."

"Ma'am, Bryn and Rota provided enough intel to give us an idea of what we'd be facing, but no one forced us. We didn't know about the problem with firearms—a few M240s would have come in very handy—but a few of us can handle swords and knives and those staffs you keep in your gym, and others have martial arts training. We weren't completely unprepared."

"Not even for giants?" she asked. "For magic?"

He shrugged. "We learned fast."

Not fast enough, Mist thought, remembering the recruits and Einherjar who had given up their lives for something as fragile as a dream.

In spite of what she said to Dainn, Mist knew that there wasn't a hope of winning without mortal help. And lots of it. But this couldn't be the way.

"Ma'am," Taylor said, so softly that she had to strain to hear him. "I can see you wish this hadn't happened. But we know you're the one. That's why we'll follow you to the death, and not complain about it."

"I don't want your deaths," she said, hoping against hope that she could prove worthy of this man's faith and the others' sacrifices. "But it's not going to get any easier. You won't have much time to get up to speed."

"We figured that, General."

Mist winced at the title. "I think we'd better stick with something a little less . . . formal. How about 'commander'?"

"That's pretty formal. What about 'Chief'?"

"If that's what you recommend, it'll do for me. And since you have military experience, Captain, I'm putting you in charge of the people who came with you. While you learn more about what's going on here, you'll assist Rota and Bryn in acclimating and training your squad to survive the next fight. It may come in a few hours or a few days or weeks. Lives depend on your ability."

"Understood, Chief."

"One more question, and then I'll leave you to rest. Do you think any of your people could be trained to use a forge to make bladed weapons?"

"Better than that, ma'am," he said, flashing another grin. "We've got a blacksmith and two troops who can make swords and knives as well as handle them."

Mist released her breath. "That's very good news. Now you'd better get some sleep, Captain Taylor. You'll need it."

This time he did salute. "We won't fail you, Chief."

Mist turned away quickly before he could notice how close she was coming to losing her last crumbling fragments of composure. She dragged herself back to her own blankets in the factory's smallest office. Now, more than ever, she couldn't afford to make mistakes due to lack of sleep.

Falling onto her simple bed fully clothed, Mist drifted off almost immediately.

She woke to the sense that someone else was in the room. She rolled over, drew Kettlingr from its sheath, and had it at her attacker's throat before he could move in for the kill.

Then she smelled him, recognized the pattern of his breathing, the silhouette of his body against the dim moonlight spilling through the half-covered windows.

"Dainn?"

31

Mist tossed Kettlingr aside and jumped up. He stepped back, utterly silent, and shook his head.

"I was told you were gone!" she whispered. "How did you—"

He placed a finger across her lips. With his other hand he laid a piece of paper on the ground beside her blankets, a note covered with a few brief lines of Runic script.

"Dainn," she said, pushing his hand away from her lips. "How did you get back here? What the Hel is—"

She never got a chance to finish. Suddenly his mouth was on hers, and she opened to him, wanting him with every part of her body, dragging him down on top of her as she fell, her fingers digging into his shoulders and hair and back. Desire was everything, and there was only one being in all the world who could satisfy her. Only one she could—

His weight pressed her to the ground, his mouth on her neck as his fingers worked at the top buttons of her shirt. She found the zipper of his jeans, only half aware of what she was doing. And then, suddenly, his heat and warmth and hunger abandoned her, and she was alone again. She didn't even see his shadow vanishing from the room.

Feeling as if someone had slugged her in the stomach, Mist rolled over and grabbed the note he'd left.

Danny is safe. Say nothing of him. Do not trust Freya. Not all is what it seems.

Mist touched her lips. They felt bruised, but she wasn't angry. She'd had as much to do with what had happened as Dainn. Each of them safe in the darkness, silent, acting on the most basic instinct shared by gods and mortals alike.

He could be anywhere now. Refusing to return to her.

Or refusing to return to Freya. What had really passed between them on the steppes? Had they spoken? Did he know Freya wished him ill?

Why had he warned Mist so urgently not to trust her own mother?

And how much do you *trust her?* Mist asked herself. She hadn't spoken of Danny, and now Dainn's note confirmed her instincts. But what had he meant by *"Danny is safe"*? If Loki had taken him back, how could he be?

Not all is what it seems.

She looked at the alarm clock on the floor a few feet away, her bleary vision just beginning to clear. So short a time since she'd spoken to Dainn on the steppes, begging him to hold on.

Sleep took her again before she could even consider finding some vital work to drive the crazy thoughts from her mind. When she woke, still half caught in an erotic and very disturbing dream, it was nearly 9 p.m.

Still dazed with bewilderment and grief, Mist gave herself a quick sponge bath, changed her clothes again, and wandered outside. The night was crisp and surprisingly clear, all the clouds swept aside as if by some magic beyond Mist's understanding.

And perhaps it *was* a kind of magic. Mist crossed the parking lot to the warehouse that was being set up as a secondary shelter. The wide room was dark save for a few floor lamps the Einherjar had brought in and a string of colored lights hung along one wall, invisible from the street. It was a rather pitiful display, as was the tiny tree decorated with cheap glass and plastic ornaments.

A tree. Mist counted backward, ticking off each day on a mental calendar she hadn't so much as glanced at in a week.

Tonight was Christmas Eve.

"Hey," Rick said, coming up behind her as she stood staring at the tree. His face was marked with cuts and bruises from the battle, but otherwise—somewhat miraculously—he hadn't suffered any serious injuries. It was clear, however, that he was grieving for his lost comrades. Especially Bunny.

"I'm sorry," Mist said quietly.

He waved his hand as if to dismiss any hint of sorrow. "You look a little out of it," he said. "Something I can do?"

Mist shook her head. "I didn't even realize that Yule Eve had come already. I still forget sometimes how important this celebration is to mortals, given that you believe it's the day of your Christ's birth."

"For some of us, yeah. Others just like the celebration. Not much of one tonight, though."

"I wish I had a better gift to give you than the prospect of more danger and suffering."

"That's the whole point of Christmas for a lot of people," Rick said. "The idea of sacrifice. I guess it ain't so bad to look at it that way. Sacrificing for the greater good."

Mist gripped his arm. "You're a brave man, Rick. You and all the Einherjar."

He glanced away. "Now that the elves are here, won't the . . . the *real* Einherjar start showing up, too? Are we going to have to change our name?"

"Not if I can help it," Mist said. "We'll work something out." She squeezed his arm and let him go. "How is Sleipnir?"

"His temporary stable seems to be working out okay, though Hild said he's still depressed, or whatever the word is for a horse."

And Sleipnir would probably stay that way, Mist thought, until he was reunited with Danny. Or Odin. If either reunion ever happened.

But at least they had another one of the Treasures. Something good had come of all this pain.

"Is it true that Dainn's gone?" Rick asked.

"I don't know where he is," Mist said, carefully holding her voice steady.

"He wasn't so bad after all, once you got to know him."

"Not so bad," Mist murmured. "I'll see you at the funeral."

The funeral service was brief and secular, given that spiritual beliefs among the allies ranged from the teachings of the White Christ through veneration of the Aesir and even more esoteric traditions with which Mist was only vaguely familiar. No one, even the companions of the fallen, had cared to linger after the Alfar had given the bodies to the earth. Freya had not attended.

Anna was waiting for Mist in the factory "kitchen" when Mist finally returned to the main camp. "You should be sleeping," Mist said, locating a beer in the portable fridge and a can of tomato soup in one of the crates that served as temporary cupboards. She forced herself to grab one of the saucepans hanging on the wall and pour the gloppy stuff into it.

"I couldn't," Anna said, moving restlessly around the table brought over from the loft. "There's something I should have told you a long time ago, or at least right after you got me away from Vidarr. But things moved so fast." Her eyes welled with tears. "You went through that portal with Dainn and the boy, and then there was the battle, and before that I was just plain scared."

Mist could hardly focus on the young woman's words. She added water to the soup and tried not to fall asleep on her feet as she stirred it in and put the saucepan on the small burner of the camp stove. "Tell me," she mumbled.

"Ryan had visions of the future, right?" she asked. "I . . . I can see the past. Sometimes."

Mist dropped the spoon in the saucepan with a clatter. "How?" she asked.

"I don't really know. Sometimes"—she hunched her shoulders and began again— "All my life I've had . . . I guess what you'd call dreams that weren't mine. Only they weren't just dreams. I *experienced* things I knew couldn't have happened to me, like being interrogated by Nazis."

Nazis. Like the ones who'd nearly killed Rebekka and Geir and Horja. "You thought it was happening to you?" she asked.

"When Orn led me out of the apartment to find you, I thought we were being hunted. And when Loki first caught me, I saw him as . . . well, one of the Nazis. I think." She shrugged apologetically, as if she really believed what she was saying might make Mist laugh. "Sometimes it's all a jumble, as if I'm seeing things from Rebekka's and Helga's lives at the same time."

"Rebekka?" Mist asked, remembering that only a few hours ago she'd thought she could never be astonished again.

"That's . . . another thing I should have told you," Anna said. "I knew before I ever met you or realized you weren't mortal that my great-grandfather and a woman named Mist had been lovers. After you and I talked for the first time, I wondered if you knew about Rebekka. The way you acted—"

"I did," Mist said. "That was something *I* should have told you."

"You helped save her, didn't you?"

Mist was grateful that her exhaustion made the bitter memories a little less immediate. "Who is Helga?" she asked.

"She married Geir when the Nazis were run out of Norway," Anna said. "They adopted Rebekka."

Mist wanted to shake herself. Helga. Horja. Could anything be more natural?

"You knew her too," Ann said, "Because you fought beside her. Geir told me a story about his taking care of Rebekka in Sweden while Helga went back to fight in Norway."

"But you said you . . . remembered being interrogated by Nazis," Mist said slowly. "That could never have happened to Rebekka. She was too young."

"But Helga wasn't," Anna said. "The one thing they had in common is that both of them wore the pendant. Rebekka almost never took it off, but she gave it to Helga when she left to fight, for good luck. It must have worked, because Helga came back." Anna rubbed her bloodshot eyes. "She was tortured, though. By Nazis who wanted something from her. They thought she knew something she didn't."

"Gods," Mist whispered, beginning to see where the story was headed.

"Yeah." Anna shivered. "But they weren't able to get what they wanted from her before she escaped."

"Was Orn with her?"

"That's where things get confusing. Sometimes I see him with Helga, in a cage. But it's hard to tell if I haven't added a little of my own life into the mix."

"But all three of you wore the pendant," Mist said. She left the pot on the boil and moved toward Anna. "If these Nazis knew the pendant was connected to Orn, they were probably after him." She dragged her hand over her face. "Horja—Helga must have understood by then that there was something different about him."

"If she did, she never told Rebekka." Anna squeezed her hands together tightly. "When I first saw Vidarr, I was sure he was one of the Nazis. Not like Loki. I was absolutely *sure*."

"But you never saw *me*, did you? In your dreams?"

"Yes, I did. I'm sorry. I didn't tell you because it scared me so much when I met you, and—" She extended her hand in a gesture of apology and regret, then let it fall. "I never saw Orn with you, though."

"Because he never showed himself to me in all the time I lived in Midgard," Mist said wearily. "How much did you see of the rest of my life?"

"Only fragments, or I would have known what you really are. I wish I could tell you more."

"Assuming your dreams are accurate," Mist said, "at least we know why Vidarr behaved as he did. He must have lost track of Orn and the pendant back then, but when he got another chance, he took it . . . even if it meant working with Loki. It looks to me like he wanted more from Orn than a message from his father."

Anna cleared her throat nervously. "There's one more thing. I wanted to make sure it made sense, and that I wasn't seeing things that weren't there. This time, I think it's good news."

Mist wandered back to the stove, barely aware that the soup was starting to boil over. "I could use some right about now," she said.

"When Helga died," Anna said, taking a seat at the table, "she left Geir some stuff that he passed on to Rebekka. For some reason Rebekka hid it, and Geir never asked her what happened to it." She frowned. "Oldefar mentioned it in passing before he died, but I never really saw any of that part of Rebekka's life in my dreams. I think she buried the stuff in Norway or Sweden, and after my parents moved to the United States, I never thought about it again. But now—"

Now, Mist thought, fresh energy pumping through her veins. She turned off the stove. "Horja's Treasures," she said.

"I'm sorry," Anna said, pressing her forehead against the tabletop.

"Quit it with the apologies. What's done is done, and it's not too late unless Loki figured this out first."

"I may be able to find more with Vali's programs," Anna said, lifting her head. "Maybe sleep *will* help me."

If these were the kinds of dreams Anna had, Mist thought, how could she ever sleep at all?

"You loved Geir, didn't you?" Anna asked. "I know he never stopped loving you, and neither did Rebekka."

"I failed them," Mist said, turning away.

"I don't know how," Anna said. "I don't need to. Love, guilt, anger . . . it's funny how all those feelings can get mixed up in your head. Just like my family's memories."

"Funny," Mist said with a short laugh. "However long you may live, that lesson never seems to sink in."

"I'd say we're all human, but . . ." Anna caught Mist's gaze, her own eyes brightening. "Shouldn't someone go to Norway right away and try to find the Treasures?" She grinned, her teeth only chattering a little. "*I* should go. Maybe I can access more of Rebekka's memories. I may be able to figure out exactly where she hid the them."

Mist fell into a chair at the opposite side of the table. "Do you have any idea what you're saying? You might be risking your sanity. Not to mention your life."

"I've been doing that every day since Orn dragged me out of my apartment." She sobered. "I know it's dangerous. But it's just as dangerous sticking around here. And you can always get another programmer."

"Don't joke about that," Mist said, reaching across the table to touch Anna's hand. "Orn may come back for you."

"I'm sure if he comes back, it won't be for me." She blinked several times. "Sure, I miss him. But I haven't done much of any use so far. This time I can really help."

Mist was silent for a moment, wondering again how she could be worthy enough to have people like this young woman risk their lives for her.

For Midgard.

"*If* you go," Mist said, "it won't be alone. I'm sure I can convince Lord Konur to send one of the Alfar. And I'll ask Bryn, Rota, or Hild if they can accompany you." She rubbed her forehead. "You do realize that if Helga had been your great-grandmother by blood, you'd be descended from a Valkyrie yourself."

"But Rebekka was adopted."

"I know. That doesn't mean you couldn't be one in every other sense." Mist slapped her palm lightly on the tabletop, afraid she was about to tip over into the maudlin again. "If you're going on a perilous journey, you need to get some real rest. That's an order. And at least for tonight, try not to dream."

Anna rose, saluted broadly, and gave Mist a lopsided grin. "I'll do my best, ma'am."

Ignoring the burnt smell of spilled soup on the stovetop, Mist slouched over the table and rested her cheek on her folded arms. The factory was caught in a rare moment of silence, and she felt a new weight settle on her shoulders. A very personal one that didn't matter in the grand scheme of things, but managed to hurt anyway.

She was lonely. Lonelier than she'd ever been in her life.

What had Anna said? *"I'd say we're all human, but . . ."*

I'm not human, Mist thought. Except that she was, inside. She was weak, and vulnerable, and made mistakes. Even the Aesir did that. They weren't really much different from mortals, when it came right down to it. They were just a Hel of a lot more powerful.

She closed her eyes and thought of the men and women who so loyally served without question. She had no right to ask for comfort, physical or emotional, from any of them, not after what they'd suffered. She was the leader, the commander, and there was always a chance that any man she might approach would feel an obligation to acquiesce because of it.

But sometimes, for a moment or two, she wished she could accept that comfort for just one night.

One night, she thought. What she might have had with Dainn. Now, when it was too late, she could finally acknowledge that she'd never been completely alone when he was around.

It wasn't likely that she would ever find that a second time.

Unless he came back. And she was pretty sure she'd never see his grave, enigmatic, beautiful face again.

32

"We can already see the difference," Bryn said, settling with the others around Mist's forge—the only real source of warmth in the factory warehouse except for the space heaters scattered around it, doing little to pierce the constant chill. The snow was falling heavily again, and while the city was still largely paralyzed, Mist hoped the forecast of warmer temperatures would take care of what remained of Loki's ice.

"Where were these new Jotunar you saw?" she asked.

"On the corners where the dealers usually hang out," Bryn said. "We typically see one Jotunn standing around somewhere, disguised as a mortal, and one regular guy. To judge by their behavior, I think the Jotunar are keeping an eye on the dealers. Maybe even studying them."

"Jotunar studying pushers," Mist said. "Did the mortals know they were there?"

"Yeah," Rick said. "They were scared, and I think either the giants are shaking them down, or—" He broke off, flushing a little. "You said that Loki's going to be recruiting a lot of lowlifes. I think maybe the Jotunar are learning the ropes so they can take over."

"That could be pretty lucrative for them," Vixen said.

"And allow Loki to flaunt his influence among the less legitimate businessmen in this city," Mist said. "He'll have been picking up mortal followers for months, but now that he's got more Jotunar, he can really get down to business."

"And we don't know when he'll get more from Ginnungagap," Rota said. "It could be any time, now that he can open the bridges."

"But you and Freya can expose these Jotunar, can't you?" Captain Taylor asked, his quiet but commanding voice catching everyone's attention.

"Loki will be countering every move we make," Mist said. "And Freya still hasn't seen fit to share her game plan with me."

"Maybe she's leaving it up to you. You've been handling the ground game all along." He paused, looking Mist in the eye. "She doesn't seem to know much of what's going on."

If only Freya could hear you now, Captain Taylor, Mist thought with a silent laugh. *She might try to demote you.*

Over my dead body.

"I noticed she's not around much, either," Rick said. "Maybe she's doing some goddess thing no one else can do."

"Things *Mist* can't do?" Tennessee asked.

"There are still a few of those," Mist said dryly. "But if she—"

"This is all of great interest," Konur interrupted—leaning against the wall near the doorway, just the way Dainn used to do—"but we are also here to discuss the journey to Norway." He gestured to the tall, unusually fair elf beside him. "Hrolf and several other of my Alfar have agreed to accompany the mortals in their quest."

"*Our* quest," Mist reminded him. "And Rota has also volunteered." She nodded to Anna, who had barely spoken. "You'll take the flight bound for New York and Norway tomorrow . . ." She glanced at the mantel clock. "I mean today."

And we can only hope that Loki hasn't gotten Danny to open another one of those intra-Midgardian portals, she thought.

Just another thing Mist knew she couldn't do much about. For now, anyway. She got up from her seat on the worn carpet remnant near the mismatched chairs.

"At times like these," she said, "when we face a new and danger-ous venture, it seems only right that we honor the courage of those who will journey into the unknown. Once, the Vikings celebrated

Yule in the middle of January, but now the custom is to exchange gifts at the time tradition claims the White Christ was born." She looked at each face in turn. "We don't have a proper feast, nor a boar to sacrifice, nor a Yule log to burn. But I have something *I* can give." She ducked her head. "Rota, Rick, do you mind bringing the drinks? Bryn and Captain Taylor, I'll need your help as well."

While Rota and Rick fetched the glogg, she led Bryn and the captain to her private office. She'd laid the velvet-lined cases on the ratty old desk the mortals had found for her. They held a dozen knives and daggers, all that remained of her hand-forged, bladed weapons; she'd already distributed the swords and axes to her Sisters and those Einherjar and other mortals who thought they could use them.

She still felt very lucky that several metalworkers and fighters had come with the new batch of recruits. Or maybe it wasn't luck at all. It was her need that had called them here. Need she had no control over, and a power she still despised and prayed she'd never have to use deliberately, no matter what she had to do to make up for the loss.

"Beautiful," Captain Taylor said, picking up one of the less decorative knives. "You made these, Chief?"

"I used to," Mist said.

With a certain reverence, he and Bryn carefully stacked the trays and carried them to a shelving unit just outside the workshop.

Once Mist had everything arranged to her satisfaction, she followed Bryn and Taylor back into the workshop, where Rick and Rota had already distributed the mugs of glogg. The hot beverage steamed, sending its glorious fragrance through the room. Even Konur and Hrolf had accepted their share.

Mist lifted her own mug. "*Skal*," she said. "To victory."

"To victory," the others echoed. Everyone drank, and then there was a long, pensive silence as each of the council members considered how difficult the path to victory would be.

"I've got something else," Mist said, setting her mug down. "If you'll all come outside . . ."

They trooped after her and stared curiously at the weapons on their trays.

"The only gifts I have to give," she said. "Please take whatever you think suits you."

After another moment's pause, Rota chose a dagger with an unusually ornate grip and slid it from its sheath. "Gorgeous," she said.

Taylor was next. He chose the plain knife, while Hrolf chose a dagger adorned with interlocking vines and birds in an old Nordic design. Rick's was the broadest and heaviest Mist had crafted.

One by one the others selected their weapons. Only Konur abstained.

"Nothing for Eir," Rota murmured.

"Believe me, she wouldn't want a weapon of any kind," Mist said. "And Gabi sure as Hel isn't getting one."

"I think this calls for another toast," Rick said.

Still admiring their weapons, everyone but Konur, Taylor, and Mist returned to the workshop.

"They seem devoted to you," Konur remarked.

"They know a good gen—*chief* when they see one," Taylor said.

"I would gladly have passed this duty on to someone else," Mist said, "but sometimes such choices aren't ours to make."

Konur inclined his head. "The Alfar follow you, by Freya's will."

As if she'd been summoned by her name, Freya walked into the warehouse. She wore tight-fitting leather pants, a close-cut shirt that showed off plenty of cleavage, and high-heeled boots. She exuded so much allure that even the phlegmatic Taylor reacted, staring a moment before he averted his gaze.

"I see you have been busy in my absence," the Lady said, looking the captain up and down. "Have you glogg for me as well?"

"If you want some," Mist said. "It's in the workshop."

Mist followed her in time to witness the reactions of her council.

Most of them had already seen her in the elven form she still wore, but there wasn't a single man or woman in the room who didn't respond to her natural glamour. She could easily have bent every one of them—mortal, elf, and Valkyrie—to her will with a crook of her finger.

Mist despised Freya for that. But she had too many questions to waste her time on anger, and she very much wanted to know what her mother had been up to during her absence.

After the council members had left to return to their various camps and beds, Mist stood face to face with Freya near the forge, sensing that this wasn't going to be a pleasant conversation.

Freya pursed her lips as if she'd read Mist's thoughts. Mist hoped that was only a cliché and not the literal truth.

"I see that you left no dagger for me," the Lady said.

"I thought you already had enough weapons in your arsenal," Mist said. "You can't keep throwing your glamour around, especially not with my mortal followers. They need their minds clear."

"I will do my best."

Sure you will, Mist thought. "Where have you been?"

"If you will be patient, I have something to show you. Something I believe you will find of great interest." She shot Mist a sly glance from under her thick lashes. "We shall have to join our minds for a brief time."

So she couldn't do it without cooperation, Mist thought. "I don't make a habit of that sort of thing," she said.

"Except with Dainn. Is that not correct?"

Once again Mist was left wondering how much Freya knew about her activities with Dainn before the Lady's initial appearance and throughout her subsequent absence. And what Dainn might not have told Mist about his communications with the goddess he had served.

"First you tell me what this is about," Mist said.

"As it happens, it regards Dainn and his present activities," she said. "That does interest you, does it not?"

"You already had a pretty firm opinion on that, as I recall," Mist said, grateful that Freya didn't know what Dainn's note had contained.

"Ah, but I have gathered new information that I believe will convince you that my opinion is quite sound."

Mist did everything within her power not to show her dread. "Okay," she said. "But I should warn you that Dainn provoked me into a serious case of psychic self-defense the last time he dug too deeply into my brain. I doubt I can hurt you, but . . ."

"I shall keep that in mind," Freya said, chuckling at her own joke. She took a seat on one of the battered chairs and patted the one next to hers. Mist sat as far away from her mother as she could.

"Hold my hand," Freya said.

Mist kept her hand where it was. "How is this supposed to work?"

"We will be traveling in a way mortals call 'astral projection.' Our bodies will remain here, but our souls and minds will travel."

"Seidr?" Mist asked. "The witch magic?"

"In a manner of speaking. Will you trust me to guide you?"

Reluctantly Mist scooted closer and took Freya's hand in her own. She felt a touch of the glamour, and then it was gone.

All at once she seemed to be flying over the city, looking down on the mortals scurrying on the ice that, along with the quakes, had so disrupted their lives. Like a banking plane, she circled around until she and Freya were hovering over a building Mist didn't recognize at first.

Then she knew it was Loki's headquarters . . . and she understood, with a pang of horror, what Freya was about to show her.

As if Loki's wards had lost all their strength, she and Freya passed like ghosts through the outer wall of the ground floor. They glided along corridors and up through one ceiling to the next until they had reached the top.

Sick to her very soul but unable to escape Freya's hold, Mist slipped through a door. The room was in fact a suite, with a sitting room richly furnished and another door to a bedroom, dominated by a bed large enough to accommodate six people at one time.

Loki was lying stretched on his belly, the silk sheets barely covering the lower half of his torso. And on the floor close to the wall, curled up in a fetal position, lay Dainn—his eyes open, his hair tangled, his face as expressionless as the day Mist had first met him.

Her stomach heaved, and all at once she was back in the workshop, Freya's hand tight around her own. She pried herself free, jumped up, and started for the door.

"Now you know," Freya said. "He has gone to Loki. He has chosen our enemy."

"Is that what you've been doing all this time?" Mist asked, turning in the doorway. "Hunting up more reasons why I should hate him?"

"I think this reason alone should be sufficient." Freya slumped in her chair, her face pale with exhaustion. The Seidr had clearly taken its toll, but Mist felt no sympathy.

"He didn't want to be there," she said

"He chose." Freya favored Mist with one of those mournfully compassionate stares. "I know how deeply this disturbs you, but you still have no conception of the depth of Dainn's relationship with Loki. Though Loki's disguise was flawless and Dainn believed *I* was his lover, Loki saw to it that no one else in Asgard knew of the affair, concealing it even from the All-father. Yet all who knew Dainn as a wise counselor, Odin's special confidante, saw him change. Saw him begin to lose his stability without understanding the reason." She touched her own cheek as if to wipe away a tear. "When I learned of this I attempted to interfere, but it was too late. By then he believed *I* had urged him to negotiate a peace with Loki on behalf of the Aesir."

"And after he knew he'd been deceived, and was to be cursed for a betrayal he didn't commit," Mist said, "he tried to *kill* Loki."

"He has had his chances to try again, has he not?" Freya asked, the warmth gone from her voice. "Ask yourself what happened between him and Loki on the day you fought Laufeyson in his dwelling. Why was Dainn so powerless then? Why did he find it so easy to surrender?"

As much as she despised how her mother had used Dainn—used both of them—Mist hadn't thought herself so capable of hating the goddess who had borne her. The image Freya had called up was one Mist had never quite managed to forget, in spite of all the times Dainn had proven his courage: Loki trapping the elf against the wall of his apartment, Dainn unable or unwilling to fight back.

In exchange for my life.

"He was trying not to make things worse for me," she said.

"But there is more," Freya said, "though it pains me to tell you. Dainn bears a scar on his palm that matches Loki's. They represent a blood-oath made not long ago, after Dainn first came to you, and these marks will not fade unless the oath is broken. Both must agree to the severance. Loki never will. Dainn belongs to him now."

"How do you know all this?" Mist asked, remembering Dainn's bloody palm, the way he'd tried to hide it from her and made up some excuse about cutting it on Gleipnir when he'd escaped to find Anna.

"I saw the wound when I met Dainn on the steppes," she said, "and Loki's stink was all over it."

"And you didn't see fit to mention this before, when you were trying to make your case against him?"

"You must accept the facts. Dainn is profoundly vulnerable where Loki is concerned. The Slanderer may work his tricks again, turn Dainn's creature to his own purpose—even convince Dainn that *I* am the enemy."

"Do not trust her," Dainn had written. Odds were that he'd already gone to Loki by then. Had he been rational when he'd written those words, or was he already . . .

"I'll never believe he'd betray us," Mist said.

"I am more sorry than you can imagine," Freya said. She rose, approached Mist and stopped, reaching out to stroke Mist's cheek. Honey-warmth penetrated Mist's skin, filling her with unspeakable joy.

Freya was right, she thought. Hadn't Dainn deceived her again and again?

No. No no no.

Jerking free, Mist strode out of the workshop, crossed the warehouse floor, and walked blindly into the falling snow. It was soft and gentle, but Mist felt only the cold her own body had turned against her. She walked at a jarring pace along Illinois, ignoring the faint call that pursued her.

Not all is what it seems. Had Dainn referred to himself and Loki? How could she ever guess what really lay beneath those six words?

And Danny . . .

Mist stopped abruptly. Freya hadn't used *him* in her argument.

And the blood-oath could mean anything. Dainn might have made it with Loki to protect *her*, for all she knew. He'd never willingly give himself to the godling who'd nearly destroyed him, who would so gleefully destroy everything he cared about.

Suddenly her thoughts returned to that first fight with Loki in Asbrew, and what Laufeyson had said at the end. *"Don't trust her. And don't trust* him."

Now she wondered if he'd meant Dainn all along, because Loki knew something she didn't. Something about Dainn that the elf would never tell her.

As for *her* . . .

Freya. The same warning from Dainn and Loki. Maybe it was coincidence. Maybe it meant something much worse, something Mist couldn't even bring herself to contemplate.

Traitors. Svardkell's word. Vali. Vidarr. And now . . .

Dainn would never have passed those words on to me if he thought he might be exposed, Mist thought.

Yet Dainn said Svardkell had died before he could say more. Was that another lie? Wasn't a little truth more convincing than none at all? And if he'd lied, was Svardkell really her—

Mist leaned over and emptied her stomach.

He's gone, she thought, her belly filling up again with a terrible certainty. *He's gone over to the enemy.*

Maybe it was for Danny. Maybe he thought he could deceive

Loki into trusting him, and turn that trust against the Slanderer. Maybe he had the best reasons in the world, and hadn't dared confide in Mist.

But he was gone. And Loki *had* deceived him before. If Laufeyson used the right kind of pressure, or even persuasion, to encourage Dainn's relationship with Danny, the boy could become an even more powerful weapon in Loki's hands.

Dainn had made a choice. And if Mist ever saw him again, she might have no choice but to kill him.

Loki frowned at the monitor. Dainn was still with Danny, working earnestly to win the boy's attention, and his failure thus far had irritated Loki considerably.

But there would be time. And Loki knew he shouldn't overlook the continuing good reports from his "employees." Vali, with the dubious help of Loki's IT team, had located another of the Valkyrie: Skuld, guardian of Thor's Belt of Power, Megingjord. Now he had two of the Thunder god's famous weapons, and he felt quite certain he could encourage the lovely Rota into giving up the third, if he played his cards right. He suspected they had much in common.

He turned up the volume and listened to Dainn speak to Miss Jones. They knew, of course, that he was watching everything they did and said, but Dainn seemed indifferent, and he appeared to have encouraged the mortal woman's suppressed inclination toward defiance as well.

No matter. Loki had no intention of ever setting her free in spite of earlier promises. And once Dainn got through to Danny again—which Loki had no doubt would happen . . .

Nothing would be beyond them. The three of them, together.

Orn laughed.

Vidarr sat at the bar, drinking one whiskey after another. The once-called "Silent God" had regained his reputation at last. His blue eyes were dazed, as if he had forgotten where he was.

But then again, he had not been quite himself since Loki had given him the thrashing he so richly deserved

"*It was for him,*" he had said to Orn, over and over like a silly parrot that only knew one phrase. "*It was always for* him."

Orn knew better than to believe Odin's son. He cocked his head to examine the flat chip of stone lying on the table at his feet. He recognized the picture on it. It was not a good likeness, but it was important.

The *pendant* was important, though he didn't yet know why. He still had much to learn, to remember. But he had touched the Spear. It wasn't enough, but it was one of the strongest, and he had been different ever since.

Different enough to know he had to hide, even from Anna. Different enough to understand how to make Odin's sons create a new ward around this place, so that no outsiders would realize they were there. Not the evil one, not the traitors, not Mist.

And he would not have to hide long. Soon Vidarr would serve a new purpose, and continue to serve until he was no longer useful. One by one the others would be found.

Until *he* was whole at last. Then they would all get what they deserved. Mist, Odin's sons, the Slanderer, Freya. And this world would at last become the paradise it was meant to be.

With a soft croak, Orn stretched his wings, settled more comfortably on his perch, and watched Vidarr slip into unconsciousness.

ACKNOWLEDGMENTS

With thanks, as always, to my agent, Lucienne Diver; my eagle-eyed editor, Melissa Frain; the excellent Amy Saxon; my husband, Serge Mailloux; the Krinards, Lonners, and Weinmanns; C. J. Cherryh, for thirty-five years of inspiration; and the booksellers and readers who make it possible for me to write what I love.